The Liar's Gift
By
Sidney L. Jackson

To God Be The Glory For This Work

The Liar's Gift

ISBN 978-0-578-88733-3

© Sidney L. Jackson 2021

All Rights Reserved

Published by El Cid's Books

1833 Rangewood Ct.
Plainfield, NJ 07060
http://www.elcidsbooks.com

Other Books by Sidney L Jackson
(Formerly El Cid)

The Big Lie – El Cid - - Publish America
ISBN 978-1-4489-5137-6

Darkness Is Not Eternal El Cid - Publish America
ISBN 978-1-63508-928-8

Darkness Is Not Eternal Sidney L. Jackson (Digital Version)
HMG ePublishing ASIN:BO7X13X4J9

Kingdom Planet (The Final Kingdom) - El Cid - Lighthouse
Christian Publishing ISBN 978-1-52385-6886

Man's Law And Divine Justice - Sidney L. Jackson
Lighthouse
Christian Publishing
ISBN 978-1-64373-2497

Cover Design by:
Tyrone R. Kinnard
Tykin Artworks
Outthinkers@yahoo.com
(609) 638-4850

Chapter 1 - The Set Up

"In the beginning was the Word, and the Word was with God. And the Word was God...John 1:1 - NKJ) For all who are familiar with the Christian Holy Bible this is not an unfamiliar chapter beginning. The essence of the chapter in John's Gospel establishes who the creator of this world is and what His mission was. To help the reader of this work understand all that happened after the world's creation and how the concept of truth and lie came about, it would be necessary to detail a portion of the book of Genesis. Since it is not the intent of this book to engage in that effort, it is hoped that the following story would provide enough insight into understanding the difference and perhaps encourage the reader to investigate further by reading Genesis for yourself.

Sufficient for now however, let it be stated here that the progenitor of the truth was and is the Word (Jesus Christ).

The following tale relates to a situation that is all too common in everyone's life, but the effect of deception is more devastating for some than others. Whether the ruse is perpetrated on the sophisticated socialite or on the less experienced debutante; whether it is played out in the urban confines of a city or in the spacious countryside, the outcome is still the same. In this saga the victim, a woman who categorically falls somewhere in between the two, is the unwitting target of the one who can deceive us all.

She was a spiritual church going lady, but he didn't care. Many times before, since the very beginning, he had polished the proverbial apple to such an appealing luster that it was hard to resist. To the undisciplined eye it was mouth watering and begged to be tasted. Combined with his guile and well honed skill at deception, when she became his target it was hardly a fair match. The circumstances surrounding the game favored him in all aspects of the contest.

After the death of her military husband who was killed, several years ago fighting in a foreign war, Sarafina struggled in her attempt to live a happy life. The untimely demise of her beloved spouse had presented her with challenges that she had never had to face before. In the years that they had been married he was always the one who took care of everything. As a career military wife she had become somewhat accustomed to the family being shuffled around the country more than one time, but it was not until that cloudy Monday morning, the day when the soldiers arrived at her door bringing the bad news along with a letter of commendation, that she began to realize her life was never going to be the same again. Since that time the vicissitudes of life itself had dealt her a hand she felt was given by a cheating dealer. Moving from one city to another from one house to another always trying to escape the hurt and pain of sudden loneliness she was determined to find some consolation that would uplift her spirit. She finally settled in Newtown, NJ.

In the early years of her residency there she thought she had come to a place where at least she would be able to raise her two boys comfortably. She had landed what she believed was a good job and it offered some stability. Even though the city was a large metropolis, in a way she was glad about that because she wanted to lose herself in the hustle and bustle of a booming society. The neighborhood she found had been advised to her by some friends she met when her husband was still alive. They saw it as an up and coming section of the city and it was relatively safe for her intentions.

Taking up residency in a third floor walk-up apartment it provided enough space for her and the boys to be comfortable. For a while it seemed that her life was beginning to move in a positive direction and she was starting to enjoy it. Through the church she joined she found a sense of new purpose and even became a leader in one of the civic organizations. Things were going okay for a while and then as fate would have it things began to change. Initially, it was hard for her to see why, then as time ran it's course and it seemed like every day presented a new challenge for her and the boys, then she finally realized what was happening and the reason became undeniably clear. It may just have been because of the man she met. This is her story.

****

"Jameel git outta that bed and wake ya brother up. Don' make me call you again." The voice rang through the apartment and reverberated off the walls as Sarafina rushed to go to work. She was already in the long hallway, when she heard the sound of movement in the boy's bedroom so she continued on. Trying to raise two adolescent boys, as a single mother, in a

2

neighborhood that had become all too typical of an urban inner city setting, was difficult. Too often the frustration of seeing her boys threatened by the wiles of street life came to a head and she just broke down and cried. As badly as she wanted to move again and find a better place, whenever it seemed she was close to making it happen, life got in the way and the burdens of her heart didn't roll away. Her clerical job at a small manufacturing plant paid enough to keep food on the table, pay the rent and have a little bit left over, but it was far from seating her in the lap of luxury.

"Git up Cinque! You heard momma jus like I did. I'm movin and you better move too. Come on man, I ain't playin' wit you, you better move. I ain gittin in trouble cause a you – now git up. You know today at school there gonna be some action and we wanna be there. Talk is a big party goin down tomorra night and ereybody to be there. So come on git up and les go."

It was Friday morning and as the boys struggled to accept the new day, Jameel got to the bathroom first and saw the note left on the mirror over the sink.

"Come strait home from school today and don't go to that hangin corner. I want to talk to both of you."

He took the note down and began to wash. Minutes later he exited and a hurried Cinque charged in.

"Why you take so long man, you know I gotta go?"

"Ah shut up boy and go head in. I'm gonna make some brekfas, what you want?" "What we got?"

"Frosty Flakes." "Yeah, fix me some."

The two teenagers, Jameel sixteen and Cinque fourteen, finished breakfast, grabbed their backpacks and headed out the door. As they started to run down the creaking stairs, Jameel stopped short and turned around to make sure the door was locked behind them. This was something Sarafina had always told them to do if they wanted to keep their things. They continued down the three flights and jumped off the small porch headed to school. It seemed they were going to be late, but they both ran the long three blocks in record time and made it in the school's front door just as the first bell rang.

Passing the school guard and through the metal detector, Jameel turned right and headed to homeroom 102. Cinque turned left and walked up to the second floor to homeroom 213. Jameel was a junior who was doing okay, but hated school. Cinque, a freshman, showed some academic promise, but it was only the first half of the year and only the second marking period. Both boys were constantly reminded by mom how much they needed an education, so they were at least trying to finish high school.

At Midland High, in the center of the city, the population was pretty well mixed racially and gender wise so there was a good spread of street culture from all sides. Many of the students were bused from different parts of the city due to the latest zoning modification and change in the city requirement to boost the appearance of a non- segregated facility. It also didn't hurt their image when they applied for various educational inner-city subsidy education grants.

As the students hustling to their respective rooms settled in, the second bell rang signaling the start of the late arrivals list. In room 102, all 25 kids responded to the role call and it was an unusual day; everybody showed up. There was something in the air that caused an excitement permeating the whole building. In room 213, likewise all 30 students were present. This room was more subdued however, because they weren't sure what all the buzz was about.

"Hey "J" wha'sup?"

"Ain nut'n Raj, how you doin?"

"Man I'm okay, I be betta if I can jus get me some money. I need some stuff real bad. You heard 'bout tomorrow right?"

"Yeah man, you goin?"

"Yeah, I'm goin, but I gotta stay in the background. You know dem Cripplers tryin to`cruit me."

"Yeah, I heard."

"You know, Dolitha gonna be there lookin for you. She got a real thing for you." "How you know that?"

"She tol me yesterday when I saw her."

"Yeah well I got to hit that, so I guess I'm goin. Maybe I can get my moms to cut some slack and lightn up on the curfu."

Rajon was Jameel's classmate and a close friend who seemed to know everything that was going down both in and out of school; especially when it came to the street life.

He wasn't a bad student, but it was suspected that he might be into some things that kept him from being good, both in and out of school. The Cripplers, a local gang that had overrun the hood, sought him because of his street acumen and wanted him in.

The bell rang signaling the start of the day and Jameel headed to his first class. Just as he left his room, he ran right into Dolitha who happened to be in the corridor, although her first class was on the other side of the building.

"Hi J. Hy you doin? Did Raj tell you I was lookin for you?" "Hi D, yeah he told me. I was gonna fine you later. Was'up?" "I wanna know if you goin to the party tomorrow? I'm goin." "Yeah prably me and my brother goin."

"Okay, I'll be lookin for you. Now call me if you ain gonna be there, here's my number."

She gave him a slip of paper then hurriedly turned around and headed in the opposite direction while Jameel scurried to his class. As he was about to turn the corner to his classroom, he heard a loud scuffle. Slowing his pace he eased his head around to check it out. Two boys were going at it and battling with some serious intent. Hands and knees were flying as they pummeled each other. As other students came into the area, the crowd was mounting when suddenly what appeared to be a silver blade hit the floor and slid right up to Jameel. Not thinking, he picked it up just as the security guard and a teacher came near. The two boys, somewhat bloody, were separated and hauled off to the principal's office. The guard took the knife from Jameel and told him to follow to the office.

Once in the office all three boys were kept separated while the principal, vice- principal, guard and the teacher tried to find out what was the problem. The larger of the two fighters was grilled because it was not the first time this had happened for him. The principal knew Jameel and that he was not one to get into this kind of trouble so he told him to go to class and that he would be called later.

Neither one of the remaining boys was talking, but it became clear that the large kid who was wearing what looked like the identity of the C's club was trying to stare down the principal. Finally, after some time without any progress in finding out who started it and what it was all about, the police were called, the knife was turned over and the two boys were taken out of the building. That was the beginning of another day at Midland High.

The remainder of the school day was alive with talk about what happened that morning and what was to happen Saturday night. The talk was going around that because of what happened today, the Cripplers and the Bandits, the other rival gang in the 'hood, were scheming. However, unknown to Jameel, what also was circulating was a rumor that he had been involved in the knife fight.

After the final bell rang and the scurry out the door started, Rajon caught up with his friend and with a rush of excitement told him about what he heard. A few minutes later, Cinque came over and verified it. Rajon told J he should go to the hang and get it straight. The hangout was a corner grocery store not far from the school called the Minute Mart or M&M. Looking at the sparse shelf stocking, products other than canned goods and produce were definitely being sold. Jameel agreed and asked Raj to come with him.

"Man, you know I'm down wit you, but I can't go there. The C's already scopin the hood for me anyway. I'll check you later and we can rap."

"Okay man, later. Cinque you and me goin down to M&M's for a few. I gotta rap with Razor and let him know what went down at school. He can handle it for me, he know his sister like me."

"Jameel, you know momma said come home."

"Yeah bro., I know that, but we ain gona be there long. Jus long enuf for me to tell Razor the true story. Mom ain gonna be home for a while anyway. Let's go."

Once they were near the store they could see that a few C gang members had already gathered on the corner sensing the same excitement that was at school. There was a slight difference here though; the excitement was tinged with a feeling of tension. Razor the leader of the pack, dressed in his usual combat outfit of baggy khaki pants and a loose fitting hooded sweat shirt saw Jameel coming and went inside. Two of his soldiers turned and followed him as Jameel and Cinque approached the corner. They both went inside.

"Hey Razor, wha's up? Look, can I talk wit you for a minute man?"

"Yeah "J" anytime. Les go over here where we can rap in private. I already done heard about the git down at school. How you get in it? I thought chu was cool with us. My boys tell me they heard you sided with the B's. What's your story?" "Razor, man you know I ain into none of that. I was caught up on the sidelines when that blade slid up to me an I picked it up. I ain sidin with them and I wasn't in the deal. You know me man, I jus happened to be there when everything went down. You can aks yo sister she there too. Thas what happened."

"Aw-ight man, I hear you, but I'm gonna check with Sista anyway. You comin tomorrow? We got som'm planned you might wanna see. It's been a long time comin and we gonna settle things. You don' wanna miss it. Don' show up in the wrong outfit, you feelin me?"

"Yeah man, I'm cool. See you tomorrow."

As Jameel turned to go from the secluded corner of the store that Razor called his private office, Cinque, who had stayed near the counter watching Razor's two soldiers, caught up with him and they quickly headed out the door. They moved quickly from the area as the number of gang members grew. The growing crowd all wore the quasi club uniform which was readily apparent to anyone who might chance to come into the area.

Jameel and Cinque kept up a good pace and when they made it to the block that was deemed unofficially the territorial dividing line, beginning a neutral zone, they slowed down a bit but were definitely mindful that they had to get home.

"Jameel, if momma home early, what'chu gonna tell her?"

"I don know, I jus hope she ain't there. If she is, I jus have to think up somthin. Whatever I come up wit you better go along. I think I'll jus say we lef school late cause we checkin' out basketball practice. She know I was gonna try out and I'll say I still can. You down wit that?"

"Yeah!"

It was about 5:00 o'clock when the boys reached the house and they scampered up the stairs two at a time stopping at the door to listen. Hearing no sound inside, Jameel opened the door and breathed a loud sigh of relief. Cinque echoed the breathing pattern and they both went into their bedroom. Sarafina, usually got home around 5, but for some reason today she didn't. At 6:00 o'clock, the hunger pangs set in and the boys turned their attention away from the video game and wondered where mom was. As Jameel went into the kitchen to see what he could find to eat, the key turned in the door and Sarafina entered.

"Jameel, Cinque you here?" "Yeah mom we here!"

"You know I tol you I want you straight home from school cause I want to talk to you. Well, I know you must have, so sorry I'm late. Anyway, I stopped by the church to see Rev. Joyner about this program he's talking' bout startin to git the gangs out the area.

I know both of you got friends that might be hangin with some of them. I don't wanna see you get in that mess an I don't want you to be afraid to go to school either. Somethin gotta be done and I want to help. I jus want to let you know that I'm gonna be doin

that when it starts and I might ask you to help. It may be a while yet, but I know it's gonna happen. You got any questions?"

"No mom, what we gonna eat?" said Jameel. Sarafina then went to the kitchen and fixed dinner.

It was about 9:00 AM Saturday morning and the bright sun penetrated the thin shades in the boy's room. As Jameel rolled over and rubbed his eyes, he could smell bacon and eggs coming from the kitchen. Sarafina was usually up early on Saturday making breakfast for the boys. Until recently, after breakfast she would just be doing household chores most of the day. Now she was headed out to meet with her volunteer civic group.

The group called themselves CONNs (Change Our Neighborhood

Now) and was made up mostly of women who had come together just a few weeks ago after an assault was made on one of them. Today they would be making the final plans for the big event that everybody was talking about. This was what the big excitement at school was all about. What made it such a must do thing for the kids was that the party was going to be at the new recreation center where all the youth groups came out for basketball games. The idea that it was being sponsored by an adult group didn't bother them because they had their own plans underway. The CONNs believed that doing this first time party event would bring their youth together. The kids had their own reason.

"Jameel, Cinque come on – breakfast is on the table."

About ten minutes later, Jameel came in and plopped himself down in a chair at the table. Sarafina, still putting things on the table, then said: "After you guys eat, I want you to wash your plates and then clean your room. Before you go out anywhere, make sure you take the garbage down and put it in the cans 'round back. Watch out you don't spill none in the hallway either. I'm going to my CONN meetin, should be back 'bout 2:00. Make sure to lock the doors, if you do go out."

Just as Sarafina was finishing her last statement, Cinque came in and sat down at the table.

"Momma, me and Jameel we goin to that party tonight right? The whole school gonna be there."

"You can go."

"What time we gotta be home?"

"It will be over at 11:00 and I want both of you here before 12:00 – no later." After Sarafina finished talking she grabbed her bag and walked out the door.

Cinque then looked at both plates and said: "Did you eat one of my pancakes? Why you got three an I only got two?"

"'Cause your's are bigger than mine, see. When you finish, put yo plate in the sink so I can wash it. You can clean the room. Pick yo stuff up off the floor and put it in the closet; I'll take care of mine. When you finish that you can help me take down the garbage and then we thru. I'm goin down to Rajon's house and see what's goin on. If you go out, make sure you lock the door behind you. Check it!"

"I ain goin nowhere. I'm gonna watch tv and then play some video games. What time you comin back?"

"I'll be back around 2:00, the same time mom said she be here."

Once Jameel finished his share of the chores, he bolted out the door, down the stairs and out onto the street. Rajon's house was about four blocks away in the opposite direction of the school. As he was walking down his block, he noticed that there was a greater number of cars riding through than normal. It was about 11:00 O'clock and usually hardly any cars came through this block around now. He looked inside that last car and he could see that it was filled with what looked like the B's boys. He felt a chill because this was not where they were supposed to be - on the wrong side of the line.

There were at least five cars in the group and it seemed like they were playing I Spy. He quickened his pace, moved along to Raj's apartment house and ran up the stairs. He banged hard on the door. Several minutes later, Rajon opened it after hearing it was him.

"Hey man, you know what I just saw in my block?" "No what?"

"A whole lotta B's rides movin in the area. They was scopin us out. You think we aughta let Razor know?"

"Man, I ain got nut'n to say to him. He the one tryin to 'cruit me. If you want him to know, you tell him."

"I ain goin down that way today. I ain goin nowhere before tonight. What you got to snack on?"

"Here, take some chips they good for kiliin' the munchies."

The boys laid back eating corn chips and playing video games until it was almost 2:00 when Jameel asked what time it was. Rajon checked the clock and told him it was about quarter of - Jameel then jumped up and said:

"Hey man I gotta go. I wanna be there when my moms get home. She can tell me if her group knows 'bout the B's being 'round here. See ya later."

"Aw'ight man, later."

Jameel walked out and headed home. It was still going through his mind about the cars he saw earlier and it started to bother him. He couldn't help thinking about what Razor said to him yesterday about settling things. In the pit of his stomach he had a tight feeling that he couldn't shake. He arrived at his house and walked up to his apartment. It was now a little after 2:00 and he wondered if mom had beat him home. As he walked in the door he saw that Cinque had left some papers and stuff in the hallway and he knew that as the oldest he was going to hear it when mom got home.

"Cinque, where you at. Come git this stuff outta here before momma get back. I tol you before she be here at 2:00."

Cinque came out of the bedroom rubbing his eyes. He had fallen asleep. "Aw'ight, lighten up I'll move it. Momma here yet? I hope she bring us some chicken."

Just as Cinque was removing the hallway debris, Sarafina walked in and announced that she brought a bucket of chicken and potato salad. Cinque finished his clean up chore then wasted no time in getting to the kitchen and dug in. Jameel sauntered in a few minutes later and sat down.

"Mom, know what I saw today?" "No what?"

"Coming right down the street in front of the house was a bunch of cars with some of those Bandits guys in 'em. They wasn't doin nuthin but you know they don come ' round here."

"Well, I hope they was just passin thru and not up to something. I have to start getting ready for tonight and I even have to run back out to pick up a few things. Why don't you and your brother stay inside until it's time to go to the party." "Okay, mom."

Sarafina walked out and Jameel went into the living room. Just as he got there, the phone rang.

"Jameel here who dis?"

"Hi J, it's Dolitha, hy you doin?" "I'm okay, hy you doin?"

"I'm fine, I jus wanted to let you know I been thinking about you an I can't wait to see you tonight. You still comin, ain't you?"

"Yeah, I be there."

"When I was thinkin about you before, I had a funny feelin. It felt real strange. You know that girl Sista likes you and she gonna be there looking for you too. But you gonna be wit me right? I hope she ain' gon' start no mess."

"Don' worry, I ain' into her no how. So jus chill an we can have a nice time. I'll see Ya later."

After he hung up, Jameel went into the bedroom where Cinque was playing video NFL football.

"Boy, you don' know how to play that. Lemme git wit you so I can show you somthin while I whip yo butt."

The two boys played video games for the rest of the afternoon. Time passed quickly and soon it was almost 7:00 O'clock. They had finished the chicken for dinner and were now preparing to get ready to go to the civic party. Jameel checked his clothes to make sure that his color scheme didn't indicate a preference for either of the clubs. He even looked over what Cinque was going to wear and made sure that he was okay.

Sarafina was on the phone talking to her group making last minute follow-ups. It seemed that everything was in order and they were ready. She then went into her bedroom and started to get herself ready.

"Jameel, Cinque are you boys going with me?" "No mom we gonna walk there, it ain' too far."

"Okay, but remember I said be back here before 12:00."

Sarafina finished dressing, having to be at the rec center early she left the boys on their own. At about 8:00 O'clock Jameel and Cinque headed down the stairs and onto the street headed to the center. Jameel looked around to see if any of the cars he saw before were in the area. It was clear and the traffic was like it usually was on a Saturday night.

By 8:20 they arrived at the center and saw their friends and classmates going into the building. As they approached the door, they could see inside that the large room was already filling up with kids and some adults. The DJ hired, for the night, was playing their favorite jams and kicking it into high gear. The sound was at such a high volume that normal conversation was nearly impossible. It mattered not to the kids as they moved on the floor to the rhythm of the beat. Conversation was not what they were there for. Jameel and Cinque eased into the room and joined a group from school who were standing in a corner on the far side. Jameel greeted his friends and introduced his brother. Some of them already knew him, some didn't, but greeted him. As Jameel looked around the room, which was rather dim for the occasion, he spotted Dolitha and immediately started for her. Unknown to him, he had been spotted by Sista over in another corner and she was starting toward him. Jameel got to Dolitha first.

"Hey girl, you lookin' good."

"Thank you J, you like it. I wore it jus for you."

When Sista saw that Jameel was already with Dolitha, she stopped short and abruptly changed directions. It was not too hard to tell that she was nursing a bad attitude and the heat from her furor must have raised the temperature in the whole room about 20 degrees. She headed straight for her brother who, with his boys, had occupied a major area of the room and on the dance floor. She whispered something to him and it seemed that his demeanor also changed.

The C's were well represented, but only a small wardrobe indicator on each one showed who they were. As Razor began to walk across the floor, his posse also moved in a group and eased toward where Jameel was talking to Dolitha. But just before Razor reached Jameel, a commotion was heard at the entrance door. It seemed that the B's had arrived wearing their full "colors". There was no attempt to subdue their wardrobe and some of the civic advisors were having a problem deciding whether to admit them. The voices were animated on both sides and it was beginning to escalate into a major confrontation. However, in an attempt to try and maintain some kind of peaceful order it was decided to let them in after convincing their leader to maintain civility.

Razor, seeing what went down at the entrane door, motioned to Jameel to follow him.

Jameel, not knowing what was happening, followed him into a back hallway near the boy's room.

"You lied to me man an' you know I don' like that. Sista tol me you the one in the fight an you try to take out Mo. You know you gotta pay for that. After we take care of this otha bidness, it's yo turn."

"Hey man, I tol you what happened it was'n me. Yo sister the one who lyin." "Can't deal wit you now, but I will see you later."

After that, Jameel headed back in the dance room behind Razor who headed toward his posse. It was now about 10:00, and even though the music was blasting and it seemed that things were going okay, something else was happening. The kids were dancing and partying, but there was a definite underlying tension that was mounting in the room.

Although the C's and the B's intentionally did not come close to each other, some prearranged condition had already been established. At about 10:30, when it was good and dark outside, members of both groups started toward the door. Not as a block, but they eased out in small bands until all the gang members on both sides exited.

The area around the civic center, although the center was a nice recently built modern building, was slated for neighborhood improvement and was yet spattered with vacant lots. It was clear that in the one closest to the center, the action was going to be. After a while, Jameel finally took his eyes off of Dolitha and looked around. He saw that the room had emptied of both clubs and he went to find Cinque.

"Cinque, we gotta split. I see somethin goin down an we don' wanna be 'round here." "Okay. We goin' home? We gonna walk or wait for mom?"

"We leavin now, walkin. We'll see mom when she get home. Now come on les go."

Jameel went to Dolitha and explained that he had to leave and he would call her tomorrow. He told her that something had come up and he couldn't go home with her but he would definitely call her. Disappointed, she said okay, but she told him again about the feeling she had earlier. The two boys then walked out the door headed home. The vacant lot was in the direction that they had to go and they saw that several cars had amassed in the area. The closer they got to the lot a feeling of tension began to grow in

Jameel. Finally they were at the lot and could see that the two clubs had already squared off and the battle was under way. Doing his best to avoid involvement, Jameel grabbed Cinque and turned to cross the street when two of the C's got out of a car that was parked behind them. Two large C members grabbed Jameel and began dragging him into the fracas. Cinque was scared and he couldn't help his brother much, so he just followed them. The battle was in high gear and both sides were determined to wipe each other out. As they moved in that direction, Jameel noticed again a lot more cars than usual. As the battle raged it was clear that knives and chains were in use, but then all of sudden – pop, pop, pop then datta' datta' datta' dat – datta, datta, datta, dat was heard and bodies began dropping.

In a minute the crowd broke up and both sides were running out of the area, except for the three boys lying dead in the center of the field. Among them was Razor.

Jameel and Cinque were able to getaway, but as they were running people from the housing complex across the street came to windows and front doors and were looking at the fleeing warriors as well as the carnage. Minutes later blaring sirens and the glare of flashing lights lit up the area and it was filled with police and SWAT people everywhere.

Jameel and Cinque arrived home out of breath and shaking. They ran up the stairs and burst in the door. Still breathing hard and shaking, Jameel ran into the bathroom and threw-up. Cinque ran into the bedroom and got in the bed with the pillow over his head. It took a while, but Jameel calmed down came out of the bathroom, went into the kitchen and drank a large amount of water. He then went in to check on Cinque who was still shaking but okay. Jameel spoke first and said:

"Man, I don' ever wanna do that again. They were gonna take me out. I can't believe it."

"I don' even wanna see that again" replied Cinque. Did you see Razor on the ground?"

"Yeah, him and I think two of the B's. It's gonna be somethin tomorrow. Cops gonna be all over this place. I hope momma get home okay."

"Maybe we should go back and see."

"No, boy she be in the car an we be walkin. We prably can't even get near there anyhow. We jus wait here."

Less than a half-hour went by and the boys heard the key turning in the door. Sarafina entered and immediately ran to the boy's room.

"Are you guys okay? Did you hear 'bout what happened? When did you leave and why didn't you let me know you were going? I'm jus glad you're here and alright. You musta lef before it happened. They had a big fight in that lot near the center and I hear three boys got killed. Did you see or hear any of that?"

"Yeah mom, we were jus goin by the lot when all that stuff was happenin. Me and Cinque ran. We saw some boys on the ground, but only know one of 'em. We heard a lotta noise, sound like shootin so we jus kept runnin."

"Well, it's over now I'm jus glad you both are okay. We got to do somethin'' bout this neighborhood. Lesee if they got anything on the news yet. Then I'm goin to bed.

Don' forget we goin to church in the morning." "Okay mom."

It was just before 8:00 AM on another bright and sunny day. On Sundays, Sarafina usually tried to sleep a little longer, but today was something special. She got out of bed, did her morning routine and then turned on the TV. The news was just coming on so she sat down in the living room and listened.

Good morning from TV channel 10. This is Max Papier, your on the spot news reporter, giving you the latest on what was a gruesome shootout in the center city section last night. According to police reports, it happened around 10:30 PM and involved the two notorious street clubs called the Bandits and the Cripplers. Three men were killed and two others were taken to Mercy General Hospital with minor cuts and bruises. They are being held for questioning. Also according to police, this was an incident that has been brewing for some time. The dispute seemed to center on which group would have control of the territory where the new recreation center had just been built and other major improvements are being made under the inner city urban renewal project. Police say that they have several eye witnesses and arrests are expected to be made. And now for the latest on the weather in your area…

Sarafina had heard enough so she turned the channel and went in the kitchen to make breakfast. Not long after, both Jameel and Cinque came in without being called and sat down.

Jameel said: "Mom, did you hear any more 'bout last night What all happened?" "Yes, I jus heard the news an they say three men were killed and two hurt. They say it was about which one of those clubs gonna rule. I hope they catch somebody. Now when you finish eatin, start getting ready, we goin to church."

Cinque answered and said: "Aw mom, do we hafta go? I'm still sleepy."

"Yes, you are going, so don' give me lip. Jameel you can go in the bathroom first, but don' take all day."

As they were preparing to go to the neighborhood church, news was spreading around the block that some of their own boys were involved in last night's fracas. Even non- church folk were up and milling around outside. At around 10:45, Sarafina, Jameel and Cinque came out, ignoring the unusual activity, got in the car and headed to church. As she pulled away, some of her neighbors were seen pointing and talking which made her wonder.

After a short ride she pulled up to the church parking lot and luckily found a spot right away. It was almost 11:00, so she and the boys hurriedly got out and went inside. The service was just about to start, so they were quickly ushered to seats near the rear of the sanctuary.

The choir sang an opening hymn and then the assistant pastor opened the service with prayer. The rest of the service moved through the normal program routine until finally it came to the part where Rev. Joyner would deliver the sermon for the day. He was a tall imposing figure with a deep, rich baritone voice that spoke with authority and conviction. As he stepped into the pulpit, all eyes were glued on him. The congregation was especially attentive today in light of what had happened last night. Everybody wanted to hear his view and he did not disappoint.

Rev. Joyner started in: "My Lord and my God we are your people and the sheep of your pasture who have come to hear a word from you. This is a very somber day in our homes and even here in your house. We know that you, in your infinite wisdom, are still in control, but we feel the need to ask for Your grace and mercy in this our time of need. Hear our prayer O Lord and wrap your loving arms around us and give us peace."

Thus he concluded his opening prayer.

"Brothers and sisters I'm sure that all of you by now have heard what happened in our streets last night. The time has come when we can no longer stand by and watch what's going on. We need to organize and focus on making this city a better place to live. So today, I want to talk a little bit about community responsibility and what each of you can do to help. I'll be talking from the book of Nehemiah Chapter 1, verses 2 thru 4 in the King James translation and the second Book Of Chronicles - Chapter 7 – verse 14.

Nehemiah, as you may know, was an important person, a VIP in the king's house in Persia. Even though he was a slave, he became the cupbearer to the king - a position with great responsibility and trust. Now Nehemiah was no longer living in his old neighborhood, which was the city of Jerusalem, but his compassion and concern for their welfare was profound. There came a time when one of his brothers had occasion to come to him and he asked about the conditions back home. The report was that the city had been burned, the wall surrounding it had been destroyed and the people were in dire straits. Nehemiah upon hearing this, didn't turn his head and look the other way, but he sat down wept and mourned for days. But more than just crying, he began to fast and pray for his neighborhood. His compassion and concern for his brethren, compelled him to act. He acted, not without a plan, but asked for guidance from above. After some time, and in prayer for guidance, he developed a strategy in which he would approach the king. Then he made his request to the king, which he spoke very carefully, as to not anger the king, and asked that he be permitted to return to Jerusalem and help rebuild the community. Since Nehemiah had found favor with God and consequently the king, he was allowed to go home.

When he got there after a long journey, it was confirmed in his eyes what had been reported to him. Three days after he arrived he went out by night to really see what needed to be done. He assessed the neighborhood and developed his plan. When it came time to address the people, he recognized the need to motivate them and bring them together. This was going to be a daunting task because the people had turned away from their dedication and worship of the God that brought them out of foreign captivity and back to their homeland.

To exhort the people, Nehemiah reminded them of what they had already been told, in the second book of Chronicles Chapter 7, verse 14 – "If My people who are called by My name humble themselves and pray, and seek My face and turn from their wicked ways, then I will Hear from heaven, will forgive their sin, and heal their land."

So you see my brothers and sisters, we need the compassion of a Nehemiah and faith in our God to bring about the changes needed in our community. I will be reaching out to some of you very soon to talk more about this. Right now let each and every one of you go into his or her prayer room and seek your own guidance for how you can help."

The sermon was moving and very inspiring. The whole congergation, particularly Sarafina and even the boys were focused on what the preacher said. After spending a few minutes fellowshipping with some of the members after the service concluded, she and the boys went out to the car and headed home. The few minutes that it took to get home, seemed longer than when they were coming. This was probably because they were anxious to get home and hear the latest news about last night. While they were parking their car, Jameel noticed that some of the same cars that he saw yesterday riding through the block were back. He brought it to Sarafina's attention, but she was not concerned.

They got upstairs, changed into more relaxing garb and had a light lunch. The boys went into their room and started playing video games while Sarafina turned on the news to get the latest. There was nothing new, no more than what had been said earlier so she went in her room to take a nap. She had gone into a much deeper sleep, than she thought was needed. It was about three hours later, when she heard a loud knock on the door.

"Open up, open up – police!"

Somewhat shaken she gathered herself and went to the door. Looking through the peep hole she saw that it was two uniformed policemen, so she opened the door.

"Are you the mother of Cinque Peterson?" "Yes, why do you wanna know?"

"Ma'am we have a warrant to take him in for questioning about the shooting last night."

"Oh no, not my boy, you got to be mistakin."

"No ma'am, no mistake we have an eyewitness that described him and named him. So we have to take him. Where is he?"

After a long hesitation Sarafina said nothing, but didn't move either. The policemen than went around her through the apartment and found the boys bedroom. They were still playing their games.

"Which one of you is Cinque?" "I am, what chu want?" "You're coming with us!" "What for, I ain done nuthin."

Jameel then said: "He been with me all day. He ain done nuthin," "This is about last night. Come on son let's go."

Sarafina was still standing near the door when the two policemen were about to take Cinque out. The tension had reached its' peak. Sarafina was totally distraught and fearing the worst for her baby boy. Him being locked up was the last thing she would have ever conceived in her mind. When she could no longer stand it, she moved between the cops and grabbed hold of Cinque.

"O no, no, no you can't take my baby. You can't have him. He didn't do anything."

At that moment Jameel also got into it to help his mother. The cops just knocked him down to the floor and pushed Sarafina aside as they hustled out the door with Cinque in tow. Moving quickly to their patrol car, they put him in and sped away.

By this time, Sarafina was uncontrollable. Tears rained down and she cried O Lord help me, help me. After some time, when she calmed down a bit, she placed a call to the church and got the answering machine. Fortunately, there was an emergency call number for the pastor which she dialed immediately.

With a highly emotional and quivering voice she blurted out: "Rev. Joyner, - Rev. Joyner, this is Sister Sarafina Peterson. The police have just taken my son. They said it was about the shootings last night. They took him an I don' know what to do. They won't even let me see him."

Rev. Joyner said: "Sister Peterson, please calm down. You get yourself together and meet me at the police station in one hour. I'm going to make some phone calls."

Sarafina went into the bathroom and took some aspirin and told Jameel to get ready to go with her to the police station in a little while. Jameel eager to know what was going on asked her: "Mom, what they gonna do to him? What did pastor say?"

"I don' know, but he said to meet him. I guess we'll find out soon."

An hour later at the police station, the night desk duty officer received them and said this was highly unusual, but he had received instructions from the mayor through his Captain to let them see the boy. Cinque had been taken into custody and placed in a holding cell in the juvenile detention ward of the city's correctional facility. It was getting late so no other legal action could be administered until the morning. They were then led down a long dim corridor and down a flight of stairs to a series of cells. In the last one on the aisle in the darkest corner they saw a very frightened and shaking young man who obviously had been crying. He was huddled up in a fetal position. As they approached the cell, he unfolded and came to the locked gate and said: Momma, why they got me in here. I ain' done nuthin an they won't lemme' go. Why they holdin me here. They say I killed somebody, but I didn't do nuthin. Rev. Joyner, you said that if we truly believe in God and have faith and trust in Him He will fight your battles. I been prayin and trustin since I got here. I jus wanna know…**when He gonna show up.**"

Chapter 2 - A Test Of Faith

On Monday morning Midland High School was all abuzz about what had happened over the weekend. The police had been canvassing several homes in the neighborhood questioning people about what they saw that night in the vacant lot near the new recreation center. The shootings that occurred Saturday night as a result of the clash between the rival B's and C's clubs left three young men dead and two wounded. The mayor was coming down hard on the police to provide him with answers. The police in turn were shaking up the whole neighborhood trying to come up with some hard facts. Other than the two eyewitnesses who had come forward, no one else was talking. The students at Midland had made their own assessment.

It was early in the school day and the students had just returned from their weekend break. Jameel Peterson and Dolitha Davenport, two of the students who had been at the civic center's youth party preceding the Saturday night shootout, were huddled together in the hallway just before classes started.

Dolitha was saying: "J, I heard 'bout your brother. Why the cops pick on him, I know he wasn' in it."

"Yeah, you right, he was wit me the whole time that mess went down. Cops came to the house Sunday night an' dragged him out, in front of my moms and everything. I tried to stop 'em, but they pushed up on me. They wouldn' listen to nuthin we said. They say somebody saw him do the shootin'. Dey crazy."

The bell sounded for the start of classes and the two separated after agreeing to meet later on when school let out. In almost every class, there was murmuring about the shooting. So much so that the teachers started asking what all the talk was about. Most of them knew about the fight that had happened in school on Friday, but were not aware of the incident on Saturday. It was as if what they knew about the gang activity in the community had taken a turn for the worse and that teaching any subject was going to be a challenge today.

Several of the C's club members who attended MHS were spreading the word, in their own special fashion, that nobody better be talking to the cops, even the teachers or anybody else. The word was out that they would be doing their own investigation and if anyone was found to be giving information, they would pay. The special brand of fear they spread throughout the school, was respected by all students and some teachers.

Even though there were members of the B's club in the school, the C's had the numbers.

Jameel hooked up with his friend Rajon after his first class and they headed toward the library. In the library, where they both had a common study period, they talked about what happened. Jameel said: "Raj", you know the cops got Cinque yesterday. He in the place right now. My moms supposed to go down there this morning an' try and get him out. What chu hear on the street?"

"J, I heard this mornin' on the way in that it was Sista that ID'd him. I don' know why she say nuthin, she wasn' even out there. I saw her still inside when all that stuff was goin down. I think she jus tryin to get back atchyou 'cause you was disn' her at the party."

"Man, you think she really do that? Thas whack!"

"Yeah man, you know she kinda strange anyhow. What chu' gonna do?"

"Afta school, I'm gonna catch up wit her and see was'up. Maybe I can get her to 'fess up and tell the truth. If she don't, I dono whas gonna happen to Cinque."

"You be cool man, 'cause you know Sista's brother Razor was lookin' for you Saturday. He thinks you was in the fight Friday against his boy Mo. I think Sista tol him that. Now that he dead, the rest of the C's may jus wanna jack you up anyway. So if you do catch up wit her, be cool. The word's out too that Hakeem, Razor's lutenant, steppin' up to be leader. An I know he worse than Razor."

"Okay man, I'll watch out, but I can't jus let her slide wit that crap. See you later." The two separated and went on to their next classes.

It was now about 10:30 AM and Sarafina, Cinque's mother was just arriving at the police station with Rev. Joyner. They entered the building and immediately saw that Cinque had already been brought upstairs from the cells and was sitting in lieutenant Meeker's office. After stopping at the front desk, they were directed to the lieutenant's office. His door was open and he beckoned them in. Cinque, still somewhat shaken, stood up to greet his mother and said: "Mom, they let'n me go." Rev. Joyner then chimed in: "Praise the Lord."

"You must be Ms. Peterson," the lieutenant said. "Yes, I am. Can I take him home now?"

"Yes. It appears that the eyewitness, who gave the statement about your boy was mistaken. When she was questioned further this morning, it seems that her story didn't make sense. Ms. Peterson, I apologize for the way that my officers handled the matter, but they were under a lot of pressure to come up with somebody. We're trying hard to keep this gang situation from getting out of control. Are you the reverend who contacted the mayor last night?"

Rev. Joyner then answered: "Yes, I'm Reverend Joyner and Mrs. Peterson is one of my church members. The mayor is a good friend. Now I know that the city is being hit with an escalating gang presence and I want to work with you to put an end to it. But the way that this boy was treated yesterday, in front of his mother, on a Sunday night after having been in church earlier was uncalled for. As I said, I want to work with you, but I will not tolerate the mistreatment of any of the people in this neighborhood."

The lieutenant apologized again and Sarafina and Rev. Joyner left the building with Cinque and headed home. Rev. Joyner, after praising God for His Divine intervention, separated from them and left for his day job. Sarafina after thanking the Rev. for all of his help, went on her way. For the third consecutive day the sun was shining bright, the air was somewhat brisk and it seemed to be a good day. As the duo approached home, Sarafina noticed that there were some strange cars circling the block. She immediately thought about something Jameel had told her on Saturday when he said that he had seen some strange cars filled with the B's. This brought a chill to her body and she hurried up the stairs to her apartment. Cinque had also spotted the cars, but he was just so glad to be at home that it didn't bother him.

Once inside, Sarafina picked up the phone and called the school office. She spoke to the principal and explained to him what had happened and promised that he would be back in classes tomorrow. The principal acknowledged her call and said he would be looking forward to seeing him. Next, she called her job and tried to explain to them what happened. Her supervisor was less receptive to her call than the principal. It seems that even at Gateway Safe & Lock, where she worked, the rumor mill was alive with misinformation. It had been circulating that Sarafina's boy committed the act that was all over the news. Mr. Lukinbill, an older man very set in his ways and very quick to judge, had heard the gossip and believed it. As one of the plant managers, he was in a position to hire and fire at will. He told her to come in tomorrow, but come straight to his office.

Meanwhile, at MHS the school day had ended and Jameel was searching for Sista. He waited outside the main entrance for some time and when he was sure she would have come out by then, he started asking around if anyone knew her whereabouts. No one had seen her all day and they thought that she hadn't even come to school. Jameel decided then to find Dolitha and ask her. Dolitha was waiting for "J" on the other side of the building where they usually met.

"What happened to you? I been here fifteen minutes waitin."

"Aw I was 'round front lookin' for Sista. Rajon tol me this mornin' he heard she the one who tol police she saw my brother do the shootin. I wanna aks her why she trippin like dat an get my brother in trouble. I didn' see her. You see her today?" "No, I don' think she here today. Maybe she feel guilty and stay home."

"Yeah you prably right. Come on les go. I'll walk you home."

As they were leaving the school grounds and turning the corner, a black sedan with dark tinted windows pulled up beside them and the windows rolled down. The man sitting in the front passenger side was Hakeem, the new C's club general.

"Jameel, I wanna see you. Come on down to M&Ms (the neighborhood hang out) in a half hour. Don' make me come lookin' for you."

Before Jameel could answer, the window rolled up and the car sped away. Dolitha looked at "J" and told him not to go. Jameel was a little shaken, but didn't want to appear that way so he faced Dolitha and said: "I ain gonna let him punk me. I'm goin down there, but I ain goin inside. He can talk to me on the street. You call Rajon and tell him whas' hapnin'. Tel'm also to call me tonight."

"J, you be careful. I'll call later too."

Jameel decided that he was going to go home first and see what happened with Cinque. When he walked into the apartment, Cinque was sitting at the kitchen table eating. He was glad to see him and went to the table and hugged him around his neck.

"What they do to you in there?"

"They ain' do nuthin' to me. It was jus scary in there 'cause it got real dark and there was only one other guy in there next door, an he was sick all night. He kept hollerin' he needed help, but no one came. He was throwin' up too. I tried to go to sleep, but he kept me awake jus about all night. I guess I did go to sleep sometime ʻcause when they came, to get me, it was mornin' an they tol me I was goin' home. I still don' know why I was even in there. Mom say somethin' about some girl lied on me." "Yeah, I found out it was Sista, Razor's real sister. She trippin' on somethin. I tried to find her afta school today, but she didn' come. I'll see her tomorrow and see whas' her story. I gotta go back out down to M&M's for a minute. Mom here?"

"Yeah, she layin down."

"Jus tell her I was here an I'll be back soon. Save me some of that Chinese stuff."

Jameel skipped down the stairs and headed toward M&M's. He was feeling more confident as he took each step closer. He wasn't afraid of Hakeem or his reputation, but he wasn't sure just how many C's were going to be there and what they might do. If it was going to be just him and Hakeem, he knew he'd be okay because they were both about the same size. Hakeem was a little older though and had dropped out of MHS about a year ago and became a staunch member of the C's.

"J" was right near the corner where M&M's was when he saw that about five of the club members were waiting just outside the store. He hesitated for a moment, looked more closely then decided to go ahead. As he walked up, one of the members approached him and said: "Hakeem, ain' here, he hadda' go take care of som' otha bidness, but he lef a message for you. He say you and him got som' unfinished bidness that Razor lef undone an' he'll see you later." Jameel, looked straight into the soldier's eyes and said: "Yeah aw'ight, but you tell'm Razor knew his sister lied on me ʻbout Mo. Make sure you tell'm that." Jameel then backed up, turned around and walked away glancing back every few steps to watch his back.

It was now about 6:30 PM when Jameel arrived home for the second time. Sarafina was up now and she greeted him when he came in.

"Cinque said you were here before, wher'd you go?"

"Hi, mom – I jus went down to M&M's to see somebody."

"You know I don' like you hangin around there, nothin but trouble there. Okay sit down and eat."

Around 8:00 O'clock the phone rang and it was Rajon for Jameel. "Hey Raj whas'up?"

"Man, you tell me. Dolitha tol me that Hakeem called you out. What happened? "Yeah he tol me to meet him at the hang an we would talk. When I got there he wasn' even there. One of his boys, I didn' know, said he had to leave so I jus chilled. He lef' a message for me sayin he see me later. I think he punk'd out."

"Don' bet on it, I seen him get down. Anyway I'm glad you didn' get in it wit him. What chu gonna do now?"

"I ain' doin nuthin, it's his move. I'm jus gonna do my regular stuff, ain' gonna worry none 'bout him."

"That's cool man. Okay see ya tomorrow." "Yeah, ok later."

Tuesday morning Sarafina got up a little earlier than usual. She couldn't shake the foreboding feeling resulting from her telephone conversation with Mr. Lukinbill yesterday. As she prepared the boy's breakfast, she wondered just what this meeting could be about. She had missed a day's work before and after working there for the better part of three years, she never had a problem. Yet somehow, the tone of his voice had sent her into an anxiety mode that would not subside. She slept, but not peacefully and in rising early her body reminded her of its deprived state. She managed to finish their breakfast grab a quick bite for herself and then started dressing for work.

"Jameel, Cinque ya'll get up now and come an eat. I'm gittin' ready to leave." "Okay mom, we up." Jameel said as he struggled to get out of bed.

"Come on Cinque, we gotta get up."

"Aw jus a few more minutes."

"No man, come on git up now we gotta go."

The boys got up and headed for the bathroom as Sarafina was walking out the door.

She was about two steps into the hallway when she turned and hollered back, "Now don' be goin to that M&Ms today, come home."

There was no response, but she knew they heard her so she kept going. Jameel once again edged out Cinque and got into the bathroom first. Cinque then went back to bed.

After a few minutes, Jameel came out and went into the kitchen. Not seeing Cinque there he rushed into the bedroom where Cinque had gone back to sleep. Shaking him hard he said: "Cinque, git up, git up, you gonna make us late."

"Okay man, I'm comin."

It was a struggle, but both boys were able to get it together, finish breakfast and move on to school.

MHS was having its usual flurry of activity for the morning as the students scurried to get to homerooms before the bell rang. The murmuring that was rampant in classrooms yesterday had become just the usual gossip type conversations today. The weekend's event had been relegated to yesterday's news and again it was business as usual.

Everything appeared back to normal except for what was still on Jameel's mind. He was still determined to find Sista and see why she did what she did.

The rest of the day was uneventful until the end when school was letting out. Jameel spotted what he thought was Sista running out the front door. He immediately started running after her and caught up with the girl he spotted. He grabbed her and when she turned around it was just a look alike he didn't know.

"Oh girl, I'm sorry. I thought you was Sista. You know who she is?"

"Yeah, I know her, you think I look like her, well I don't. What's your problem?" "Naw, ain' nuthin'. I was jus lookin' for her `cause I need to rap wit her."

"Well she ain' in school an won' be back `till Thursday. You know her brother got killed Saturday right?"

"Yeah I know, thas part of what I need to talk to her `bout. Well, thanks. You see Dolitha?"

"Do I look like 411 to you? Now move an let me go on." "Wow girl, ain' no need for you to get attitude on me. Later."

Just then Rajon and Cinque came over and the three of them headed in the same direction. Jameel asked Raj, if he had seen Dolitha? The answer was no.

Sarafina had arrived at work a little early and went by Mr. Lukinbill's office. He had not gotten in yet nor had his secretary, so she took a seat in the waiting area. She noticed that a copy of the local newspaper, early edition, was left on a lamp table next to her seat, probably left by the night watchman. She couldn't help but notice that right on the front page was an article about the weekend's gang rumble and who had been taken into custody. There right in front of her eyes, it showed a picture of her child being taken out of the apartment building where they lived. Her heart stopped for a minute and she felt feint. It took a while, but she gathered herself together and then thought how could they have taken this picture. It happened so fast.

Just then she heard someone coming down the hall and she discarded the paper. It was Mr. Lukinbill coming around the corner and her heart started to pump a little faster. She stood up and Mr. Lunkinbill spotted her. He acknowledged her and asked if she could give him a few minutes and then he would call her. She said yes and sat back down. By now her anxiety level was running at a peak and the thoughts that were going through her head were running wild.

It was about fifteen minutes later when he buzzed his secretary who had come in, to ask Sarafina to enter. Her heart pounding, she stood up and walked in.

"Sarafina please sit down. I know you have been with us for some time now and your work has been good. However, I heard something yesterday that was a bit disturbing. I know that on Saturday there was some kind of gang confrontation in the area and I understand that one of your children was directly involved. Is that true?"

"No Mr. Lukinbill – not true. My youngest boy was identified by someone who was mistaken. The police did take him in, but it was all a mistake. He was let out as soon as they got it straight."

"I'm glad to hear that, but the issue has come to the attention of the plant owner and he wasn't happy. I'm going to explain what you told me to him. I will be talking to him later today or early tomorrow. You go ahead to your station and I'll let you know what happens. Thank you for coming in."

Sarafina, somewhat relieved got up and headed to her area. She still felt a little uneasy about why the owner should be so upset, but she attempted to put it out of her mind as she went to her desk.

Jameel and Cinque went straight home after school, but "J" was a little worried about why he didn't see Dolitha there. Once inside he picked up the phone and called her number. The phone rang and rang, but there was no answer. This sent him into a higher state of anxiety because he knew that her mother was usually home since she didn't work and she should have answered.

"Cinque, I'm goin over to Dolitha's house and see if she aw'ight. You know she wasn' at school today. Tell mom when she git here where `om at."

"Okay. When you be back?"

"I donno, soon as I see whasup wit her, soon I guess. Later."

Jameel walked out and headed toward Dolitha's house that was right around where his friend Rajon lived. When he hit the street he saw some new cars circling the `hood and he became a little tense. Knowing that Hakeem had already warned him about "seeing him later", he wasn't sure just what that meant and he knew Hakeem knew where he lived. The cars were moving slowly, but didn't seem like they were stopping so he kept walking, but quickened his pace. As he got closer to Dolitha's apartment building he could see that there was a large crowd gathered in front. They were standing around talking loudly to each other and pointing up toward the roof. He could see even from where he was and in the early twilight, that there was a man walking on the edge of the ten-story building. His steps were unsure and as he wobbled a bit from side to side he appeared to be drunk. Screaming sirens could be heard at a distance, but definitely moving near. The crowd pointing up and hollering were fueling the moment by chanting "Jump, Sparrow, jump. Come on jump." The man they called Sparrow, was kind of the neighborhood junkie/alcoholic who was always in your face begging. He wasn't dangerous, but not a favorite of the neighbors.

Jameel, was still looking up at the man as he got closer and closer and felt a real sense of pity in his heart. Although he didn't know Sparrow well he had seen him up close several times and knew that this was just a very troubled man, who had been dealt a series of bad hands in life's poker tournament. Sparrow started looking down as the crowd continued egging him on and then in an instant – he jumped. The police were arriving and the crowd, not believing that he would really do it, stepped back as the body plummeted with contorted moves toward the cement. The sound it made was like that of an over ripe tomato being thrown hard against a stone wall. Blood splattered everywhere as his neck broke and his head was almost completely turned around. The crowd still in disbelief was getting out of the way as the police began to cordon off the area.

Lieutenant Meeker was on the scene and approached the body. There was obviously nothing that could be done for the man, except to remove him.

In all the excitement, Jameel didn't see Dolitha move in behind him. When she embraced him he jumped around and nearly punched her out. It scared her more than she scared him.

"Girl don do that, you crazy?"

" Wow J whasup wit you? You look like somebody afta you."

"Yeah, you could be right, you know what happen' yesterday. Why you wasn't at school today, thas why I come down here."

"I had to go wit my mom to the Social Service people, they hasslin' again 'bout her checks. I'm okay. Nice to know you was thinkin' 'bout me. Thas sweet. You wanna come up?"

"Naw, I gotta get back home, my mom be lookin for me now. I'll see you tomorrow. You comin to school right?"

"Yeah, I'll be there."

Jameel kissed her and turned to head home when he saw Rajon in the crowd. "Hey Raj, whassup?"

"Ain' nutin' man did you see that dude jump. Crazy mutha. He been actin' more whack lately than usual, musta got holda some bad S—t. Well, he feelin' good now. What chu doin here?"

"I jus came to see about Dolitha, you know she not at school today. Well lemme go on home, I'll see you tomorrow."

"Yeah, later."

The police were still at the scene asking the crowd who the man was and trying to get a straight story about what happened. As per normal, nobody wanted to provide the cops with anything much less good information. Lt. Meeker, who had been the one to get Cinque released was becoming more and more anxious about the gang activity growing and wasn't sure that this incident might not be related. But after going nowhere with canvassing the crowd and seeing the body being hauled to the morgue, he told his men to pack up and leave. Another frustrating event witnessed by an all-knowing crowd who would not be revealing anything. He shook his head, got in his car and left.

Jameel arrived home about 7:00 PM and was prepared to explain to his mother about why he hadn't come straight home from school, but as he walked in he could hear her on the phone. From the gist of the conversation, he could tell that she was talking to Rev. Joyner. Not wanting to eavesdrop, he headed to the kitchen and sat down to eat.

Moments later Sarafina was off the phone and went into the kitchen.

"Cinque, said you went to see about that Dolitha girl from school. Is something wrong with her?"

"Naw, mom she jus wasn' at school today an wit all thas been goin on, I jus wanted to see."

"You really like her huh?" "Yeah mom, she aw-ight."

"Well I'm glad to hear she's okay, but you better keep your mind on your schoolwork. You too close to finishin' to get in trouble with some girl. You hear me?"

"Yeah mom, I'm cool."

"That was Rev. Joyner on the phone and he was tellin' me 'bout a funeral for that boy they call Razor who got killed Saturday. The funeral gonna be tomorra night at Higginbothams place over there on 5th street at 7:00 O'clock. You and Cinque can go if you wanna. You know where it is right?"

"Yeah, I know. I donno if I wanna go to that though, could be bad." "Well you decide an let me know before I leave in the mornin'." "Okay mom."

Rev. Joyner had called Sarafina because he was a little hesitant about giving the eulogy for the young man called Razor. He knew about his participation with the C's and wasn't quite sure about what he could say. He had only learned of his real name just this morning and had nothing positive that he could add. Knowing that Sarafina was one of his prayer warriors he had called to ask her to pray with him to get guidance on the matter. He started in saying:

"Heavenly Father, gracious and Almighty God, I come to you with a bowed head and a humble heart seeking your guidance on the matter that has come before me. You know my needs and you know what is weighing heavily on my heart concerning the funeral tomorrow. Let your will be done in this solemn ceremony and the words of my mouth and meditations of my heart be acceptable in your hearing and in your sight. I don't know what can be said about a young man who chose to live by the dictates of his heart that were not in keeping with your statutes or your commandments, but chose to live outside of the kingdom circle. But Lord, I know that it is not my right to judge him nor to grant him the holy pardon that You may assign. All I ask is by the power of the Holy Spirit, that you touch my heart and let me speak to the people to deliver Your word.

Lord, hear this petition and grant me this request in the precious name of Jesus and it is in His name that we pray. Amen."

Sarafina joined him saying Amen. She also told him she would attend the funeral to help out. He agreed, thanked her then they both said goodnight.

The next day at school, Jameel, Dolitha and Rajon met before classes started and decided that they were going to attend the funeral tonight. Although it was not something that Rajon really wanted to do because he was still being sought as a recruit by the C's, and wanted to keep a very low profile, but he said that he would go with his friends.

Dolitha wasn't overly enthusiastic about going either, because she had one of those foreboding feelings again and she reminded Jameel about what she told him Saturday before the shootout. He acknowledged that she had been right about Saturday, but he couldn't see anything happening at a funeral home. Especially at "Higgy B's Last Stop" as all the kids referred to the funeral home, because it was not too far from a police satellite station. The bell rang signaling the start of classes and the group broke up.

During the rest of the school day there was a slight tinge of excitement swirling around the planned funeral and also the talk about Sparrow jumping off the roof last night. To the kids this was all that was needed to avoid another boring school day. To the teachers, this was what presented an ongoing challenge on how to get and keep their attention in class. As the students transitioned from class to class, Jameel was still on the lookout for Sista. Although he was aware that she was probably involved in whatever last minute family arrangements had to be made before tonight, he couldn't help but think that she might have come in. As Rajon had said once before, "Sista always acted kinda strange." He didn't see her so he finished out the day in his normal routine fashion.

When Sarafina arrived at work that morning in her normal time schedule, she was still somewhat apprehensive about what Mr. Lukinbill might have learned from the plant owner. She saw him in the hallway and all he said was good morning and nothing more. This gave her a feeling of ease and she went on to her work area. Even though her desk was outside of the production area of the plant, as she passed some of the other workers she could sense that there was something going on with them. She suspected that she had been the topic of conversation yesterday and there was still a carryover of talk today. She tried to ignore her feelings and went to her desk. When she got there, she couldn't help but notice that a copy of the article regarding the shooting and her son that she saw in the paper was left for her to see. She snatched the paper off her desk, looked around and then threw it in the trash. There were three other women right around her, but no one said anything and the rest of the day went with some tense moments among the group.

Sarafina kept thinking to herself, that this was all started because of a big lie.

Around 6:00 O'clock Sarafina and the boys had finished eating and were preparing to go to the funeral home when the phone rang. It was Rev. Joyner for her.

"Sister Peterson, this is Rev. Joyner how are you?" "I'm fine, how are you?"

"I'm okay but I'm down at the Higginbothams Funeral Home and I was wondering if you could come down here now? I need your help."

"Sure Reverend, I'll be there in a few minutes. Jameel, Cinque are you guys ready to go now?"

"Naw mom, it's too early."

"Well Rev. Joyner asked me to come down there now, so I'm gonna leave. Can you get there okay?"

"Yeah mom, go ahead we can walk." Sarafina put on her coat and left.

Higginbotham's Funeral Home was located near the heart of downtown right near the corner of 5th street and 8th Avenue. It was a fairly modern building with a long canopy overhanging the walkway and large glass doors in the entranceway. Since it was the only funeral home in the neighborhood, he got all the business from both the saved and unsaved, sinners and saints alike. His motto was "When you're gone you're gone, I don't know how you lived, but I will take care of you now."

When Sarafina walked in Rev. Joyner was in the office speaking to Mr. Higginbotham. He saw her and beckoned her in. "Mrs. Peterson, this is Lawrence Higginbotham."

"Please call me Larry. It's a pleasure to meet you Mrs. Peterson the Rev. has told me a little about you and I hope that this send off will be acceptable to you."

"Thank you Mr. Hig…, I mean Larry, it's not me who the ceremony should be acceptable to but the boy's mother. Is she here?"

Then Rev. Joyner said: "That's why I called you down early, we have not been able to find his mother only his sister who they call Sista. She said that their mother has not been around for sometime and that she and "Razor" lived by themselves. She said she had the money to pay for the funeral and burial and she would take care of everything. I'm a little uncomfortable with where she got the money. Something's not right.

Sarafina, I know that you've been working with some of the women in the neighborhood through your CONN's (Change Our Neighborhood Now) group and I thought maybe you could shed some light on who or where the mother might be."

"I'm sorry Reverend, but I don't know anything about this boy, his mother or his sister. I wish I could help, but I don' think any of my group knows."

"Thank you Sarafina. Well, Larry, you got your fee and we've come this far, so I guess we have to go with it. I'll do the best I can with the eulogy."

People started coming in, mostly youngsters and a few adults. Larry and Rev. Joyner went out to greet them and then several young men came in as a group wearing the obvious uniform of the C's. They sauntered in surveying and checking out the room. The casket was still open so they leisurely walked up to it and did their little private ritual for Razor. The gathering crowd became a little uneasy as the young men each stepped forward to do his thing. For a few minutes, there was a little tension in the room, but then Rev. Joyner took charge and the funeral service began.

Just as the service was getting underway, Jameel, Cinque, and Dolitha walked in the door and sat in the back. No Rajon. Apparently, at the last minute he changed his mind. Rev. Joyner started out saying: "Greetings family and friends. This evening we come to say goodbye to a young man, named Malcom Jenkins, who was better known to all as Razor. He was beloved by some and feared by others and he is a child of God.

Although, some may not have agreed with his life style, he was still a child of God. There are some who would say that his life was lived for naught, but he is still a child of God." Rev. Joyner went on to deliver a beautiful eulogy, under the circumstances, emphasizing where possible the fact that Razor, in all that he had done or was known for,

was still a child of God. At the conclusion of the service, the C's gathered together to say their final goodbyes and headed for the door. Before they got there however, Jameel said to Dolitha "Les beat them out" and he grabbed her hand and walked through the glass doors.

It was dark now and beside the few lights from the parlor, there was only the street light across from "Higgy B's" casting a dim illumination on the area. As Jameel and Dolitha exited just ahead of the group of C's, the lights came on from a dark colored SUV with tinted windows. The car pulled right up to the front of the home, windows rolled down and shots rang out. Datta, datta, datta, dat. Datta, datta, datta dat. The loud noise broke up the crowd inside and glass from the doors flew everywhere. People were screaming and hitting the floor while Rev. Joyner and Larry scrambled to get to the office to call for help. The call for help got through and the police were on the way.

Meanwhile, Sarafina, who was still at the front of the room where the casket was, looked around for her boys. The shooters had sped off so she quickly walked outside. The horror of what she saw sent her tumbling backward into the wall. There was Jameel lying on the ground with blood spurting from his body. Dolitha was huddled over him crying uncontrollably and holding him desperately. Sarafina recomposing herself ran over and wrapped her arms around him too then cried out: "Oh no, oh no, no, no - Jameel, Jameel. Lord, Lord, Lord help me." Rev. Joyner and Larry saw the boy lying on the ground through the office window, and came running out with a blanket.

"Is he alive? Is he still breathing? Here put this on him" Rev. Joyner said.

The police were just arriving and an ambulance was right behind them. "Stand back, make way, make way" they hollered.

The police moved in and began emergency rescue maneuvers. Jameel was still breathing but very shallow. The ambulance arrived and the EMT's placed him on the gurney then headed to Mercy General Hospital. Sarafina was beside herself, but managed to get in the ambulance also. Larry said to Rev. Joyner: "Let me lock up here and I'll meet you at the hospital." Rev. Joyner nodded okay, ran to his car and followed the ambulance.

At Mercy General Hospital the emergency team went quickly into action upon the ambulance's arrival and Sarafina was escorted to the emergency waiting room. Rev. Joyner arrived and went in to comfort her. It was sometime before they heard anything from anybody and Sarafina was just about totally spent. Finally, a young doctor came into the room and spoke to them: "He's out of surgery now, but I can't give you any false hopes. He sustained a lot of blood loss, but he's hanging on. You can see him now if you want to, but you won't be able to talk to him, he's heavily sedated."

The night nurse led Sarafina and Rev. Joyner up to the third floor down a long corridor to the ICU area and into his room. There was Sarafina's boy hooked up to monitoring machines and tubes and IV's. Her own heart skipped a beat or two and she had to be held up by the reverend. The sight made an indelible imprint on her mind and she broke down. Rev. Joyner tried his best to console her, but it wasn't doing much good. He then turned to the nurse and asked her if there was a chapel here. She answered yes and led them back down the hall and around a corner to a rather small dimly lit room called "The Chapel."

Once inside, he closed the door and led her to a bench near the elevated cross at the front. He sat her down, said some words of comfort to her and then went and kneeled at the foot of the cross. Then he prayed:

"Heavenly Father, it is by Your grace and by Your Mercy that we are given our daily bread. We are given the things that sustain us; the very air that we breathe; the rain that freshens the air. We are given all that is needed to survive. You told us in Your holy writ, that in this life we shall have trouble and that we shall be confronted by the evil one. You said that to every thing there is a season. Lord, I don't know what season this is for this family, but I pray that in Your infinite wisdom You might shed light on this room and illuminate as only You can. Let the Angels that are assigned to that young man in the room down the hall be instructed to restore and refresh the spirit that dwells inside him. Let it be done so much so that the life that You have given him shall not end here, but will continue. And Lord I pray that you wrap your loving arms around his mother.

Comfort her and grant her Your peace. I ask for this merciful blessing in the glorious name of our Lord and Savior Jesus Christ and in His matchless name I pray. Amen."

Rev. Joyner had not quite finished his prayer with his head bowed and eyes closed, when he sensed the presence of Sarafina as she came and kneeled beside him. He turned to her and said: "It's going to be alright. The effectual and fervent prayer of the righteous, avails much. We must believe and keep faith in his Goodness." Sarafina with tears still in her eyes turned to the Reverend and said: "I'm tryin to keep faith, and I wanna believe, but why is all this happenin' to me? Why am I goin through this?" Then she turned toward the cross and said: "Lord, You gave me this boy at a time when I didn' think I could have none. You took his father away early in the war, but You kept me goin. You hold his life in Your hands. Lord I know that you can heal him and I believe You will, but Lord help me understand. Show me some sign that you hear me and are willing." Even while she was still speaking, the whole room began to glow and a warm feeling of comfort came over her and then right there on the cross she saw it.

Chapter 3 - Revenge

For the last three days the weather had been near perfect. The sun shone brightly, skies were a magnificent powder blue and not a cloud present. The temperature hovered around the upper 60's and except for a slightly brisk wind blowing occasionally these were a weatherman's dream days. On this third night however, the sky had gathered an army of angry clouds and it was pouring. The rain was coming down in torrents and the thunder and lightening were playing a Wagnerian symphony across the heavens. Only a few hours earlier, just a few miles away from Mercy General Hospital where the storm was now beating heavily on the roof, the horrendous incident had taken place.

The shooting that took place just outside Higginbotham's Funeral Home had Jameel Peterson gunned down in a drive-by. Now inside the hospital, Jameel was fighting for his life while Sarafina and Rev. Joyner were huddled in the hospital's chapel in deep meditation and prayer. Sarafina, in her earnest prayer had petitioned God for a sign that would indicate to her His will in this situation. As she focused intently on the chapel room cross, the room glowed with a warm and comforting light and there on the previously plain cross, appeared the image of Jesus Christ crucified. Then she heard the words that seemed to be coming from His mouth; "Do not fear, for I am with you; do not be dismayed, for I am your God. I will strengthen you and help you; I will uphold you with my righteous right hand." (Isaiah 41:10). The glow that came over the room entered her body and she felt such reassurance and strength that she no longer embraced the fears of the night. Rev. Joyner saw her demeanor change and wondered if she was near feinting again. But when she turned to him and asked did he see the image on the cross, he hesitated, looked at her curiously and answered that he hadn't. Then she said to him: "I have seen with my own eyes the Glory of the Lord and my faith has been restored. I don't know why you didn't see it, but right there on that cross, in plain sight, was my Jesus crucified and He spoke to me." "Hallelujah" the reverend said as he reveled in the glow of her countenance and he too felt more at peace.

Meanwhile, down at police headquarters, Lt. Meeker instead of going home, since it was long after his shift had ended, was in his office. Some of his men who had been at the drive-by scene with him also came back to the station.

"Lieutenant, these kids are crazy and out of control. It won't be long before one of us ends up in a box if we can't turn it around" said Officer Wheeler.

"Yeah, I'm dreading that day, but it sure looks like it's going in that direction. I'm going to get hold of that preacher who was in here the other day for the boy we brought in over the weekend. What's his name, what's his name, what was his name? Ah, wait a minute here it is on his card, Reverend Cleophus Joyner from that church in the neighborhood across town. I think its called New Life something or other. Oh, wait a minute it's right here on the card – New Life Temple of God. Tomorrow, I'm going to call him and see if we can't work together on a solution. Well, thanks for coming back guys, but there's nothing more we can do here now so let's call it a night. I'll see you in the morning."

"Okay Lt, see you tomorrow."

At the Peterson apartment where Cinque had been taken by one of the funeral home staff, he sat by the phone anxiously waiting for some word about his brother. Finally it rang, but it was only Rajon who had already heard through the street tele-network what had happened. He asked Cinque what the status was on Jameel.

"Cinq, did Jameel make it, is he aw-ight?"

"Dono yet, still watin for mom or somebody to call and tell me. When they took'em I saw him breathin, but it wasn' good."

"Wow man, he can't go out on me like that. I hope he make it. You comin' to school tomorrow?"

"I dono yet, I hafta see."

"Aw-ight, if you do I'll see you there. Later." "Okay Raj, later."

Not more than ten minutes after Cinque hung up with Rajon, the phone rang again and it was Sarafina.

"Cinque, are you all right?"

"Yeah, mom om okay. What about Jameel?"

"He's not out of trouble yet, but I believe he'll be all right. You know Rev. Joyner and me have been prayin, so it's all up to God now. You could say a little prayer for him too."

"Yeah mom, I will."

"Okay baby, I'm going to stay here until I find out more about his condition. Will you be okay?"

"I'll be fine."

"Good! I'll call you again when I know more."

The next day Sarafina, after spending the night sleeping on a couch in the waiting room, woke up at about 5:00 AM after a fitful night's sleep. She tried to find a doctor, a nurse or somebody who could tell her about Jameel's condition. After a short walk to a night nurse's station she spoke to one who told her as far as she knew there was no change in his condition and she would have to check back when the attending physician would be in. This news was not at all reassuring, and she started to agonize in her mind over whether to go into work. Remembering that it was just the other day that she had to go into the manager's office about missing work, she was leaning toward going in. Then she made up in her mind that she was not going anywhere until she knew something more about her son. She then went and found a telephone to call Cinque. He answered with a sleepy voice.

"Hello."

"Cinque you alright? This is mom." "Yeah mom – how's "J"?"

"No change right now, but I'm going to keep on staying here until his doctor comes in and can tell me more. Do you want to go to school?"

"No - I wanna stay here and wait 'til you let me know somethin'." "Okay. You got food there so you can make some breakfast." "Right mom, I'll be fine."

"Okay then goodbye." "Bye."

After she talked to Cinque her mind started rehashing what had happened last night and she just couldn't bring herself to accept this was not some hideous nightmare, but then she realized her firstborn was really in this hospital fighting for his life. She just couldn't bring herself to understand why God was allowing all this to happen to her. First, over the weekend Cinque had been taken in by the police because of somebody's lie, and now Jameel in the hospital probably because of an extension of that same lie. She was starting to tear up again when she saw a doctor come in. He saw her and came over.

"Hello Mrs. Peterson I'm doctor Romane. We met last night, but you were so distraught you may not remember. I have some good news for you. I just checked in on your son and he is awake and talking. He's not completely out of the woods yet, but he's stable and may be on the way to a full recovery. Something amazing must have happened overnight because his healing where the bullets were removed seems unusually quickened. I will have the nurse contact you if there is any change." Sarafina couldn't help herself as she hollered "Hallelujah, praise the Lord. Oh thank you, thank you doctor. You don't know how much I needed to hear that from you." "I'm always glad to deliver that kind of news. I have to run now; other patients to see. Will I see you here later today?"

"Oh yes, yes. I do have to go home now and see about my other son, but I'll be back around 5:30. Will you still be here?"

"Probably not, but I'll leave word with the nurse on duty which doctor you may see for the latest status. Okay Mrs. Peterson you have a nice day."

"Goodbye doctor and thank you again."

The feeling of relief that came over Sarafina reprised that which she felt while praying in the chapel. Basking in her newfound comfort she looked up at the wall clock and regained her grasp on the issues at hand as she headed home. When she got there she went straight to the boy's room and found Cinque sitting up on the side of the bed.

"You couldn't sleep either huh?"

"No mom. I was turnin' all night. Did you meet the doctor?"

"Yes and he said that Jameel is awake and doin' better. Ain't that good news?" "Yeah, mom thas' great. When we gonna see him?"

"I got to do a few things, like call the school, but we'll go later like around 5:30." "Okay, mom."

At M&M's that morning, the talk was animated about what had happened last night. Hakeem, the C's club leader had already issued his preliminary orders about what kind of retaliation they were going to have against the B's for messing up Razor's send off. He didn't mention the fact that it was Jameel who got hit and was in the hospital. He was more concerned that his boys were just behind "J" and could have been hit. What he did say in talking with his soldiers was: "I saw Jameel go down in front, anybody git his stats?"

"Yeah, 'Keem I saw the EM's load him up an he still breathin, but not lookin' good." "Well, I guess it's okay 'cause he was due to git somethin from Razor anyhow. Aw-ight listen-up, tonite we goin over to the Bricks, where them dudes hang out at, an we gonna show'em. It's time we take'em out; take'em all out. All y'all make sure you got enuff amo for the run. If you short, see Hammer, he load you up. Meet back here at 8:00 O'clock an we movin' out. Don' be comin down here late either. Be cool 'till then."

They began to disperse and the store was now officially opened for it's normal, abnormal business.

The Bricks, a Public Housing complex on the East side of the city was made up of a mixed population including some of all ethnic groups. The B's club, the rival faction of the C's on the other side of town, was responsible for the drive-by that took place last night. In an area of the complex where the over used and under repaired basketball courts are, the nettings were missing from the rims and the cement cracked in several places. This was the known meeting place for the B's club members. For those members who were not still occupying space at MHS, they were usually out on the courts.

It was mid morning and several members had come out to talk about last night. As the group gathered together giving high five's and boldly gesturing about their caper, the leader came in laughing also. He went right to the group's center and began speaking.

"Last night was okay, but I heard we only took down one of them and he wasn' even a C. We gotta do betta next time. Remember we gotta get four of them to make up for them takin out Danny and Squirt in the lot last week. Now I know they gonna be comin afta us 'cause we messed up Razor's thing, but I donno when. So we need to stay ready. You feelin' me? PK, I wanchu and Devon to go down to Midland and find out what you can about what they gonna do. Take Rambo wit chu, but don' let him git off on nobody."

Ricoh, the leader was about 6'2" and fairly stocky. He was a little older than the rest of the group being in his mid twenty's. He had grown up in the streets of the city and had never attended MHS but knew all about everything that went down inside and around there.

At Midland that day, the news had already spread about what happened last night and Jameel being in the hospital. Cinque had come in late after Sarafina told him Jameel was better, but he was trying to keep a low profile because everybody was coming up to him asking about "J". Dolitha had also come in, even though she had nearly been hit by the shooters herself. She was all over Cinque pushing him to tell her the latest status. Had Jameel not pushed her down when he saw the SUV coming toward them, she might also be lying in the hospital.

"Cinque, how's "J"? Is he gonna make it? When can I go see him?"

"My mom talked to the doctor this mornin' and he said he was betta. He is awake and talkin, so I guess he gonna make it."

"Wow, thas good. Can I go down there today, will they let me see him?" "Om goin down later today wit my mom, maybe you can go wit us." "That would be good, what time you goin'?"

"She said about 5:30, I guess we goin then." "If I go home wit you you think she mine?"

"Naw, I don' think so, she might wanna talk to you anyhow, since you was wit "J" when he got hit."

"Okay, wait for me afta school. Wait out in front okay?" "Yeah, okay, see you later."

Dolitha turned and headed for her classes and Cinque did the same.

The C's boys that came to school today were walking around with major attitudes and several minor skirmishes with the B's took place in the gym, in the cafeteria and in the parking lot. Nothing was major enough to get the police involved, but the teachers were definitely on high alert that something else happening was almost imminent.

The principal, called an emergency staff meeting after the school day ended and cautioned them to be extra vigilant about any suspicious activities and report it immediately.

The rest of the day had gone without any major crisis and Cinque met up with Dolitha. It was only about 3:30 and Cinque, after thinking about what he had said earlier about Dolitha going home with him, now wasn't so sure he should let her go home with him when his mom was not there. He told her that maybe she should come by around 5:30 and meet them. She said that was okay and she would do that. Cinque then headed home.

Sarafina feeling good about "J's" progress, decided to go to work even if she was very late. She was prompted by her earlier meeting with her boss. She knew that her co- workers would probably have heard the news by now and wasn't sure how they were going to handle it with her. The last time something happened affecting her family, a big lie had caused some major misinformation to be circulated throughout the plant. Now she was a little apprehensive about who was spreading lies. She went in and made her way to her station. The other girls around her acknowledged her, but nothing more than that was said. She had even seen Mr. Lukinbill, and he just nodded at her. Feeling a little less leery, she went right to work, even though in the back of her mind she still had an uneasy feeling about what was going to happen next. Then she remembered that the doctor had given her a good report, and her anxious feelings subsided for the remainder of the workday.

Sarafina got home a little before 5:30 and was headed up the stairs when she heard someone call her.

"Mrs. Peterson, Mrs. Peterson can I talk to you. I don' know if you remember me, but I'm Dolitha Davenport an I was with Jameel last night."

"Yes, I know you - what are you doin' here?"

"I talked wit' Cinque this mornin' at school, and he said that maybe I could go see "J" wit you."

"Yes, thas fine. I think he'll be glad to see you. Come on up for a minute and let me get Cinque, then we'll go okay?"

"Yeah, great!"

Cinque was waiting at the door when they walked in and he was surprised to see that Dolitha had already caught up with his mom. He was about to tell Sarafina about what Dolitha wanted to do, but now that was not necessary as he surmised that had already been done.

Sarafina walked into the apartment and asked Dolitha to wait in the living room while she stepped into the bedroom for a minute. She was considering changing clothes, but when she looked at the clock she thought better of it and just wanted to get down to Mercy. She came out of the bedroom and then stepped into the bathroom to freshen up a bit. Ten minutes later the trio was headed down the stairs and on their way to the hospital. Once in the car, Sarafina in a motherly tone, politely asked Dolitha, where she lived and what her relationship was with Jameel. Dolitha, a little uneasy responded that she lived in the neighborhood just a few blocks away and that she and Jameel were just good friends, but that she liked him a lot. Sarafina got the message, just smiled and kept on driving. Although not showing it much, Sarafina felt pleased with her. She was definitely pretty, well built and appeared to be someone worthy of her son.

As they approached the hospital, they had to go by Higgy-B's and Sarafina noticed that the police were again out there. She couldn't be sure what they were doing, but she could tell they were talking to people around that section. She slowed down, looking for Lt. Meeker, but didn't see him. The hospital was just a few more minutes away so she resumed her speed, found a place to park and headed in.

Once inside, after checking in with the receptionist, she was directed to another room where they had moved Jameel. He was no longer in the ICU, and she was feeling a new high as they entered the elevator to the second floor. On the floor another nurse directed them to room 214. Sarafina, Dolitha and Cinque moved with a sense of urgency as they neared the room and looked inside. There was Jameel sitting up watching television and talking with his roommate who also was a young man about his age. Although they didn't know each other, being about the same age they had much to talk about. Sarafina moved to the bed first wrapped her arms around Jameel and kissed him.

"I'm so glad to see you sittin' up, and talkin' and everything. Last night, you really had us worried. How you feeelin'?"

"Aw mom, Om okay, just sore, but I feel a lot better than last night. They just finished feedin' me an' the food here is really bad. Not like yours. I ate it 'cause I was real hungry, but it wasn' nothin."

"Well, you get better fast, an when you git home you'll have a good home cooked meal. Look who I brought wit me."

At that point Dolitha stepped toward "J" and hugged him.

"I was worried a lot 'bout you. They wouldn' let me go to the hospital wit you last night, so I didn' know what was goin on. You look good though, so I guess you gonna be aw-ight. When they gonna let you go home?"

"I dono, the doctor said I hafta stay here 'till they sure I don' have no infections or nothin'. Maybe a couple more days an he'll see if I can leave."

"Thas not bad, seein' you was hit a few times." "Yeah, what they say at school today."

"Oh, ereybody talkin 'bout what happened, but nobody knows who really did it. You know who they think did it?"

"Yeah, I know an Om sure who did it. I'll deal wit it when I get out."

" Now Jameel, the first thing you want to deal with is getting completely well. The police are already after the shooters."

"Yeah okay mom."

Just then Cinque stepped in and said: "Yo bro. How you doin'? I didn' know whether you was gonna make it. You sure didn' look so good las night."

"Yeah, bro. thanks for the reminder. What you up to, you go to school today?" "Yeah, I went. Ain' nothin new happnin, 'cept ereybody talkin' 'bout you. They all aks 'how you are. I tol them you be aw-ight."

They continued the conversation for about an hour more talking about everything. Sarafina was so happy to see Jameel in such good spirits that she knew God had answered her prayer. Dolitha knew right then that her whole heart belonged to this man and she just wanted him out of there and with her. The night nurse finally came in and reminded them that visiting hours were over and they would have to leave.

The pale green glow on the clock hanging from the wall in M&Ms showed that it was just a few minutes before 8:00 PM. Cars started pulling up to the store while several of the C's came from around the corner walking. Getting out of the first car, Hakeem walked over to Hammer and said: "What it look like man?"

"We reddi to roll on your word 'Keem, but I think two more soldiers comin." "Aw-ight, we wait a cupla minutes, but I tol erebody before don' be late. How we fixed for tools?"

"We good man. Got 'bout 4 T-9's, 2 shotguns, 3 Glocks and a few 32's with plenty of shot."

"Good! We reddi. Aw-ight here come Buster and Shariq. Les go!"

The scene outside M&Ms looked like a staging area for a militia assault. The street soldiers piled into four vehicles ranging from a SUV to an old luxury sedan and moved the convoy out toward the Eastside of town.

The night air was brisk and not too many people were walking around in the Bricks complex. As they approached the courts, Hakeem noticed that not a lot of activity was going on. When they got near the fence around the courts they started to pile out of the cars ready for some action. The scene that greeted them was definitely not what they expected and they all turned to Hakeem for new directions. There in front of them was a totally empty playground. There wasn't a soul in sight, not even the old winos that sometimes hung around in that area at night. Hakeem immediately starting looking around as if sensing they had stumbled into some kind of a trap. But no, nothing could be seen. Realizing then that the B's must have been tipped off somehow, he motioned for his boys to get back in their rides and leave.

Several minutes later the first of the group arrived back at the hang (M&Ms) and waited for Hakeem who had the key to the store. Thoroughly disappointed, the perverse high that they had felt in anticipation of the action was now turned to a new low. Getting out of the car, the five occupants started grumbling to each other about what happened and each one offered a different causal theory. Just then, Hakeem pulled up and jumped out of his vehicle. He hurriedly went to the front of the store opened the door and turned off the alarm. He motioned for them to come and bring the weapons. The expression on his face showed a high degree of anger. In other words, he was totally pissed. It was if the devil that normally guided his actions had abandoned him.

The soldiers were milling around in the store with just one dim light on so as not to attract the attention of any patrol car that may be circling the area. Waiting for the rest of the posse to arrive they were each a little antsy about what Hakeem was going to say. He had made his way, by himself, to the private corner of the store he called his office and was in deep thought. Once the rest of the crew had arrived and the weapons were again stored in the store armory, Hakeem came out from his seclusion and faced the group.

"I dono how they got wind, but we gonna fine who did it and waste'em. Aw-ight, who you think it was?"

Hammer, the next in line for command, stepped up and said:

"I dono too, but tomorrow me and Shariq goin down to Midland and lay into some of them. We fine out who did it, no lie."

"Aw-ight, Ham thas a bet–git back to me tomorrow. Meanwhile the rest of y'all stay low tonite and check wit me tomorrow, late. We gonna set up again for Saturday nite wit no snags. Right?"

"Yeah, `Keem we down wit chu." "Aw-ight later."

The group broke up and each was leaving the store just as a police patrol car was passing by. The officers looked in their direction, but didn't stop or even slow down. A neighborhood resident that had been looking out of his third story window across the street, witnessed all that had gone down including the police apathy, wondered to himself was this a sign of what the neighborhood was coming to?

It was Friday morning at MHS and the week had been a tumultuous one. From the fight in the school corridor last Friday through the gang clash and shooting over the weekend to the neighborhood roof jumper and the drive-by hospitalizing one of their own, this period had truly not been boring. The students were still filled with tension and excitement while the teachers were hunkered down to try and weather the current storm and continue to teach. Cinque and Dolitha were both in school today and when they met, they talked about how good Jameel looked last night. As they went about going to their classes, Dolitha spotted Sista and was going over to say something to her, when a member of the C's moved in beside her and redirected Dolitha's path. Not wanting to cause a problem, Dolitha just went on to class, but wondering what that was all about.

Around the beginning of the lunch periods, Hammer and Shariq showed up and tried to enter the building through the normal front entrance.

The security guard, not recognizing them as students, suspecting they were C members, turned them away. He then informed the principal who, anticipating a possible problem given the climate between the warring factions, alerted the police. Hammer, determined to get in somehow, got on his cell phone and called a member inside. His call just rang and rang until he remembered that his boys couldn't have their cells during school. So he and Shariq just hung around the back delivery door until someone came out. Soon the janitor came out to empty the trash and they both snuck in, unseen.

Once inside the building, they went down to the lower level where the cafeteria was and soon spotted a group of B members. It was easy to recognize them because they wore their colors/symbols in either a mark on their belts or a handkerchief hanging out the back pocket. Since there were several of them, Hammer decided to wait until one of them went off on his own. It wasn't long before the opportunity came and the group disbanded and went off in different directions. Hammer and Shariq quietly eased up behind the single B just in front of a vacant classroom and pushed him inside. Shariq grabbed him in a restraining wrestling hold while Hammer punched him hard in the face, twice. Reeling from the first punch, blood spewed from his mouth on impact of the second.

"Who tipped ya'll off, mutha? Who tol you we comin' las nite?"

Hammer yelled at him. When he got no answer, he hit him again hard in the stomach and the boy fell to the floor clutching his gut. Just as Hammer was about to kick him, he heard a noise in the corridor that sounded like someone coming. Hammer and Shariq ran out the door and around the corner before anyone got to the room. The fallen B just got up staggered to the nearest boy's room and washed his faced.

Hammer, mad because he didn't get the information he sought, found one of the C members and asked where he could find Sista. A little surprised to see Hammer inside the school, the C boy said he thought she might be in the library now. After a short search, Hammer found Sista in the library. Boldly he walked in and sat down beside her receiving no admonition at all from the librarian.

"Sista, you know we tried to get them las nite to make up for them messin' up Razor's thing. Nobody was there. You know who tipped'em?"

"Yeah, I think so. You know ya'll was talkin' 'bout doin' somethin at the funeral Wensday nite. I think that boy, Cinque, Jameel's brother heard you and dropped the quarter."

"You think he tol the Bs? Why he do that when they shot up his brother?" "I dono, maybe he think ya'll did the shootin'"

"Is he here today?"

"I dono I havn' seen'em?"

Hammer hearing what he needed to hear, got up walked out of the room and gathered Shariq who was waiting in another vacant classroom nearby. Not wanting to be caught in the halls when no students were there, they waited until the next bell rang for a class change. Hearing the bell, they cautiously went to the back delivery door, which was the only unsecured exit, and walked out.

The B member who got roughed up, found his boys and reported what had just happened. The word was out and all their members went on high alert trying to find Hammer and Shariq in the building. Not having any success, they agreed to meet after school and search the area. A cell phone call was made to Ricoh and the word came back that the whole group was to meet tonight at the courts. Hearing this, they disbursed and headed away from the school.

Dolitha, Rajon and Cinque met up after school as usual and started walking home together. They hadn't gotten far, when Sista approached Dolitha and said: "You wanna see me?" Dolitha sensing that Sista was preparing for a throw down that she wasn't ready for, thinking quickly she just said: "I jus wanted to tell 'bout "J". I saw him at the hospital last night an that he is aw-ight. He'll be home soon. Jus thought you wanna know." Sista's whole attitude changed and she just said "Yeah, okay. Thanks for the info." Then she turned and walked away. Dolitha could see though, not far behind her were several C's just waiting for some action. Cinque came over and said: "Whas the matta wit her?" Dolitha then said: "That girl got some real problems. She's strange." Not realizing that some new trouble had been set in motion, by this strange girl, Dolitha, Cinque and Rajon headed home.

When Hammer and Shariq arrived at M&Ms that afternoon, they found most of the guys already there including Hakeem. They greeted their leader and starting giving their report.

"'Keem, we found one of them dudes and started jackn him up for the info when the man start comin an we had to split. Anyway we foun' out it was Cinque, Jameel's brutha who tipped'em. This is what Sista said. What we gonna do?"

"You sure thas what Sista said? Don' make sense, he know who shot his brother." "Yeah, well thas what she said."

"Aw-ight, we gotta talk to Cinque." "Jus talk?"

"Yeah for now. 'till I fine out if he really did it. Don' make sense to me. I know she already lied on him once, I dono why she don' like'em, maybe she tryn' to set him up again."

"Aw-ight, 'Keem we see him at the school Monday an bring him here. We might could see him 'fore that. What 'bout the hit Saturday, we still on."

"Yeah, it's on we gonna clean up the Bricks."

Later that afternoon as the sun was going down, a number of Bs assembled on the Brick's court. The topic of the evening, of course, was the attack on one of theirs.

Ricoh, looking at the cut lip and puffy face of his soldier, swore loudly in words not usually spoken in polite company, determined that the time had come for an all out war. The assembled troops put out a loud yell, a vote of approval, and high five's were passed all around. Ricoh then told the group that he wanted just the war counsel to meet him in his apartment in a half hour to make up the attack plans. And so it was, the beginning of a new level of strife between the young adolescent residents of the city had come. The devil that indwelled the leaders on both sides had mustered a new corps; a new brigade and divided them amongst themselves. In this upcoming battle, he knew he would be the only winner.

At Sarafina's apartment that evening, she and Cinque were just finishing dinner when the phone rang. It was about 6:30 and on the line was Rev. Joyner.

"Sister Peterson, how are you? I'm sorry to call you so late, but I need to speak with you. Were you busy with something?"

"I'm fine Pastor, and I was just finishing dinner. No I'm not doing anything now." "Good! I'm calling you because I got a call from that Lt. Meeker who we met down at the police station Monday. He called me earlier today and wanted to talk about how we could work together to stop this rise in gang activity. I meant to call you earlier, but I got tied up at my job. Anyway, what he said was that he would like to hear from the community what they think about what could be done. I told him about your work with the CONNs group and that you had already made some attempt to bring both sides of the gangs together. I didn't mention that it was your group that sponsored the Youth Civic Dance last week at the recreation center the night of the shoot out in that nearby vacant lot. I don't think the two events should be related. What's important is that your group is trying already to do something. By the way how many men are involved with the group?"

"Right now rev., we only have two. It seems that most men in this neighborhood think that their role in community action is not needed or else they are more concerned about who wins the MHS basketball or football games."

"Sister Sara, I truly understand that and I'm going to speak on that subject this Sunday. Unless we get our men out and involved, especially the fathers of some of these boys, then we will have lost the battle at the very onset. Will I see you in church Sunday? Maybe we can enlist some of the members to join your group, both men and women. When is your next meeting?"

"I plan to be there hopefully with both my boys. Our next meeting will be the following Saturday. That will give you time to try and get more of the church members to join us."

"Good! I'll let Lt. Meeker know that we're working on a plan and I will be getting back to him soon. God Bless and I'll see you Sunday."

Friday nights usually found most of the neighborhood men either in the bars or they were at the football game. Tonight was generally no different. However, the football game being played this night was unusually important because it would determine whether the MHS Jaguars would be headed to the playoffs or not. The stands were filled to capacity and sprinkled throughout were factions of the C's and the B's. Security was high and the police had stationed themselves in key positions near the entrances, exits and all along the corridor walkways. The tension in the air was not just from the excitement coming from down on the field, but there was a definitely foreboding feeling pervading the stadium.

It was late in the fourth quarter with just minutes to go and the Jag's were up by 3 points. The visiting team had the ball and was moving toward the Jag's goal. All of a sudden the lights went out in the whole stadium and the fans went berserk. Although it was only a few minutes until they came back on, the interruption was enough to set off the melee that ensued. Fans from both teams started pushing and shoving and bedlam broke out. The police that were there were not enough to control the crowd and a stampede erupted as people stormed toward the exits. On the field, the referees had no choice, but to cancel the remainder of the game and get the players to the safety of the locker rooms.

Reinforcements were called in and eventually order was restored. Several attendees had to be taken to Mercy while still others elected to patch themselves up at home. The big question being asked now, is what happened to the lights? More importantly to Jaguar fans, did we make the playoffs? The police were extremely busy trying to piece together what had happened and determine who could have been responsible. There was nothing solid that they had to go on but a small lead from an eyewitness who was standing near the control booth. In the control booth was a master switch that governed the stadium lights. According to the witness just before the event, he saw some members of what he thought looked like the B's club hanging around. Other than this, there was nothing else to go on. The game was over the crowd had dispersed and the only losers were those that got hurt in the action. No further investigation was forthcoming.

According to police, for lack of evidence there was nothing more that could be done.

On Saturday morning as was his custom Cinque slept late and not hearing his mom up early as usual, he enjoyed the even extra sleep. Sarafina, was exhausted having gone through a rough week so she clung to the bed for few extra winks also. Around 9:30 AM she got up and headed to the kitchen to get her eye-opening cup of coffee. Cinque hearing the movement also struggled out of bed.

"Mom, you makin' brekfas'? he said."

"Yes baby, in a minute. Jus let me get myself together here."

Cinque hearing this then stumbled into the bathroom and washed up. Sarafina followed shortly after. It was now around 10:00 O'clock and as she was listening to the news on the kitchen radio the report came on the football game. It was reported that in the melee that took place several people were hurt and some taken to Mercy General. No one had been seriously hurt and no one had been apprehended and there were no suspects being sought. The cause of the power outage had not been determined, but some say that it was not due to natural causes. The outcome of the football game was a sad ending for the MHS Jaguars who had their hopes set on going to the playoffs. What decision will be made regarding that issue will be made sometime next week when the officials have their meeting. Sarafina, after hearing this just shook her head and wondered whether the gangs could have had anything to do with this. It seems things were just starting to go wrong at all events these days.

Around Mid afternoon, Hakeem had assembled his troops at M&Ms and they were going over the plan for the evening caper.

"Hammer, you git word that them dudes gona be out tonite?"

"Yeah, 'Keem don' think nobody messed up this time. I slid by there 'while ago and look like they shootin' hoops and stuff. Don' look like they 'spectin nuthin."

"You talk to Jameel's bruther yet?"

"No man I didn' see'em. We can deal wit that later I'll fine'em."

"Aw-ight, les check out the tools and meet back here at 8:00."

At the hospital Jameel was being examined by Doctor Romane. The doctor was still somewhat astonished at the amazing healing that was happening with his patient. Where the bullets had been removed, it was as if the area around the incisions had been accelerated in the healing process by a hundred fold. He had never seen anything like this and he told "J" just that.

"My mom is a prayin woman", he said. "I think thas what's doin't it."

"If she has that kind of power, I want to put her on staff here" the doctor joked. "I will check in on you one more time tomorrow morning. If things keep moving along like this, you can go home. How do you feel?"

"'Cept for bein' sore, I feel good. Jus wish I could git a 'burger or somethin beside this stuff here."

The doctor laughed and said: "Nice to see you're in good spirits, you'll be fine and you can eat all that junk when you get home. Is your mother coming here today?"

"I think so, she should be comin' here soon."

"Okay, I have to go, but I'll see you again tomorrow." "Okay doc. see you later."

The doctor left and a few minutes later in walked Sarafina and Ciinque.

"How you doin' son?" Sarafina said. "You lookin real strong, feelin' alright?" "Yeah, you jus missed the doctor he was here an said I'm doin good. I might be gittin' outta here tomorrow. He said afta he come then, if everythin's okay, I can go home."

"Hallelujah, Jesus" she exclaimed.

"I knew when I saw that image on the cross in the chapel, everything was gonna be alright."

Cinque then came over and said: "Bro. did you hear 'bout what happened at the game las' nite?"

"No, what happened?"

"Durin' the game, right near the end, all the lights went out an ereybody went crazy. People got stomped on an all messed up. Some say the B's did it."

"Were you there?"

"No, but I herd it on the radio this mornin'."

"Glad you wasn' there. It's gettin real crazy everywhere. Whas up at school?"

"Ain nuthin'. People still aksn' `bout you though. An you know who aks everyday." "Yeah, how she doin?"

"She fine."

"Mom, when I get outta here tomorrow, can we get a pizza or somethin' this food here ain gittin it."

"Once the doctor say you can go, we'll get the biggest pizza we can find, okay?" " Good, I can taste one now."

The trio stayed and talked for another hour right up until it was time for them to leave and then Sarafina and Cinque said goodbye and left.

It was now about 7:45 and darkness had set in outside. The usual cars had arrived at M&Ms, the troops were in place and the tools had been handed out. Hakeem was giving his last minute instructions and the soldiers were gearing up for the action. The nosy neighbor was in his window across the street witnessing the scene and thinking again to himself, Lord what is this all coming to. The soldiers piled into the vehicles, the engines revved up and the mission was underway. The convoy of cars sped away from the hang and headed in the direction of the Bricks.

Back at the hospital Jameel was feeling good after first getting a good report from his doctor and then a nice visit from his brother and mother. In the room, he was now by himself, since his roommate had been released earlier that morning. No television was on because the service had been turned on in his roommate's name, so he attempted to busy himself with some magazines that Sarafina had brought him. While he was reading a sports journal, he started thinking to himself about that night that he got hurt and all that had happened that week. He rehashed in his mind the run in with Hakeem, the roof jumper, the fight in school and his getting hurt. It seemed that so many things were happening so fast that he couldn't get a handle on why it was all coming right now. He pondered his relationship with Dolitha and was looking into his future about where that was going. In his reverie it seemed that the hospital halls had suddenly gone very quiet and no one else was around. The lights appeared to have dimmed and he thought to himself, I hadn't noticed that before. Maybe they're trying to save money on the light bill after visiting hours. The feeling started to get a little eerie and he got up slowly and eased toward the window to see what was happening on the street outside in the dark.

When he turned around however he was startled and jumped as he saw something strange standing in the doorway.

Chapter 4 - Massacre

Mercy General Hospital was located in the North Eastern section of the city. It was just outside of the center city section and was a good facility. The doctors and staff were competent, friendly, and people serving. Most of the city residents were pleased with its services and few had any qualms about how it operated. On any given day, more than half of the beds were occupied with paying customers and it was operating in the black. This was unusual, being that it was in an urban setting where the unemployment rate was fairly high and many of the local patients lacked insurance. What kept it operating profitably was the number of patients coming from the affluent surrounding suburbs to take advantage of its excellent cancer and kidney treatment center. It was a situation that worked out well for the locals and the commuter patients equally. However, if there was one drawback for the hospital it was in its security which Jameel found out on his last night there.

On Saturday night, soon after the visit by his mother and brother a slight feeling of apprehension came over him. He had not had this feeling before and it was probably due to the fact that up until then he had a roommate. Never before had he noticed that lights were turned down low after a certain time and that the noise level became eerily quiet. Now that he was alone in the room, his senses were heightened and he was aware of the slightest movements. He got up slowly and went to look out the window to see if anything was going on in the street. The glow of a full moon came through the window and he got the feeling that something was behind him. As he turned he was startled by something standing in the doorway. He jumped at first, but then realized that it was a person. Standing there in the dimly lit hallway just outside the room was Sista with something in her hand.

From where he was Jameel could not completely make out what it was, so he moved cautiously back toward the bed where the call for help button was. When he moved toward the bed Sista walked in. She was dressed in tight fitting dark blue genes, sneakers and a loose fitting black hooded sweat that could hardly hide the more than ample chest it covered. Her medium length jet-black hair was tied up with a kerchief in the silver and black colors of the C's. As she moved closer, Jameel could see now that what was in her hand was a rolled up magazine that she brought for him. His level of tension eased and he greeted her.

"Hey girl, was-up? What chu doin' here so late?"

"Hy, hy you doin'? I jus hadda see you. But I wanted to see you when nobody else here. There wasn' nobody on the desk downstairs so I jus came on up. The janitor down there tol me how to fine yo room. Here I brought you somethin'. You gonna be in here long? You don' look hurt no more to me."

"Naw, doc says I could be outta here tomorrow, maybe."

"Jameel, you know I really like you. I wanted to be wit you Saturday at the dance. Why you dis me like that? You didn' even see me. All you saw was that Dolitha girl. Why you do that?"

"Is that why you set my brother up like that, `cause I didn' talk to you? Girl, thas whack. You know he spent a whole nite in the lock-up `cause a you."

"Yeah, well I'm sorry `bout that, but you made me real mad, an I hadda do somethin'. Anyway I know he got out, so it wasn' no big thing."

"It was to him an my mom. You `caused a lot of trouble for nuthin'"

"Yeah like I said though I'm real sorry, but you made me very mad. You know I do anything for you - even right now, if you want to."

"Girl,you crazy? First of all, om still a lot sore, and then second we can't do nothing in here now, people be walkin' all over here. I'll see you when I git out. Now tell me whas goin on out there?"

"Aw-ight, I'm gonna look for you when you git back at school. Whas goin on is that the C's right now over at the Bricks taken care of bidness. They gettin back at them for messin' up Razor's send off. It should be jus `bout over by now, so I gotta git back home an' fine out what happened. You know the B's the ones that shot you up don't you? They wasn' even lookin' for you, but you came out Higgy-B's first. Thas why you got hit."

"Yeah, I figured that, an I'm gonna settle up wit them too."

"You won' hafta, it's already done. Look I gotta go. I'll see ya when you get back." "Yeah, aw-ight, later. Thanks for comin'."

Sista said goodbye, but not feeling that she got through to Jameel the way that she wanted to and that there was still something more that she was going to do.

The convoy of C's pulled up to the Bricks courts and unlike the first attempt, the playground was filled with the enemy. They were all over the yard. Some were sitting on the benches passing around their favorite smoke, some were sharing a bottle of their favorite beverage while others were actually on the court throwing the ball at the netless rims. The lighting around the courtyard was exceptionally bright. It was one of the few services that was being maintained. The idea was intended to occupy the kids by giving them a place to play after dark and hopefully keep them off the streets. The idea was a noble one for its intended purpose, but in the next few minutes the scene in the area was like something from a combat movie. The C's jumped out of their vehicles ran up to the fence and started shooting through it. Blam, Blam, Blam, Datta, datta, datta, datt, datta, datta, datta, datt, and then pop - pop, pop, pop, was all you heard as the scramble began. Bodies fell in all directions and those that were still able to run headed inside the buildings. Others scrambled over the fence and out of the area. The massacre took only about ten minutes, but the casualty rate was high. There were at least ten bodies on the court, and it was hard to tell how many were hit, but able to make it out. Hakeem smiling, motioned for his soldiers to get back in the cars and leave. The action plan had worked and the mission accomplished.

It wasn't long before the blaring sound of sirens and the flashing emergency lights were lighting up the streets. Once again police and SWAT were rushing to the scene. When they arrived, all they saw was a mass of dead bodies drowned in a sea of blood and a few onlookers who scattered as the police stepped in. A call went out to Lt. Meeker, but it was discovered that he had gone away for the weekend to visit family in another state. Sergeant Calloway then took charge and started his investigation. The curious few that didn't run away were hesitant to talk with the police and give any useful information. The one thing they did give the police an earful of was that something had to be done.

They couldn't live like this. Sergeant Calloway just shook his head and said to the crowd: "How do you think we're going to end this, if you won't help us?"

One man finally stepped forward and said:

"I know who did this? Erybody here know. It was them boys from over there by that M&Ms place on 12th Street. They call themselves C's. Y'all even know dat."

"Sir, can you identify any of them?"

"I dono 'xactly who they be, but it's that gang. I know dat."

"Sir, would you be willing to come with us to look at some pictures and see if you recognize one of them."

"I ain' gonna look at no pictures, then they be comin' afta me. Naw, no, not me." "Well, thank you sir. Come on boys let's go, no more we can do here. Sanitation will clean up tomorrow."

The city's coroner's vehicles and the ambulances were still taking away bodies when the police left.

Back at M&M's the guys just arrived and gathered in front of the store laughing and trading high five's as if they had just won a championship in a major sporting event. No remorse, no feelings at all for the bloodshed they caused. There was no apparent concern about the police or any fear of being caught. It's hard to envision anyone being this callous and apathetic about life in general, but here it was the result of years of pent up frustration and anger unleashed in a flurry. The act they committed made a dramatically bold statement about the type of young men these had come to be. Hakeem finally arrived, opened the door to the store and the weapons were quietly returned to the armory that was concealed in a secret room at the back of the store. They didn't stay long in the store, but relinquished their arsenal, casually walked out, got in their cars and drove away like nothing happened. They were all on their way somewhere to party and get high.

Ricoh wasn't out on the courts tonight, but stayed home entertaining a lovely companion. When he heard all the shooting and commotion outside his window, he knew immediately what was happening, but there wasn't anything he could do to help his posse. He could see all the commotion going on from his window so he just chilled.

When the police left and the crowd thinned, he went down to the yard and saw the macabre sight. The rage that he felt at that moment if it could have been harnessed would fuel the city's energy needs for the next ten years. He walked around the courts looking for clues or any indication which of his boys went down. It was so messy though, that even he couldn't stay out there long so he went back. Once inside, the rage just spilled over and he yelled at his guest to leave. He picked up the phone and started calling around to see who would pick up. After calling several of his ranking soldiers and getting no answer, he was getting totally frustrated and even angrier. His brain was on fire and he couldn't begin to formulate a vision about what to do. Out of utter frustration he picked up the bottle he had shared with his companion and drank himself into a stupor, falling asleep.

Hakeem and Hammer separated themselves from the group and headed in the opposite direction. Though they knew that most of their guys were headed to Al's Big "A" bar on 6th Avenue to celebrate the victory, the duo eased across the neutral zone and went into Baxter Terrace where Razor lived. Baxter Terrace was a series of two story garden type apartments that had been in earlier years the pride of the low-middle income housing developments. But in more recent years, it had succumbed to the downward spiral of a population trying to survive in the dire economic conditions of the day. It was here that Razor had established his command post outside of M&M's. Since his death, Sista was still living there, but uncertain how she was going to continue to do so.

Hakeem and Hammer strolled through the commons area and across the yard to Unit 5. They entered the building and located the bell for Apartment B10. Since it was a buzz to enter unit they had to wait to gain access. After pushing the bell several times, they finally received the responding buzz that unlocked the door. Once on the second floor, it was a short walk to B10. When they reached the apartment they found the door partially open and without knocking entered. Sista was sitting there on the couch in the living room facing the door and was not surprised to see the duo coming in.

"I know you was comin', but I thought you be here before now" she said. "Yeah, well we hadda go back to the hang and put away the tools. You okay?"

"Yeah, I'm good for now, but who gonna pay the rent next week when the man come lookin' for it?"

"Don' worry 'bout nothin' I take care of dat. Afta Mundie when the big deal go down, you gonna have 'nough dough to last for a good while. I tol' Razor long time ago, I take care a you if 'e go down an I keeps my promises. What chu got to drink here?"

Sista pointed to the bar in the corner and said:

"Razor use ta keep some stuff over there, but I ain' been in it. You can see what's there."

Hakeem went over to the bar, looked behind it and was surprised to find that it was pretty well stocked. Razor, even though he had some odd ways was a good host. When he had his meetings at the place he made sure that his associates were well fed and thirsts quenched. The alcohol included a variety of name brand liquors and on the bottom shelf was a box containing a number of joints of his favorite weed. Hakeem called Hammer over and said:

" Man, will you look at this s—t, I knew that he was doin' okay, but not this good. Sista, you know I gotta come by here more, now he gone." Sista responded saying: "I don' care when you come here, but don' think you movin' in. Jus keep the rent man offa my back an we be okay. I know how Razor set you up in the first place, so don' be tryin' to move on me."

"Hey girl, chill, om jus sayin' that he got some good stuff here an' I don' wanna see it go ta waste."

As Hakeem continued to avail himself of the well stocked bar and continued speaking to Sista he began to focus on her massive charms.

"Girl, who takin' care of you?"

"What chu mean, who takin' care of me?" she said.

"You know what I mean. Who satifsfyin yo needs?"

Sista realizing that this conversation was not going in a direction that she wanted to pursue cautioned Hakeem by saying:

"Hakeem, you don' want none of this, 'cause it ain' for you." "Well if it ain' for me, who it for?"

"Not you, now you betta go."

Hakeem, thought about pursuing the issue, but Hammer motioned to him that it was not a good idea and he dropped it. Finishing his last drink, Hakeem and Hammer left the terrace and headed home. Sista, after the guys left, went into the bathroom looked in the mirror and said to herself: "There's gotta be more to life than this?" and she went to bed.

Sunday morning had the whole city on edge about what had happened at the Bricks complex last night. The news reporters were in a huff trying to put together a report that had some sensibility to it. Not having any concrete information to go on, it was mostly reporting on speculation and innuendo. The police were not much help because they didn't have any reliable witnesses or evidence linking anyone to the crime. It was like an invasion had occurred, but the spaceship had come and gone.

Sarafina got up that morning and according to her usual custom she was making breakfast when she heard the early morning news reports on the kitchen radio.

Good morning, this is your WXBN radio news reporter Bob Winston giving you the latest headline on another incident happening in our city. Last night between the hours of 8:00 and 8:30 a multiple shooting took place at the Bricks Apartment Complex in the East Ward. The casualties were high and the death toll stands now at eleven. Police are baffled at how the assailants could have come and perpetrated the assault without any witnesses seeing what happened. They're calling for anyone who saw the shootings or has any information related to the incident, to come forward and identify any of the perpetrators. They're asking that you call the following help line at (800) 922-4111 to give your information. Your identity will not be revealed.

In other area news, it was also reported that …

Sarafina, after hearing the initial report stopped her cooking and had to sit down. She was so overcome by the news that she just couldn't reel in what was happening in the city that she had come to love. Before she finished making breakfast, Cinque strolled in and sat at the table.

"Well you're up early, still couldn't sleep?"

"Naw, mom, I was thinkn' `bout "J" an I thought he be home now."

"Well, you know he might be comin' home today, but don't you worry `bout him, he'll be alright. We're goin' to church this mornin', so afta breakfas you get ready, okay?"

"Yeah, mom, I'll be reddi."

At New Life Temple that morning, Reverend Joyner had come in a little earlier than usual. Even though he had already prepared his sermon, he wanted to get in and relax before the service began. Although it was early morning, it appeared this was going to be another bright and sunny day. At the outset, it appeared that this was going to be a day reminiscent of the series of days that had happened last week. Rev. Joyner went into his study and kneeled down to seek the Lord's guidance once more before facing the congregation. The heaviness in his heart, having heard the early news reports about last night was burdening him. He cried out:

"Lord, Lord, I beseech You by the mercies of God that You would intervene according to Your infinite wisdom and rain down blessings upon your people. We have come to a cross roads in our journey and seek your guidance on how to go forward to achieve what you are calling us to do. Lord, we know that You are in deed still in control of our lives, but we need guidance from the Holy Spirit to move forward and achieve the goals that you set before us by your commandments. Feed me now Lord so that I shall not want, guide me now so I shall not go astray and I will deliver Your word to the people according to Your vision for your people."

At Sarafina's house, she was still preparing for church and was admonishing Cinque to get himself together to be ready to go when she was. The phone rang at about 10:30 and it was Doctor Romane calling. She picked up the phone:

"Hello."

"Good morning Mrs. Peterson, this is Doctor Romane from Mercy Hospital, how are you?

"I'm okay doctor thank you for asking. How's my son doin?

"That is why I'm calling. I've just checked in on your son and his recovery is nothing short of a miracle. He is fine and I'm releasing him to go home. You may come and get him at any time."

"Halleujah Jesus" Sarafina exclaimed with a loud voice. " I'll come and get him right after my church service this morning."

"That will be fine. Just let the receptionist know that I spoke with you already and that his release has been approved by me. If you need anything else, don't hesitate to call me, you have my card."

"Thank you so much doctor, you've been truly a blessing for my family and me. May God bless you in your service."

Sarafina and Cinque, after the phone call, continued to get ready and within the hour they were both ready to leave. They exited the building, got into the car and headed in the direction of the church. She was reminded though of the activity they witnessed last Sunday when they were going to church. This time it was not there. Even though another crisis had taken place in the city, the non-church goers were not out this morning.

Sarafina wondered at this, but had no answers.

At church that morning, the usual ritual ceremony took place and the service proceeded as per normal. The choir sang and the assistant pastor led the congregation in prayer. When it came time for the pastor to speak and deliver his sermon, once again the whole congregation focused intently on him. He stepped reverently into the pulpit and addressed the congregation.

"Members, family and friends, I greet you in the precious name of our Lord and Savior Jesus the Christ. It is once again that I come before you with a heavy heart and a troubled mind to remind you that we must be in the last days before Jesus returns to judge our society. As we mourn the loss of all the young people that fell victim to the atrocities that occurred last night, we must be reminded how far we've strayed from His teachings. When we reflect on how our God over the years has brought us through many trials and tribulations, we need to be reflective that it is only by His grace and mercy that we've been allowed to come this far. I want to speak to you this morning, for a few minutes from the scriptures as set forth in the book of St. John the apostle. For it is in the book of John's Gospel that it is said that Jesus came not to condemn the world but to save it. He came so as those that are in need of healing would receive the blessings of the Father and His kingdom. He came that those who are downtrodden shall be uplifted; those that have been cast into bondage shall be freed and those of the poor shall receive the glory of God.

It is through His message that we shall know that the kingdom of God is at hand, and it will be by His mercy that we all shall be saved. The time has come when all of the people shall know that the Lord, Jesus the Christ shall be known in all the earth as the forth- coming ruler and it will be His kingdom that shall prevail forever.

I will be speaking to you from John Chapter 4 versus 10 thru 15. The scripture reads as follows:

> Jesus answered her, "If you knew the gift of God and who it is that asks you for a drink, you would have asked him and he would have given you living water. Sir, the woman said, you have nothing to draw with and the well is deep. Where can you get this living water? Are you greater than our father Jacob, who gave us the well and drank from it himself, as did also his sons and his flocks and herds?
>
> Jesus answered, everyone who drinks this water will be thirsty again, but whoever drinks the water I give him will never thirst. Indeed, the water I give him will become in him a spring of water welling up to eternal life. The woman said to him, Sir, give me this water so that I wont get thirsty and have to keep coming here to draw water."

"Saints, we have come to a crisis in our neighborhood where even as the woman at the well in Samaria, are in need of healing water. We have come to the point where the water in the well of healing is the only thing that will bring about the healing that this community needs to make it whole. As Jesus said to the woman at the well, if you continue to drink from the normal waters of this well, you shall continue to thirst. But if you drink from the waters that I give to you, you will never thirst again. Folks, what is this water that He speaks about. This is the water that can only come from looking to Jesus our Savior who has the power to heal and quell the thirst that we seek. It is by His mercy and His grace that we shall be able to turn around the atrocities that are occurring in this neighborhood. We need to come and drink from the fountain, the well that He has made available to us. That is the well of prayer and belief from which we can drink of His healing water. It is not a well that exists only in Samaria, but it exists right here in our town, right here in this sanctuary, if we will only avail ourselves of the water springs that are right here. Saints, I encourage you, I beseech you to come forward and humble yourselves before our God and seek His mercy and His blessing so that the water that you will receive today shall be everlasting. The times that we are in, shall be corrected in due time according to His will. By His grace and by His mercy we shall see His salvation prevail in all that we do in His name. Amen!

Saints if we continue to do nothing and stand by watching our community degenerate into a war zone, then it shall be only our fault when it happens. As Jesus said to the woman at the well, drink of the water that I give you and you shall never thirst again. So it is that we need to drink of this water. I'm now asking you, men, women, and our own young people to get involved in a community action to initiate the healing process. As you leave this morning, there will be a sign-up sheet in the lobby. Please step-up, sign-up, and become part of the solution to our community problem.

At the hospital, Jameel was excited about going home and just wondering where his mother was. It was now about 2:00 PM, the sun was high in the sky and as he looked out his window he could see that it was a great day. In his mind a thought came back about his visit late last night by Sista. He knew that she was a little strange, but he couldn't help thinking about what she said to him regarding what was supposed to be happening when she was there. Since he didn't have a radio in the room and the television service had been disconnected when his roommate left, he had no way of knowing what went down. While he was still pondering the issue in walked Sarafina and Cinque all smiles and rushing to hug him. As Sarafina hugged him, Jameel recoiled a bit reminding her, that he was still sore. Cinque just grabbed his hand and low five'd it. After the greeting the trio picked up his belongings, looked around the room to make sure nothing was left and headed to the elevator. They signed him out then exited the building heading for home.

"Mom, remember you said we could get a pizza when I got out. We gonna do dat?" "Yes, we can stop by the Pizza Heaven near the house and pick up the largest pie they have, okay?"

"Thas a bet."

The ride was pleasant, the day was beautiful and it seemed that everything was going to be fine, so thought Sarafina.

Ricoh opened his eyes and the room was spinning. He attempted to get up despite the throbbing hammers that were pounding away inside his head. He was angry at himself for getting that drunk and passing out on the couch, but it seemed like a good idea at that time. To compound his misery, flashes of last night's scene flew into his mind's eye. He struggled to his feet and staggered into the bathroom. Leaning on the sink staring into the mirror, the reflection that looked back at him just confirmed how he felt. He opened the medicine chest and searched for anything that would provide him with the relief he sought. Finding the blue plop, plop, fizz, fizz box he reached for it in the hope that it would be a miracle cure for his malady. After drinking the mixture, he wobbled back to the couch and picked up the phone. His first call was to PK, his second in command.

"Yo, wha's up, this PK."

"PK, man am I glad to hear you. This is Rick. What happened las night?"

" Man, they really caught us nappin'. They hit us 'fore we could even move. Nobody herd'em comin'. Them fools hit three of the young boys jus out there shootin' hoops, they wasn' even wit us. They got eight a us 'cludn Rambo, I think he dead. What we gonna do?"

"Om still tryn' to think. Can you come here now, you okay?"

"Yeah, I jus got grazed. Big momma fix me up good. I'll be over in ten minutes." "Good, see you then."

Once inside the house Sarafina, Jameel and Cinque sat down to enjoy their large pizza covered with "J's" favorite toppings. Jameel bit into his extra large slice and just hummed, mm, mm, good as he devoured the piece.

"Mom, this is good - sure beats that hospital stuff" he exclaimed as Cinque echoed his sentiments.

Sarafina delayed eating her share and went into the living room to turn on the TV news. The afternoon news on Sunday was somewhat sparse as this was the height of the football and basketball seasons. What news there was of the massacre was just basically a repeat of what had already been reported earlier. The police were still struggling trying to come up with a way to bring in the ones that they knew were responsible. This was extremely difficult without eyewitnesses.

PK arrived at Ricoh's apartment, knocked and went in. Struggling to put on a happy face even though he was still hurting Ricoh said "Hey man, good to see ya." They greeted each other with their special grip and moved to the couch.

"What happened to our lookouts? Who `posed to be workn'?"

"Man, we had it covered, but they came down 9th from the North end `an hit us `fore the runners could get back."

"Yeah, well that won' happen again, you hear me. Not again! Who you know is lef from here? We hafta get a new plan `cause dat otha one ain'gona work now."

"I know Devon he okay and I think Skeeter make it out too. I can call `em an say get over here now."

"Yeah you do that, an then we'll come up wit somethin'. I don' wanna wait too long `fore we hit'em back wit all we got."

PK started calling the troops and Ricoh, even though the fizz fizz had not fully worked, was beginning to formulate a plan.

It wasn't long before five of the soldiers were walking in. Ricoh greeted each of them and they sat down. "Y'all know we was hit hard las night an its payback time. What we gonna do is move quietly tonight, jus like they sneak'd us. We gonna move on M&M's where dey be at alla time." Just as Ricoh was laying out the plan, PK spoke up and said:

"Rick, I `don think they be in dere on Sundays."

"Yeah, dey be in there, I know dat. But om gonna ride by in a little while to jus make sure. I'll call you `an you can get them together. We gonna do this `bout 7:00 so get the stuff ready, aw-ight?"

"Yeah man, thas cool."

"Okay y'all can go now, but hang loose 'an wait for PK's call." The group broke up and each went his way.

About an hour later, Ricoh got in his car and headed to the West side. Instead of going the normal route that one would take to get from his house to M&M's he purposely went in the direction that the C's had used to come into his turf. He went up 9th Avenue almost to the end turned left onto 2nd Street and went past Mercy General Hospital. He thought to himself, this is why my lookouts didn't spot them. Nobody would come this way to get to the Bricks. When he got to 7th Avenue he turned left again and headed down toward the hangout. He knew he had crossed the neutral zone, but was sure that his car was not known to the C's since he very rarely drove it anywhere.

As he approached M&M's it became painfully obvious to him that making a hit on that place tonight was not a good idea. There were so many patrol cars circling the area it was like flys around a sugar bowl. He knew then that they were looking for anything and anybody that they could haul in for what happened last night. He also spotted what he thought to be the C's lookouts who were also covering the neighborhood. Unlike the Bricks courts, there was no easy backdoor kind of access since M&M's sat on a corner smack dab in the middle of several stores and apartment buildings. Ricoh also noted this in his mind and thought from now on, we need a new meeting place. He then turned around and went back home. Once inside he phoned PK and explained to him what he had seen. PK, although a little disappointed, agreed with him and asked what he was going to do now.

"I dono yet, but call the guys an let'em know ain nuthin' goin' down tonight. I gotta lay back down 'cause my head is still bad. I'll call later when I git back up."

"Okay man, later."

After finishing the pizza Jameel and Cinque went into their room and picked up on their NFL video games. Sarafina went back in the living room and called one of the members of her CONNs club.

"Lydia, this is Sarafina how ya doin'?"

"Oh, I'm okay, how are you? I been hearin' 'bout all thas happen' to yo boys. You sure you alright?"

"Yeah, I'm makin' it okay. God is good. I called 'cause I wanna talk to you 'bout somethin' the club said cupla weeks ago. Remember we was talkin' 'bout gittin' the churches to do somethin'?"

"Yeah, I remember."

"Well, in my church this mornin' pastor asked for people to sign-up for this community action group he gonna run. I dono how many sign-up, but

I think he gonna let me know this week. I was thinkn' we aughta get them to join wit us to git somthin' big going. Since we already started workin' on tryn to change the neighborhood, they should help us. What you think?"

"If he can get the men in your church to come out, I think it would be great. We 'don need no more women in this club."

"I ain' thinkin' 'bout them joinin' our club, I jus wanna git a lotta people together so we have some say wit the mayor and his folks."

"I go along wit dat. When you think he gonna let you know what he got?"

"If I don' hear from him by Wensday, I'll call him an see. Then I'll let you know. If I don' talk to you before - we have a meetin' Saturday an I'm gonna bring it up then anyway. Okay?"

"Okay, goodnight." "Goodnight!"

Ricoh woke up again around 8:30 feeling a little better but not fully recovered. He said to himself "I ain' never gonna do dat again, but went to the refrigerator and reached for a beer. He then called PK and said: "PK, it's me, Rick. I figured out what we gonna do."

"Yeah, what?"

"If I got it right, don't Razor's sister go to Midland?" "Yeah, I think so, what?"

"Well, we gonna grab her an hold on 'till one of them, like Hakeem, come to git her wit some dough. We kin keep her in the store-room in the Super's basement right here in the project. He still cool wit us right?"

"Yeah, he usta be one a us, but I dono if he be down for this." "I'll deal wit him, he be aw-ight."

"How we gonna get her?"

"I want you to get a message to our people in the school and fine out how she rolls. Fine out where she live an what time she go home from school."

"You know she be wit them mos time."

"Thas aw-ight, she gotta be alone sometime. Fine out when."

"Aw-ight I'll git word to the school tomorrow an git on it. We should know somethin' Tuesday, I'll get back atcha."

"Aw-ight, meantime we needa start recruitin' again tomorrow, to git some replacements, right?"

"Yeah, cool - I know jus who we needa go afta. We should go by that Spencer grade school, I seen some good p'tentials there."

"Okay, I'll hook up wit you tomorrow. Later." "Yeah, later."

At M&M's that night, just as Ricoh had said Hakeem and some of his posse were in the store. In the semi-darkness with just one light on, they were talking about how the police had stepped up patrols in the area and what they needed to do to stay low profile. Not that they were concerned about them coming in the store, but the street network had already informed them that the cops were out to pick up anybody that they could even remotely link to the shootings.

"Man, I ain' seen dis many cops 'round here since we been comin' in here. Look like they plannin' a raid or somethin'," Hakeem said.

"Yeah, you think they got somethin?" Hammer responded.

"Naw, if they did, they already be pickin' up somebody. They jus tryna' scare us into doin'somethin stupid. We jus chill a few days 'till things cool down an they go away. Be sure none y'all walkin' 'round packin' nuthin'. You git pick'd up for dat, you on your own, feelin me?"

"Yeah, 'keem we cool" the group responded.

They hung in the store sitting around passing the smoke and sharing some brew and getting high until about 11:30 PM then they broke up and left. Once again a patrol car passed by saw them exiting the store, but nothing was done or even said.

On Monday morning Lt. Meeker returned from visiting a relative out of state. He wasn't in his office ten minutes, before the calls started coming in from irate citizens wanting to know what was being done about the violence that had occurred over the last couple of weeks. He poured a cup of coffee and rang for Sgt. Calloway to come in.

"Ray, what the heck happened here Saturday. I can't even sit down for a minute before that phone rings again. What do we have going?"

"Well lieutenant, just like always, there was a crowd out there who know everything, but say nothing and they want us to use our crystal ball to solve the mystery."

"Do we have any leads, any witnesses willing to speak up?"

"Like I said, they know, but ain't saying. There was one guy though, I think if we stay on him, promise him some money and tell him we'll guarantee his safety, he might finger one of them for us."

"How much we looking at?"

"For him I think a fifty would do it and maybe we can put him on the payroll for future reference, know what I mean?"

"Yeah, I have to check the slush fund and see what I got. Meanwhile, go ahead and tell the guys to ease up to this man without scaring him and start the ball rolling.

Right?"

"Okay lieutenant you got it."

"Now I have to come up with something to tell the mayor; he should be calling in here any minute now."

Sgt. Calloway left and Lt. Meeker started going through the reports and files trying to piece together some kind of a story of police progress to tell the mayor and the city council.

At Midland that morning another week was beginning with some horrible news that happened over the weekend. The students knowing more about the inside details of the action than the police, were trading tales about what was going to happen next. The members of both clubs were walking the halls eyeing one another, but neither side wanted to instigate an action that would draw attention to themselves and consequently their clubs.

Just outside the school PK, following the orders from his general, had contacted one of theirs that was still attending MHS. He told him about the plan that Ricoh had come up with and what his role was. The B member accepted his assignment and relayed the message to his associates inside. The orders were to find out what Sista's daily schedule was and what would be the best time to grab hold of her. One of the soldiers, however, who knew about her and Jameel, came up with a better suggestion. He told PK about Sista's crush and that it would be easy to set her up and make her come to them. When the word got back to Ricoh he endorsed the idea whole-heartedly and left it up to PK and the soldier to pull it together.

Dolitha, Cinque and Rajon were all at school today and as was their custom they met in the morning before classes and just talked about the weekend's happenings. Rajon who was the best street reporter in the neighborhood had all the facts. He was telling the others that the B's got caught with their guard down and this was a good sign that the balance of power was definitely shifting to the C's. He was just getting warmed up with all the details on how it happened when the bell rang directing students to report to homerooms and start the school day. So they broke up their little gathering and went inside.

Ricoh got up that morning, fully recovered from Saturday night's alcohol bout, got dressed and went to see the superintendent of building #1. This is where he proposed that they would keep Sista until the money exchange could be made. He knew the building well because he had stored some of their illegal weapons there for short periods. He reflected about the number of storage rooms that were just perfect for what he had in mind. The series of rooms each was like a little 5x10 U-Haul storage bin having its own light. He thought that he would put a little cot in there with bedding and things would work out fine.

Reaching building #1 he went straight to the super's apartment that was also in the basement. His name was Willie, also known as Slick Willie, and having been a former member of the B's was still semi active with them in making some of their deals happen. Ricoh knocked on the door: "Willie - hey Willie, open up man it's Rick." After a few minutes footsteps from inside could be heard coming toward the door.

"Hey Rick, whas up?"

"Man, I got somethin' 'bout to go down an I need to use one of them rooms again." "Sure man, what chu got?"

"Can't tell you ereything now, but I'll clue you later." "When you gonna need it an how long?"

"Maybe two three days, startin' Wensday. I'll be comin' late night through the 'livery doors, so make sure they open."

"Man, you gotta give me a betta time than that, I can't jus leave them doors open." "Aw-ight, I'll be gettin back to you later tonight an give you what you need to know. Cool?"

"Yeah, okay. You gonna have somethin' for me?" "Yeah man, you know I always take care of you." "Aw-ight see you later."

"Yeah, right."

At the end of the school day, the B soldier had already worked out the plan and called it in to PK. What was going to happen was that a note would be delivered to Sista in the cafeteria saying that Jameel wanted to meet her at the Public Library on 8th Avenue near her house about 7:00 PM. She would have no reason to suspect anything so she would come alone. When he doesn't show up, she will probably leave after fifteen - twenty minutes and take the quick way to her house on Short Street on the back side of the library. It's usually dark on the street then and we can drive the van up and get her. We just have to be ready and make it quick.

When the plan got back to Ricoh, he approved it and everything was set in motion for it to happen Tuesday night. Ricoh in turn called Willie and told him when to have the delivery doors open. He also told him to let him know what room he would be using and to put a bed in with some sheets, pillows blankets and stuff. When Willie heard this he immediately thought the wrong thing, and agreed to it laughing. The plan was now set and Ricoh was savoring the moment and looking forward to seeing Hakeem's face when he is told that they have Sista.

At school on Tuesday the main talk now was about what's going to happen with their football team. The outcome of the abruptly ended game that took place last Friday night was still undecided. The officials were due to meet on Wednesday and the students were posturing in favor of having another game. The team was more interested in finding out if they had to play another game, would it be played giving them the lead that they earned when the game was called. This was a big thing for the players as well as the coaches.

So everyone was anticipating a favorable decision in the middle of the week.

Nothing unusual was happening in the halls today. The atmosphere was relatively calm, given the anxiety status between the clubs. Dolitha, Sista, Rajon and Cinque were all there and it was just business as usual. When her lunch period came, Sista went to the cafeteria and got her lunch. She was sitting down eating with some of her girlfriends, when another girl came over and dropped a note on her tray and walked away. She didn't know this girl and thought it a little strange. She picked up the note and read it anyway. The note said: "I want to see you. Meet me tonight at 7:00 PM at the Public Library. I'll be in the Science room waiting for you. Jameel." Even though she thought it strange, the excitement she felt about this possible rendezvous was overwhelming and she decided to go.

After school Sista couldn't wait to separate herself from the C's that usually hung around her. She told them that she had some errands to run and that she needed her space. Actually she was running home to find something she thought would be enticing to Jameel to wear. The library was about a fifteen minute walk from her house so she waited right up until quarter of to head over there. She put on what she thought would get his attention and started out. The walk didn't take the time that she thought so she arrived a few minutes before 7:00 and went to the Science Room.

She found a table in the corner, put down her book bag and went into the stacks to get a book to read. When she returned she looked all around the room, but didn't see "J" anywhere. She sat down and pretended to be reading when she was really eyeing the room intently every few minutes. After performing this routine for about twenty minutes, she decided that he wasn't coming and she was going to call him when she got home to find out what happened.

When she exited the library, she decided to take the quick route down Short Street and save a couple of minutes. As she turned the corner, she noticed that it was darker than usual and there was no one else on the street. She thought for a minute about not continuing, but then said to herself: "I've done this a hundred times before." She was about half way down the street when a large black cargo van came up beside her. The side doors opened and two big B's jumped out and grabbed her throwing her into the vehicle. She put up a struggle, kicking and biting, but they were too much for her.

Quickly her mouth was taped shut and her arms were tied behind her and she was blindfolded.

Her heart was pounding and she knew that she had been suckered into a trap. Out of just pure fear, she decided to lay still and see what was going to happen. The van sped down the street and turned onto what she thought she could hear as a real busy street. She was trying to get a bearing on where they were headed, but couldn't be sure. After several minutes the van turned again and it felt like they were going down hill. Suddenly it stopped and the doors opened. She was then pulled out by two outside men and escorted roughly through a door. She was then pushed down what she envisioned as a long hallway and thrown into a room. The blindfold was removed, her arms untied and she could see her attackers. She knew they were B's, but didn't understand what this was all about. They turned around walked out and turned the light off from outside the room. Once they left she felt for the bed that she saw when they first removed her blindfold.

She felt sheets, a pillow and what felt like an old large quilt. It was a bit damp and cold in the room, so she felt just a little better with these few comforts. She lay down on the bed staring up in the darkness and wondered what they were going to do to her. After what may have been an hour, maybe more, she heard footsteps and voices in the hallway as some of them were coming. She could hear them laughing and talking about what they were going to do and her heart really started pounding. As they got closer and closer she got off the bed and found her way to a corner. She was cowering waiting for something to happen, when suddenly the light came on and the door opened.

Chapter 5 - Kidnapped

Near the corner of 5th Street and 5th Avenue on the upper West side, just this side of the boundary, was an old abandoned warehouse. It was a four level cement and brick building with huge industrial windows on the upper floors. Some years ago, it was run by the Gateway Safe And Lock company. Most of it was boarded up except for a rear delivery door along side the freight dock. Sitting inside at a desk in the freight office, Hakeem, Hammer, and three street soldiers kept watch through a partially covered window. It was now a little before 8PM and the darkness outside had already set in.

There was no electricity in the building, so they had strategically placed a few battery- powered lamps. The lighting was just enough to illuminate the desk area and left the corners almost completely dark.

They were waiting for the merchandise contact so they could complete their deal.

Last night they picked up a large shipment from the airport. Several keys of a #1 quality product were now stored in a corner of the room. The meeting was scheduled for 8 PM and it was now about 8:10. Hakeem was starting to get a little antsy so he got up and walked outside. The soldiers waited in the corners. A few minutes later he came back inside and said: "I know dey ain tryna mess wit my head `cause I ain in no mood. We give'em ten mo' minutes an then we outta here an look for a new buyer." The words had just rolled out of his mouth when the headlights of a black sedan shone through the window. The car pulled up to the loading dock and four men got out. Hakeem put his soldiers on high alert and focused his attention on the door. The men came up to the door, looked inside first and then knocked. "It's open," said Hakeem. The men walked in cautiously surveying the dimly lit room and the leader said: "You ready to deal?"

"Om reddi, are you?" Hakeem responded. "Where's the stuff?"

"I got it, where's the money?" "Right here."

The leader, standing in front of the desk, placed a large satchel on it and opened it up. There inside were stacks of $100's and $50's neatly placed. Hakeem picked up some of the stacks and fanned them to make sure they were all of equal amounts and then placed them back in the case. He nodded to his soldier in the far corner and he stepped into the light with a large duffel bag that he placed on the desk. Another man opened one of the bricks inside and tasted the product. With a smile he nodded to the leader and the exchange was made. Inside of fifteen minutes the deal was completely transacted and the leader with his men and Hakeem with his soldiers departed the warehouse. Everybody was happy.

The next day at another part of town in the basement of building #1, Sista was anticipating, with a pounding heart, what was about to happen to her. The ceiling light in her confinement cubicle came on and the door opened. In walked Ricoh, PK and two of his soldiers. He threw Sista's book bag, which contained her pocket book and cell phone, on the bed. "Go get it" he said to her. Sista slowly moved from the corner and sat on the bed.

"Take out yo cell an call Hakeem, tell him we got you. Then lemme talk." "What chu gonna do to me?" she said.

"Nuthin' if you do jus like I say, now call'em."

Sista looked inside the bag retrieved her phone and punched in the numbers. "Hakeem here whas up?"

"'Keem, this is Sista I'm in trouble." "Trouble, wha kinda trouble?"

"The B's got me an they holdin' me over here."

"Gimme dat phone" Ricoh yelled as he snatched it from her hand.

"Hakeem, this is Ricoh. Now you listen up an listen good. Yeah we got her an its pay back time for y'all comin over here, you feelin' me?"

" What chu want?"

"I want $10,000 by tomorrow night or we first gonna have some fun wit her an then ship her back to you in stages."

"Man, I ain got dat kinda dough, you crazy?"

"Don' play me 'Keem, I know what chu picked up from the port las night an yo deal shoulda gone down by now."

"How you know dat?"

"Don worry `bout it, I know thas all." "Aw-ight man, how you wanna trade."

"Tomorrow at 5:00 O'clock bring da money in $20's and $50's in a plain gym bag to Ciscero's Diner down there on 8th Avenue and 13th Street. Come by yo self an I'll be waitin wit yo people in a booth in the back. Don git stupid on me an she be aw-ight." "Yeah okay I be there."

"Don be comin' late `either cause I ain gonna wait too long." "Yeah right, I'll see ya."

Ricoh hung up and handed the phone back to Sista. "I gotta go to the bathroom" Sista said.

"Well I guess you got a problem, `cause ain no bathroom down here." "No, you got a problem, you brought me here, didn't you think about dat?" "Aw-ight, aw-ight, jus hol on, let me go tell Willie you gotta use his." "Willie, who Willie?"

"You don need to know, jus hol on, I'll be right back. Watch her."

Ricoh then walked down the hall to Willie's apartment and told him what the situation was. Willie of course had no problem with it and said to send her down. Ricoh told him he wasn't sending her down, but was coming back with her because he didn't want Willie messing with her and screwing up his deal.

"Aw-ight come on" Ricoh said to Sista and she got up and followed him. While she was walking she was trying to figure out where she was. She knew it was an apartment building basement, but she couldn't determine in what housing development. When they arrived at Willie's place she walked in and he showed her where the bathroom was.

Ricoh stayed there to make sure nothing went wrong and when she came out he was ready to walk her back to the bin. When she was slightly out of ear shot, "Whas a matta, you don' trus me man?" Willie said.

"Not wit somethin' like that. I know you be tryin ta git on that in a NY minute." They both laughed and Ricoh caught up with Sista.

"You did all dis jus to git some money?" Sista said.

"Naw, it ain jus the money, it's about payn y'all back for what you did to my boys. You lucky I don take you out anyway an set him up to take the money when he show" Rick responded.

Sista thought about this and didn't say anymore because she knew that he might be thinking about doing just that. They got back to the storage bin and Ricoh grabbed her bag and took out her phone.

"You can keep the bag, you ain goin nowhere nohow," he said. "You gonna leave me in here all night?"

"Yeah, what chu wanna go to a motel? You'll be aw-ight."

That ended the conversation and Ricoh and his soldiers left. Sista noticed that they didn't turn the light off so she started looking around to see if there might be a way out. There was a window high up on the wall that she hadn't seen before. She pushed the bed over by it and stood on it, only to see that there were bars on the outside. So much for that she thought and sat back down on the bed curled up in the quilt and soon went to sleep.

Dolitha called Jameel that night to find out how he was doing and when he was coming back to school.

"Hy "J" hy ya doin? she said."

"I'm aw-ight, soreness goin away slow, but om gettin there." "When you comin' back to school?"

"Doc said I could go back Thursday, I jus hafta wear this wrap for another cupla days. Whas goin on dere?"

"They still talkin' 'bout whas gonna happen wit our football team. They dono yet if the team gonna hafta to play dat game again or not. What chu think?"

"I dono, if they hafta play again, they betta give us the points ahead that we had. Was Rajon there?"

"Yeah, he was there."

"What he say about what went down at the Bricks Saturday?"

" He said that the B's got caught sleepin' an the C's ready to take over the city." "Yeah, I dono 'bout dat, but I think a real war 'bout to start an we betta not sleep on it."

"What can we do?"

"Ain nuthin we can do, but watch our own backs. I jus hope they don start no mess inside the school. Look like erey time they start somethin, I git caught up in it. I don' need no more of dat."

"Well "J" can't wait to see you, but I gotta go now. Glad to hear your better. I'll see ya on Thursday call me tomorrow, okay?"

"Yeah aw-ight, later."

At police headquarters Wednesday morning just before the shift change a harried looking Lt. Meeker trudged into his office and flopped down in his chair. He picked up the intercom and called for his department to meet him in the conference room in ten minutes. He then got a cup of hot coffee, gulped it down picked up some files and headed to the room. After they were all assembled, he said:

"Men, last night the chief and I spent about two and half hours getting eaten up by the mayor and the city council. The mayor's not happy, the council is like wise and that made the chief unhappy; so you know where that leaves me. Listen I know these last few weeks have been like a nightmare, but we have got to come up with something soon or we're all going to be looking for new jobs. That reverend from the church across town was also there and he had some ideas. I think his name is Joyner, Rev. Joyner. Anyway I want to work with him so I'm going to assign a couple of you guys to be ready when he calls. It looks like he's putting together some kind of citizen's community action group and they may be able to help us. Sgt. Calloway, where do we stand on getting that guy from the Bricks to ID somebody?"

"Lieutenant, we've been talking to him and I think we're making some progress but as of right now he's not ready to come in."

"Well stay on it, we've got to come up with something and very soon. Also, I want whoever is patrolling that area around the corner of 11th Street and 7th Avenue, where that Minute Mart is, to step up your vigilance. I understand that there may be some illegal stuff going on in there. The overnight boys have reported some late night activity going on in there but they don't have anything to go in on. Okay, men, that's it let's get out there and find me something I can use to get the mayor off the chief – and me."

The meeting broke up and the officers went out to start their shifts.

Sista woke up to see the sun beaming through the window that let her know she had survived the night. The beam was concentrated on a small area of the room, but it seemed to cast brightness all over. For a brief moment she felt a sense of well being, but the stark realization of where she was set in and her fears returned. She was amazed at how rested she felt even though she had spent the night on a narrow trundle bed with a hard mattress and she remained fully dressed. She guessed the sleep was so good because of the many adrenalin rushes last night that completely fatigued her body. The regenerating sleep through the night gave her the rest she needed. As her body started to adjust to the start of a new day, nature's call presented a sense of urgency. She recalled last night's situation, but realized that now there was no one to let her out. Feeling trapped she ran to the door and tried the knob desperately. Finding that the door was still locked she banged on it hard and started screaming. To her surprise she heard a voice just outside saying: "Hol on, hol on I'm comin'." It seemed that after she pointed out to Ricoh his lapse of thinking about her bathroom needs, he had left a soldier outside the door all night. In a few minutes, the door was opened and she told her guard that she had to go.

"Aw-ight come on" he said and led her down the hall back to Willie's apartment. Ricoh had also arranged for Willie to allow her to wash up and do whatever else she needed to do.

Sista threw her overcoat on the couch rushed into the bathroom and took care of her urgency. But she also noticed that there was a washcloth, towel and a new toothbrush on the sink. She thought to herself, is this for me? Hers or not she took advantage and attended to her hygiene. When she finally came out she wasn't thinking about what she was wearing which had been intended for Jameel's eyes only, and it caught the attention of Willie's eyes. The short tight skirt that barely covered her georgous big legs and the clinging sweater that emphasized her gifts just served to bring the man to his feet and headed in her direction. As he reached for her, the soldier still in the room, stepped between them and reminded Willie what Ricoh had said. The look of extreme disappointment came over him, but he backed off. Sista grabbed her coat, hastily put it back on and headed back to the room.

On the way back she asked the soldier: "How long y'all gonna keep me here? An what am I 'pose to eat?"

"You jus chill. Rick be here soon."

Not exactly what she wanted to hear, but having no choice she went in the room and lay back down on the bed. About an hour later she heard voices outside again and knew that somebody was coming. The door opened and in walked PK and Ricoh. PK had some egg and bacon sandwiches in a bag that he gave to her with some orange juice.

Unabashed, she grabbed the bag and devoured the food. When finished she said: "How long you gonna keep me here?" Ricoh responded:

"You heard the deal las night, we gon keep you here 'til 'bout 4:30 then we headin' over to the diner. What you got another date?" he and PK laughed.

"You mean I'm 'posed to jus sit here doin' nuthin 'til then?"

"Well, I kin think a somthin we can do to pass time" Ricoh said. Sista not liking the sound of that pulled her coat tighter around her and just stared at him.

"Don' sweat it girl, I ain' gonna do dat, not now anyhow. I got some otha things to do 'fore tonight."

Ricoh then motioned to PK and they both left, closing the door behind them. Sista looked at the window again, resigned herself to the fact that she was there for the day and went back to sleep.

Hakeem got up about 10:00 AM and reflected on the business deal last night and the conversation that he had with Ricoh. He was a little mad trying to figure out how Sista had let herself get snatched like that. He knew that some of the posse was supposed to be around her all the time. He also knew that he still had the bag so he got dressed and headed to the store to stash the money. Once at the hang he went in the back and placed the funds in the secret safe. There were actually some customers in the store and the store manger and clerks that worked there serviced them. Hakeem chuckled to himself thinking about how slick this operational cover was.

He left the store and went straight to Hammer's place. He knocked on the door and went in. "Hey man whas up?" Hammer said. Hakeem without responding to the greeting said: "I got a call last night afta we split up, from that dude that run the B's – Ricoh. They got Sista, I talked to her. I wanna know how dat happen."

"Man I dono, the school posse 'pose to cover her. You wanna go over there an fine out?"

"Naw, not now, we kin deal wit dat later. Right now, I gotta figure out how to git her back witout givin up the dough he aksin for."

"Dough, what dough?"

"He wants $10K for us to git her back." "$10K, he crazy? Why he think we got it?"

"Somehow he knew 'bout the pickup 'an the deal las night. We gotta leak down there at the port an we gotta sniff that out soon, but not now. We 'pose to meet him at Ciscero's at 5:00 today an bring the dough in a gym bag. He wants me there alone." "What chu gonna do?"

"Well, om thinkin 'bout settin him up so when I give up the dough inside an come out wit her – then y'all git him when he come out. Make sure y'all git the money back." "Man, he ain' stupid you don' think he be thinkin a dat."

"Yeah, I guess you right, but what else can we do. I ain gonna jus give him all dat dough."

"We ain got no choice if we want her back."

"We gotta git her back, she know too much 'bout the bidness." "Yeah well guess we gotta do it then."

"Aw-ight I'm goin back to the hang an git the dough together. Tell a cupla soldiers to be ready to roll at 5:00 jus in case we need'em. I want you to roll wit me up to the joint anyway, jus don go inside."

"Yeah aw-ight when you wanna meet?" "Meet me at the hang at 4:30."

"Aw-ight, see ya later."

Lt. Meeker after the meeting went back to his office and started looking through the files and reports to see if there was anything that he missed. There was nothing. Nothing he could string together to make a good case. He decided then that he had to get out of the office and hit the streets. He got in his car and headed first for the Bricks where the recent shooting took place. When he got there, he saw a patrol car just outside the courts and slowed down. Keeping out of sight he watched his officers talking to some of the residents. He wondered to himself, if one of them was the man they were trying to get to come down to the station to look in the book and perhaps point out somebody. He wasn't there long when he saw Sgt. Calloway coming out of one of the buildings and walking up to the other officers. Upon seeing this, he moved closer and they saw him.

Pulling up to the officers he rolled down his window and spoke to Sgt. Calloway. "Is one of those our guy?"

"No lieutenant our guy has gone missing and can't be found anymore. Maybe he's hiding or he just may have disappeared. Strange things happen down here. We're trying to get a handle on his whereabouts from these guys. Not much luck so far." "Alright Ray keep at it, I'm going to ride around for a while and see what I can spot." "Alright lieutenant, I'll talk to you later."

Lt. Meeker took off and headed next to Higgenbotham's Funeral Home where the second shooting was. He looked around the area noticing that the front glass windows had been replaced already and it was back to business as usual. From there he went back across town toward 11th Street and 7th Avenue the area where he had instructed his men to be especially vigilant. He rode past the Minute Mart and noticed that several patrol cars were also circling the area. They acknowledged him and he just rolled by. He circled the block and came back again noticing that there were apartment buildings across from the store with good views and wondered whether any of the residents there would have noticed anything suspicious on the night of the Bricks shootings. He filed this in the back of his mind and thought that he would bring it up with Rev. Joyner to see if anyone from there might be members of his church or the new group they were assembling. Not really coming up with anything concrete he went back to the station.

At the Peterson house that morning things were getting back to normal. No new crises occurred, Jameel was on the mend nicely and had been cleared to return to school tomorrow. Sarafina was getting excited about the possibility of getting help from the church for her CONN's club, especially about getting some of the men involved. Cinque, a big school football fan was anxiously waiting for the decision from the officials regarding the Jaguars make up game. All in all things seemed to be going well.

Sarafina told the boys she was leaving and said especially to Jameel that if he needed anything from the drug store to call her and let her know.

Jameel told her he was fine and for her to have a good day. Hearing that, she headed out the door. When she got down to her car she already got in and started the engine before she noticed the note that was left on the wipers. She got out and took it off. It said: "We're watching you. Don mess wit our `hood – it's our turf. CONN's don belong here. You know who dis is." Suddenly what had started out as a bright and positive day had now turned into one in which she needed to be concerned. She wasn't quite sure about what the note really meant. Her CONN's club had not done anything yet, except for the youth dance that they had given two weeks ago. It was no secret though, that the whole neighborhood knew about their existence and what their mission was. Maybe she rattled somebody's cage or was starting to get too close to something. She put the note in her bag and continued on to work.

Cinque finished his breakfast, told Jameel later and walked out. He took the normal route to school and as usual arrived there in time to meet up with Rajon and Dolitha before classes began. The main topic of conversation this morning was still Jameel's state of health, but after Cinque told them "J" would back tomorrow they moved on to the football team. They rehashed what had happened at the last game and wondered if anybody had been blamed for what caused it. They also tried to get Rajon to finish giving his report about what happened at the Bricks complex Saturday night. Once again as he was starting to fill in the blanks, the bell rang and the story ended. They moved to their respective homerooms and the school day began.

The artificial peace that was being forced between the two rival groups in the school was really being stretched now that each group was aware of what was due to happen this evening. As they passed each other in the hallways, it was all they could do to not bump into one another. Even the teachers sensed that there was a new tension in the air, but they couldn't identify a cause. Teaching at Midland was always interesting, but in the last couple of weeks teaching there had become more of a challenge. The students were all aware that a new level of strife had been created since the shootings after the dance two weeks ago. They were also keenly cognizant of who among their fellow students could have been involved. As a result most of the students walked the halls cautiously and were constantly looking over their shoulders for anything strange. Even in the classrooms academic progress was suffering.

Principal Steinberg, who had been in his position for four years now, was also keenly aware of the changes that were going on affecting his students and the teachers. He was sensitive to reports about the build up of gang activity in the area and was doing his best to try and keep his teachers motivated under these new conditions. Until now he was able to direct his energy to keeping things under control, but over the last few weeks it seemed that control was eluding him. He had a good idea about who among his students were club members, even who was on which side of the rivalry, but there was nothing he could do until they violated school policies. Other then the few fights that didn't amount to much, they didn't do anything disruptive enough to cause suspension or expulsion. It seemed that they knew just how far they could push the law.

In the early afternoon, Ricoh left his apartment and went to the diner. He wanted to check out the parking lot to see just what staging possibilities Hakeem could set up just in case he might act stupid and try to pull something. He pulled into the lot and drove around. There were several cars there because it was still the lunch hour. Ricoh knew that at about the time his meeting was set, there would be more cars there because Cisceros was known for a good dinner crowd. He envisioned all possibilities but couldn't see how a clean hit on him could be made when he would be coming out of the diner with the money. In any event, he was going to station his soldiers at what he thought would be strategic spots. He also ran the idea through his head about having his soldiers take out Hakeem and Sista when they came out, but decided that given the number of people around, it wasn't a good idea. Satisfied that he had done his homework, he left the parking lot and went back to the Bricks.

He arrived at the complex and went to building #1 where Sista was being held. He noticed that there were still some patrol cars riding through the area and he wondered if they had come up with something. Wanting anxiously to know what they knew he sought some of his lookouts that were left in the B's. The information he received wasn't to helpful, but as his spotters said, the police know who did everything, but they can't do anything without eyewitnesses. After this brief conversation he turned around and headed to Willie's place. It was now about 3:30 and he thought he would hang with Willie until it was time to go.

At about 4:30 he left Willie and walked down to the storage bin. He stopped just outside the door and listened. He didn't hear anything coming from inside and he figured that Sista was still sleeping so he quietly opened the door. He was right she was sleeping. He walked in and shook her. Slowly she woke up rubbing her eyes and said:

"What time is it?"

"It's time to go" he said.

"I gotta go to the bathroom."

"Yeah aw-ight, but git yo stuff you ain comin back here."

They walked back to Willie's and she took care of her needs. Willie gazed one more time salivating at the thought of what might have been and resigned himself to the fact it's not going to happen. Sista came out looking refreshed and followed Ricoh out to his car.

She was happy to see the daylight and felt that her ordeal was about to be over.

Somehow though she had a feeling that something wasn't right and a feeling of foreboding came over her. As they rode across town to Cisceros diner she kept looking out of the window to see if she could spot any of her people. They arrived early and went in. Ricoh motioned for her to head toward the back. She walked straight ahead and found a booth right near the rear entrance. They sat down and waited. Sista asked if he was going to buy her something. He said yes, get a cup of coffee because we won't be here long. He ordered coffee also. While they were drinking their coffee Ricoh kept staring at the front door expecting Hakeem to walk in any minute.

At 5:10 Ricoh nervously said to Sista: "Yo man ain stupid is he?" "What chu mean?"

"You heard me tell em don be late right? Where is he?" "He tol you he be here. He be here."

Just then the front door opened and Hakeem slowly walked in surveying the room and looking for them. About half way through the diner he spotted them in the booth in the back. He proceeded slowly. Ricoh was looking hard to see what kind of bag Hakeem had and he was also checking to see if there were any bulges in Hakeem's jacket.

Hakeem arrived at the table and put the bag down by his side. He looked at Ricoh and said: "Aw-ight les do this, let her out."

"Aah, jus a minute dude, push the bag over here. We ain done yet."

Hakeem pushed the bag over to Ricoh who moved it with his feet under the table to the wall. He then slowly picked it up while keeping his eyes on Hakeem. He opened it and looked inside. It appeared that everything was as he instructed so he said to Sista: "Aw-ight you can go." As Sista got up from the table so did Hakeem who turned to Ricoh and said: "You got dis one, but I'll see ya again." then they walked out of the diner. As Hakeem opened the door, he paused before going out to see if everything was all right. He had positioned his soldiers around the lot for insurance, but he also noticed that Ricoh had done the same thing. He just laughed to himself and motioned Sista to his ride.

Once in the car, Hakeem started grilling Sista about how she got snatched up. She told him she was thankful for him getting her out, but she was very tired and just wanted to get home. He didn't push her and just drove her to the terrace. She could see though that he was not finished with this conversation and there would definitely have to be some explaining to do later.

Sarafina got home that night after going through a workday that was not unusual except for the thoughts constantly going through her head about the note she received that morning. Her first thought after getting inside was that she should call somebody and let them know about it. She wasn't quite sure whether it should be Lt. Meeker or Reverend Joyner, but she decided to think on it for a little while. The boys were there playing video games as usual and she poked her head in just to make sure everything was okay. "Hi guys" she said and without turning around they both said: Hi mom, you bring some chicken?"

"No not tonight. We'll finish what we started last night."

After dinner Sarafina asked Jameel if he was ready to go back to school and did he call Mr. Steinberg to let him know he was coming. He said that he had and the principal was ready for him to return. She then turned to Cinque and asked whether he had done his homework. Cinque reported that he had finished it in school during his study period. Satisfied with that Sarafina went into the living room and decided then to call Reverend Joyner for two reasons. First to find out who signed up Sunday and second to tell him about the note she got. She dialed his number and got the answering machine so she left a message. She then decided to call Lydia, her friend from the CONN's. Lydia answered after a few rings:

"Hello"

"Lydia, this is Sarafina how you doin?" "I'm okay, how are you?"

"I'm fine but somethin strange happened to me today." "What?"

"Well when I went to my car this mornin' there was a note on it. It said the CONN's don belong here an to leave the 'hood alone. It didn 'xactly say who it was from, but it said that I would know who. I'm not sure what to do wit it."

"Girl, you needa call the police."

"I thought 'bout that, but then I said maybe I aughta talk wit Rev. Joyner first." "Yeah, I agree wit dat. Did you call him?"

"I tried 'fore I call you, but got his machine. I'll try him again now. I'll call you again afta I talk wit him."

"Okay, see ya."

"Talk to you in a while, bye."

Sarafina hung up the phone and dialed Rev. Joyner's number again. This time he picked up on the second ring.

"Hello, this is Reverend Joyner."

"Reverend Joyner this is Sister Sarafina how are you?" "I'm blessed Sister Peterson how are you?"

"I'm fine, but I have something to talk to you `bout."

"Okay, but you know I was just about to call you. Isn't that strange?" "Yeah well what were you callin me for?"

"I wanted to tell you about the results of the sign-up on Sunday and to see how we can move forward with the next steps. There were 30 members that signed up and among them were twelve men. That's a good sign we just have to wait and see who really means it. I'm thinking that on Sunday I will announce that we will have a meeting at the church on Tuesday evening to lay out our neighborhood improvement plans. I'll also have some flyers made and handed out around the community. Do you think you can get your CONN's to come out?"

"Yes, I don think that'll be a problem, but you know I got a strange note this morning when I went to my car."

"You did, what kind of note?"

"It said they are watchin me an the CONNS don belong here. It also said that I know who sent it."

"Well do you?

"Don' really know, but I think its them C boys that ride `round here." "Did you tell the police?"

"No. I wanted to talk to you first."

"Alright, let's wait on that for now, unless you get another one. We'll talk about it at the meeting, okay? See you at church Sunday?"

"Yes I should be there."

"Okay I'll see you then. Goodnight." "Goodnight."

Sarafina hung up and Jameel came into the room.

"Mom, you finished talking? I tol Dolitha I would call her before I come back to school tomorrow."

"Yes, you can call her."

Jameel picked up the phone and dialed. "Hello, this Dolitha?"

"Yeah hi "J". I wondered when you were gonna call. How you doin?" "I'm good. I'll be in tomorrow."

"Thas great, can't wait to see you." "Anything good happen there today?"

"Not much, but Sista wasn' in school today. Sometime I don see her all day, but I really don think she was in at all. I don' really care if she don come back, jus thought I let you know case you lookin' for her."

Dolitha laughed after she said that.

"Aw come on girl, you know where om at. What else go down?

"Nothin, you know tonight they gonna know `bout playin that football again. We should fine out tomorrow."

Sarafina walked back into the room. "Aw-ight, I gotta go, see ya then." "Okay, bye."

Once he was through, Sarafina got back on and called Lydia back.

"Lydia, it's me again. I talked with pastor an he said 30 people signed up – including 12 men. He's callin a meetin for Tuesday night at 7:00 at the church an he wanna know if all of us can be there. I think we should go, don' you?"

"Yeah, we should all be there. You gonna call everybody?"

"No, you gonna help me. I'll call the first 6 on our roster an you can call the rest, okay?"

"Yeah I can do that."

"Okay then we can get together later an see who gonna come. Okay? "Yeah okay, later."

The ladies hung up and Sarafina was excited about the possibilities of what this could bring about regarding what the CONN's had in mind from the beginning. The note she got this morning however, was still on her mind and she pondered it.

The rest of the week was uneventful when compared to what had happened over the previous couple of weeks. There was a quasi calm between the rival factions both in school and on the street. The teachers felt a little more at ease and the principal was pleased at what he thought was a return to normalcy. The decision had been made about replaying the key football game and it was decided in the Jaguar's favor. The game would be replayed next Friday night and the Jaguar's would be spotted 3 points at the start. Jameel returned to school and his friends were very happy to see him, Rajon and especially Dolitha. Sista saw him and tried to get him alone several times, but it was not to be. She wanted to tell him about her ordeal, but didn't get the chance so she decided to just be patient.

On Sunday Rev. Joyner after preaching his sermon and commend-ing the congregation on signing up for the action group, announced the meeting on Tuesday. He was adamant about the need to not stand by and watch the community fall apart as he reminded them about his Nehemiah sermon last Sunday. When they dismissed there was an air of excitement among the people and it promised to be a good turn out for the session.

Flyers advising the details of the meeting were handed out and a number of people took extras promising to distribute them around town. Rev. Joyner was pleased, Sarafina felt a surge of new energy; congregation members were excited, and even the boys felt like something good was coming.

Tuesday morning came and the Peterson family got up with a renewed sense of something exciting about to happen. They went through their normal routines and left the house at their usual times. Jameel and Cinque met up with Rajon on the way in and Rajon filled them in on what was the latest street news. Sarafina got to work and everything seemed to be working according to plan. She was a bit surprised though to see that some of the church flyers about tonight's meeting had made their way into her office. Since she hadn't brought any in, she wondered to herself who else could have placed them there. The rest of the day went by quickly and 5:00 O'clock came. She wasted no time in leaving the building knowing that she wanted to get to the church a little early to help with setting up. The boys also left school promptly to get home quickly to meet mom per her instructions that morning. Sarafina arrived home at 5:30 fed the boys with some fast food take out and they were ready to roll.

Arriving at the church about 6:45 she and the boys walked in. Already there to her surprise were Lydia and several members of the CONN's. Rev. Joyner had already greeted and welcomed them and said to Sarafina how pleased he was that they were ready and willing to work. Sarafina acknowledged his greeting and agreed that they were all ready to work. Within ten minutes of the proposed start time, the church Fellowship Hall was filled almost to capacity. Rev. Joyner with his booming baritone voice quieted the group and brought the meeting to order.

"Members, family, friends and neighbors, it gives me great pleasure to see so many of you here that have responded to the call. We come here tonight in response to the senseless killings that have taken place in our community over the last few weeks. I believe that we have a neighborhood that is in need of healing and have prayed for the wisdom and courage to start a work that will come up with a solution to solve the problem."

At that point a loud Amen came from amongst the group. Also, the door opened and to everyone's surprise in walked Principal Steinberg along with the head football coach. More surprising to Sarafina, also walking in was a woman from her office and a man from inside the plant area.

"We are here to commit ourselves by working together hand in hand with the Change Our Neighborhood Now (CONN's) group that has already begun a good work toward that end. I've put together a tentative action plan that I'm going to ask you all to look at and briefly discuss so that when we leave here tonight we'll have something to start with."

The reverend then handed out the strategy plan to the group and asked them to take a few minutes to look at it and afterward they would talk about it. The group didn't take long to agree to the document and commended the pastor for his diligent attention to what was needed to get the job done. So with the consensus of the group in order, assignments were made and they were ready to be dismissed. However, just before he let them go he made it a point to remind them about Nehemiah's work on rebuilding the wall and that the people accomplished their task because they had a mind to work and were not afraid. Another Amen issued forth from the group and they were dismissed.

Sarafina, Lydia and the other CONN members left the church that night feeling that they had really started something big. They were anxious to get their piece started and decided to have their own follow up meeting on Thursday to get things going. Sarafina got home that night feeling good and with a sense of accomplishment. The boys didn't quite understand all that had been discussed in the meeting, but they knew that whatever mom's group was going to do, they would somehow be involved. Jameel felt a sense of tension about this, but Cinque just didn't feel anything one way or the other.

Wednesday morning was starting out to be another beautiful day. Even in the early morning the skies were already blue and there were no clouds in sight. Sarafina got up a little early feeling energized and ready for the new day. The boys were not so energized, and getting up was more of a chore. They managed though and the Peterson family made it through their routines and readied themselves for the tasks of the day. After breakfast, Sarafina issued her usual final instructions for the boys for that day and headed out the door. Following her normal routine she made her way down the hall, down the creaking stairs and outside into the building parking lot. When she approached her car and looked at it, she was stunned falling backwards almost to the ground. What she saw she couldn't bring herself to believe she was really seeing.

Chapter 6 - The Key

What started as a beautiful day, all of a sudden turned ugly. Sarafina got up this morning feeling energized with a carry over surge from a most positive community meeting last night. Now she was staring, unbelievingly, at a car that had been vandalized. She continued to stare in disbelief for several minutes wondering how this could have happened right outside her house. The windows had been smeared with some kind of dark goop and the front tires were completely gone. Now the front end sat up on a couple of cinder blocks. After several minutes, she composed herself and approached the vehicle. There on the windshield was another note. With hands shaking she plucked it from the wipers. It read: "You were warned. Now believe."

She stuffed the note in her pocketbook then looked at the car more closely. The initial shock had prevented her from seeing clearly that the goop on the windows was just some kind of paste and when she rubbed it with her hand it started to come off. She thought to herself at least this is something I can fix. But the tires, although hardly new, had to be replaced and she wasn't sure her insurance would cover it. She turned around headed back to the apartment and went inside. Then she called her office to advise them she would be in a little late. Next she called the police. Jameel hearing her come back in asked what happened and she told him.

"Mom, what chu gonna do?" he said.

"I'm gonna wait for the police an then I'll take the bus to work. I can deal wit it from there. Don you worry 'bout nuthin, it'll be all right. You boys go ahead to school."

She left the apartment and went back outside to wait for the police. Ten minutes later a patrol car arrived and the officers surveyed the situation, took her statement and told her she could pick up their report in a few days. They also asked if she had any idea who did it?   She hesitated and then said no. She wanted to talk to Rev. Joyner first before she told the police anything more, especially about the notes she had received. Then she walked to the bus stop and headed to Gateway.

When she arrived at work and got to her desk she saw that the message light on her phone was blinking. She picked it up and retrieved the message. It was from Mr.

Lukinbill asking her to come to his office. She said to herself, here we go again. When she got there he was on the phone, but motioned to her to come in and sit down. In a few minutes he concluded his call and asked her what happened. She explained to him her incident that morning and he responded with a kind of an odd statement. He said that he wondered about what was going on with her and her family over the past few weeks. It seems that unusual things have been happening to them. She told him that she thought it was just a series of coincidences. He said okay, but he was going to be keeping an eye on her for the next few weeks. Feeling a little despondent she said fine and went back to her desk. She was getting a little concerned about her job security all because of what had started as a lie and was now escalating into something that could threaten her employment status.

When she got back to her desk, she made two calls. The first was to her insurance company to find out what they could do. The second was to Rev. Joyner to let him know about what happened. The insurance company told her just what she thought she might hear. Coverage to replace the tires, without the car being involved in an accident was not available on her policy. Since it was an older car, she had no comprehensive coverage. The call to Rev. Joyner ended up in her leaving a message on his machine explaining in detail what happened and that she would call him again tonight.

Later that afternoon, Hakeem arrived at the hang and met some of his boys. He asked whether the message had been delivered and they confirmed it. He then told them that the big man would be coming around tonight to talk about a new deal so all he wanted here was Hammer, Buster and Shariq. Everybody else should stay away. The big man was the owner of the store and the warehouse and was the one who negotiated the deals that the C's carried out. When he came around it was always understood, per his instructions, to not have any more than Hakeem's key people be there.

Hakeem also told the soldiers that he was still mad that somebody was able to snatch one of his people and make him lighten his bank account heavily. The boys got the message and went straight to MHS to see whom they needed to tap. The fact that Sista had been taken by the rival B's did not sit well with Hakeem and he was intent on finding out where the breakdown was in his security system. Whoever was responsible would have to answer to him directly and pay the price.

At Midland when Hakeem's soldiers arrived they were somehow able to get a message through to the troops inside the building. Not being able to get into the school themselves, they sent instructions for an inside contact to come out during a lunch period. The time now was about 1:30 so the wait wasn't long before one of the inside troops appeared.

"Hakeem ain happy `bout Sista gittin snatched the otha night" one of the visiting soldiers said.

"Who `posed to cover her."

The inside contact responded and said: "Man, me an tyron had her covered, but she tol us to chill that night `cause she needed some space to take care a some errands. She didn want us goin wit her."

The soldier wasn't sure how to react to that or what he should take back to Hakeem. If Sista told the guys to chill, then she was on her own from there. This meant that it was something Hakeem would have to deal with directly with Sista. The conversation ended with the agreement that the cover boys were not at fault, so the visitors left.

When they got back to the hang, Hakeem was still there and the report was given. "I don know whas up wit her, she know she can't take chances like that by herself. She musta had good reason. I'll be over her place tomorrow an straightn it out" Hakeem said.

"You don think she doin nuthin wrong do you?" said the lead soldier.

"Naw, but she git real strange sometime an I dono where she be comin from. Thas aw-ight, like I said I'll straightin it out. You did good so you can split, see you tomorrow."

Back at MHS the word was circulating about last night's church meeting. The fact that there was a community action group that was more than just the CONNS alone now, was putting a wrinkle in both rival factions feelings of immunity. However, it was not likely they would be joining forces to combat the CONN's efforts, but it was likely that each group had to do something to stop the effort. Their thoughts then turned to the big game coming up on Friday night and the stadium would once again be filled to the brink. To the rivals, it seemed that this might be another opportunity to display a show of force and let the community know that they had no fear. But who was going to do what would be the big question.

The non-verified talk was that it was the B's that caused the first black out at the stadium and the panic that ensued. The police never resolved anything from that nor did they have anything to go on, so the case was just left hanging. The C's fully aware of this status, were bent on either duplicating the havoc or taking it one step further to let everybody know that they were indeed in charge. Even though most of the students were excited about going to the game, there was an underlying current of apprehension because of the rumors that were running rampant about what was going to go down.

Principal Steinberg, having also heard the rumors, was once again on high alert and he cautioned his staff to keep their eyes open.

In the evening when Sarafina got home she ran to check out whether anything else had been done to her vehicle and then rushed to get on the phone and talk to Rev. Joyner.

The car was in the same condition that she left it so she went inside. The boys were treated to a large pepperoni pizza so they were completely occupied engrossed in devouring the meal. The phone at Rev. Joyner's house rang several times, but the machine didn't pick up which gave Sarafina a bit of concern. Finally though just as she was about to hang up, he picked up and answered:

"Hello, this is Rev. Joyner."

"Oh, Rev, Joyner, this is Sister Sarafina. I was about to hang up, your machine didn answer."

"Yes, I was just changing the greeting and I had it off line for a minute. How are you?"

"Well I'm okay, but I got another note today an my car got messed wit." "What do you mean messed with?"

"They painted the windows, well not really paint, but they smeared stuff all over them an took my front tires."

"What? When?"

"Yeah jus like I said they really messed up my car. They had to do it overnight last night."

"Will your insurance cover the damage?"

"No, they tol me I don have comprehensive so I'm not covered for that. The stuff on the windows I think I can wash off, but I dono what to do about the tires. I don have no money for no new tires."

"Don't you worry about that, I'm sure the church will be able to help you out. My concern now is that whoever did it targeted you for a reason. Did you call the police?"

"Yes, this time I filed a report. They said I can git in a few days."

"Good, I think the gang is trying to send you a message to stop the community action and I'm just wondering how far they'll go. Once we get the car fixed, is there someplace else you can park it?"

"I dono right now, but I'll fine somewhere. I don wanna keep doin this."

"Right. Tomorrow I'm going to talk to that Lt. Meeker and get him to step up his patrols around your building and parking lot. We can't let the gang get any satisfaction from this and think they won't be caught. I'll call you tomorrow night and let you know what he said. Goodnight!"

"Okay, I'll talk to you then. Goodnight!"

As soon as she got off the phone with Rev. Joyner Sarafina called Lydia. "Lydia, you jus git in?"

"Sarafina? No, I've been here, why you call before?"

"No I didn call before, but I wasn sure what time you got in. Well I got another note today an they also messed wit my car this time."

"What? What'd they do?

"Took my front tires and put goop all over the windows." "Wow! You call police?

"Yeah, this time I did. They took a report that I'll git end of the week. I also talked to Rev. Joyner an he said he gonna talk wit that police guy to get some patrol cars to ride around here more."

"Well, thas good. I dono though if they gonna catch anybody, 'cause it don seem like they really want to."

"Yeah girl, sometime I wonder 'bout that too. Well anyway, jus thought I'd bring you up to date on whas happnin wit me. Thas it. I'll see ya tomorrow at the meetin, right?"

"Yeah, it should be a good one. Talk to you later, bye." "Bye."

Around M&M's that night the usual milling around of C members outside was missing. The corner was seemingly naked stripped of its covering of bodies that had no other purpose than to just be a presence in one spot or another. Inside the store in the back, where the secret room and the armory were concealed behind a well-disguised facade, were a conference table and several comfortable chairs. The lighting was not overly bright, but sufficient to conduct a meeting. Cleverly hidden in a picture that hung on the front wall was an oversize peephole that allowed observation into the store. The main area of the store had its normal night-lights on and a lookout was seated on the floor leaning against a merchandise counter facing the entrance door. The time according to the green reflecting glow from the clock on the wall said it was 8:30 PM.

There was no set time for the big man to show, but when the message was sent he would be coming by on any given day, Hakeem and his lieutenants were expected to be available anytime from 8 PM until he arrived. Hakeem, Hammer, Buster and Shariq sat around at the table discussing what had happened to Sista, but were really just passing time until the big man arrived. Hakeem said that he thought Sista's behavior was always a little strange because she was just like her brother. Everybody agreed because they remembered Razor was really strange, but he was a good and fearless general that had set up this whole operation and got the contact going with the big man. With this they had to give her a lot of slack and respect. Also, they were all aware that she knew things about the operation that they didn't.

About 9:30 three men dressed in dark suits and hats pulled down low walked up to the door of the store. Keys were inserted in the lock and the door opened. The lookout had seen them approaching and moved to the back where he gave the special knock. The hidden observation portal slid open and he alerted Hakeem that their guests were here. Hakeem got up and looked out of the peephole and verified that Mr. Mazzetti, a.k.a. Mr. M and his associates were in the house. Before they got to the portal, he slid the door open and invited them in. "Mr. M, come on in - sit down. How ya doin?" he said. His soldiers got up and gave their seats to the men dressed in dark suits. Hakeem sat in the one chair left opposite Mr. M.

"Can I git y'all a drink or somethin?" Hakeem continued.

"No thanks, Hakeem we won't be staying long. How'd thing's go with the deal? You have any problems?"

"No, Mr. M ereything was cool. I got yo money right here."

Hakeem motioned to Hammer to hand him the satchel. Hammer picked up the bag and brought it over to the table. Mr. M's lieutenant sitting at his right hand stood, picked it up and opened it. He picked up several stacks from inside and fanned the packets then nodded okay to Mr. M.

"Good" Mr. M said. "I hear you had a little trouble with those boys crosstown. Is that right?"

Hakeem was a little stunned because he didn't think Mr. M. would know about that, paused a moment composed himself and then said:

"Yeah, Mr. M. they got hol of Razor's sister for a minute, but we got her back. It wasn no big thing, I took care a it."

"You know she knows a lot about this operation, and we don't want her to turn up on the wrong side, right?"

"Yeah, Mr. M. I know an it won happin agin." "Make sure it doesn't, I don't like surprises." "Okay Mr. M, we got it covered."

"In two weeks there's going to be another shipment coming in at the airport just like before. You will do exactly like you did the last time, except that you will not use the same van. Got it? You will not use the same pick up men and the time will be earlier. You'll get a call from my people next week with the exact date and time, so be ready. You clear on what I'm telling you?"

"Yeah, I got it. I'll wait for yo call." "Okay - boys let's go."

Mr. M. got up and his soldiers did likewise. They picked up the satchel and left the store. Hakeem walked out with them and saw parked near the corner, the prettiest Bentley Continental he had ever seen. The thoughts that ran through his head had him reeling with a sense of how he pictured himself in a few years. He really saw himself driving one of those and retiring from the street life, but living just as Mr. M. did. The trio got in the car and sped away, but not before a patrol car rode by the store and spotted them. Hakeem had ducked back in the store so he was not seen.

Lt. Meeker came in early Thursday morning hoping there would be some good news waiting for him on his desk. Since he and the chief had been raked over the coals recently, he was still feeling the tension. His department still hadn't come up with something they could hang their hats on to make a case and arrest someone for the shootings. Each day it seemed he was no closer to solving anything and the frustration was causing a rise in his pressure. Everyday he admonished his men to step up the hunt, but at the end of each day there was nothing really new.

Finally, this day, around 10 AM he got a call from the night desk sergeant who had already gone home from his shift. He told the lieutenant that last night his men around 2330 hours had spotted an expensive looking Bentley leaving the area of that Minute Mart on 7th Avenue. He continued and said that his officers got the plate number, but didn't run it last night. He has it in his report and he was going to fax it over in about an hour. The lieutenant anxiously asked him why it was going to take an hour and the sergeant replied there was no fax machine in his house. The lieutenant begrudgingly thanked him for the information and told him that he looked forward to reading his report.

Not long after that another call came in. This time it was Reverend Joyner. "Lt. Meeker, this is Reverend Joyner how are you?"

"I'm okay Rev., how are you?"

"Doing fine thank you. You and your chief held up pretty good the other night under that barrage from the mayor and council and I just want to encourage you and to say that I know you have a tough job. Please remember that you're not alone in this struggle and that there are many in the community who support you and your troops." "Thanks Rev., I appreciate that coming from you it means something."

"There's something else I wanted to talk to you about that may be the beginning of something promising. Yesterday Mrs. Peterson, you remember her she's the one that your guys mistakenly picked up her son after that vacant lot incident, had her car vandalized. There was also a note left on it. This was the second note that she has received threatening her if she doesn't get her group to back off with the community improvement effort. I'm sure that I told you before that she is also one of the leaders of that CONN's club you are aware of. Anyway, what I think is important is that the note came from that gang called the C's that frequent that neighborhood. She must be upsetting them."

"I do remember talking to her with her son. What makes you think that the C's are responsible?"

"Because in the note it says she knows who sent it. They're the only ones it could be."

"Did she report it to us?"

"She reported the damage to her car, but not the notes. I can get you a copy of both notes, if you want."

"Yeah, soon as you can get that to me. You said the car was trashed yesterday?" "Yes, actually sometime overnight Tuesday after our meeting."

"Do you know what officers took the statement?"

"No, but I'm sure you can get that information from your dispatch records."

"Okay Rev., I'll check it out. While I have you on, there's something I wanted to ask you. I was riding by that Minute Mart on 7th Avenue the other day and I noticed that there is an apartment building right across the street that some of the apartments have a clear view right into the store. What I want to know is if any of your people live there or if any of those CONN's live there?"

"Yes, I know where you're talking about, but I don't believe any of my members live there. I can't answer for the CONN's, but I will ask Mrs. Peterson. Why do you ask?"

"I just wanted to know whether anybody there saw anything suspicious going on the night of that massacre over at the Bricks Complex."

"Yes, I see. Well when I speak with her again I'll ask and let you know. Is that all?" "Yes Rev., thanks for the head's up and the encouragement. I told my men that you would be working with us, so any time you get something please let me or my guys know."

"Yes, will do. Goodbye."

Thanks again. Goodbye reverend."

Just as the lieutenant hung up with Rev. Joyner, a clerk came into his office and placed the sergeant's report on his desk. He quickly picked it up and looked for the Bentley automobile information and the statement about Mrs. Peterson's car. The report said that a Bentley Continental Sedan, license plate number NJ IM1-2SN was seen at 2330 Hrs. in the vicinity of 11th Street and 7th Avenue. This was unusual for that type of vehicle to be in this area at that time. The report also provided details on the Peterson car vandalism on 8th Street, but there was no mention about any note. Lt. Meeker called the clerk back and asked that the license plate be run through Motor Vehicles for a registration check. Minutes later the clerk returned and advised that the vehicle was registered under the name of: Gateway Safe and Lock Company. The registered owner was a Mr. Antonio Mazzetti.

Later that evening the CONN's held a meeting as a follow-up to

Reverend Joyner's Tuesday night session. About fifteen people showed up, which was a sharp increase over what their usual attendance was. Sarafina greeted everyone and was really surprised to see the man who worked inside the plant at the Gateway Company.

"Hi everybody, it's good to see all you here tonight. I'm glad you can make it. Y'all know why we're here so I wanna get started on tryna set up some ways that we can git started doin what Rev. Joyner aksed us to do. I dono if you met Lydia, but she's the Vice-President and when om not here she's the one to see. Okay, first we needa git the names and addresses of the new people here so I'm sendin around a sheet for you to put yo information on. Please write or print good so we can read it. Thank you. I dono if y'all heard, but my car was vandalized after the Tuesday meetin an I got a note sayin for us to back off changin anything. This mus mean we gittn close to somebody."

There was a laugh from the crowd.

"It's not gonna scare me, but I jus wanna let you know what we're lookin at so you know what you gittin into. What we wanna do tonight is share any information that you have 'bout whas been happenin lately. Anything on the shootins or jus anything.

'Cause if we don tell the police den they can't or won't help us."

When Sarafina finished speaking, a woman from the crowd spoke up and said:

"I don't know if they want to help us anyway. The police fly through here all the time and don't ever stop nobody unless somethin happens. Why do you think we gonna change that?"

"You're right I've seen that myself, but if we don start here tonight to do somethin, then it's never gonna change. And now that we have a lotta people gittin on board an we have a whole church wit Rev. Joyner wit us, I think we can git somethin done."

Several thas rights, yeah's, and uh-huh's came from the crowd as they acknowledged and agreed with Sarafina. The mood in the group was definitely one of wanting to do something to improve the community. At that point, the man from the Gateway plant stood up and said:

"I know who behind the gang over here on this side of town; them C boys. I know he the one got them organized."

Sarafina said: "You do?"

"Yeah, I work for him. An you work for him too."

Sarafina was a little taken aback wondering what this man was talking about. She asked him to explain what he meant.

"The same man that owns the Gateway Safe And Lock Company,

where you work is the one be settin all their drug deals and otha stuff."

"How you know this?" Sarafina said.

"Some of the men that work there in the plant, they also work for him outside the plant. I hear them talkin sometime an they be plannin how a deal gonna happen usin them C boys. I hear'em, but they dono I be listenin."

"Wow, thas really a surprise. If your right, then we got a bigger problem then I thought. Can you prove any of what you said?"

"I dono how to prove it, I jus hear dem talkin."

Sarafina told him and the group that she was going to get this information to the right people and she took what the man said wrote it down on a note to give to Reverend Joyner on Sunday. She then continued the rest of the meeting and after getting all the new people's names and addresses she divided them into teams of three and told them that they were going to be starting a neighborhood watch patrol themselves. They would ride around in groups of three and watch everything that goes on. The group was high on the idea and they were ready to do it. The meeting ended on a high note and they all left feeling focused.

When Sarafina got home, she was still having a hard time processing what she had heard from her co-worker. If her boss's boss was really behind all of the recent events, then this could partially explain why Mr. Lukinbill was coming down on her lately. She then thought to herself that she really had to be careful. She thought about calling Rev. Joyner now, but then looked at the clock and it was too late. What she had just become aware of she was now trying to tie together with all the shootings that had happened recently. It all started to make sense except for the original lie about Cinque, that piece didn't fit in the puzzle.

Ricoh, PK and Devon were sitting around drinking and smoking at Ricoh's apartment. They were still laughing about the money they had collected from the C's for returning Sista. Although this was the main topic of conversation, they were also discussing what to do about tomorrow's big game.

"Man, that was the easiest $10K we made yet. Did chu think he was gonna give it up that quick?" PK said to Ricoh.

"I wasn sure, but I know one thing, that girl got somethin on him. When I tol him we got her, he didn even try to argue long. I dono if he doin her or not, but she's important to all of dem."

"Yeah, we gotta keep dat in mind. What we gonna do wit the dough?"

"Well we gonna have some fun first and buy some mo of this stuff an then we needa git some more hardware for the new `cruits. By the way PK, how's dat goin?"

"Good, man. Me an Devon was over at that grade school today got some real hungry 8th graders ready to come in. We gonna test'em next week an see who git in."

"Aw-ight, good. Now we needa talk about tomorrow. I heard dat the C's may be tryna do somethin at the game. What y'all wanna do?"

"Rick, you know every cop an his momma gonna be out dere tomorrow. We be crazy to try an hit that place agin like las time. Let the C's roll up on em an git all caught."

Devon said. "On top of that I wanna see dem git caught early so the Jag's can win dat game an go to the playoff's. I got some money on the game."

"Yeah you right. Hit'n there again, might not be smart" said Ricoh.

The trio continued to drink and get high for the rest of the night.

Across town Hakeem was at the hang tonight standing around outside with some of his soldiers. The meeting with the big man yesterday had cleared the corner plaza for just one night, now it was back to loitering as usual. The bantering among the troops was an indication that they were all feeling good and just waiting for the next deal to go down.

Just like employees at a fortune five hundred company, they knew their payroll was secure and they were just looking forward to another payday. After a while as it was starting to get dark, Hakeem motioned to them to go inside. Like good soldiers responding to a command they ceased the bantering and moved into the store. They didn't go into the back room, because not many of the street troops even knew that it existed. This group just huddled around the aisles. Hakeem stood behind the checkout counter and started to address the group.

"Y'all know tomorrow they got that replay game over dere at the stadium. Las time we was dere, them B's turned the motha out. This time we gonna rock the house. I know some of y'all got dough ridin on the game, so we gonna chill 'till the 'Jags take it home. Afta dat we gonna let ereybody know who we are an what we can do. Ain like the cops can stop us. An that CONN's crap, we already takin care of. Y'all down wit dat?"

Except for one soldier in the crowd, everybody was in agreement with Hakeem's plan. However, the one soldier stood up and said:

"'Keem, man this is kinda whack ain it. Ya know what went down at the las game, dey gonna have eery cop in and around the city dere tomorrow. We can't win man." "You ain wit the action hoss? Yo heart ain wit us?

"Naw man that ain it, you know I'm down wit chu, but dis don make no sense." Hakeem ordered that the soldier be brought up to the counter. Three of the larger soldiers in the group went over and escorted him to the front.

"I want y'all to look at whas gonna happen to us, if we let this kinda troop keep runnin' wit us. Dude, you ain worth the gold we be layin on you if you ain gonna follow orders. I said we gonna rock the house tomorrow, an thas what I mean. If you ain wit us, then you against us, an I don need you."

Hakeem gave a motion to the big guys to take the soldier out of the store. He has not been heard of since.

Hakeem then continued to set up the plan and instructed his troops that at the end of the game tomorrow, he would give them a signal by starting a fight at the front entrance of the main gate. At that time, the relay would signal all of the troops stationed around the stadium to start fights with anyone and get a riot going. At the end of the melee they were to get away however they could and assemble at the hang. They were to leave all signs that it was the C's who pulled it off this time. Hakeem was proud of his plan and his soldiers bought into it. They left the hang that night with another mission in mind and ready to carry it out.

Friday morning came and Sarafina was excited when she got up. What she had learned last night was really giving her a sense of intrigue and she felt like she was the leader of a bonafide mission to save the city. She went through her usual morning routine and headed out the door to work. She was so excited that she forgot to bring the note that she had made to herself with the information about the owner of Gateway. She got to her car, which had the tires replaced from a gift by the church and headed to work. The goop on the windows she had discovered was easily removed with some stringent cleaner and water.

When she got to work she tried to locate the man that had come to the meeting and given her the information. She walked inside the plant, which was not where she normally would go and looked for him. Everybody she talked to knew who he was, but nobody had seen him this morning. This made her wonder about what may be going on. Not locating him she went to her office and sat at her desk. The thoughts building up in her mind set off a series of ideas that started to really scare her. If what the man had exposed last night had been relayed to Gateway's top gun, then his life would have been in real danger. Sarafina couldn't help but envision this possibility and wondered whether she should call Lt. Meeker. She gave in to the urge and placed the call.

"Hello, Lt. Meeker here."

"Lt. Meeker, this is Sarafina Peterson I need to talk to you." "Yes Mrs. Peterson how are you?"

"I'm fine, but I have some information that I need to give you." " Good! What kind of information."

"Last night my group had a meeting to follow-up on the one Rev. Joyner had on Tuesday."

"Yes, he called me about that."

"Well there was a man who came and tol us `bout who's behind the shootin's. "You say someone told you they know who was responsible for the shootings?"

"Yes, he said the man behind it is the owner of Gateway Safe And Lock Company." "How does he know this?"

"He said he heard them talkin `bout it in the plant." "Are you sure?"

"Thas what he said." "Alright can we talk to him?"

"I tried to find him this mornin an he ain in today. Thas strange?" "Okay, Mrs. Peterson thank you for the tip. I'll follow up on it."

Sarafina hung up feeling that she had done the right thing. She was still very concerned about her coworker and wondered whether she should try walking out to the plant again or should she try to make a call to him. She decided going into the plant again would draw unnecessary attention to her so she thought to try and find a way to call him. Since he was a production line worker, phone calls were not usually allowed. She decided then that she would take time during her lunch hour to casually stroll through the plant area under the guise of expanding her company operations knowledge and check on him. When her lunch hour came she did just that. When she got inside the plant, she again asked some people about the man and got the same response. This made her very suspicious.

Lt. Meeker, armed with the information from the vehicle check and now receiving the tip from Mrs. Peterson began to be thoroughly interested in Mr. Mazzetti. It had never occurred to him before that there could be any possible connection between an established company in the city and any of the gang activity that was going on. Now with this tip, it started to come together. Knowing that there was a major event scheduled for tonight, he hesitated to assign any of his troops to follow-up on what he had just learned because they would be working overtime. Even though he also would be working tonight, he couldn't let himself squander a tip like he just received. He decided that he would ride over to the Gateway Safe And Lock Company and talk to this man.

He got there and went inside. Identifying himself he asked to speak to the plant manager. Mr. Lukinbill received him and took him into his office. After a brief discussion, Lt. Meeker told him whom he was there to see. Mr. Lukinbill was very concerned about why he was looking for this man. The lieutenant explained to him why he was there and Mr. Lukinbill paged the man. There was no response and Mr. Lukinbill said to the lieutenant that the man must not be in today. Lt. Meeker asked him to check because it was rather important. Mr. Lukinbill summoned one of the plant supervisors and had him come to his office. Upon arrival the supervisor confirmed that the man had not come in today and that there was no call in to say why. Mr. Lukinbill apologized to the lieutenant and told him that when the man came in tomorrow he would have him call. Lt. Meeker thanked Mr. Lukinbill, handed him his card, and said he would look for the call.

Not long after Lt. Meeker left, Mr. Lukinbill was on the phone to Antonio Mazetti.

He told Mr. Mazetti what had happened with the visit. Mr. M told him to relax and when the man came in tomorrow find out why the lieutenant wanted to talk to him and then get back to me. Mr. Lukinbill agreed and went on with the day's business. Meanwhile, Mr. M., not wanting to dismiss what he had just heard alerted his soldiers to go and pay a surprise visit to the hang and talk with Hakeem. This was something he couldn't just ignore.

Hakeem wasn't at the hang when Mr. M's men arrived. It was too early in the day for him to be out. After questioning the store manager, who really knew nothing about the store's true business, the soldiers decided to leave and come back later. Hakeem meanwhile was on the phone at his place talking to one of his soldiers going over his game plan for tonight. It seemed that everything was ready so he hung up and hit the street. About an hour later he arrived at the hang to find Mr. M's people waiting for him. They met him at the door and motioned for him to walk with them to their car. He nervously accompanied them and got in. Once inside he asked what was up.

"Mr. M had a visit at his place of business this morning by a police lieutenant from downtown. You know he don't like surprises and this one caught him off guard. The cop was looking for a man who works there. Why would he be doing that, he wants to know?"

"Why you comin to me? How I know?"

"Wrong answer," and one of the men grabbed Hakeem's throat. "Let's try this again. Why were the police at the plant today?"

Hakeem struggling to speak said:

"I, I, I really dono but I kin fine out. I can fine out now." The man released the hold on him and sat back.

"We'll give you fifteen minutes to get us a good answer. Get out! We'll be back then."

Hakeem got out of the car and ran back to his ride and sped away. Once out of the area he got on his cell to Hammer.

"Hammer whas goin on, the big man jus sent his people down here to lean on me 'bout somethin with the cops and his plant this mornin. You know 'bout it? I got fifteen minutes 'fore they comin back for an answer."

"Naw 'Keem, I dono nuthin 'bout dat. What I do know is that dat woman we tryn to git to back off us had a meetin last night. Maybe it had somethin to do wit that. You kin tell'em that."

"Yeah cool, good. Thas what I'll tell'em an lay it on her. Yeah man, thanks, I'm good. See ya later."

"Aw-ight blood, later."

Hakeem went back to the hang and waited for Mr. M's men. They arrived at about the same time. Hakeem tried to compose himself as he walked over to their car. Without getting in he spoke through the window to the front seat passenger.

"I know what happened." "Get in" came the reply.

The back door opened one of the men got out and he got in. "Alright talk" the soldier said.

"There's a woman 'round here we havin trouble wit. She been talkin wit the cops

'bout whas goin on."

"What's that got to do with Mr.M?"

"I think she work over there at the plant, she may know somethin."

The men looked at Hakeem and believed his story so they released him. The soldiers called Mr. M and told him the story. Hakeem went back to his apartment and immediately alerted his troops to call off the action for tonight. His heart wasn't in it anymore.

That night the big game was played to a packed stadium. The officials had indeed given the Jaguars a three-point advantage to start the game and the home team came out fired up and ready to play. The mood of the crowd was pure excitement and everywhere school colors from both sides were flying high. Jameel and Dolitha, Rajon and his girl were sitting together and enjoying it. Cinque was there, but in another section with his friends. The only downside to everyone's pleasure was the prison like presence of law enforcement personnel in every corner in every aisle in the stands and on the field.

What was anticipated to be a rough night for the police turned out to be an enjoyable evening for many of them. They were able to watch a good competitive football game and with the exception of a few minor skirmishes between some over zealous fans or some patrons who had one or two too many to drink, the affair went without a major incident. Representatives from both rival factions were in attendance and in significant numbers, but the overwhelming presence of the law made it highly unlikely that a repeat of the last game was going to occur. If anyone was not thoroughly enjoying the evening it may have been the mayor, who after surveying the number of police personnel on overtime, knew that his budget was taking a severe drain.

On the field the Jaguars were playing as good a game as they had played all season and it became convincingly evident late in the fourth quarter that they were going to move on to the first round of the playoffs. The crowd for the visiting team had quieted down accepting the fact that it was just a matter of minutes before the hopes in their team would fade with the ending of their season. The score was 28-14 with just two minutes to play. The Jaguars had the ball and it was just a matter of running out the clock. High five's on the Jaguar's sidelines were being exchanged, pats on the back for the coaches and the congratulatory handshake to the principal was given.

At this point, the only thing left to be determined was who the Jags would meet in the playoff first round and what new challenge would be happening at MHS next week.

Chapter 7 - The Connection

The Bricks Complex on Saturday morning during the fall season had the look of an urban ghost town. Except for those having to go to work, most of the residents remained inside either nursing a hangover or recovering from some other type of indiscretion. The big game played last night had to be a big contributor to their ill health. As was their usual custom, most of the men from all sides of the city attended athletic events. This Friday's event had more than the customary drawing power because it meant that should the Midland High School Jaguars win this football game, they would move on to the playoffs. Getting to the playoffs was big because the Jags hadn't made it to that level in a number of years.

In building #3 on the tenth floor in apartment 10S Ricoh was up and looking out the window. From his vantage point he could see the courts where just two weeks ago a massacre had occurred. His mind conjured up the scene on that night when he went down there to view the aftermath. The gruesome picture that came to his mind's eye showed a bloody mess and he felt deep remorse. More than remorse he felt a strong sense of retribution needed. He looked at the fence where some of the residents had placed a large memorial wreath with a number of hand-written notes on it. It wasn't so much that the tenants mourned the loss of all those young people who died, because they all knew what they were into, but it was more about sympathizing with each other over their feeling of helplessness. Ricoh, with his morning beer in hand, pondered what should be done to exact the revenge that would appease his nature. Yes, he had made his rivals shell out a large monetary sum from which he now enjoyed the benefits, but somehow, this didn't give him the feeling of closure that he sought. Several of his main people had been lost in the melee, including Rambo his most trusted soldier.

After his extended reverie, Ricoh composed himself and sat down on the couch to try and come up with a new plan to hit the C's. Strangely, what popped into his mind was his knowledge about the large shipment that had been delivered to them recently and the large amount of cash that he envisioned had been exchanged in the deal. His thoughts raced ahead to a plot to interrupt the next pick up at the airport. He already had a reliable bug at the port and he was sure for the right amount of currency this mercenary would provide him with the necessary details to pull it off. Satisfied that he had come up with the start of a workable plan, he laid his head down on a cushion and went back to sleep.

On the other side of town, Hakeem was also just getting up. His demeanor was a lot different than Ricoh's because first he was still a little shaken about how he had been treated by Mr. M's people; and second who was this man that brought about the action. He said to himself, if this man got something on Mr. M, then it wouldn't be a minute before M would take it out on me. His first task was to find out who the man was and what it was that he really knew. Also he remembered what Hammer said about the CONN's meeting and wondered if his warning message had any affect on that Mrs. Peterson. Maybe something more needed to be done for her or more correctly, to her.

He picked up the phone and called Hammer.

"Hammer, dat you?" "Yeah Hakeem – whas up?"

"Man, I been thinkn `bout what happened yesterday with me and Mr. M. You know he kinda shook me up. I thought I was in bettrn that. Jus go to show who got the power."

"Yeah, you got dat right. What chu wanna do?"

"We gotta fine out who dat man was they said got the cops to come out to that lock factory. Once we fine out who he is, we needa fine out what he know `bout Mr. M. Man, if it's big enough, maybe we kin use it."

"`Keem, don go gittin crazy on me man. You know who you dealin wit. He could take us all out in an hour an not sweat the effort."

"Yeah, you right, but I needa get somethin to cover my butt case he wanna come down on me again."

"What chu gonna do?"

"Put the word out to fine the man and coax the info from him. Don mess him up too bad though, jus git the info."

"Aw-ight 'Keem it's done. I'll git back to you when I know somethin, later." "One mo thing Hammer. It seem like my message to that CONN's woman didn't have no power. Either that or she got no sense. I think we hafta do somethin else to git her attention. I ain sure yet what, but be ready. Las time I rode by that parking lot, they had a whole bunch of cop cars ride'n by so we can't mess wit her ride no more. We may have to mess wit her then.

Hammer got off the phone and immediately contacted other members of the club. The command was given and the orders were quickly funneled down to those soldiers who needed to get involved. Hammer thought that he would also get involved directly so he got in his car and rode by where Sarafina's parking lot was. He wanted to see for himself what kind of police presence was around. When he got there he saw that it was just like Hakeem said, police constantly riding through the block. His next thought was to find out who was in the CONN's, and better yet who was at that last meeting. This was not a hard task because the CONN's were actively seeking new members. He wasn't about to change his own stripes, but what he would do is get one of the younger troops to get in as a mole.

Today was Jameel's final post-op check-up and he and Sarafina were getting ready to go to the hospital to meet with Dr. Ramone.

"Jameel are you ready yet?" "Comin mom, be right dere."

"Now Cinque we shouldn't be that long. If you go out, make sure you lock the doors an check behind you."

"Aw-ight mom. I don think I'm goin out though." "Okay, we'll see you later. Les go Jameel."

The ride to Mercy General didn't take that long and following her normal route she arrived there in less than fifteen minutes. On this route she passed by Higginbotham's Funeral Home. As she was passing by she noticed a man coming out that looked a lot like her co-worker from Gateway. She slowed down and tried to get his attention. He spotted her and quickly ran around the corner and disappeared. When she turned around to try to relocate him, it was like he was never there. She thought to herself now what was that all about. Why is he acting strange? His name didn't immediately come to mind, but she remembered that he had signed up on the member roster at the meeting. So she decided to give him a call when she got home.

At the hospital, Dr. Ramone was waiting for them when they arrived and was pleased to see Jameel who he called his miracle case.

"Jameel, how are you young man?"

"I feel fine doc. No more soreness. I'm ready for anything."

"Yes, I bet you are. Well let's have another look at you just to make sure."

He went through his final exam routine and pronounced once again that he was completely baffled at how given the number of injuries he sustained he could have so completely recovered. Sarafina said without any hesitation:

"Nothing but the grace of God." Looking at Jameel again the doctor said:

"I must agree with her, because there's no other way to account for it." Then he turned to Sarafina ,

"I ought to put you on staff here and ask that you just pray for my patients" he said laughingly.

Turning back to Jameel he said:

"Okay you can put your shirt on now, you're finished. You don't need to take any more of those anti-infection pills. You have a clean slate."

Sarafina and Jameel feeling real good about that report walked out of the hospital, got in the car and went home. Before arriving at the apartment she said to Jameel:

"I'd better stop an pick up some chicken, or Cinque won be happy." "Yeah, mom you right."

They walked in the door and alerted Cinque. "Cinque, we're back."

And almost as if on cue Cinque hollered back, "Hi mom, you bring some chicken?" "Yes, Cinque come on and get it."

After setting up the table with the bucket and the sides Sarafina went into the living room to call her co-worker. She looked for the CONN's roster that they had just revised to include the new people and found it on the coffee table. As she thumbed through the list she was trying to remember which name went with his face. Finally when she came across it, it clicked and she identified him. His name was Malcolm Long, a rather large husky man about 6'3" tall and well over two hundred pounds. His physique was like that of a heavy construction worker, but surprisingly his demeanor was very pleasant. She also noticed from his address that he lived in Roundtree Gardens. This was the row house development that was right across from the Minute Mart and she remembered that Rev. Joyner had recently asked her whether she knew anyone that lived there. Putting that thought aside, intending to alert the pastor on Sunday she dialed the number.

"Hello."

"Hello, Mr. Long?

"This is Long, who's this?

"Mr. Long this is Mrs. Peterson from the CONN's how are you? "Yeah, Mrs. Peterson I'm fine how you doin?"

"I'm fine. Didn I see you comin out of Higgiby's today? I tried to stop you, but you ran away."

"Yeah, I was there saying goodbye to an ole friend. I saw you, but I didn wanna talk to you on the street. You know I heard that the police came to the job looking for me, the day I was out. I dono now if it was such a good idea pointn out Mr. Mizzetti

being behind all them Crippler boy's actions. That man got the power and the means to make somebody like me jus disappear. An I ain talkin 'bout those street boys, I mean some real power."

"Mr. Long…"

"You can call me Malcolm, even though I didn really know you before, we do see each other almos every day at work."

"Okay Malcolm let me ask you this. Do you believe you're doin the right thing?" "Yeah its right, but I don wanna die over it."

"Malcolm do you believe in God? "Yeah, sometime when I need Him."

Sarafina laughed to herself, but continued:

"Well please let this be one of the times you do believe in Him 'cause you, we all need Him now. Are you coming to work Monday?"

"I dono, I hafta see what I can fine out 'bout whas gonna happen wit me." "Malcolm remember we have the police already watching our work place, I don't think even Mr. Mizzetti would do anything there."

"You may be right, but I'm gonna check anyway."

"I hope you haven't given up on workin with the CONN's have you?" "Naw, I'll work wit you, long as it's safe."

"Thas great 'cause we need you. Okay, I'll see you Monday right?" "Yeah maybe. Bye."

Sunday morning was another bright and sunny fall day. Inside the Peterson apartment Sarafina had prepared the usual big breakfast and called the boys to the table. As they were eating she noticed that Cinque was just nibbling at his food and picking at his pancakes. Extremely unusual for a growing boy with a voracious appetite she asked him what was wrong. He told her that he didn't feel good and that he was hot. She felt his forehead and confirmed that he probably had a slight fever. She went to the bathroom and brought back some cold medicine and gave it to him.

"Okay, you go back to bed. I'm goin to church, but you drink lots of water while I'm gone. Jameel stay here and look afta your brother."

Jameel, without showing it, was elated at the command because he didn't really want to go anyway.

"Aw-ight mom, I'll watch him."

When she arrived at New Life Temple she was early and the members were just milling around in fellowship before the start of the service. She did notice however that even at this early hour there seemed to be a larger number of concregants than usual. She spotted one of her friends and went over to her.

"Good morning sister Janey how are you?" "Oh I'm truly blessed, how are you?"

"I'm fine. Don it look like we got more people here today?"

"Yes, sure looks like it. I believe it's because of the movement that pastor started to help stop all this gang stuff. I think people really want it to stop and they want to help."

Sarafina agreed with what she said, but she felt a little slighted that she had not been given credit for actually starting the movement that pastor Joyner had bought into. She dismissed the thought as no big deal feeling that the truth would come out in the end and went on with the conversation.

"If we continue to grow like this there's no tellin what we can do to get the changes we want."

"Yes sister, Hallelujah Jesus."

As they were finishing their conversation, the ushers were motioning people to the pews and the service began.

According to tradition, the praise and worship portion took place leading up to the choir singing. New Life Temple had gained the reputation throughout the city and the surrounding towns of having an excellent choir. Today they seemed especially spirited when they sang the praises of God and it set the stage for an equally spirited sermon from Rev. Joyner. As he moved to the pulpit, the filled to capacity sanctuary was already hollering Hallelujah, praise God, Hallelujah Jesus - so deeply moved by the choir's rendition of the gospel song "Stand". Reverend Joyner was the type of preacher that thoroughly prepared his message so it wasn't that he was unready when he stepped behind the sacred desk, but the spirit that was in the house today was just so overwhelming that he had to recompose himself before beginning.

"Members, family, friends and neighbors once again I come before you and in the presence of God, to speak a word that has been given to me from above. I stand here humbly to proclaim that there is a road ahead that is rough and a mountain to be climbed that is very steep. We are about to undergo a test like we've never seen before in that we are taking on a new challenge that we've never known before. My people it is by God's grace that we have come this far and it is by God's grace that we shall see it through. Today I'd like to talk for a few minutes from the book of Hebrews and the subject is a test of faith. The text is Hebrews chapter 11 verses 1-3 and it reads as follows:

Now faith is the substance of things hoped for, the evidence of things not seen. 2) For by it the elders obtained a good testimony. 3) By faith we understand that the worlds were framed by the word of God, so that the things which are seen were not made of things which are visible.

Faith is the substance of things hoped for the evidence of things not seen. Now what does that really mean? My brothers and my sisters what it means is that before this church stood on this sacred ground, our founders had a vision and by faith in that vision we now have the church. What it means is that before we had our wonderful Mercy Hospital, a few doctors had a vision and through faith we now have the hospital. More than that we in this church have developed a vision of a community where violence will cease, peace will reign and we can all feel safer when we sleep at night. This vision can and will be made manifest, but can only be so with God's help, His grace and our true belief in Him and most importantly we must have the faith to bring it to pass."

Reverend Joyner continued on with his fiery sermon until when he finished, the Amen's, Hallelujahs, and glory to God shouts filled the house and echoed throughout the building. The congregation was truly inspired and ready to go out and perform whatever would be necessary to fulfill the vision. However, even in the midst of all that piety, there were still some who said quietly, it can't be done. So the seeds of failure were mixed in with the seeds of success.

All through the sermon Sarafina listened intently to every word that came forth from the preacher's mouth. It was as if he wasn't addressing the church, but his message was directed only to her and he was speaking only to her. A chill came over her and she wondered was God speaking to her through him or was she just feeling the breeze from the fans around the sanctuary. Unable to decide she let it go.

After the service was over, she mingled with other parishioners for a few minutes, then remembered that she had something to give to the pastor. The note that she had written down about Mr. Long and the Roundtree Gardens was still in her pocketbook. She made her way downstairs to the pastor's study and requested a minute with him. The deacons on duty bid her to wait while they checked. One of them stepped into his study and returned right away beckoning Sarafina to enter. When she went inside Reverend Joyner greeted her and asked her to sit down.

"Pastor that was a wonderful sermon today and I thank you for the message. I'll only take up a couple of minutes of your time, but I have something that may be important. I remember you askin' 'bout if we knew anybody who lived in those houses across from the Minute Mart. Well somebody who jus joined the CONN's gave his address as one of them houses. Its called Roundtree Gardens and here's his information." "That's great sister Peterson, I'm sure Lt. Meeker will want to talk to him."

"I dono 'bout that. He's the same man that I tol him knew who was behind all the shootins and they went to talk to him last week."

"Really! What happened?

"When Lt. Meeker got there they couldn't find him 'cause he didn't come in that day. When I talked to him he said he was afraid that something might happen to him if he kept on talking to people."

"Thank you for that. When I talk to Lt. Meeker, I'll make sure that he doesn't go back there to talk with him. Maybe they can get him to come down to the station.'

"They might could get him to do that, but I know he won't say nothin if they go to Gateway."

"Okay sister you did your part, now let me do mine, I'll take it from here."

She left his study and headed home. There was a slight sense of urgency on her trip home because she couldn't shake the feeling that there was something in the message that she heard this morning that was intended just for her. Could it be a warning or an alert about something? She exceeded the speed limit a bit and arrived home in less time than it took her to get to the church. She rushed up the stairs and burst into the apartment calling out to the boys.

"Jameel, Cinque you all right?"

Quickly the response came back from Jameel: "Yeah mom we okay. Whas a matta?" "How's Cinque?"

"He aw-ight, jus went back to sleep. He was up for a good while. He drank the water like you said."

"Oh good. I guess I jus let something get to me that I shouldn't. You go on back to what you were doin, I'll be fine."

Jameel looked at her a little strange and wondered what that was all about, but it didn't take long before he let it pass by and went back to watching television.

That night Hakeem was on the phone with Sista telling her he needed to come by to talk with her. She was hesitant at first, but when he told her that Mr. M had paid him a visit, she thinking that it was all about another deal getting ready to go down told him to come on over. When he got there she opened the door, but her greeting was very cold.

"Okay Hakeem what Mr. M say? He got somethin big workin?" "I dono yet, but that ain why I wanna talk wit chu."

"Now you said he pay you a visit. What chu mean?"

"Yeah, he sent some of his people by to jack me up 'bout some dude pointin fingers at him."

"Who you talkin 'bout?"

"I dono that either 'till the guys git back to me an leme know. I jus wanted to let you know that somethin's goin on an it ain good. I also wanna fine out how you let your self get snatched last week."

Sista's attitude really went south at that point and she lashed out.

"Hakeem what I do is my business, I don need to report to you ereything I do. What happened, ain gonna happen again. I thanked you for comin to git me, what else you want?"

"Hakeem looked her up and down for a minute and started to say something, but then thought better about it. What he finally said was:

"You know we got posse who's job it is to watch out for you, if you don use 'em then that breaks down my security."

"I know, I know. Like I said that was a bad move an it ain gonna happen again les drop it okay?"

"Aw-ight. Why Mr. M so big on you anyway 'cause a Razor?" "It's a long story."

"I ain got nowhere to go an I need to fine out so maybe I can keep him offa me." "Well if you mus know 'bout three years ago when I was jus fourteen an Razor was jus startin up the C's. He was hangin with Bumpy from New York who use ta do work for Mr. M. Razor met him an he like the way Razor did things. So when Bumpy went away, Mr. M. aks Razor if he wanna replace him. Razor said sure an thas when the C's really got strong. Razor use ta go places wit Mr. M's people an he saw him do some things himself an he saw where people got hid. He passed that knowin to me for insurance an I still know. I also know that Mr. M ain the top, I know who he answer to. Thas why he treat me good."

"Why don you tell me some of this stuff an leme protect myself."

"You mus be crazy, if I tol you, an you tol him what you know 'cause you wanna back him up, he'd know that I tol you an that would be it for me, fool."

"Yeah, okay but I gotta figure out somethin. What chu got to drink here?"

"Hakeem, if thas all you wanna talk to me 'bout, then you needa go. The las time you start drinkin here, you got some strange ideas an start actin funny. I ain in the mood for a replay."

Hakeem finally said okay and started to leave, but when he was about to walk out the door Sista said:

"Mr. M say anything about when the next deal comin?"

"Naw, not yet. Why, you can't be runnin outta money this fast?"

"No, I'm good for a while on what chu gave me, but I jus thought maybe he had somethin else workin. Thas aw-ight, see ya."

"Aw-ight, later." Hakeem left.

Monday morning Sarafina got up early wanting to get to work earlier than normal to see if Mr. Long made it in. The plant workers started their shift an hour earlier than the office people. When she arrived she went straight to the plant area and poked her head in. Looking around for a few minutes she spotted him on one of the machines way in the back. She was happy to see him and felt a kind of easiness believing that what she said about God made a difference in his decision to come in. She turned around and made her way to the office.

It was much too early for any of the other office personnel to be in, but when she looked in the direction of Mr. Lukinbill's office she noticed that the lights were on. Just out of curiosity she got up from her chair and walked over there. To her surprise he was there and on the phone. His door was closed so she didn't even try to go in. He spotted her gave her an acknowledgement greeting, but continued talking on the phone. She returned the greeting turned around and went back in her office. On the way she chuckled to herself "I wonder if he's talking to Mr. Mizzetti?" she had no idea how right she was.

The morning seemed to go by more quickly than usual because it seemed as if she had just sat down when Sarafina looked up from her desk and saw through the glass petition Mr. Long being escorted by his supervisor toward Mr. Lukinbill's office. It was 11:00 O'clock. At first she didn't think much of it, but then she reflected that she had never seen him in that office before. The thought about the police visiting the factory last week looking for Malcolm and what he said about being made to disappear ran through her mind. She couldn't help but wonder if this might not be an omen that in one way or another it could very well happen. Could they be letting him go? Terminating him?

She attempted to put the thoughts aside and return to her tasks, but still couldn't ignore the fact that he was in with Mr. Lukinbill an extended amount of time. Mr. Lukinbill was not one to spend a great deal of time with any of the employees in his office on any issue. Finally Mr. Long came out alone and seemed to be headed back to the plant. The expression on his face gave no indication one way or the other whether he had been traumatized by what had just happened or whether he had been congratulated on a job well done. This really set Sarafina's curious mind on a sprint. Her thoughts were racing fast and speeding toward conclusions for which she had no foundations. The idea that he might be in some sought of shock and not able to express it popped into her head. Then she thought that he might be trying to hide his feelings to save face before his peers. In any event, she knew she had to find out.

When it was time for her to go to lunch she got up and went out into the plant. Since she had been there a few times before, recently, there was no surprise anymore seeing her in the area. She looked over to where she had seen Malcolm that morning, but he was not at his machine. Her first thought was one of panic, but then she said to herself, "I'm at lunch maybe he is too. I'll find a way to come back here when they break for the day and see if he's there". This seemed to satisfy her for now and she proceeded to the cafeteria where she spotted the office worker who came to the meeting the other night. She made her way over and asked if she could join her. Because her mouth was full, the woman just motioned to Sarafina to sit down.

"I'm sorry, but I forgot your name. I know you came to the meeting the other night." The woman looked at her very strange and said: "What meeting you talking about?" Sarafina very surprised said:

"The CONN's meeting".

"I don't know anything about no CONN's and no meeting."

Sarafina just looked at her and wondered whether she could have been mistaken in recognizing her at the meeting, but then she looked her over closely and reconfirmed in her mind that this was indeed the woman who was there.

"I dono why you actin like this, but its okay if you don wanna talk to me here." The woman just said:

"Thank you" and kept on eating.

Of course this sent Sarafina's mind on another tear and she couldn't figure out what was going on around this place. There was definitely something happening and the intrigue was getting to her.

At 3:45 she again got up from her desk and headed toward the plant. The shift ended at 4:00 so she thought for sure that she should be able to see Mr. Long if he was still at work. Sure enough he was back at his machine finishing up for the day and cleaning his area. She tried to get his attention without being too conspicuous, but he was too far away. Then she decided since she had his telephone number, she would call him tonight and find out what went on in Lukinbill's office. She turned around and went back to her office. Before sitting down again she noticed on the far side of the room the woman she had lunch with and she was staring at her. No expression whatsoever, but just staring at her with a blank stare. She was tempted to go over to her, but thought better of it. If the woman didn't want to acknowledge knowing her at lunch, why would she want to here. Sarafina made another note in her mind to look her up on the roster and see if she could put a name to her face, since she didn't give it at lunch, and then she would call her. The rest of the workday was uneventful and at a few minutes after 5:00, Sarafina packed up and headed out the door. Before leaving she looked over to where the woman had been sitting, but she was already gone.

When Hakeem got to the hang late that morning a message had been delivered that Mr. M had found out who the man was and he was taking care of the situation himself. Somewhat relieved at the news, Hakeem figured the heat was off of him, but he still wanted to know who it was. There was another part to the message so he listened in – it said that he was to do nothing more in trying to find this man, in other words back off. Hearing that he knew that he had to jump into action and call off his hounds before they located the man and did something Mr. M had not authorized. His first call was to Hammer.

"Hammer you there?" "Yeah `Keem whas up?"

"Man, Mr. M lef a message down here at the hang to back offa findin that dude he was aksin me `bout. He already found em. We didn git to him, did we?"

"Ain nobody check in wit me `bout dat yet, but I'll fine out an git backatcha." "Yeah, aw-ight but do it soon, I don want them doin nothin to him an the big man think I did it."

"Yeah, I got chu. Later." "Okay, bye."

Hakeem hung up and then went to talk to the store manager. "Who took this call?"

"I did" the manager said.

"Didn it soun like Mr. Mizzetti, you know the one who own the store? Did he say it was him?"

"No. He didn't say, I just forwarded it to your voice mail and that was it." "Yeah, okay you cool, thas it."

He couldn't help but wonder if the call wasn't some kind of a set up. Some strange things had been going on around him lately and it made him very uncomfortable. He figured though that he did the right thing in calling off the hounds because this way if it wasn't Mr. M he would still have some time to get his boys back on the case. But if it was Mr. M and the dogs had latched onto the man, then he'd be the one to pay.

At police headquarters that day Lt. Meeker was finally getting the feeling that his department was making some progress. Linking the owner of the Gateway Safe And Lock Company to the recent incidents was very strange and he knew that he needed to tread lightly on how he pursued the case. Gateway was a big employer in this city and also a heavy campaign contributor to several of the political pundits, including the mayor. He had backed off going back to the factory to try and speak with Mr. Long because that would cause too much controversy, but he was still intent on getting the man to come down to the station to talk. In conversations with Rev. Joyner he had learned that Mrs.

Peterson had persuaded Long to join their organization and he also found out that the man lived in the building that was his particular interest. His next mission was to ask Rev. Joyner to try and get Mrs. Peterson to convince Mr. Long to come in and see him. The lieutenant knew that this may be a daunting task because it didn't appear to him that Mr. Long would be one to just walk into a police station - for any reason.

He was pondering what to say to Rev. Joyner when his phone rang. "Hello, police headquarters, Lt. Meeker."

"Lt. Meeker this is Mayor Stanton how are you?"

"Yes good morning Mr. Mayor, I'm fine how are you?"

"Well depending upon what you're going to tell me then I'll know how I feel." "Feel fine Mr. Mayor we're getting some breaks. Some good information is starting to come in and we're following up on it even as we speak."

"Are we close to putting something positive in the papers?"

"I don't want to jump the gun on putting out anything yet, because it may involve some people at some high levels. I want to be sure."

"What do you mean high levels? I thought we were talking about some gangbangers." "Yes mayor we all thought that way in the beginning, but now the information that I'm getting is leading to something bigger than that."

"Meeker, you make sure you keep me informed if your investigation starts to point in the direction of any of my people or anything like that you hear me?"

"Yes Mr. Mayor, of course you'll know what we know when we know it, but like I said these things are just starting to come in so we need to make sure that everything checks out."

"Okay, you stay on top of it, but make sure you keep my office informed right?"

"Yes sir."

"Okay goodbye." "Bye."

Lt. Meeker hung up, but wasn't so sure that making Mayor Stanton privy to what he knew at this point was such a good idea. Especially since his whole case revolved around a man who hadn't exactly identified anybody and a car that was just at the wrong place at the wrong time, regardless of who it belonged to. Not a very strong case by any stretch. He picked up the phone and tried to reach Reverend Joyner. No answer, so he left a message on his answering machine and turned to something else. He was still searching for reliable witnesses and his thinking went back to the man from the Bricks that sergeant Calloway was working. He pressed the intercom button and paged him.

"Calloway here."

"Yeah Ray, its Meeker." "Yes lieutenant."

"Bring me up to speed on what's happening to that witness from the Bricks Complex that we were going to get to come in. Did you ever find him?"

"Yes we did lieutenant, but as of now he's not coming down here. I have a suggestion though."

"Yeah what is it?"

"I think if we set it up the night before and go there early in the morning in a plain car after the working crowd has gone and when nobody else is out, with some of the books and pictures of the most likely's, he might get in the car."

"You really think that'll work?" "Yeah long as we include the $50."

"Okay, I got the $50, make it happen and let me know."

Sarafina arrived home that night feeling anxious to get on the phone and talk to both Malcolm and the woman from the office. After checking whether the boys had done their homework she prepared dinner and they ate. During dinner Jameel said that he noticed a lot more police cars riding around and he wondered if all that was because of what had happened to her car. She told him that part of it was, but more so because they think that the C's are getting ready to do something else around here. Jameel then asked her if she knew what that was. She said no not exactly, but you know they want the CONN's to stop their activity. She also told him not to worry about anything it will be all right.

After dinner Sarafina went into the living room and grabbed her roster. She scrolled down the list trying to again associate a name with the face that had come to the meeting. Not too far down the list she spotted Janet Johnson and immediately made the connection. It was not too hard to do because when they first met and she heard the name she said it again to her herself because it was so close to the famous celebrity. She noted the number and dialed it.

"Hello, this is Ms. Johnson."

"Hi Ms. Johnson this is Sarafina Peterson from the CONN's and from Gateway. I had lunch with you today."

"Yes Mrs. Peterson, I'm so sorry about that, but I have to be careful there. I know that they're watching everybody who even talks to you. Did you know that they are tracking everything you do?"

"I know Mr. Lukinbill said he'd be watchin, but no not 'bout anybody else."

"Well the word is out, so you need to watch your back. What can I do for you?" "You already tol me what I needed ta hear an I thank you for the info. Did you know Mr. Long before that meeting?"

"I knew him from the plant, but not really to speak to. We talked a lot more after the meeting and he told me a lot about the owner of the place. That's another reason why I'm telling you to be extra careful, from what he told me."

"You know the police came there looking for him last week?"

"Yeah, I heard. Good thing he wasn't there. I wonder if he knew they were coming." "I talked to him Saturday an I don think he knew. He was surprised when he found out, but was glad he wasn there too. He tol me they could make him disappear. That got me really worried so I went in early today to check on him. He seemed to be okay. I'm gonna call him when we finish. Are you still gonna work with the CONN's ?"

"Yes, I want to, as long as it doesn't get too dangerous. We may be getting into more than we are able to handle."

"Long as we get smart people like you to join, I think we'll be fine."

"Why thank you and I hope so, because something really does need to be done to change our community. Okay I'll see you tomorrow."

"Right, bye."

Sarafina hung up feeling a lot better about what happened at lunch today. She was concerned though on hearing that she had been targeted as the office outcast and wondered whether she should say something to Mr. Lukinbill tomorrow. She put it aside and looked again for Malcolm Long's number. Finding it she dialed.

"Hello."

"Malcolm, this is Mrs. Peterson how are you?" "Oh hi, yeah I'm okay what's goin on?"

"I came in early today and went into your area to see if you came in. I was glad to see you there."

"Yeah well I said to myself an no use in duckin, if they gonna fine me they fine me. They can do it there or anywhere. I figured the cops wouldn't come back there twice anyway, 'cause Mr. Mizzetti would see to that."

"I saw you go in Mr. Lukinbill's later. What did they do to you?"

"They ain do nuthin to me. Jus aks what I thought the police wanna talk to me about. When I told them I didn know, they started talkin about job stuff and a big order we got comin in.”

“Oh, well thas good. I thought they might be tryin to get you out.”

“Naw, I don think so. I’m the lead machinist there. They ain got nobody else that can do what I do. I said they can make me disappear but when I thought about it, it wouldn be so good for his bidness. How you doin there? They ain said nothin to you yet about them cops comin in?”

“I think I’m okay so far and nobody said nuthin to me ‘bout the cops. But I talked to Ms. Johnson before, you know her she work in the office too, an she said that everybody there been tol to stay away from me. Thas not good.”

“Yeah I know her, when I came to your meetin we walked in together. She seem to be good people so she prably tellin you the truth.”

“Well, tomorrow I might talk to Mr, Lukinbill an see whas to that.”

“Lady, you be careful dealin with that man too, remember who he reports directly to.” “Yes, I will. Maybe I’ll see you tomorrow too. Goodnight.”

“Yeah okay bye.”

Soon as she hung up with Malcolm the phone rang. She looked at the clock and it read 10:30. Somewhat surprised she answered it.

“Hello.”

“Hi Sister Peterson this is Reverend Joyner and I’m sorry to call you so late. Were you retiring?”

“No I was jus on the phone, its okay.”

“I got a call from Lt. Meeker down at police headquarters earlier today and he sounded rather urgent about something he wanted me to ask you to do. I don’t usually do someone elses bidding, but I know he is trying to help us, so I guess we have to help him.”

“What’d he want?”

“You know I had told him before that you knew that Mr. Long and that he had joined the CONN’s.”

“Yes.”

“Well what he wants is for you to try and get him to come down to headquarters and look at some pictures in the files to see if he can identify anybody that may have been at that Minute Mart across from his house on the night of the Bricks incident. He also wants to talk to him about a Mr. Mizetti who I believe owns your Gateway Company."

"Wow ain that strange. I jus finish talkin wit him. Wish you hadda call before I coulda aks him then. I don wanna call him back tonight, but I'll try an see him tomorrow an aks."

"Okay sister Sara, that's all I can ask. I'll wait to hear from you and then let the lieutenant know."

When Sarafina hung up this time she said to herself: "I'm goin to bed, I don care who else call. Enuff excitement for one day." Before retiring she peeked in on the boys and as usual they were sleeping with the TV still on. So she quietly eased in and shut it off.

Tuesday started out as a beautiful day. The sun was shining and the skies were cloudless and blue. Even with the chill in the air, there were signs that summer was still hanging around. Sarafina felt good about going to work today because she wanted to get to Mr. Long and carry out pastor's request. She finished her normal routine and after leaving her final instructions with the boys for the day, she made her way down to the parking lot. Since the incident with her car she had started parking over in the far corner of the lot now, so it took her a few extra minutes to get there. She felt more confident that the police were patrolling the area regularly, but she also thought it didn't hurt that she had found a better parking spot.

Arriving at the office on her normal schedule she went in. Aware of what Ms.

Johnson told her yesterday she looked around in a little different way to see if any one was eyeing her strangely. For the few workers that were there on time, she didn't seem to notice anything different much less strange so she sat down and settled in. Everything was going as per normal until around 10:30 when the intercom lit up. It was Mr.

Lukinbill calling to ask her to come to his office right away. She didn't like the sound of that, but what could she do. Slowly she finished the task she was into and locked her computer. As she approached the office all kinds of thoughts were racing through her mind. She got to the door and he beckoned her to come in.

"Please close the door and sit down, Mrs. Peterson."

She complied and placed herself in the big chair in front of his desk.

"You've been with us now for 3 years and seven months, is that right?" he said. "Yes, that sounds right why are you aksin?"

"Do you feel any sense of loyalty to this company and your job?"

"I'm not sure what you mean."

"I mean you wouldn't do anything to hurt this company would you?"
"Oh no, not me."

"Well, Mrs. Peterson it has come to my attention that that's not quite true. Aren't you the leader of a group called the Change Our Neighborhood Now or better known as the CONN's?"

"Well yes I'm one of the leaders?"

"Aren't you the one that got the police to come here looking for one of our employees and to implicate our owner in some kind of illegal doings?"

"No. I don even know what you talkin about."

"Well I think you do Mrs. Peterson and I had a long conversation with our company president yesterday and this is his decision. As of the end of today your services here will no longer be required. At the end of today you may go by personnel and pick up your current check and two months additional severance pay. Please have your desk and all personal belongings cleared out by then. That's all you may go."

Sarafina was devastated. She grew weak instantly and could hardly get out of the chair. Tears welled up in her eyes, but she held them back. Finally she composed herself enough to move but before she walked out she said: "I think you set me up for this an I dono why but I will fine out" and then she left. She got back to her desk and looked over to where Janet sat and gave a sign to her of her throat being cut. Janet who was looking at her, mouthed the words "Oh no", and then looked away. Sarafina immediately started to clean out her desk and walked out. She didn't even wait for the end of the day nor did she pick up her severance package. Her anger over rode her senses and she just had to get out of there. The mission to talk to Malcolm was no longer of any importance and she abandoned the idea.

When Sarafina got home it was well before the boys would arrive and she just broke down and cried for a bit. After a while she got it back together and was trying to figure out what she was going to tell them. She looked in the mirror and the face that reflected back was a mess so she washed it, remade it and figured she would just tell them the truth. She didn't feel much like cooking and when she looked in the refrigerator there wasn't enough of anything leftover to even piece together a meal so she decided to go out and get something. It was then that it dawned on her she had left the job without getting her money. She just said: "Oh well I'll get it tomorrow."

She drove around for a while trying to clear her head and decide what she should pick up to eat. She even went as far as the high school hoping that she might even see the boys when they came out, but realizing that it was only around 2:00 O'clock she knew it was much too early for that so she kept going. When she pulled out of the school waiting area and pulled back into the street as she started leaving the area she noticed that a car seemed to be following her. She decided to test whether this was true so she made some turns that were not in the direction of her planned route. On the last direction change that would have assured her she was being tailed she turned, but the car kept going so she breathed a little easier. When she looked around and saw that she was close to one of their favorite Chinese take out restaurants she pulled into their parking lot and went in.

She picked up the order and headed home. As she neared her own parking lot she looked in her rear view mirror and saw that the same car that had been following her before was behind her again. She was so close to her parking spot that she just pulled in hoping that the car would just go by as it did before. She pulled into her spot and got out with her bags hoping to get inside her building quickly. The car pulled up behind her and before she could make her dash, two rather large men in dark suits got out and started to approach her.

Chapter 8 - Groundwork

Her heart was pounding as the two men continued to approach. She looked around in desperation to see if there was anyone to help, but there was nobody. Her last resort was to scream at the top of her lungs and hope to attract some attention from someone, anyone, anywhere. Just as she opened her mouth to initiate a primal shriek, one of the men reached in his pocket with one hand and pulled out a badge. With the other he reached out toward her in an effort to bring calm.

"Mrs. Peterson, Mrs. Peterson calm down please. Calm down! We're not here to hurt you. I'm Detective Sergeant Halleran and this is Detective Cato, we work with Lt. Meeker down at the precinct."

With a great sigh of relief, Sarafina stumbled back onto the hood of her car and sat down. It was all she could do to continue clutching her bags without dropping them.

"Why you been followin me?"

"We were at the school looking for someone when we saw your car there. The description had been given to us from the incident report you filed. Lt. Meeker asked us to stop by your place when we finished and talk to you about this Mr. Long. So when we saw you leaving the school, it seemed like this would be a good time to catch up with you and talk."

"You scared me half to death comin up b'hind me like that. I almos dropped my food."

"Sorry about that we didn't intend to scare you, but now that we're here can we go inside and talk."

"What you wanna know?"

”Please Mrs. Peterson can we go inside.”

“You know the last time you people came ta my house, ya took my son out for nothin.”

“Yes we know all about that, it was a mistake. We’re not here to do anything like that, just talk.”

“Okay come on.”

She escorted them into the building and up the stairs to the apartment. Still being upset about what had happened to her earlier, she really wasn’t in the mood for this interrogation. In the back of her mind though, she was thinking - why couldn’t they have just talked to me on the telephone? In any case they started in.

“This Mr. Long, you know where he lives?”

The question really piqued her curiosity, because she had given that information to the Lt. “Didn’ Lt. Meeker tell you where he lives, he got that?”

“Er no, I guess he forgot. You want to give it to us?”

Sarafina now getting more suspicious said: “I think I oughta call Lt. Meeker.” Suprised at this response the sergeant blurted out - “That’s okay ma’am don’t bother we’ll be leaving now. We’ll have him call you tomorrow and vouch for us.”

Then they walked out.

This incident just added to her anxiety and she had to go and lay down. The headache building up in her was definitely the result of extreme tension and she knew that she had to do something to calm herself or she’d really be sick. In the bathroom she found the aspirins, popped a couple in her mouth then returned to the bed. When she woke about an hour later it was time for the boys to be walking in. Almost as if on cue, she heard the key in the door and in they came.

“Mom what chu doin here? You sick?” Jameel asked.

“Well I have somthin real important to tell y’all, but les eat first. I brought your favorite Chinese food.”

While they were eating it was difficult for Sarafina not to bring up the subject, but she wanted to let them finish their meal without worry. She talked about everything else and attempted to keep the conversation light. Prompting them to tell her about their day she asked what was going on. Jameel was concerned about a test he had coming up and she encouraged him telling him he would do fine. Cinque wasn’t concerned about anything except that the football team was going to be playing in the first round of the playoffs Friday against a team that had won the state title the last two years in a row. He wasn’t so sure the ”Jag’s” could win.

After dinner instead of the boys going in to play video games and she to watch TV in the living room, she asked them to join her. Once they were all together in the living room she said that she had something to tell them and she didn't want them to be upset because everything was going to work out fine.

"Boy's somethin happined today thas gonna change some things 'round here for a while."

She was trying as much as she could to keep her tone upbeat and act like this was just going to be a temporary thing until she could find something else to do; another job or something. It wasn't easy for her because since the death of their father in the war some years ago, she had really struggled for a while, but had now been at this job for almost four years and their lifestyle had come to at least some kind of stable pattern.

"They let me go from the job today an we're gonna hafta cut down on some things." "What chu mean let go mom?" Cinque said.

"She ain workin there no more, boy" Jameel answered.

"I hope it's only a little while 'til I fine somethin else, but anyway thas whas goin on. I got some money comin tomorrow that I'm gonna pick up. It should get us through the next few weeks. Now ya'll don worry we gonna make it."

"Mom can I do somethin to help?" Jameel said.

"You jus keep on goin ta school and studyn. Cinque that go for you too. We jus gonna hafta spend less for a while. No more Chinese take out, chicken take out an stuff like that 'til I fine a new job. Okay?"

"Yeah mom we gonna be okay" Cinque said.

They all agreed that things were going to be fine and then each went about doing what they normally did after dinner. Sarafina felt much better in having told them. It was like getting a heavy weight lifted off of her. She contemplated calling Lydia and telling her, just to have a girl to girl kind of comfort talk, but then she remembered about the visit from the two detectives and decided to call Rev. Joyner instead and ask his advice.

"Hello, Reverend Joyner."

"Reverend Joyner this is Sister Peterson did I catch you at a bad time?" "Oh no, I just got in but that's okay. How are you?"

"Well I guess I'm okay, but today I got let go from my job an I'm not really sure why. They tol me it got to do with the "CONN's gettin the police to go to the factory an somethin else 'bout the owner. Then later two detectives came by here wantin to fine out where Mr. Long lives. I din't tell them 'cause they should have known from that lieutenant They said that he sent them, but when I said I was gonna call him an check, they backed off an left. What you think a that?"

"That sounds rather strange. You sure they said they were with Lt. Meeker? Did they show you identification?"

"Yeah, one of them pulled out a badge and he 'tol me they names, but I forgot. An yeah he said they worked wit the lieutenant"

"Well tomorrow I'm going to call him and find out about that. Meantime will you be okay?"

"Yeah I got some money comin tomorrow should last a while. I can also get some unemployment checks once I go sign up. I think I'll be okay. But I wanna know 'bout them cops. If they don work for the lieutenant who they work for?"

"Sister Peterson, you've had a rough day, try to get some sleep and I'll check on you tomorrow. I'll also put you on my prayer list tonight."

"Oh thank you reverend I appreciate that. Goodnight." "I'll talk to you again tomorrow. Goodnight."

That same night, Buster and PK were sitting with Ricoh at his place listening to a plan on how to intercept the next shipment being delivered to the airport for the C's. Ricoh was telling them that he had already talked with his mole down there and for a 20% cut of the sale he would arrange it for us to have access to the container with the stash. He couldn't tell yet how big the stash or what the street value is but from what he knew about the last one, it should be worth between $150 - 200K.

"Man with this kinda dough we can live large for a few years, but we hafta leave here for a while" said Ricoh.

"Ricoh how you gonna get to the stash before them? Yo mole ain gonna tell them the wrong day is he? He ain crazy" said PK.

"Naw, what we gonna do is set it up so it look like the Feds found out an they raided it on pick up day. How you like being a Fed for a day?"

They all laughed.

"Man how we gonna do all this?" PK said.

"Soon as I get the right date, then we get that dude in NY, you know the one that do all them phony papers, to make us up some badges and some Fed papers so we can git in an out a there in a hurry. We jus transfer the stuff to our van an move out. It should'n take no more than 15, 20 minutes to do the whole thing. All I need is two soldiers an you two. You jus got to get yoself fixed up to pass for Feds. Think you can do that?"

"I dono man, I ain never try to look like one" Buster said. Again they all laughed and passed around the peace pipe.

"I think we got about a week before this go down, so y'all got time to fine out what you needa look like. Git it right 'cause we gotta get by security at the port, besides my man, an we can't mess up his thing."

"We'll be aw-ight you jus make sure yo man ain settin us up too. You really think Hakeem gonna believe the Feds got his stuff?"

"Yeah, - what he gonna do investigate 'em?"

This one got the biggest laugh of all and they closed the discussion with that. From there it was all down hill on the earth and the group went on a mind trip vacation in the sky. The next morning when Sarafina awoke at her usual time she looked at the clock, smiled, rolled over and went back to sleep. The boys got up on their own said to each other that they weren't going to bother mom, fixed their own breakfast and got off to school. She slept for almost another 2 hours and when she finally did get up it was about 8:30. Hearing nothing stirring in the apartment she knew the boys were gone. She trudged into the kitchen made a cup of coffee and sat down. The news on the radio didn't have anything particularly exciting, but it was nice not to hear about any shootings that had happened overnight or even recently. She savored this unscheduled time off as if she had taken a vacation day, but when the thought arose concerning her situation, the mood wasn't so mellow anymore.

The money that was due her she knew would be there, but decided the sooner she had it in her pocket and not theirs the better off she'd be. With this in mind, she finished her coffee went in the bathroom to get ready and go down to the office. It didn't take her long to get ready because she was on a mission and wanted to complete it ASAP. When she got out to her parking lot she carefully looked around before going to the car. Since yesterday's events with her getting fired and then right after, the detectives following her she felt that she had to be more vigilant of her surroundings. Not seeing anything that appeared out of the ordinary, she ventured forth to the car. This time though, before entering she even looked the car over carefully. Saying to herself: "Am I going overboard with this?" she wondered if she wasn't beginning to blow things out of proportion. Convinced that until she heard back from Reverend Joyner she wasn't sure what to think. With all that was happening around her lately she couldn't be sure whether these detectives were legitimate or could even be working for Mr. Mizzetti.

After all it was strange that when she mentioned she was going to call Lt. Meeker, they all of a sudden decided to leave her house. If he had sent them, why wouldn't they wait and talk to him. This didn't make any sense to her and she was determined to find out whether she was in any danger and who was behind it.

She arrived at Gateway and having relinquished her employee ID stopped at the receptionist who was glad to see her. The receptionist greeted her warmly and after a few minutes of small talk was permitted in to go to personnel. She didn't venture into her former office area because she was not ready just yet to confront any of them. She especially wanted to avoid Mr. Lukinbill at all costs because of what she said to him before she left. However, as fate would have it, as soon as she walked into personnel there he was talking to the clerk. He was just as surprised to see her as she was him.

"Well Mrs. Peterson I didn't expect to see you here again" he said.

She looked at him with a bit of a scowl and said:

"I didn pick up my money 'fore I left yesterday so I came to git it. Didn expect to see you either."

"You know you've caused quite a stir with our boss Mrs. Peterson and he's really upset with you."

She smiled at him then said:

"If what I'm findin out is true he got reason to be upset."

This caught him by surprise and he wasn't sure how to respond. His expression changed dramatically and he didn't know whether to smile in return or get angry. He decided to remain cordial and just say goodbye and leave. The personnel clerk took Sarafina's information and located her package. Package in hand and feeling good about standing up to Mr. Lukinbill, she left the factory and headed home.

At Midland High School these days all the surface talk was around the football team playing their first playoff game in years on Friday. There was a genuine excitement among students and faculty and the atmosphere was filled with that kind of high expectation that comes when the first bonfire rally is held at the beginning of the season. The hallways were decorated with booster type banners and even the rooms had some promotional material supporting the team. However, lurking underneath all of this enthusiasm was still the high spirits of contention between the two rival factions that functioned in the same building. Having to restrain themselves whenever they passed by a member of the opposite pole was getting to be more difficult as each school day passed. The strain on the teachers and the principal as the school year moved toward the end of the first semester was getting to be an obvious distraction. Although Mr. Steinberg, who was considered in many educational circles to be an excellent principal, was doing his best to maintain some semblance of control, any given day there could be an outbreak that could set off a major melee. The mere threat of something like this happening was always present in the back of the minds of the staff that tried their best to perform proficiently daily.

As it got closer to Friday the level of enthusiasm for the game grew and the yearning for educational achievement diminished. Mr. Steinberg, being an experienced educator, was aware of this and declared that on Friday there would be no real classes, but a monster pep rally, provided that the students would excel in their classrooms from this time, which was Wednesday, until then. The idea was well received by all and a slight improvement in classroom work was made. Even the negative interactions between the two rivals was somewhat mitigated because of it. Total peace had not been reached, but there was a kind of detente status for a couple of days.

The Peterson boys, Rajon and Dolitha at the end of the school day as usual gathered together to walk home since they all lived in the same direction. Sista was still pursuing Jameel, but had not made much headway in getting him to refocus his attention. She was still biding her time waiting for the right opportunity that she was sure would come. She had even made some overtures to Dolitha to try and strike up some kind of pseudo friendship in order to find out more about what he was really into. Dolitha was less than interested in elevating their relational status, so that strategy wasn't working well either.

On the way home Jameel spotted the same SUV that was used on the night that he got hit outside of Higgyb's. He scrambled to find something to write with so he could take down the license plate number. By the time he got something, of course the vehicle was much too far away. He turned to his group and asked:

"Anybody see what the plate numbers were on that car jus passed us?" "Why you aksn?" Dolitha said.

"'Cause thas the car they used that night I got hit." "You sure?" Rajon asked.

"Man, I'll never forget that night. I wonder what they doin 'round here. Sista tol me when I was in the hospital it was the B's that did it. They shouldn be 'round here?" "I know it was them, I tol you that too" Rajon said. "But they ain got no real power now though, 'cause they still tryin to rebuild. So it ain no big thing if they ride 'round here, they know bettern to try nuthin."

"Yeah man, but I sure would like to get that plate number if I see'em again so I can give it to the cops. I'd like to know who it belongs to."

"Yeah me too" Dolitha said. "It would make me feel better if they all got picked up." They arrived at Jameel's house first and Cinque left the group.

"Cinque, tell mom I'm walkin Dolitha home an I'll be there in a little while." "Aw-ight I'll tell her."

The trio continued walking to Dolitha's house that was in the same block as Rajon's. Rajon split off and it was just Jameel and Dolitha.

"You wanna come up for a minute?" Dolitha said. "Ain yo mother home?"

"Yeah she should be there, so?"

"She won say anything if I come up?"

"No, she let me do what I wanna do mos of the time 'cause I take care of her really." "Yeah well maybe next time. I gotta go."

"You know I keep invitin you up, but you always gotta go. What chu fraid of?" Jameel laughed then offered:

"I'm afraid of you girl, you might take advantage of me."

Dolitha laughed and punched him playfully. Jameel smiling too, kissed her on her cheek turned around and went home.

When he got there mom and Cinque had already eaten, but left a plate on the table for him.

"Mom I'm home."

"Hi. Your plate is on the table, put it in the oven for a minute or two and warm it up." "Okay."

Sarafina was on the phone talking to Reverend Joyner.

"I spoke to Lt. Meeker today and I asked him about those two detectives that you told me about. He said yes they do work for him, but he didn't send them to find Mr. Long or to talk to you. He was surprised himself when I told him what had happened. He said he would talk to them about it and let me know."

"You think they might be working for Mizzetti?"

"I don't know, but they had no business asking you for anything. There was something else the lieutenant asked me about. He wanted to know whether you had talked to Mr. Long about coming to the precinct."

"No, since I was let go the day I was gonna talk to him, I put it in the back of my mind. But now that I had that run in with those detectives, I'm not sure if I should try and get him to do anything. He might really be in danger."

"Sister Peterson, I think we're getting close to finding out something really big and I think he may be the key. We need to trust Lt. Meeker, even if the detective's can't be. When are you having your next group meeting?"

"I had scheduled one for tomorrow night, but now that I'm not working I don' know." "If you can, I think you should still have it. You should try and keep on doing all the things that you usually do until you can't do them because of funds. That will keep your mind occupied. If you can have it, I'd like to come myself along with the lieutenant and speak with M r. Long. He should be there right?"

"He said he would continue comin, so I guess he be there." "Where do you meet?"

"At the rec center in the basement, 7:00 PM."

"Okay I'll get hold of the lieutenant tomorrow and make sure he can be there and I'll be there too. I think we're finally really onto something if Mr. Long hangs in." "Yeah maybe an if we don get him killed."

"Let's not even think like that. I'll see you tomorrow."

"Goodnight."

At police headquarters the next day, Lt. Meeker had the two detectives in his office questioning them about the confrontation with Mrs. Peterson.

"I got a call from Reverend Joyner, you know the mayor's friend, about you two guys cornering a Mrs. Peterson and asking her about a possible key witness that I'm interested in. What was that all about?"

"Well first of all Lt, we didn't corner her" said Sgt. Halleran. When we were on watch over at the high school like you told us to, we saw her ride by. I knew that you were looking for this guy Long to grill him, so I thought we would just talk to her and see if we could get a lead on where he was."

"I told you to watch the school, not go chasing around after somebody I already have a lead on. I also heard that when she said she was going to call me, you left. Is that right?"

"Yes, lieutenant because there was no need to get you involved."

"Listen, I don't know what you two were up to, but I don't like it. Now listen and hear me good, unless I tell you differently, you're not to bother the woman, her club members, Mr. Long or the Reverend. I'm busting my tail trying to come up with some positive witnesses to these recent shootings and these people may be the only ones that can get them to come in. Now back off, is that clear, do we understand each other?"

"Yes lieutenant we got you." "Okay now get out of here."

A little while later, the lieutenant received another call. This time it was from Rev. Joyner.

"Police headquarters, Lt. Meeker." "Good morning lieutenant, how are you?"

"Hi rev., I'm okay I guess. You got good news for me, I can sure use it."

"Well that depends. I may have something that could turn into good news if you can come to a meeting with me tonight."

"What meeting and where?"

"It's the CONN's meeting and its going to be at the recreation center at 7:00 PM tonight."

"What's so special about this meeting that I should be there?"

"I have a good feeling that Mr. Long will be there and you may be able to get him to talk to you directly about what he knows. He may even be able to point out some people for you."

"You say you have a good feeling, what does that mean?"

"Well it's more than just a feeling, I have it on good authority that he should be there. I suggest you bring some of the pictures you want him to look at and maybe he'll identify somebody."

"All right reverend that sounds like a plan. Are you going to be there?"

"I wouldn't miss it."

"Okay, see you there at 7:00."

It was a long time before Hammer got back to Hakeem about whether their soldiers had made contact with Mr. Long and he was getting a little worried about his own security. Finally the call came in.

"Hakeem this is Hammer." "Yeah Hammer, whas up?"

"Jus wanna update you on the search for that Long guy." "Yeah, where he at?"

"They couldn't fine him over the weekend, but he go to work ereyday at that lock factory an when he come out they can't get to him 'cause he be ridin wit too many people. So nuthin been done."

"Aw-ight thas good, 'cause I tol you Mr. M gonna handle it hisself. Where you at now?"

"At M&M's."

"Aw-ight stay there I'm on my way. We needa go down to the port and check up on that leak we got there, 'fore we get a call for the next pick up."

"Aw-ight, I'll be here."

Within the hour Hakeem and Hammer were on their way to the airport. The arrangement that they had with the contact there was for them to be notified two days in advance of when the goods would be in. After that on the day of delivery, Hakeem would come down one hour early before actual pick up and pay the contact his fee. The contact would then ensure that the container passed through security and be available for Hakeem's van to enter the storage area. The goods would then be transferred from the container to the van and that was as simple as it could get. Only a few people were supposed to know when the shipment would arrive. As a cover the bill of lading would indicate that it contained coffee being sent to a major supermarket warehouse for distribution. The plan was simple, but involved some key people that had to sign off.

Hakeem was the least of them.

It was really hard for him to understand how Ricoh could have known about the last shipment pick up. Except for the primary contact, who else would or could leak the information. He first thought about the contact being the leak, but then he said to himself: "That'd be crazy 'cause erebody would know he did it. An why would he wanna mess up the good thing like he had goin." So he ruled that out. He was going down there to find out from him who else could possibly have knowledge about what the deal was. When they got to the airport they parked in the regular short term parking area and then made a call to the contact. They arranged for the contact, who was a fairly high level employee able to leave his post at will, to meet them in the luggage pick up area.

The contact agreed and the meeting was set for 1:00 PM that was fifteen minutes from now.

They got out of the car and started walking into the terminal area. Since it was an afternoon in the middle of the week, there wasn't a large crowd in the terminal nor was there any other action going on that would make it anything other than a normal airport day. They went downstairs to the luggage pick up area and sat down on a bench in the rear of the building. Making it a point to keep well out of sight and be as inconspicuous as possible until they spotted their contact they rushed to the bench. Just as agreed, the contact came down the escalator a few minutes before 1:00, spotted the duo and motioned them to start walking in a direction that he pointed to. They heeded the call and started walking toward where the contact was headed. There was a passenger waiting section that also served as a break area for some airport employees. The contact directed them there. Once inside he moved to a seat in a far corner and the duo came and sat down beside him. Hakeem positioned himself on one side and Hammer on the other and the conversation began.

"What can I do for you gentlemen?" the contact said. "Somethin ain right wit security."

"What are you talking about?"

"The last package that came in, had some people knowin 'bout it that shouldn know." "Make sense man, I'm not following you."

"Somebody knew 'bout me pickin up the last shipment right after I picked it up. How that happen?"

"Who you talking about?"

"You don needa know, jus tell me how that could happen."

"It can't. Nobody knows about our deals except you, your boss, me and my boss." "How well you know your boss? You truss him?"

"More than I do you."

"Well, I jus came to tell you 'bout the problem today 'cause somethin else should be comin in soon, an I don want it to happen again. Check yo people here somebody may be peepin in the cases you don know 'bout."

"Don't worry I'll handle it, but nobody looks in a container without my permission, just so you know."

"Aw'ight we outta here, but if it happen again I gotta let my boss know." "Of course gentlemen."

The conversation ended. Not really satisfied because he didn't know anymore now then he did when he came in, Hakeem wasn't sure whether the contact could be lying or not. If he was lying though what did he have to gain, Hakeem kept saying to himself. The ride back to the hang was unusually quiet because both men were deep in thought about what it could mean if their next shipment would be compromised or intercepted by anybody. Finally just before they got to M&M's Hakeem spoke up and said:

"I heard what that dude said, with his smooth behind, but somehow I don' truss him. What chu think?"

"Yeah, I got the same feelin'. He seem too smooth for his own good, but it don make sense for him to mess up down there. I'm sure he know who makes the deals." "Yeah he mus know, but maybe he think he too slick to get caught."

"I dono man, what chu gonna do?"

"Ain nothin we can do but jus wait for the next delivery an see what happens." They arrived at M&M's and went inside.

The next day Sarafina after having another leisurely morning started to get some things together for tonight's meeting. She was starting to enjoy these days of not having to get up early and running to mix with a crowd of people and cars rushing to get somewhere. She knew deep down inside that it wasn't going to last, but she was going to enjoy it for as long as it did. For the time being she had some money, but she also knew that wouldn't last long either. Also for the time being she had some peace of mind, but that too wouldn't last long. All in all she resigned herself to the fact that she was where she was because that's where she was. Looking at her roster from the last meeting, she was going over in her mind who would be the most effective leader should she have to step down. Of course Lydia would be the next in line by command, but she wondered whether her heart was really into all this. Sometimes she got the feeling from her that she would rather be doing something else. Janet, the new member was really a sharp lady, but Sarafina didn't think she was a fighter and at the first sign of a real skirmish, she'd be gone. Mr. Long, she knew would be there in a pinch, but he certainly didn't want to be out in front. Nobody else on the roster jumped out at her so she abandoned the idea for now thinking she would get back to it later and continued to prepare.

On the other side of town Ricoh was also preparing. He was busy trying to put the final touches on his intercept plan. A plan he thought would not only provide him with the retribution that he sought, but could also give him the escape capital that he was always looking for. While he was going through all the details the phone rang.

"Yeah, this Ricoh whas up?"

"Ricoh, this is your airport agent," he said intentionally not giving his name.

"I was just paid a visit by Hakeem and his boy. Did you tell him you knew about his last pick up?"

"Oh man, yeah it slipped out in the heat of me tryna get a point over."

"Are you a total idiot or what? What you've done is blow off everything we talked about. I can't put myself in a position where if the next shipment goes wrong they'll all be looking at me. And I'm not talking about no Hakeem, he's small potatoes.

He'd be the least of my concerns. But the big guy who calls the shots would be very upset and I don't need that. So you can forget it."

"Aw cut me some slack man please. I almos got it all worked out. We can do this." "No we can't, at least not now. Maybe sometime much later after some more deals go down smoothly, then we can talk again, but right now it would be crazy. I'll call you again when I think it might be safe to try. That could take some time so don't get your hopes up."

"Come on man, I know we can do this. I know we can make it work." "Ricoh its over, finished" and he hung up.

Ricoh was so thoroughly disappointed that he just sat staring out the window not knowing exactly what alternative move he could make. Without the airport contact, there was absolutely no way he could carry out his plan.

Sarafina was so engrossed preparing for the meeting and deciding what message she wanted to get across to the group, that she totally lost all track of time. When she finally looked up at the clock it was almost 3:30 and time for her boys to be walking in. She jumped up from the couch and went in the kitchen to see what she could whip together for their dinner. Fortunately she had thawed out some meat she had planned to cook yesterday and it was ready to go. She grabbed a large can of string beans and a box of instant mashed potatoes and went to work. She was an excellent cook with a great deal of experience in whipping up good meals in a hurry. Coming from a large family in which she was the oldest girl and expected to be the family cook because her mother worked, this was nothing new.

In minutes, she had everything working and was just putting on the final touches when the boys walked in.

"Hi, mom." they both said.

She didn't stop doing her thing, but she hollered back: "How was school today?" Almost simultaneously the reply came back: "It's okay."

With this reply she accepted that nothing unusual had happened and it was school as usual. A few minutes more and she told the boys to go wash up and come to the table. Reminding them that she had a meeting to go to, she said she would be leaving in about an hour. Homework was the next point and she covered that quickly. Both boys accounted themselves promising that it would be done before she got back.

At 6:45 she was ready to walk out the door and made a final check to make sure the boys were carrying out their promise. All in order she left. When she arrived at the recreation center it seemed that there were a lot of cars there that were not there normally. She found a parking spot and ventured inside. Walking past several people in the lobby she made her way down to the basement where they usually met. When she walked in the room she was really surprised. The number of people there already almost doubled those that were at the last one. She was a bit overwhelmed and wondered if they were there for the right meeting. She made her way to the front and saw Lydia.

"Lydia, are all these people here for our meeting?"

"Yes, it seems that your efforts have caught on and the community is tired of what's been happening. By the way we have two special guests tonight. Look over there."

Sarafina looked over in the far corner and there sat Rev. Joyner along with Lt. Meeker. She immediately started looking around to see if Malcolm Long had come. Not yet! Since it was still a little early, even though the place was full, she wanted to give people who would still be on time a chance to be there at the beginning. She made her way over to Rev. Joyner and the lieutenant

"Hi y'all good to see you here. How are you?" "Fine Mrs. Peterson." the lieutenant said.

"Very good Sister Peterson. It's good to be here" was the response from the Reverend. Sarafina asked the reverend if he wanted to say a few words after she opened the meeting and he declined. He said that he and the lieutenant were there mainly to talk with Mr.

Long if he comes tonight. He then added that perhaps at the end of the meeting, depending on how late it gets, he might want to add something, but definitely not in the beginning. He reminded her that this was her show. She then looked at the clock and it showed it was now about five minutes after the hour so she made her way back to the front.

The center had provided her with a podium and a PA system that she was very happy to get because she didn't exactly have a booming voice like the reverend. She turned on the mike tapped and blew in it. Pleased with the sound she started in.

"Friends and neighbors it's so good to see all y'all out here tonight. It really makes my heart glad ta know you wanna help right the things that have gone wrong in this community."

There was a loud applause when she said this, and it made her feel more relaxed. "Tonight after we pass around again the sign up sheet 'cause I know we got some more new people here, I wanna go over the patrol schedules and what we need to be doin when ridin on patrol. I wanna let y'all know also, that tonight we have here a representative from our police department, so he can help us know what we shouldn't do."

She looked over in the corner at the lieutenant and it was obvious that he didn't want to be recognized because he was in plain clothes, but he smiled and waved anyway. While she was recognizing the lieutenant in walked Malcolm and Janet and sat quickly in the back. She acknowledged them silently and continued on.

"As we talked about las time, the patrols will be in teams of three an we don want anybody tryna be a hero just watch an write down anything that don seem right. We will then turn in a report twice a week to the police an let them know what we see. Is that okay with erebody?"

The roaring agreement and endorsement from the crowd really gave her the feeling that she had something big going. She looked over at Rev. Joyner and saw him beaming with pride. She went on with the rest of the meeting covering some other things such as the logistics of who was going to cover what areas, who would be working together, what to do if they see something that needed attention right away etc. It was another positive meeting and she was excited about the turn out. She was getting ready to close the meeting when she again looked over to Rev. Joyner and asked whether he wanted to speak. This time he accepted and started heading toward the front.

"Brothers and sisters in the Lord I greet you in His holy name. As your leader said earlier it is such a good thing to see that you are all responding to the call to come out and do something to help your community. There is much work to be done, but when we work together there is nothing that we can't accomplish. I know its getting late so I'm not going to be the one to hold you, but I just want to end by saying let us not grow weary in well doing, for in due season we shall reap if we do not lose heart.

What that means is that we may not see the benefits right away for what we're doing, but if we persevere, we will witness the right end. With that Sarafina closed the meeting.

She came down from the front quickly and went to Malcolm and Janet. She asked Malcolm if he could stay a little while longer and talk with Reverend Joyner and Lt. Meeker in the office. Malcom agreed as long as Janet could be with him. Sarafina motioned to Lt. Meeker and Rev. Joyner to join her in the little office just outside of the meeting room. Once they were all inside Lt. Meeker took charge and first wanted to know who Janet was and why she was there. Malcolm told the lieutenant that if he wanted to talk to him, then she would be staying. Lt. Meeker looked at him and then agreed.

"Mr. Long do you live in the Roundtree Gardens?" the lieutenant said. "Yeah, been there ever since they built it `bout five years."

"Do you remember the night that the shootings took place at the Bricks Complex over on the east side?"

"I sure do. I was lookin out my window that night `fore it all happen an I seen those boys that hang out at that Minute Mart puttin stuff in cars like they was goin to war. I wasn the only one that seen'em whole lotta people saw'em but ain nobody say nothing `cause they scared."

"Mr. Long would you be able to identify any of them if I showed you some pictures?" "Yeah, maybe. I ain had no looking glasses or nothin, but I know some of em anyway `cause they be `round there alla time."

"Okay. Would you look through this book and point out anybody you recognize as being there that night."

"Well leme see here what chu got."

While Malcolm was looking through the book, Rev. Joyner asked what the next step would be if he identified somebody. Lt. Meeker replied that he could then start bringing these guys in for questioning and maybe get a search warrant to go into that Minute Mart and see what's in there. Rev. Joyner was very pleased with that response and sat back in his chair.

"Hey lieutenant, see this guy here, I know he one of `em."

The picture that Mr. Long pointed to was that of Hakeem. He had prior convictions for atrocious assault, burglary, armed robbery and drug possession. Another conviction and he could go away for good. His whole name was Hakeem Brown and he was originally from New York City. The lieutenant looked at Mr. Long and said:

"Are you sure this is the man that you saw that night?"

"I saw him that night, last night an a whole bunch a nights. He be down there alla time. I saw him put some of those guns in the cars that night."

"Would you be willing to say this in court, if the time comes?" "Yeah, I ain `fraid of him, but he not the one to be scared of." "Who else are we talking about?"

"The man you really should be lookin at, is the one who own that store, the lock factory an that warehouse at the end of town."

"You're absolutely sure about this right?" "You mean `bout the big man?"

"Yes."

"Yeah, I hear his people inside the plant talk a lot `bout what he does an how he uses those boys. Now if I agree to talk in court, you gonna guarantee me I'll be safe, right."

"If you help us we'll make sure of that. Anybody else in that book you know."

Mr. Long went back to looking at the book. Lt. Meeker turned to Rev. Joyner and said: "This could be a tremendous break for us. Tomorrow I'm going to discuss it with the captain and try to get a search warrant to go into that Minute Mart and see what we can come up with. If they're really using that store as a weapons warehouse, then we're in good shape. The only thing that bothers me is what the connection is between the owner of the store and the gangs. You know if this is the same man that owns that Bentley that was seen down there recently, then I have to be very careful. He's a big man in this town and even with your friend, the mayor."

Reverend Joyner just looked at him and nodded his head.

"Lieutenant, here go another one of 'em. I see him down there a lot too."

The second picture that Mr. Long pointed to was Hammer's. His real name was Claudius Miller and like his leader he too had several priors and if convicted again would be looking at some serious time out of the public eye.

"Once again I'll ask you Mr. Long are you sure and would you be willing to identify this man in court also?"

"Yeah, both of 'em wit the rest of that gang needa be put away. Then maybe the streets be safe an all this shootin stop."

"Well thank you very much Mr. Long. I'll be in touch with you. Is this your right telephone number?"

Malcolm looked at what the lieutenant had written down from the roster sheet and confirmed his number.

The group came out of the office and Malcolm and Janet separated from the rest and left the building. Sarafina, the lieutenant and Reverend Joyner continued talking and agreed that they may have just got the breakthrough they've been looking for. Lt. Meeker was cautiously optimistic, but kept saying to them that if this Mr. Mizzetti was really behind all the action, then this town was in for a real shake up. Sarafina looked at the lieutenant and told him that if he was then it was more important than ever that it get stopped now, before he was able to take over the whole town, with the C's running the streets. The lieutenant assured her that that wouldn't happen, but she wasn't so sure.

They finished their conversation with the lieutenant saying to them that he would start first thing tomorrow to try and get a search warrant for the Minute Mart. He would let the reverend know of his progress.

When Lt. Meeker arrived at his office the next morning he was feeling confident about the breakthrough he had last night. He felt the captain would be pleased that they now had something to start bringing people in on. He prepared his report and warrant request and walked into the captain's office.

"Good morning captain, how are you?"

The captain was less than in a cordial mood finishing a cup of coffee. He motioned to the lieutenant to come in and sit down.

"What you got, Meeker?"

"Well sir, I went to a meeting that the group called CONN's, you know the community activist group that's been helping us, had and they produced an eyewitness."

"Oh really, is he reliable?"

"After talking with him, he seemed to have his head on straight so I asked him to ID some perps from the book. He nailed a couple that may be of interest to us. Anyway, I want to get a warrant to search that Minute Mart down there on 7th Avenue."

"What are we looking for?"

"Weapons, sir. According to our witness he said they may be warehousing them there." "Okay lieutenant If you think that's a good lead run with it. Here I'll sign it. Who's the judge for this?"

"I think I can get our favorite lady to sign off." "Okay, just keep me informed."

The lieutenant wasted no time after getting the signature in running over to the other side of the municipal building and getting the request to the judge. At the time he arrived in the judicial area, the judge had not come in yet, but was expected any minute. Lt. Meeker spent the next few minutes talking with some of the clerks and asking about how busy they are. The consensus was that there were too many cases and not enough judges or administrators. The lieutenant agreed and laughingly said that he would try to cut down on the number of arrests so they would have a lighter load. In the midst of the laughter from the clerks the judge walked in and wondered what was going on. She then spotted Meeker shook her head and said:

"I might have known it was you causing this. Are you here to see me?"

"Yes, your honor I have a present for you."

"A present from you, I don't need, but what you got?"

Lt. Meeker presented her with the request and she reviewed it.

"You really think they got this stuff in there that you're seeking?" "Yes ma'am on a pretty good tip we think there's something there."

"Alright lieutenant here you are. You'd better come up with something. This town needs to hear that you guys have caught somebody soon or the press is going to continue crucifying all of us."

"Yes your honor you're right. Thank you."

The lieutenant took the papers and hurried back to his office to initiate the action. He hit the intercom button and paged Sgt. Calloway.

"Yes lieutenant, - Calloway here?"

"Ray, I've got a warrant to search for weapons in that Minute Mart down there on 7th Avenue. I want you to get a team together to go in there tonight around 8:OO PM."

"Sir, we authorized overtime?"

"Don't worry about the overtime, just get the guys ready. I'll meet you there at 8." "Yes sir, see you there at 8."

The lieutenant hung up and started going over everything he had so far related to the shootings. Somehow until last night he felt like he was on a super merry-go-round, but now he felt like he was moving in a new direction.

At exactly 8:00 O'clock two police cars and a S.W.A.T. police van pulled up in front of M&M's. It was already dark and the streetlights cast a shadow over the area.

Surprisingly, the normal activity that took place outside of the store was not there. The store was closed, but the lights were on inside. The lieutenant met Sgt. Calloway and they motioned for some of the men to go around to the back of the store and then they walked up to the door. They first tried to open the door, but it was locked. The store manager seeing them came to the door and opened it.

"Who are you and what are you doing here?" the lieutenant asked.

Nervously the man answered.

"I'm the store manager and we're taking inventory."

The lieutenant explained to him that he had a search warrant and he was going to look through the place. He motioned for him and the two clerks to move over to the side behind the checkout counter. He then asked where the stock room is. The manager pointed it out and the lieutenant rushed into it. He threw open the door and starting turning over boxes and ripping open bags. His frustration at seeing no weapons, not even a slingshot, was beginning to build as he climbed a ladder to the top of the shelves. After he had looked in every corner and crack in the room he came across something on a shelf way in the back that he was totally unprepared to find.

"Ray, come take a look at this." he hollered.

Chapter 9 - The Adversary

It was the perfect night for a football game. The air was brisk, but not cold, the temperature hovered around the mid 50's and the stars were out in mass against a midnight blue sky. The moon had completed its cycle and was now showing full in all its brilliance. Fans ambled by the dozens into City Stadium pumped up with the excitement and anticipation of a contest that had been super hyped by the local radio station.

Through some quirk in scheduling, as a result of the incident that happened at the last game mandating changes, the first playoff game was being played on the Jag's home field. Although most of the adults in attendance felt that this should be a decided advantage, students from MHS were not so sure. They had supported the team earlier in the day with a major pep rally that took into account their heroes were not even expected to get this far, this season. But somewhere in the back of their minds they were ready for the worst.

In the Jaguar's locker room, Peter Winston (Pete), the head coach was going over last minute details of his game plan. He was alternating between congratulating them for having reached this pinnacle, but at the same time also admonishing them to not feel that this was the end of the line. He told them that the guys in the other locker room put their pants on just like you do.

"They're flesh and blood just like you are and they don't have any special powers. If they think they're Superman, then we'll be the Kryptonite, if they come out on fire then we'll be Niagara Falls, if they play hard then we'll play harder. You can win this game, but you must believe you can."

Then he looked into the eyes of each player and said louder and louder with each repetition:

"Can we win?" "Yeah!"

"Can we win?" "Yeah!"

"Can we win?" "Yeah!"

"Okay everybody on 3 - win. 1, 2, 3" "Win."

"Okay now let's get out there and play the game of our lives."

When he finished, the team was at the height of their emotions and herded out of the locker room bull rushing toward the field.

Security for this game was nothing like what it had been for the last encounter. There were no advanced reports of any planned gang activity and no speculation on a possible outbreak. Even though the gangs were definitely present and well represented on both sides it seemed that the recent stepped up police patrols and the institution of the new civilian community patrols was having some positive effect. Members of both the C's and the B's were heavily wagered on this game and oddly enough they wanted no distractions to occur prior to its completion. The police that were in attendance along with the stadium's own private security, were more focused on the game itself rather than what might be going on in the stands.

Normally, the C's would have been hanging out at their favorite haunt, but tonight the whole crew decided that the stadium was the place to be. Little did they know that while they were enjoying their local gridiron combatants competing in a battle for football supremacy, M&M's was being visited by the police. The raid was spawned by a witness who came forward and pointed out that the store is being used as a weapons warehouse. Lt. Meeker and Sgt. Calloway got a search warrant and carried out the mission.

During the actual search, Lt. Meeker was totally frustrated at not finding the weapons he had convinced his superior and the judge he would find. In his mind he thought: "Now I know how the US government felt in the Iraq WMD search and invasion." Setting aside his disappointment, he was bent on finding something to justify the issuance of the warrant. When he had turned over everything in the storeroom and searched high and low ceiling to floor, he was almost at his wits end when in the far corner on the top shelf of one of the storage bins he spotted an old miniature safe.

He scrambled over there retrieved it and attempted to open it. The safe door had not been completely closed so it was easy to open. Brushing away the cobwebs and layers of dust he removed an envelope containing a document that had been carefully cut in half. On his half were plans including partial names and locations for a major drug shipment and the partial details for a deal that would have happened about three years ago. At the bottom it said something, he couldn't quite understand, about a hidden façade, a secret compartment or other. His curiosity was intensely high and he kept wondering if there was something more in this room that he was feeling, but couldn't see.

This information was one side of a high level deal that he knew could be the salvation for his search efforts. His first thoughts were what was it doing here and where is the other half. If he could find that, then he would have some real answers and perhaps solutions to what's really going on behind the scenes in his town.

Back at the game, the competition was well underway and the combatants were each acquitting themselves admirably. Each team had scored on their first two possessions and it was now deep into the second quarter with the Jags holding a slight lead at 17-14. In the stands the excitement was at a fever pitch and the capacity crowd was rocking the stadium like it had never been treated before. The police and security agents were enjoying it because the fans were so focused on the game that the normal skirmishes were at an extreme minimum.

Ricoh, PK and three of the B soldiers were seated in the lower section around the 40yard line. These were seats normally held for VIPs, but Rick was able to exchange his capital influence with a ticket agent for this prime consideration. On the other side of the stadium Hakeem, Hammer and three of their crew were also seated in choice seats through perhaps the same type of arrangement. It was all about what money could buy. Representatives from both clubs were sprinkled liberally throughout the stands, but amazingly no confrontations took place. Among the guests that were also moving about the stands were some visitors from New York with a special interest in Ricoh. After they were screened by Rick's troops regarding his location, the two men made their way to his section.

Upon getting within speaking distance, Ricoh recognized one of the men as a contact that he had made some time ago when trying to get a foothold in the New York market. He greeted the man by name, Alivedi Leisar (a.k.a.- Big Al) and invited him to come and sit down. Two of the soldiers immediately relinquished their seats and the men sat down.

"Ricoh, ole buddy how you doin?" Al said. "Hey Al, long time whas up?"

"Got somethin you might be interested in comin down soon." "Oh yeah, like what?"

"Can't tell you details now, but we need to get together tomorrow night. Can you throw a party or somethin that I can bring some of my posse to?"

"What kinda party?"

"Man you know, one where there's a lotta honeys an closed to the outside. Can you handle that?"

"Yeah man, but you said tomorrow. What time you talkin?" "You can kick it off `bout 9 an we can go to whenever you want."

"Man you gotta tell me a little more than that. Do I need my soldiers ready for somethin?"

"Naw, naw man ain nothin like that. I jus wanna make sure when we talk that there be a lot goin on. What I got to tell you is big an I don want distractions."

"Aw-ight, its done. Gimme yo cell number an I'll call you early tomorrow wit the details on where and when."

"Okay cool. Talk to you later." "Yeah man, later."

The two men got up and the soldiers who were watching from the aisle returned to their seats. Ricoh then got up and went down to the main concourse area to try and find a spot where he could be heard on his cell. He went into an old phone booth that had been decommissioned closed the door and placed his call.

"Willie, Willie can you hear me?" "Yeah, just barely who this?"

"Its Ricoh man, I need another fava."

"Yeah man, what chu need now? You bringin that girl back for me?"

Ricoh laughed and then said: "Naw man, you still can't have that. What I need is to use that big room where your people have their family gatherins at."

"When you need it for?"

"Tomorrow night startin 'round 9:00 O'clock."

"Man is you crazy? I can't get that joint ready that fast."

"Willie this important. You don needa have it spotless, it ain gonna be nothin but a big party. Jus get stuff out the way so people can get in there an boogie. I'll have some ladies comin that you can mess wit."

The last part sounded real good to Slick Willie and his mind shifted gears from what he couldn't do.

"Aw-ight man, you betta have somethin good for me. I'll take care the room. You say y'all comin at 9."

"Yeah somewhere 'round then."

"Aw-ight, but y'all gotta help me clean up that place afta, right?" "Yeah right, don worry 'bout that we take care of it."

The wheels were set in motion. Ricoh then spoke to his soldiers and told them to get one of the guys ready to DJ a party tomorrow night starting at 9:00 O'clock and also get enough of all kinds of stuff to make it a good party. Having started the ball rolling, he was confident that whatever it was that his NY visitors wanted to talk about, if nothing else they would be ensured of a good time. He turned his attention back to the game hoping that his wager was being covered.

In another part of the stadium, Rajon and his girl, Jameel and Dolitha were enjoying the game and having fun. Cinque as usual had hooked up with his friends and was in another section. Where they were sitting it was mostly filled with other students from MHS and it was clear that the visiting team fans were outnumbered. Although there was no outlandish hostility or showing of any hostile intentions, the visitors were careful not to become too verbose in their cheers. All in all it was one of the best games of the year being played on the field and the fans in the stands on both sides were on their best behavior. Right up until half time the crowd actively cheered, but was passive in any physical contact. Even the traditional drinkers held themselves in check.

At the half, the score remained 17-14 favoring the Jags and Jameel and Rajon decided to go down to the concession stand for some refreshments. As they joined the throng of people exiting toward the concessionaires Jameel spotted Hakeem and Hammer and wondered whether he should greet them or not. It didn't take long before the decision was made for him. Hakeem spotted him and started to make his way toward the duo.

"Jameel, ain seen you 'round lately man, you aw-ight?" "Yeah, om okay."

"You know we wasn' the ones that did you up on that night afta Razor's thing right?" "Yeah, I know."

"Good, thas good. I didn want you to get it wrong. I was gonna deal wit you, but afta I talked wit Sista, she straiten it out an ereythins aw-ight now. You cool wit us.

Whas up wit yo mom though? Why she comin down on us, we jus tryna live." Jameel looked at him hard and said:

"My mom ain doin nothin to y`all she jus want ereybody in the hood to live too." Hakeem looked back at him and just laughed. He then motioned to Hammer and they continued down to the concession stands. Jameel turned to Rajon and said:

"You know I really don like that dude." "Yeah, me too neither." Rajon said.

They also continued down to the food stand and picked up something for the girls and themselves. The run in with Hakeem stayed in the back of his mind and he wondered whether Hakeem knew that his mom had someone in her club that was about to bring some serious trouble into his life.

When they got back to their seats, Dolitha told Jameel that she overheard some guys coming through the stands talking about a big party that was going to happen tomorrow over at the Bricks. Jameel responded by telling her that there was no way he was going over there and she shouldn't either. She squeezed his hand and said that if he wasn't going she wouldn't either. It was amazing how quickly the news traveled around the whole stadium about the party. Even those who the message was not intended for heard about it and it became like fodder to hungry cows. When Hakeem got the news, he pondered whether this could be another ruse to get him out into a situation, especially on the wrong side of town where he would be compromised. He sent word by his messengers that none of his crew was to even think about going over there.

The remainder of the game proved to be all that the fans had come out to see. For the local penny pinchers got not only their money's worth, but received a bonus in addition. It came right down to the final minutes and the Panthers had tied the score at 24. With less than two minutes remaining on the game clock, the Jags had the ball and they were advancing into the visitor's red zone. The drive however, stalled at the 15yard line. With seconds left on the clock, it was fourth down and 6 yards to go to get another first down. Not known to have an exceptional kicker, coach Pete looked at his assistants and asked: "

What do you think?"

Without hesitation they all said in unison: "Go for the win."

Coach pulled his young kicker aside and said to him:

"Son, this is your moment. I know you can do this, but you have to believe you can. Don't worry about a thing just do what you do in practice and it will be all right. Now go to it."

The youngster ran onto the field and there was an odd silence that came over a previously boisterous crowd. The team set up in field goal formation and the holder called for the ball. Good snap, good hold and the kick was on its way. For those few seconds from the time the ball left the center's hands until the time the kicker's foot launched it, fans in the stands held their collective breath and it seemed like an eternity before the ball crossed the line and went easily between the goal posts. When the referee signaled the kick was good, the stands rocked, the quiet turned to raucous pandemonium and the MHS students were having difficulty absorbing what had just happened. Except for the visiting team down on the field who were stunned by the results, the hometown fans were celebrating at a fever pitch drawing the attention, for the first time in the evening, of the police.

Moving quickly to pre-arranged stations, the police and security rushed to get in position to keep a well, deserved victory celebration from turning into a nightmare. The crowd was on their feet for several minutes and the cheers were at a decibel level far in excess of what anyone would have imagined. As it turned out, while the visiting fans were exiting, a small melee broke out and drew the attention of security. Quickly quelled, the remainder of the stadium emptying took place without any major incidents.

It was a great night for the city on the one hand, but very disappointing to some degree on the other. Lt. Meeker, Sgt. Calloway and their team went back to police headquarters for a quick debriefing. What the lieutenant had come up with in his search, he was hoping would be a real key to solving a major problem, was a big disappointment. However, his innermost feelings would not allow him to feel that he had accomplished the mission. He talked to his men and thanked them for their work and then sent them home. Sgt. Calloway volunteered to stay a few extra minutes to try to talk the lieutenant out of his doldrums.

"Lieutenant you think that guy was lying about what he saw coming out of that store? Or do you think somehow they got tipped off we were coming?"

"Ray, at this point I'm not sure of anything. I don't think our man was lying, but I'm not sure about any tip off either. I don't know about you, but somehow when we were there I got the feeling that we were overlooking something."

"Yeah, I kinda felt that too, but we looked over everything and I didn't see nothing more."

"Well, that note in the safe has to mean something and I'm going to find out where the other half is. There's got to be a connection between that store, Mr. Mizzetti and perhaps that warehouse. Thanks for staying, but why don't you take off. I'm going to stay just another minute and then I'm gone too. See you Monday."

"Okay lieutenant Goodnight!"

Sergeant Calloway left the station. Lt. Meeker sat at his desk a little while longer trying to make some sense out of the document in his hand. It was like trying to solve a puzzle with only half the pieces. After another twenty minutes, he decided that his brain had reached the level where nothing else was making sense so he went home.

About mid-morning on Saturday Ricoh was up and talking with his crew about the party. He touched base first with Slick Willie to make sure that the room was available and ready to go. Then he reached out to PK to see what goodies he was arranging to have available for his guests. Assured that the guests would want for nothing, Ricoh moved on to wondering about what this big deal could be about. He was remembering some time back when he was trying to make some connections in New York to get a foothold on that market. It didn't go very well then, because somebody by the name of Bumpy was totally in control and there was no room for any new entries into the area. But the good thing that came out of that venture was that he met this Alivedi Leisar who seemed to be interested in him and told him then to just be patient that his time would come. Big Al, as he was known, was well connected in

NY and also a mover and shaker in the business. For Al to come all the way across the river looking for him specifically, Rick knew must be an indication of something that could set him up for life. With these thoughts in mind, he settled back on his couch and a broad smile came across his face. What he failed to see is that embedded in the name of his NY visitor was something sinister.

Over at the Peterson house, it was another normal Saturday. Sarafina was still feeling elated about the last CONN meeting and how Mr. Long had stepped up to identify some of the C's. She was really thrilled that people in the community were beginning to take an interest in what her group was doing and deciding to pitch in. Jameel and Cinque were riding a virtual high still bragging about how the "Jag's" had pulled off the biggest upset of the year last night at the stadium. All in all it was a good morning for the Petersons.

About 11:30 Sarafina asked Jameel to go down and get the mail. When he returned the pile of envelopes in his hand was a bit unusual. As Sarafina took them and started looking through, what had been a good morning started to change. She noticed from the very first one from the hospital that this was a bill for services rendered during Jameel's stay. When she looked at what the charges were going to be for her, she immediately felt feint and had to sit down. Getting by that one, she moved on to open the second one.

This one was not from the hospital, but from a private physician who had assisted in the surgery and was also billing her. Right under that one was another one from a Dr. who was the surgical anesthesiologist. If there was any comfort coming, the next envelope was from the Gateway Company insurance agent. In that letter she was advised that her coverage had been terminated as a result of her leaving the company and they would only pay for a small portion of the expenses. Looking at what they would cover and what the bills totaled, she just sat down speechless.

Jameel noticed the change of expression on his mother's face and asked her what was wrong. She showed him the bills and he too became depressed. She tried to assure him that they would get through it, but he couldn't see how. Knowing that she was out of work he was not convinced about her enthusiasm. She finally said to him:

"Well first thing Monday, I'm going down to that unemployment office and get signed up for those checks. I hope they can give me something right away."

Jameel then said:

"Mom, maybe I can get a job and help."

"Thank you son, but les jus see how Monday goes and then we'll talk 'bout that."

Cinque not being aware of what was going on continued in his jovial mood and enjoyed his day. Jameel came into the bedroom and just looked at him. Rather than interrupt his high spirits he just kept the knowledge to himself and decided to wait until Monday before telling him anything.

Sarafina's mind was racing through a thousand thoughts about how she was going to get through this, but nothing seemed to comfort her. She knew that even when she started collecting any unemployment checks due her it would not be enough to pay the medical bills and still continue to provide food and shelter for her and the boys.

Depression began to set in, but then she said to herself:

"Why am I feeling like this? My God has never let me down before."

She then reached for her bible and thumbed through the Book of Psalms. Finding one that gave her the relief she sought, she put it down and tried to sleep.

That night as the time approached for the big party to kick off at the Bricks, cars began to flood the area looking for parking spots. There were all kinds of vehicles coming into the complex from high-end luxury rides to small hybrids. As was the mixture of cars so was the admixture of people. There was an assortment of women bundled in long coats who were scantily clad underneath looking for a good time and just as many men who were there to make sure they had one. As they piled into the utility room of Building #1, the B's DJ was already kicking the party into full swing with the latest dance tunes. Ricoh and his crew greeted their guests and directed each one to an area of the room according to their pleasure. It didn't take long before smoke filled the room and the aroma of a familiar plant manifested itself in all who entered. After a short time, the music was rocking at a decibel level that should have been painful to a conscious person, but the hypnotic spell cast over the area prevented all affected minds from being aware that there was anything wrong. Most of the group had gone into one area or another at which either a beverage was available or a line or joint of something else. It didn't appear that anyone was having nothing but a good time as some of the couples started to disappear into the corridors of the building. At several junctures it was not too hard to see what was going on. Unabashed and unconcerned about anyone looking in the shadows of the storage bins, couples began engaging in activities that have been around since woman was first introduced to man on this planet.

Ricoh and PK were still mingling with the crowd when Big Al and several of his cronies entered the room. One of Rick's soldiers spotted them and rushed over to alert him. Ricoh immediately broke off his conversation and went over to the new guests.

"Hey Al, I thought you said 9:00 O'clock."

"I did man, but I jus wanna make sure you had enough time to get the party in full swing. Why don you turn my boys onto what chu got for `em an then we can go talk."

Ricoh then turned to one of his soldiers and whispered in his ear. The soldier motioned to a couple of the women who were just waiting around to be called and they came over. Grabbing the arms of Al's men, they walked off disappearing into the heart of the crowd.

"Okay Al we can go over there."

He pointed to a secluded portion of the room that had been kind of cordoned off. Although it was in the room, it was not like it was a part of it. Al looked at the area and said:

"Yeah man, thas fine."

Al and his lieutenant, Ricoh and PK headed off to the corner. "Okay man whas this all about?" Ricoh said.

"Check this out." Al said as he handed a piece of paper to Ricoh. "Whas this?"

"Read it man, you can read right?"

"Look like a whole bunch of mumbo jumbo to me, man what it mean?"

"Those are codes giving details for a very large shipment of unstepped on stuff comin in next Friday at the docks."

"How you get this?"

"Don you worry `bout that? If you can get yo people together to pick it up, we can all go fishing for a long time afta."

"How much it worth on the street?" Ricoh asked. "You lookin at over $1 Mill."

"How we gonna do this man?"

"Das why I came to you, I thought you could handle it. Was I wrong?"

"Naw man we kin do it, I jus need time to git a plan together. Now explain to me what these codes mean."

Big Al started breaking down what all the various codes in the document meant and how and when the shipment was due to arrive. It was going to be up to Ricoh and his crew to come up with the plan on how to get the goods off the docks and across the border. Ricoh was so excited inside that his head was spinning. Not wanting to show his anxiety to Big Al he made an excuse to get away for a minute so he could recompose himself.

"Hey Al, I gotta make a run, I'll be right back" he said. "Yeah sure man, but don take too long. I'll be right here."

Ricoh disappeared from the room and went down to Willie's apartment. He knocked on the door but there was no response. He knocked harder this time and hollered.

"Willie its Rick, open up."

Finally the door open and a half dressed Willie looked out. "What chu want man, can't you see I'm busy?"

Ricoh peeped over his shoulder to see the half dressed woman he was entertaining. "Sorry man, I jus needed to get outta the party for a minute. Here I want you to stash this for me until afta its over, then I'll come get it."

Willie looked at the paper with all the codes and said: "Whas this garbage?" "Neva mind jus stash it, I'll explain later. See ya."

Willie took the paper closed his door and went back to his business. Not knowing what it was, the paper was thrown on the floor near the couch and soon Willie was riding again.

When he got back to where Big Al was, he saw that Al had moved to a section of the room where the beverages were flowing. He apologized for taking too long, but Al was in a good mood and said no apology was necessary. They continued in the midst of the crowd having a good time and Al said that he would expect to hear from Ricoh by Tuesday about his plan. He also cautioned Ricoh, that there would be no room for error on this move. It was a one-time shot and it had to be perfect in execution or they would all wind up not seeing Saturday. Ricoh assured him that his plan would be golden and there would be no margin for error. Al feeling more confident after Rick spoke said that he knew from when they first met, he could count on him. He even went on further to say that once Ricoh signed on with him, his future would be assured. This sounded real good to Ricoh at the time, but he had no idea what Alivedi Leisar really meant.

By the time the early morning hours came, the party had ended and the crowd dispersed. Even though the noise was loud and the crowd was less than discreet as they left, the Bricks residents had already reconciled themselves to the fact that it was just another one of those gang activities and there was nothing to be done about it.

Ricoh made his way back over to Willie's and banged on the door. This time he struggled to the door quickly and opened it. Willie looking like he had been drained of his last drop of blood, with a tired voice invited Ricoh in.

"Man, I'm not stayin all I want is that paper I gave you before."

Willie turned around trying to keep his balance and remember what he did with it, hesitated for a minute to gather himself. Remembering where he thought he placed it he moved over to the lamp table by the couch. He turned on the light and looked on the table. Not seeing it there, he started to panic and then saw it on the floor. He didn't want Ricoh to see that it was on the floor, so he started coughing and bending over. So much so that he was able to pick up the paper without drawing attention.

"Here man, here it is. Whas that all about?"

"This is somethin big comin down that might get you some big bucks. I'll fill you in later."

Of course Willie got all excited about this when he heard big bucks and his strength seemed to return.

"When you gonna tell me?"

"Soon" Ricoh said. "Soon" and he left.

Sunday morning found Sarafina waking up not feeling refreshed at all. Thoughts about all the bills she received yesterday stayed with her during the night and prevented her from entering into the REM sleep she needed. She believed deep down inside that everything would be all right, but there was something in the timing of all the events that had been happening lately that had her wondering. She eased out of bed and made her way to the bathroom. The boys were not up yet and she thought she could enjoy just a moment of solitude before they came to life. She then made her way to the kitchen and had her morning coffee. Not in the mood to fix a big breakfast, she contemplated what else they could eat. Then it was decided this was going to be a cereal and toast morning for everybody.

She then made her way back to bed and slept for another hour. By this time the boys were up and wondering about breakfast. Since they hadn't smelled anything coming out of the kitchen, Jameel went knocked on her door and asked if she was all right. When she confirmed that she was but just a little tired, he went back to the kitchen and told Cinque that mom was tired so we have to get something for ourselves. Cinque not happy to hear that because his taste buds were prepared for his usual pancakes grumbled a bit but settled down to eat his bowl of cereal.

Along about the time it would be to start getting ready for church, the boys noticed that mom had not said anything to them about preparing. Not wanting to push the issue, they both just lay on their beds watching TV waiting for the word. After an hour, and nothing, Jameel got up and said:

"Mom we ain goin to church?"

"No not today baby, I'm still very tired. I think I'm just gonna relax today. I'll call Rev. Joyner tomorrow."

Jameel inwardly was not disappointed, but he said in a somber voice: "Okay mom if you don want to," and he went back in to challenge Cinque to a video NFL football game. The balance of the day saw Sarafina trying to busy herself with things to take her mind off her situation. She got out her notes from the last meeting that Lydia had prepared for her and as she read them, she did get a boost from the progress she could see was being made by the group. What made her especially happy was the feeling that since Lt. Meeker now had something concrete to go on he could soon be bringing in some of those C guys off the streets. She was unaware that the lieutenant had already raided the store and didn't find what he went there for. She also didn't know that picking up the two men Malcolm identified could be done, but the police couldn't hold them long without some other hard evidence. For right now though, she was in a better mood and looking forward to going down to the unemployment office bright and early tomorrow to start her checks coming. Somewhat comforted by what she had read in the meeting notes, Sarafina had a decent night's sleep and was ready to go.

It was Monday morning and she was up early as if headed to work. The boys were up too and going through their regular routines. They finished what they had to do and were off to school right on schedule. She followed right behind them and walked out to the parking lot. Still being somewhat cautious before getting into her car, she reminded herself not to be overly reactive to the thoughts she had been having. She did a casual look over of the car and got in. She wasn't exactly sure where the unemployment office was, but she knew that it was somewhere down on 8th avenue. She believed that it was in the same block as City Hall on 8th, so she headed in that direction. She had the address in the packet that was given to her with her severance papers, but there were no directions on there. Once she got into the area she drove past the building and sure enough it was just about where she thought it would be. She turned into their parking lot and luckily someone was going out just as she was coming in. As she pulled into the space she noticed that the sign in front of her read that parking in this space was limited to 2 Hours. Since she had no idea how long this process would take, she wondered whether she should leave her car there. Looking at her watch she noted the time and decided to take a chance. She would ask inside about how strict they were with parking enforcement and based on what she heard would move the car or not.

It was a little before 9:00 AM and there were several people there like herself waiting to start unemployment claims. Finally when her number was called and she had the opportunity to sit down with a counselor, her first question was about the parking. She had already been there about twenty minutes and was starting to get a little concerned about how much longer this was going to take. The counselor assured her that for this first visit she would just be filling out a bunch of papers and then be directed to come back tomorrow for the orientation. The whole thing shouldn't take more than another fifteen minutes so she was in good shape. Her mind being eased a bit she focused more on what the young man was telling her. He noted all of her documents and asked her to complete a questionnaire that she filled out quickly and handed back to him. He was entering her data into his computer when he asked her whether she left the job voluntarily. When she said no, he looked at her and said that it had been reported that she had quit. Stunned, she answered the young man and said:

"Oh no, I was fired. For no reason for that matter."

The young man just noted her statement and then told her that he would have to consult with his supervisor for a decision on how to proceed. Sarafina then looked at her watch again and thought this might take longer than she thought. In a few minutes the young man came back and told her not to worry about it the claim would be entered and if there is a problem she would be notified. He also told her that her first check would be issued within a week after she completed the orientation tomorrow. He set up her appointment and then told her that was it for now and he would see her back here tomorrow at 9:30 AM.

Feeling better that she had at least started the process she looked around the room at all the people who were there seeking help. She wondered to herself, are all of these people out of work. If so, how hard is it going to be to find another job? She was consoled a bit when she overheard someone saying that most of the people there were coming in for Social Security assistance or Welfare help. She shuddered at the thought that it's possible she could be coming back in the near future seeking protection under that same umbrella. When she got back to her car she was well within the 2 Hour limit. Just as she pulled out, someone else was waiting to pull in. She made a mental note to allow herself some extra time tomorrow, knowing that parking was going to be an issue.

At police headquarters that morning Lt. Meeker came in with a tired look on his face. He too had not slept well since the raid and was pondering what it was he was going to tell his captain and the judge that issued the warrant. He walked into his office fixed a cup of coffee and sat down at his desk. Minutes later before he was really ready, the intercom buzzed and before responding he knew who it was.

"Lt. Meeker, this is the captain can you come down to my office for a minute?" "Yes captain I'll be right there."

Dreading the long walk, he was still preparing in his mind what he was going to say. He had the document in his hand, but was feeling extremely hard pressed to lay the weight of his find from the raid on this as good evidence. It really didn't tell the police much and it certainly didn't prove anything. He got to the door and the captain motioned him in.

"How are you this morning, Lt?" the captain said. "I'm okay sir how are you?" he offered.

"Feeling good my boy just wanted to hear about your action on Friday. How did it go?"

A big lump came into the lieutenant's throat and he had difficulty in getting the next words out.

"Well sir, we pulled off the search fine without incident, but when we got in there we found nothing, not even a pop gun."

The expression on the captain's faced changed quickly and a scowl came over it. "You mean I authorized overtime for six men not including you and Calloway, and you're telling me you got nothing."

"Well no that's not exactly right sir. We did come up with something we can use, but not the weapons that we were looking for."

"What do you mean something, it better be good."

Lt. Meeker laid the document on the captain's desk and started explaining what he thought he had. When he finished he wasn't sure whether he had appeased his anger or whether he just set the stage for his Waterloo. Surprisingly, the captain read more into the document than even the lieutenant had conceived. He seemed to recall that there was an investigation just about three years ago which involved a large drug shipment coming into the airport that never got intercepted nor was the case ever resolved. As far as he knew, this could be the link to that case. He told the lieutenant to step up his search to find the other half of this document and he may have something to solve a lot more than he's aware of. Feeling thoroughly relieved, he knew his blood pressure was coming back down to a normal range and he quickly agreed with the captain and got out of his office.

When he got back to his own office he got on the intercom and talked to Sgt. Calloway telling him what had just transpired in the captain's office. Calloway was happy to hear that the lieutenant still possessed his backside and agreed to immediately increase the intensity on the search for the missing piece of the document. Calloway asked whether the lieutenant thought the warehouse should be the next target for the search. Meeker replied that he wasn't sure at this point. He wanted to talk some more to that Mr. Long. He still believed that the man knows more than what he's telling.

Meanwhile, Calloway volunteered that the witness they have been pursuing from the Bricks Complex was finally ready to give some information provided the cash was right. Lt. Meeker wondered at this point, whether he was still needed. Calloway thought that it couldn't hurt, but the matter was put on hold until after another conversation with Mr. Long was had.

The next day Sarafina arrived at the unemployment office right on time. Her good fortune with finding a parking space was holding and she found one almost as soon as she entered the lot. When she got inside the building she was directed to a room where several others were assembled and waiting for the instructor to enter. After a short while in walked a man who appeared to be in his early to mid fifties; fairly tall of stature with handsome rugged features. His hair was well groomed, graying slightly at the temples that gave him a very distinguished look. As soon as he walked in, Sarafina was strangely attracted to him and had a hard time in focusing on what he was saying. She had not had this kind of feeling in so many years that it disturbed her. She must have drawn his attention because he looked at her, so she thought, in a way that he was not looking at the other women in the class.

"Good morning everyone" he said.

"My name is Asantani Leisar and I'll be your instructor/counselor for the next few weeks or until we can place you in another position. You are here this morning to begin an orientation as to what you can expect from your unemployment benefits and also what resources will be made available to you while you are looking for re-employment. We are going to watch a film that provides most of the information that you'll need and then I'm going to hand out the materials that they discuss in the film for your records. After the film you will be broken down into small groups and assigned to a specific counselor for follow-up. You will be scheduled to come here twice a week for the next month for training and also job interviews. If you should find something on your own during that period, of course, your work here is done. Okay. Are there any questions? Hearing none let us begin." He then started the film. Sarafina was having a hard time reconciling her feelings with the purpose for why she was there. She couldn't help herself, but the attraction that she had for this man was not something she was ready for. She tried to keep herself under control, but whenever he looked in her direction, she was sure that he could see right through her and it was apparent how she felt. As the class went on and the film ended, it just so happened that she was assigned to his counseling group. In the small group he had a chance to interact more closely with his charges. There were three women and two men in his group and he arranged to meet with them one on one for a few minutes prior to each group counseling session each week. The thrill of knowing that she would be talking to him one on one was setting off thoughts that were totally foreign or at least had been dormant for a long period.

When her first one on one session came she was stumbling for words so much so that he asked her if she was okay. Slightly embarrassed she composed herself and told him that she had not had to do this kind of stuff for a long time. He was very observant and quickly calmed her by telling her that she had nothing to fear and that through him she would see a great change. She felt such confidence in what he was saying and his voice seemed to be so soothing that she was ready to believe whatever he said. He asked her to not call him Mr. Leisar but to call him Asa. If Sarafina could have only seen that embedded in his name was something that should have set off warning flares throughout her whole body she would have run, not walked out of that office immediately. But this, for now, was not to be and she was already on the path in a direction that would challenge her very soul.

After only a few sessions with Asa the relationship became less formal and more intimate. She was invited to have dinner with him. There was no convincing her that he was not as attracted to her as she was to him. She tried at first to say no, but then her heart over ruled her mind and she agreed. It was arranged that she would meet him at a restaurant on the outskirts of the city on a night following one of her sessions.

Sarafina before going out, explained to the boys that she was having dinner with someone she met at the unemployment office. Jameel, being somewhat protective of his mom, wanted to know all about this man, but was assured that he was okay.

Accepting this for now, he backed off the questions and just wanted to know when she was coming home. She gave him as much information as she thought he needed to know and then went out on her date. Jameel sat with Cinque that night and they discussed the changes they saw taking place with their mom. Neither one was comfortable with this new status, but neither did they want to see mom not have a new man in her life. Jameel especially since he was really getting close to Dolitha, understood how Sarafina could be feeling and that his mom had been alone too long.

Over the next few weeks, the bills were continuing to pile up and even though the unemployment benefit had started and the checks were coming, Sarafina had not been placed in a new position and her enthusiasm was waning about her prospects. She was changing right before the boy's eyes and they weren't sure what to do about it. She was cooking much less and staying away from home much more. They even were surprised one night when they noticed her coming in with the smell of alcohol on her breath. Her personality had also made 180 degree turn and she was less attentive to their schoolwork or even the CONN's that she loved so well. She talked more and more about Asa and how he was going to help her out and where he was taking her. It seemed to them, though they couldn't be sure, that it was because of him that she was going down this new road.

Her continued absence from New Life Temple of God and the fact that the CONN's with the New Life collective group was beginning to fall apart for lack of leadership raised some questions in Rev. Joyner's mind about what may be going on with Sarafina. He called the house several times, but she would not take his calls. She told the boys to tell him that she was through with the CONN's and the church and she was moving in a new direction. When the reverend heard this he became highly suspicious about what may be happening. He asked the boys one day when he called whether she had met anybody new recently. The boys confirmed that she had and explained to him what had been going on. Reverend Joyner made up in his mind that he was going to go over to the house and see if he could talk with her.

On the night that he went by, when he was approaching her house he saw her come out and get into a late model sedan with a man at the wheel. The way she was dressed sent a shock wave down his spine and he knew right then what was happening. Sarafina had not been one when she was active in the church to pay any special attention to putting on a lot of make up or dressing in any provocative way. Although she was a natural beauty with golden skin tone and a body that would make most women her age envious, she had not drawn attention to herself in years. The reverend, seeing her dressed in a most exposing fashion, realized that it could have been due to her loneliness and her long overdue need to correct that. But somewhere inside his head he fathomed that it was something much more than that. Given that she was on the verge of doing something big and giving glory to the one that had catapulted her to her new heights, he was convinced that there were some forces at work here that needed special attention.

Sarafina got in the car and kissed Asa right before the reverend's eyes. She didn't see him, but it probably wouldn't have mattered at this point whether she did or not.

Reverend Joyner still stunned turned around and headed to his church where he was going to go into special prayer for her. Asa pulled off with one arm around Sarafina and drove with the other. They were headed to what had become their favorite haunt for dinner and he was telling her all about something that he thought would be of interest to her. He was explaining to her that if she continued to follow him and submit to him, that he would make sure all of her bills would be paid and she would be on easy street. He also wanted to make sure that she was not going back to that church or the CONN's. In her dazed eyes and her hypnotic state of mind brought on by his smooth promises of security and easy living she couldn't see clearly where she was going.

At the restaurant the waiter, who was now accustomed to the couple coming in almost regularly, showed them to their dark secluded corner. To Sarafina this was the feeling of bliss that she had missed for so many years and she was taking every advantage of the opportunity to make up for lost time. Mr. Leisar, knowing that he was on the verge of another victory and adding one more to his trail of conquests, continued to ply her with promises of well being and ultimate serenity. He ordered their favorite wine, but this time asked the waiter to leave the bottle.

As the night went on and they both imbibed heavily, it seemed to her that this was about as romantic a setting as she could ever remember being involved in. As she reminisced in her mind what it used to be like when she was with her young soon to be husband and they used to go to the mountains where they loved to sit in the car and just watch the stars and the heavens, this moment was beginning to compare with that feeling. The hour was getting late, time moved by quickly and it was time for them to leave. He got the check and paid the bill. Sarafina told him that she wanted to first use the ladies room and then she would call her boys to let them know she was all right and she was coming home soon. He just smiled at her and acknowledged what she said. When she returned he was waiting with a broad smile and he asked if she was ready to go.

Before they got into the car he asked her if she really had to go home right away because there was something that he wanted to show her. She told him that she didn't have any curfew and asked what it was he wanted to show her. He then escorted her to the car and they got in. As they headed out of the parking lot she asked him where they were going and he said to his house. Even though her senses had been somewhat dulled by the alcohol circulating through her body, she became very aware of what was happening. She then laughingly said to him:

"What chu gonna show me?"

"Oh you'll see when we get there!" he said.

It wasn't too long before he pulled up into a townhouse develop-ment near the end of the city going toward the more affluent area of the suburbs.

He pulled into his driveway and helped her out. At this point she knew that she was more than just a little past the point in her drinking where she should have stopped. She stumbled a bit getting out of the car and when he grabbed hold of her they both laughed like little school children at a picnic. Once inside, she was impressed at the decor and asked where his decorator was, slyly referring to a possible woman's touch. He assured her that he was the decorator, the maid, the gardener and the cook. He led her over to a plush couch and planted her on it. She was still inquiring about what he was going to show her and then he said:

"Be patient while I go and get it. Can I fix you a drink?"

She knew good and well that the last thing she needed was another drink but for some reason "yes" came out of her mouth before she realized. He went to the bar and fixed her another glass of wine and brought it to her.

"Now for the grand showing," he said.

He left the living room went into his bedroom and brought back a large painting of a Roman orgy with Caligula at the center.

"This is quite valuable you know worth a lot of money."

Sarafina except for the scene itself wasn't quite sure what she was looking at from an art perspective, but just looking at the frame she could tell that it must be worth a lot.

"It's beautiful" she said.

"I'll give it to you if you become one of my followers" he said.

Sarafina wasn't quite sure what that meant, but at this point in the evening she was ready to follow him anywhere he wanted to go. He carefully lifted her up and took her into the bedroom where he turned on the sounds of romantic melodies with strings.

It was not long before Sarafina and the wine had decided that whatever will-be-will be and succumbed to the wiles of the night. Asa started to undress her with very little resistance and as he planted passionate kisses on her lips, she was melting into a dream state that she was sure must be heaven. The passion mounted and as he caressed her gently the curtain was about to drop on the final act, when she saw something unbelievable in the room. Something that her mind, suddenly sober, refused to admit, but she knew it was there. Shivering she tried to stop the act to see if she could get a better look at what she thought she was seeing, but it was too late so she gave in. She closed her eyes, but she could still see it.

Chapter 10 - Crossroads

In the past two weeks it seemed as if an ominous shadow had become a permanent part of nature's decor for the city. Where prior days had been beautiful and clear, the skies were now overcast and gloomy daily. The mood of the people generally reflected the weather pattern and where smiles had been present, they were now almost non-existent.

Something was happening, something they couldn't quite identify. The period in which the initial shootings had taken place in the vacant lot near the recreation center to the massacre that occurred at the Bricks Housing complex, was giving way to a pervasive feeling of despair.

What had seemed like a brief respite in the gang violence due to the rise of the CONN's popularity, the church community's involvement and stepped up police activity, was now a thing of the past and violent doings were again on the rise. The frustration felt by Lt. Meeker and his department in not finding the weapons cache they sought nor even coming close to finding the other half of a crucial document that could possibly provide the solution to his problem, was at an all time high. Since the presence of the Leisar brothers was now an integral part of both the B gang leader and the Peterson family, the connection between the pervasive gloom and the road to destruction was apparent.

Reverend Joyner, although aware that something was happening to one of his formerly stalwart church members, was challenged to know exactly who the man was that he saw her with on the night he came by the house. What he was sure of was that who ever the man was he was exerting an undue negative influence on her life and that as a minister of God it was his duty to find out. He prayed for her, he tried to reach out to her and also tried to minister to the boys as she began racing down hill to destruction. She however, still rejected his help and prevented making contact. The boys were caught in the middle not knowing what was happening to their mom, or who this man was that was controlling her.

On that Thursday night when she had gone to dinner with the man, they knew she was going out, but when she didn't return home early, they went into a state of panic. They tried calling her on the cell phone, but the message came back that the service had been temporarily interrupted. Jameel knew that the bills were piling up and some of them weren't getting paid, but he didn't know that this was one. He tried his best to comfort Cinque and keep him calm, but this wasn't easy. Cinque wanted to call the police right away. As it got later and later Jameel was tending toward listening to Cinque's appeal. He was about to make the call. At about 3:00 AM, the phone rang. Jameel answered.

"Jameel, this is mom are you guy's okay?"

The voice sounded shaky and the words were somewhat slurred. "Yeah mom, we okay where are you?"

"I'm at Asa's house an I'm okay. I'll be home first thing in the morning. Can you guys get to school okay?"

"Yeah, mom but you sure you aw-ight?"

"Yes baby, I'm fine now don you worry 'bout nuthin, I'll be home later." "Okay mom, bye."

She hung up the phone, but felt for the first time since the death of her husband years ago, really ashamed of leaving her boys home alone. She turned to Asa, who was lying beside her, and said:

"I don feel good 'bout this, don seem right. An you know I saw somethin in here last night. Somethin kinda scary."

He partially woke up turned to her and said in a raspy voice: "Scary, what are you talking about?"

"Just before you did me, I saw right there floatin near yo ceilin a big red dragon, with a lotta heads, a lotta teeth and a long swinging tail. He seem like he was comin for me."

"Now I know not to give you anymore of my special wine. You can't handle it. Think about what you're saying. If you saw something in the room, where did it go, and why didn't I see it."

She thought about it for a minute and then said:

"I know you mus be right, but it seemed so real, so very real."

"You just had a little too much wine. Now go back to sleep and I'll take you home soon. Remember I have to go into the office in the morning."

"Okay, but I can't forget what I saw."

She rolled over and went back to sleep, but the image remained in her mind.

Later on that morning down at police headquarters Lt. Meeker was once again in the captain's office explaining what the status was on his investigation.

"Captain we got enough to pick up this Hakeem guy and his chief Hammer, but I don't know how long we can hold them. Remember the eyewitness we had swears he saw the weapons come out of that Minute Mart store, but when we went there we found nothing. Now either they moved them out or there's more to that room than we discovered."

"What do you mean there's more to the room?"

"Well sir, even while we were there, I got the feeling that there may have been another part of the building that we didn't have access to; like a hidden room."

"Hidden room? What are we into secret compartments now? You been watching too many spy movies?"

"No sir, I really believe that there's more to that building than what we saw. I'm going down there again, unofficially and physically look at the length of the building and then remember where the room stopped that we entered. If they don't match, then I'll know there's something more."

"Well lieutenant you do that, but remember the mayor's on me again and I need to get him off. How's the search going for the other part of that document you showed me?"

"Nothing new yet, but I'm checking into that old warehouse over there on 5th avenue at the end of town, I think there may be a connection with the store. The other half could be hidden in there somewhere."

"Okay do it and keep me posted."

Lt. Meeker left his office and got into his car headed back to M&M's.

Jameel and Cinque got up feeling like they hadn't even been to sleep. For them it really felt strange getting up without mom being in the house and not receiving any last minute instructions for the day. Jameel was even contemplating not going to school at all, but the thought only lasted a moment as he remembered what Sarafina said about getting to school. They struggled through their normal routines and headed out the door. Scrambling down the stairs they were on their way when Rajon caught up with them and brought them up to date on the latest street knowledge.

How Rajon was privy to all the news he was able to report on Jameel could never figure out, but from past experience he knew that Rajon was seldom wrong. This time he was reporting on the party that had happened over at the Bricks recently and that some big time drug hustlers had come over from New York to the party. Jameel conceded that he knew about the party from the last football game they went to, but didn't know about the NY visitors. Rajon went on further to tell him that he thought the B's were getting into something heavy and that their recent recruiting at the grade school was part of an effort to get enough foot soldiers to carry out their plan. Jameel was only half way interested in what was being said because he knew that he had enough to think about with his own problems.

When they got to school Dolitha joined them before going to class. The usual casual conversation took place, but one note of importance surfaced. Dolitha said that her mom had seen "J's" mom down at the unemployment office a few times and that she saw her with one of the counselors regularly. Jameel was a little embarrased and wondered what exactly Dolitha was implying so he said to her.

"What chu mean by that?"

"Oh nothin, I was jus sayin they mus have a thing goin on." Jameel was a little peeved and said:

"You needa mine yo bidness 'bout my moms. What she does down there is hers." Dolitha felt real bad that she had brought it up and quickly told Jameel she was sorry. Even though he felt offended, he knew that what she said was true and he just wondered who else knew about it. The bell rang and the group broke up and went to class.

During school that day the tension had again escalated to a height that had not been there since before the 'Jags' had unexpectedly won the first round of the playoffs.

However, after the team's subsequent loss in the second round it seemed that the gangs were moving back to trying to annihilate each other on a regular basis. The B's were regaining their former strength and it was known that the balance of power was again restored. Skirmishes were happening in the cafeteria, in the parking lot and even in the hallways once again with regularity. Mr. Steinberg, who thought he had made some inroads to gaining the upper hand in maintaining peace, was once again frustrated at the sinking back to prior levels. And so it was that along with the gloom and doom overcast in the weather, the attitudes of the students reflected the same gloom and doom.

Something was happening. Something was happening outside that was definitely affecting the inside.

When Lt. Meeker got down to M&M's he parked around the corner and got out.

Since it was early in the day, there wasn't much going on as far as the usual activity that took place around the building outside. He walked up to the store and started to step off and measured the length of the building from front to back of where it started and where it ended. Then he went inside. The manager remembered who he was and asked him if he was doing another search. He told the manager no, but wanted to just casually look in that room again. The manager asked him if he had more of those papers for the search. He told the manager no, but he would get them again if he had to. Reluctantly, the manager opened the room and the lieutenant went inside. With the outside measurements fixed firmly in his mind, he stepped off the internal measurements. Suddenly the light in his head went on and he knew that where the wall ended in the room, was not where the building ended. He turned around, thanked the manager for his cooperation and went back to his car. Once back at his office he called the captain to let him know that his theory about the room was confirmed and that he was going to pick up Hakeem and Hammer and then if they didn't tell him the truth, he was going back into the room with a sledgehammer.

Mr. Asatani Leisar dropped Sarafina off at her apartment building and offered to take the painting he had given her upstairs. She politely declined telling him that she was thankful for the gift and that she could manage it. Inside her head though, she was thinking that she really didn't want any of the nosey neighbors who may be looking to see this man going up with her. He opened the car door and helped her out with it and then she disappeared into the building. The picture was a bit larger than the average wall rendering, so the effort required in getting it up the stairs was more challenging than she imagined. After a slight struggle she completed the climb and got to her door. Listening before she entered to see whether the boys might still be inside, hearing nothing she turned the key and went in.

Going straight to her bedroom she placed it on the floor where she intended to mount it on the wall. It was a curious thing. The more she looked at it, the more she got the feeling that there was something eerie about it. Once more as she looked deeper into the scene, the vision of the dragon popped in her mind and she shuddered. Quickly she turned around and wondered whether it was really just her imagination. Remembering that she had forgotten to get the mail she went back out and down to the mailbox. When she reached inside the box, she felt a large bulk package of envelopes wrapped in a rubber band. She grabbed the package and hurried back upstairs. Tearing off the rubber band she thumbed through the mail and with each successive one an overwhelming feeling of being inundated with debt surfaced. She opened one from the hospital that was an announcement of a third attempt to collect the debt and that the account was being turned over to a collection agency. Finally, there was a note on the bottom from the landlord requesting payment for this month's rent including the late charges. She knew that in her attempts to buy groceries and pay a part of some of the other bills, she had neglected to take care of the rent. Now the meager income for the month was exhausted. Feeling really depressed, she decided to go out around the corner to the liquor store and get herself some gin. She hadn't done this in so long, it felt strange when she walked in so she quickly made her purchase and returned home.

Sitting at the table staring at the bottle and the bills for several minutes she was contemplating whether this was what she really wanted to do. For some reason she felt compelled to go into the bedroom and look at the picture again. In the picture, it seemed as if the characters were having such a good time they were encouraging her to join them in the festivities. Feeling motivated to have some fun too she returned to the kitchen got a glass and poured a small amount of gin with tonic in it. Sipping slowly at first, the liquid felt warm and smooth going down. She turned on the radio and found an easy listening station that seemed to mellow her anxiety. Before long she was pouring another drink, even larger this time than the first and she was no longer sipping, but drank it down.

As time went by and the initial effects of the drinks kicked in, she made an attempt to get up from her chair and it hit her that she was extremely high. Feeling giddy and laughing she made her way to the living room having forgotten for the moment all about her troubles. She plopped down on the couch and between staring at the ceiling and just looking around the room and laughing to herself she noticed on the coffee table in front of her were the notes from the last CONN's meeting. She had not attended a meeting in a while and when she read the notes it seemed funny to her all the things they discussed.

She was really amused that she could have even been involved in this stuff and asked herself what for?

It wasn't long before her private party was ending and a glaze settled over her eyes and then it was – lights out. Her head hit the cushion on the couch and she settled into a deep sleep. In her mind, in its inebriated state she was dancing with a man whose face wasn't clear, but she was having so much fun. And then he took her flying over the clouds high into the sky up to the top of a mountain floating above the earth. She could see from her vantage point the whole world and he was offering it to her if she would be his completely. She was reveling in the feeling and basking in the moment, but something deep within was telling her that this couldn't be real.

It was 3:45 PM when the boys walked in and saw her lying on the couch. They could smell the odor of liquor on her so Jameel decided not to wake her. He went in the kitchen and saw the bottle still sitting on the table so he took it and placed it in a cabinet. Cinque kept asking why she was doing this, but Jameel really didn't have a good answer. After putting away the bottle he looked in the refrigerator to see what they might have to eat.

There was nothing there to really make a meal out of and Jameel decided right then that he had to do something about this situation. His birthday was coming up in a month and he would be turning eighteen. In his mind, it was time for him to take care of his mom. He was feeling as depressed at this moment as he thought she was and seeing her in this new condition that neither he nor Cinque could understand, was getting to him. He looked in one of the cabinets and found there was still a large jar of peanut butter and some jelly and fortunately some bread left. He told Cinque that this was going to be it for tonight, but tomorrow he was going to get some money somehow. Cinque, not in the mood to disagree nodded his head and ate his sandwich knowing this wasn't going to satisfy his appetite at all.

When she finally woke up it was 6:30 and she felt like a construction project was underway in her head. She struggled to stand up and staggered into the bathroom. Grabbing a handful of aspirins she gulped them down and then went into the kitchen. She was looking around to see what the boys might have eaten and when she saw the remnants of peanut butter and jelly she just fell into the table chair and wept. Jameel hearing her crying came out of his room and went to her.

"Mom, mom wassa matta?"

"Oh "J" I'm so sorry. Are you still hungry?" "No, mom we'll be okay. We'll be fine."

Through her tears she just looked at him and then hugged him. Cinque feeling the pangs of hunger had already gone to sleep.

"Tomorrow mom, I'm gonna fine someway to get some money." "What chu gonna do?"

"I dono yet but I'll do somethin."

"You ain gonna drop outta school." "Naw, but I'll get somethin afta."

"Okay baby, but you stay in school an finish, right?" "Yeah mom, right."

"All right. I'm gonna go lay down in my bed, I don feel so good. You still got cereal and milk for breakfast right?"

" Yeah, we be okay you go lay down."

Sarafina eased out of the chair and gingerly made her way to her bed.

Jameel continued watching her and knew something was doing this to her, but wasn't sure what. He went back into his room lay on his bed staring up at the ceiling and wondered what it was that he was going to do to get some money.

This Saturday morning was a little different than most, first because Sarafina was nursing a hangover that was new for her and second because Jameel had gotten up real early and went out. By the time she was up he had been gone for some time. Cinque was still sleeping when she poked her head in the boy's room and asked where Jameel was. Cinque not knowing that he had even left was confused about the question. Sarafina went in the kitchen to try and get herself together made some coffee and sat down. She remembered her conversation last night with Jameel and was wondering just what it was that he was going to do. She called Cinque and asked him if he wanted breakfast, but he said that he would get it and went back to sleep. She then went in the living room, turned on the TV.

Meanwhile Jameel had gone down to the big Supermarket to try and get some work. He went inside and talked with the store manager, but was told that he would like to help him out, but there was nothing open right now. He filled out an application and was told that he would be called when something opened. Disappointed he walked out went over to the local car wash. There he was told that they had all the guys they needed for that day, but if he wanted to come back before 7:00 AM tomorrow, they may be able to put him on. He agreed with that. When he asked the manager about working during the week, he was told that they could only use him during the day because they closed at 5:00 PM. Knowing that couldn't work for him because he couldn't leave school so he walked out. Unable to think of anyplace else to try he went home. Before getting there he stopped by Rajon's house.

Being it was really early he was hesitant about knocking on his door, but decided that this was important so he proceeded. He knocked several times and then heard in a rough voice:

"Whose at my door?"

"Hey man it's me, Jameel open up."

"Man you crazy it ain even 9:00 O`clock whas up?" "Sorry to git you up this early, but I need help." "Aw-ight man come on in what chu need?

As many times as Jameel had come to Rajon's place he never saw any adults there and he wondered where his parents were. He started to ask, but then thought it was none of his business so he forgot about it.

"Hey man you know my moms lost her job an we really gittin low on funds. I needa fine somethin to get some money quick. Can you help?"

"Yeah I know how you can get some big bucks fast, but I dono if you wanna do it."

"What chu talkin 'bout?"

"I'm talkin 'bout hookin up with Hakeem an them an move some stuff." "You mean sell some drugs?"

"What chu think?" "Man I can't do that?"

"You need a lotta money right?" "Yeah."

"You need it now right?" "Yeah."

"Then thas what chu gotta do?"

Jameel just lowered his head and was torn between knowing what he needed and knowing right from wrong. He hesitated for a long moment and then asked Rajon how he got in. Rajon told him that his best shot since he knew that Sista had a thing for him was to play up to her and she could get him in quick. Jameel really wasn't in favor of this, but when Rajon told him how much some of those guys were making, he started to give it some serious thought. He thanked Rajon for his advice and said that he would talk to Sista and see what happens. Then he left and went home.

When he got home Sarafina wanted to know where he had been so he explained that he went to a few places to see if he could find a job. She was very proud of him and told him that she appreciated him wanting to help, but that she was going to get Asa to help out with the bills and the food. Jameel told her that he didn't like that man and didn't want his help, but she smiled at him and calmed him down by telling him that she liked him and that he could really help them. Jameel looked at her a long time and then through his maturing adult eyes he realized that he could no longer view her as just his mother, but she was a woman with needs and she was hooked on Asa, so he backed off.

In his study that night Reverend Joyner was preparing his sermon for Sunday and he was contemplating his subject matter. He was very concerned about how the group that had been moving so smoothly in a positive direction and gaining momentum toward bringing a change for good in the neighborhood had gone in a reverse direction since Sarafina left. He knew some of the members in the CONN's and when they had joined forces with his church members he thought that this was the answer to their prayers.

What was missing he knew was the leadership and strong belief in the cause that she brought, but he wondered why some of the other members had not been able to step up and fill the void. He decided to call Lydia and talk to her about it and see if there was something that he could include in his message tomorrow that would stir up and motivate the people to rise again.

"Hello, this is Lydia."

"Hello Miss Spencer, this is Reverend Joyner from New Life Temple how are you?" "Oh hi reverend I'm fine how are you?"

"I'm blessed thank you for asking. Listen if you have a few minutes I'd like to talk to you about Sister Peterson. Do you have a minute?"

"Yes sure how can I help you?"

"Well I was wondering whether you have talked to her lately and if so how is she doing?

I've tried to call her several times, but she won't take my calls. I even went over to her place but she was out. She has not come to a service in some time and I'll admit I'm worried about her."

"Reverend I tried calling her too, but her sons say she's not there when I know she is. I haven't tried to go by there because I felt she didn't want to be bothered with us no more. She hasn't been to several of the last meetings and the group is about to break up because they don't feel like we're getting anything accomplished. I've tried to hold it together, but I don't have her excitement to move the people like she can. As far as I know she's okay, but I actually haven't seen her. What are you gonna do?" "I have her on my prayer list and tomorrow I'm going to talk to the congregation about what happens to the sheep when the Sheppard is struck. It would be nice if you could come to my service. Do you have a church?"

"Well reverend I ain been big on goin to anybody's church in quite a while, but maybe I will come and hear what you got to say."

"Good you may want to get some of your other members to come also; it could be worth your time. I look forward to seeing you there."

"Okay I'll see what I can do. Goodnight." "Goodnight! Be blessed!"

Reverend Joyner hung up with Lydia and returned to planning his message. Before he continued though he got down on his knees and went into prayer asking for divine guidance on what his message should be to galvanize the people and get them back on the right track. He had already used Nehemiah as a role model and he wondered whether to revisit that sermon again or pursue his thinking about the shepherd and the sheep. In the midst of his prayer when he was in deep meditation, the answer came to him as the Holy Spirit entered and the answer was as clear as fresh water.

The message should be just as when Jesus was organizing his followers, even his personally chosen disciples, when the time came for him to reveal to them that he would be captured and put to death, they would deny Him and be scattered and the cause for which they were being prepared would suffer. He had to carefully word his message because he couldn't refer to Sarafina in any manner that would compare her to Jesus, but he could use the example of leadership and a cause in which he could say to the people that though the shepherd may be taken away for a time, it is the cause itself that needs to go on in anticipation of divine help from above. He felt confident that he could deliver this with conviction and motivate the group to reassert themselves and move forward.

On Sunday the church was as crowded as it had been since the violence began. Although the violence had not only returned, but had reached new levels and the people were fearful once again about where it was all going, they never stopped coming out to hear the word. And today they wanted to know what the pastor was going to say and do about it. Even though many of the members had initially flocked to the cause and had gone to some of the early joint meetings with the CONN's, the interest had waned and many were feeling it was hopeless. They came here today to find something that would re-ignite them and give them the hope they needed in order to continue.

When the time came for Reverend Joyner to step behind the sacred desk, all eyes were on him and ears attentive to his voice. He began by reminding them of what he had said earlier about what Nehemiah had done for his people and what their responsibility to the community should be. Then he launched headlong into the message. He laid the groundwork by first commending all who had come out to the meetings and participated in the early efforts to bring about a change in the community. He then went into the story about Jesus as the Shepherd leading the sheep and how when he was taken down the sheep would scatter.

His delivery was powerful and the words hit home to all that were in attendance. He was confident that for now he had achieved his mission and the people were ready to go again. However, as he looked around the congregation, he saw Lydia and what he believed were some of the CONN's members, but he didn't see Sarafina. He knew that the fight was going to be difficult because she was still the battlefield captain. However, greater than this he also knew that the battle that they were fighting was not with flesh and blood, but with powers beyond what they could see. So he reconciled himself to be content with what had been achieved today and pray that the Lord would hear their collective cry and answer according to His schedule.

In the Peterson house that Saturday night a real test of fortitude took place. Sarafina knew that the cupboard was practically bare and she had to do something. Searching in pocketbooks, drawers and clothing she scrounged up enough funds to go food shopping and get a few TV dinners, some milk and eggs. It was nothing substantial, but they were able to get through the night. Cinque was especially cranky, because his voracious appetite was not appeased, but he kept his complaints to a low key. Jameel was even more determined to remedy this situation on Monday one way or another. Sarafina told the boys that tomorrow she was going to Asa and get some help.

Sunday afternoon Sarafina made the call to Asa and after a brief conversation she was getting ready to go out. Jameel asked her where she was going and she told him she was going to get the help that she talked to them about last night. Jameel wasn't quite sure what that meant, but he said okay. A short time later she pulled into Asa's driveway and he met her at the door.

"Hi, how are you?" he said as he invited her in. "I'm okay for now, but I need some help."

"Of course, let me take your coat and we'll talk."

He removed her coat and motioned her to the couch. To Sarafina somehow the place looked different than it did when she was here the last time. Strangely, she felt as though the allure that was there before was gone, but it was still very nice. In her mind she attributed the difference to the glasses of wine that had carried her into a dreamscape.

"Now, how can I help you?"

"You said when I first came down to the center that I would be back to work by now. I ain even had no interview."

"Patience, patience, you know the job market is slow right now. Anyway, I have something in mind for you that I'm working on and it's going to take a little time to develop."

"Oh yeah, whas that?"

"I can't tell you about it yet, but you'll see. Just have a little patience." She felt a little better for the minute, but then she remembered why she came.

"You know that UE check jus ain enough for me to pay my bills an feed my boys, I need more."

"How much more?"

"Well right now, I need to get some food so we can eat until the next check comes." "I'm sure I can help you with that."

He got up from the couch and went into the bedroom then came back with a $100 dollar bill.

"Will this do?"

Sarafina looked at the bill and was surprised to see the denomination.

"Yeah this will get us through 'till then." she said as she took the bill and placed it in her pocketbook.

"Okay that's that now why don't you just relax and let me fix you a drink." Sarafina tried to say no, but her mouth and her mind were not in synch. She took the wine, drank it and that was the start of an instant replay of the previous encounter.

A couple of hours later, she looked up at the bedroom wall clock and said that she had to go because she had to go to the supermarket. He smiled and asked her if she wanted him to go with her. She politely said no and thanked him again for his generosity. He responded by reminding her that he had some other things that he was going to do for her. She left with mixed feelings. Happy that she had gotten what she came for, but unsettled because she knew what she was doing wasn't right. She left went straight to the supermarket and stocked up on groceries for the next week.

"Jameel, Cinque come help with the groceries," she hollered through the half open door.

The boys hearing groceries came running out of their room and headed down to the car. There they lifted up several bags of food and brought them quickly back up the stairs. Once inside, they rumbled through the bags looking for deserts and other goodies, but saw none. However, there was one small cake that she had placed in a separate bag and was bringing it up herself. When she got in the apartment she reminded the boys that they were still on a very tight budget and this stuff was going to have to last for a while. Once she got settled, she went back in the kitchen and started to cook. Jameel and Cinque were delighted to inhale the aroma of some home cooking, again. That evening they enjoyed a meal like they hadn't had in some time. Cinque, with his stomach completely full, thanked his mom several times and even volunteered to do the dishes.

Jameel, was also quite satisfied, but kept wondering how she got the money. At school that Monday, Jameel could hardly wait to get to his lunch period so that he could look for Sista. All last night he kept dwelling on what Rajon said about the kind of money he could make with the C's. Sista, he believed had the same lunch break he did, but he couldn't recall ever seeing her in the cafeteria. Maybe she always went out he thought, since there were a few little deli's in the area. While he was diligently searching for Sista, someone else was doing likewise for him. Dolitha spotted him first and practically ran over to catch him. When she caught up with him she grabbed his arm and said:

"Where you runnin to?"

"Hey girl, how ya doin? Listen I can't eat wit chu today, I gotta fine somebody." "Oh yeah who? Sista."

Even though she was only joking, it caught Jameel a little off guard and he stammered.

"Naw, n, no, I'm lookin for Rajon."

Dolitha picked up immediately on the hesitation and questioned him a little more, fearing that she might have been right in her statement.

"What chu need Rajon for? Don he usually eat in the cafeteria?"

"Yeah, but I think he went out today. Look I'll catch up wit chu later, okay?" "Aw-ight, see ya afta school."

She let him go and went into the lunchroom and met up with some of her girlfriends. She wasn't at all satisfied with his answers and was growing more suspicious each passing minute.

Jameel ran out of the building and down to the first deli near the school. He poked his head inside and there she was sitting at a table near the back. She was with another girl and what Jameel assumed to be her two C bodyguards. He slowed his pace and eased his way over to the table. The two C's looked him up and down and asked:

"Whas up man?"

He ignored them and spoke directly to his target. "Sista, can I talk wit chu a minute, by yoself?"

Sista was all smiles and it was obvious to the guards what she was going to say. "You want me?"

"Yeah, I needa wrap wit chu for jus a minute."

"You know its almos time to go back don chu, did you eat?" "Naw, I'll be aw-ight. Can we talk?"

Sister motioned to her people to let her out and she got up and grabbed Jameel's arm. They walked over to another table nearby that was empty and sat down. Jameel spoke first: "Sista, you said when I was in the hospital you'd do anything for me, right?"

"Yeah, you remember that huh? That was a while ago, why you comin now?" "'Cause I need yo help. I needa get in wit yo crew to make some money fast."

Sista looked at him hard for a few minutes and then said finally: "You don really know what you aksn do you?"

"Yeah, I know. I jus gotta do it, cause I need the dough. You know my mom lost her job an things gittin tough. You gonna help me?"

"'J", if I do this an you git in, you gotta know ain no gitin out." "Yeah I know."

"Well I needa talk to Hakeem and Hammer an I'll let you know. You sure you wanna do this?"

"Yeah, I got to."

Sista looked almost sad when he said that and shook her head when she got up. She ended the conversation by telling Jameel to come over to her place tonight around 8:00 and she would let him know. They separated and she went back to her crew and he raced back to the school.

After school let out, Dolitha made a beeline to where they usually met, but only Cinque and Rajon were there. She asked Rajon where 'J' was and he told her that he left a message for her he had to leave early and would call her later. This really set Dolitha wondering what was going on, but she had no choice but to wait for the call and ask him. The trio left the campus and headed home. Even Rajon wasn't sure what 'J' was about, but he suspected that it had something to do with the conversation that they had over the weekend. He thought to himself, that he hoped he hadn't goaded his best friend into doing anything stupid, and knowing Jameel like he did he felt some comfort thinking that he was smarter than that.

Jameel got home earlier than usual even before Cinque and told his mother that he left school early because he was continuing to look for a job. He told her Cinque was on his way and should be there shortly. Sarafina had already prepared the boy's dinner so he was able to sit down and eat before leaving again. He went into his room and changed his clothes, putting on something a little dressier. Sarafina noticed he had changed and thought that he was dressing to impress a potential employer, she was right, but how could she possibly know who the employer might be. She wished him luck and saw him out the door.

It was much too early to even think about going to Sista's, but he wanted to get out of the house and do some soul searching. He reflected on what Sista said to him and then back to what Rajon told him and the two sides of the equation just didn't seem to balance. On the one side he knew what the C's were into and it could get him in trouble, but on the other the money he could make would really help his mom out and maybe get her to stop what she was doing. Somehow the elements on the right seemed to carry more weight and the decision was made to go for it. He ended his walk at the library and went inside to pass the time until it was time to go to her place. Baxter Terrace, where Sista lived was not far away.

At 7:45 Jameel put down his sports magazine and looked up at the clock. He took a deep breath, walked over to the stacks returned it to the shelf then walked out and spent the next ten minutes making his way to the Terrace. With each step bringing him closer to her door, his mixed emotions wrestled with each other vying for the right to make the final decision.

"Should I or shouldn't I go up there?" kept running through his mind. Before too long he was in her vestibule and pushing the access button. The intercom responded, he identified himself and gained entry into the building. As he walked up the stairs his heart was racing and he wasn't sure what to expect when she opened her door.

Moments later he was at the door and pushed the bell. When she opened it, he definitely wasn't ready for what he saw. She was wearing a low cut loosely fitting sheer blouse that partially exposed her super size bosom in a most provocative way. The blouse was tucked into a mini skirt that barely covered her upper thighs and showed her well-formed sturdy legs. Her hair was down and flowing and the slippers she wore were just a hint of shoe covering. It took 'J' about five minutes before his body could adjust to the eye candy that was causing his hormones to go into a semi diabetic shock. She smiled and invited him in, but his feet wouldn't move. She then grabbed his arm and helped him.

"Sit down, can I get you something?" she said.

Not knowing what to ask for he said: "What chu got?"

"Do you drink?"

Trying to calm himself and appear macho he said: "Yeah, you got any gin?"

He asked for that because that's what he saw on his mother's table. Jameel might have had a sip or two of strong drink at some special occasions in the past, but he was definitely not a drinker.

"I think I can fix that for you." she said and went over to the bar. "How do you like it?"

Not really knowing how to respond to that he said: "With some ice."

She poured about a quarter glass of gin filled it with ice and handed it to him. Jameel took the glass and started to drink then stopped and asked if she was going to have one. She said that she didn't normally drink, but that she would have one just to join him.

Once she had her drink they both sat on the couch close to one another. Jameel took a sip of his drink and immediately tried to hide his distaste for what was in his mouth. Still trying to maintain his macho appearance he swallowed the sip and put the glass down.

"Did chu get to talk wit Hakeem 'bout me?"

"Yeah, I talked to him and Hammer. They ain too down wit you comin in, 'cause they don know you. You gonna have to do somethin to prove you want in."

"Somethin like what?"

"They didn say but tomorrow night you gotta go down to M&M's an meet wit them. Don worry though 'cause I tol 'em I want you in, so I know they gonna do it. But they can't jus let you walk in, you know what I'm sayin."

"Yeah, I think so, but I ain 'bout to off nobody or nothin like that."

"I don think they'll want that, but be ready to do some dealin. Maybe not tomorrow, but it gonna hafta be soon if you wanna make some money."

"Yeah aw-ight I can deal wit that."

By now the first few sips had started to settle in and a slight buzz was coming over Jameel. He reached for the glass and took another drink, this time it wasn't a sip. The taste wasn't any better, but the liquid seemed to go down smoother. She also took another drink and the two of them were on their way. Moments later he finished his glass and asked if he could have another. She bent over to reach for his glass and his eyes got stuck on the cleavage. By now the gin was having its way with both their bodies and the second drink just served to reduce the inhibitions.

She moved closer to him and kissed him. Lightly at first, but then he grabbed her and locked on to her lips with all that he had. He was flushed with excitement and his hands began to move all over her body. As he kissed her long and hard the rise in temperatures made the couch seem too hot. She paused long enough to get up and pull him into the bedroom. The heat of the moment prevented them from casually removing clothing so it was a clutch and tear situation. When they were both down to the buff, he lifted her onto the bed and as temperatures continued to soar so also was he rising for the occasion.

The kisses were deep and passionate and as he continued to fondle her, she responded likewise by caressing him. There was no stopping at this point and when the curtain on the final act came down, they both melted into the sheets as if they were all a single fabric.

After the act, Jameel lay back and watched the room spin before his eyes. He knew that if he tried to get up he wouldn't make it, so he just lay there and took it in. She was talking to him, but her words just flew right over and he was non responsive. As he lay there feeling a strange peace with the world, he wasn't sure whether what was to follow on the next day would make any difference for him. She kept talking, but to him she was in another room. Finally, after getting no verbal response, she rolled over to him kissed him hard and a new play began.

It was almost 11:30 before Jameel got himself together enough to get dressed and leave. She was smiling the whole time that he was preparing to go, and asking if he was coming back. This time he heard her and was trying to not commit to anything. With as macho a voice as he could muster after that experience he just told her that depending on the outcome of his meeting with Hakeem he would let her know. She laughed out loud this time and said: "Don you even worry 'bout no Hakeem, I tol you I'd take care a it." Feeling like the conquering hero Jameel headed out the door. Before he left, he turned and kissed her lightly on the lips and told her he'd talk to her at school.

When he got down to the street it finally dawned on him how late it was and that he had not called his mother nor did he tell her he was going to be this late. He looked for a pay phone, but the one he found in the Baxter Terrace development had a box but no handset. It was about a twenty-minute walk from where she lived to his house so he decided he would just step up his pace and explain when he got home. There was hardly anybody out on the street. Even though it was a little cold, Jameel was really surprised that there were very few cars moving about on 11th street that was kind of a main drag.

The quickest way for him to get home was to stay on 11th and go right by M&M's. He wasn't sure he really wanted to go this way because some of the C's might still be hanging out, but he decided sooner or later he was going to have to meet them so why not now. As he got closer to the store he noticed that the lights were on and it seemed like something was going on inside. He crossed over to the other side of the street, but kept his eyes wide open to see what was happening. He was feeling the chill from the night air and the alcohol had already lowered his body heat, so he quickened his pace to get by the store. He was close enough now that he could see inside. It appeared that there were a few people in there, but he couldn't make out what they were doing.

As he was passing by, a patrol car came up and parked on the corner. Minutes later another one came in from the opposite direction and parked on the other side of the street. The officers didn't get out, but they just looked into the store and waited. Soon after they arrived the lights in the store went out and it was almost completely dark inside except for the green glow of the clock on the wall and the low level lumen of the night lamps. Four officers then got out of their cars and walked over to the store. They went up to the front door and peered inside. One even got out a flashlight and pointed it in.

Apparently, they were not authorized to enter uninvited so they knocked on the door. After several knocks and no one responded, they just turned around and left.

Jameel had stopped to see what the action was all about, but when the police left, so did he. As he walked he kept turning around and looking over his shoulder to see if anybody was coming out of the store, but he saw no one. He was sure that he had seen people in the store and he wondered why the police didn't see them. He was also saying to himself if they had a warrant to go in, why didn't they. If not, why were they there in the first place. He was trying to make sense of what he saw and immediately he started to connect it to his possible meeting there tomorrow. If the police were eyeballing the place it must be for a reason and did he want to get caught there tomorrow if they might be coming back. He was still pondering this thought when he got to his house.

It was just about 12:00 when he got to his door and he quietly put his key in and opened it. He stepped softly inside hoping to not wake anybody. He was successful. Before going to his room, he went into the kitchen to get himself a glass of water and he saw the gin bottle almost empty on the table. Now he knew why nobody heard him come in. Cinque wouldn't have heard him because once he went to sleep a herd of elephants stampeding wouldn't have disturbed him. As for mom, her date with the bottle caused a deep sleep from the effects of the gin. He didn't know exactly how to feel about this. As he witnessed his mom drinking more and more and becoming more depressed each day, he wondered whether this Leisar man that she was seeing was causing her to do it, or was she just reacting to this very stressful no job, no money situation.

His head was starting to spin again and his steps were less sure now than when he was walking in the brisk air outside. He went into the bathroom found the aspirins and swallowed a few. Before going to bed he decided to go into the living room and sit down on the couch for a few minutes to try and clear his head. When he got in there, he saw the pile of bills laying out in the open on the coffee table. It became very clear to him, why mom might have taken to having a few tonight. The hospital was getting nasty in its dunning letters and even the private physicians were leaning on her. The landlord wanted the rent and the telephone company was threatening to shut off their service. He wondered whether the decision to sit on the couch to clear his head was a good idea, because if anything his head was spinning more now after reading the mail, than it had been before he sat down.

It was becoming more evident to him as he pondered the family situation once again that his decision to go with the C's to get some quick cash was the right one. The only thing that still bothered him was what Sista said about not being able to get out once you got in. He knew that making a career of doing what they did was not the way he wanted to go, but he looked at the regular job situation for someone in his category, and it was extremely bleak. His mom said stay in school, but if he did that how could he make any serious money with only half a day to work at any legitimate job. If he dropped out, she would really be disappointed and he would have to deal with that. Clear his head, sitting down in here was not the answer so he said let me go to bed maybe I'll feel better tomorrow. The one happy feeling he reflected on as he was getting up, was the image of Sista that stayed in his head. She was unquestionably the most woman he had ever seen naked and the experience he had tonight was unforgettable.

He got up headed to the bedroom, but thought to get one more large glass of water in the hope that he could flush out all the alcohol he had ingested tonight, by tomorrow morning. He drank the water and searched for a piece of bread to fill the hunger that was beginning to set in. Quickly he munched down two slices of bread and finished the water. Now he felt he could go to sleep and hopefully feel better in the morning.

He went into his room and saw Cinque hanging half out of the bed with the covers half off of him. This was not new so Jameel wasn't surprised, he often slept in this state and he would be totally refreshed the next day. Jameel removed his clothes put on his PJ's and got ready to get in the bed when it occurred to him that he hadn't seen his mother. Not knowing whether she was all right, didn't sit well with him so he wanted to just peek in on her and make sure. He light stepped down the hall and slowly opened the door to her room. There she was in the bed and her breathing was very heavy, but regular. When he turned his eyes away from her he noticed that on the floor by the far wall there was a rather large painting that had not been there before. Out of curiosity he inched closer to see what it was. As he got closer and closer, even in the dimness from the hallway light, the painting seemed to absorb him and he moved even closer to get a better look. When he was right up on it he shivered and fell back grabbing the chair near by to steady himself. Even in his inebriated state he couldn't believe what his eyes were recording. He blinked and blinked again to refocus, but it was still there.

Chapter 11 - Initiation

The press conference was scheduled for 1 PM and Mayor Stanton was in his office early desperately trying to pull together enough information to calm the public with his presentation. There was a general cry of outrage concerning the recent rise in violence and criminal activity in the city. Even the CONN's joined by New Life Temple had loudly expressed their vote of no confidence in the police department's lack of progress. They were all holding the mayor responsible. The combined force of CONN's and New Life had sometime earlier made inroads in quelling the rise, but they had now, due to a lack of effective leadership fallen to a new low. Those that were still with the group, in their frustration, were pointing fingers at the administration and the police department in the hope that their last ditch efforts would bring about some positive action.

Even now, the mayor was on the phone with Captain Tillery and Lieutenant Meeker railing about their failure to produce any arrests. He was calling for them to come over to his office right now and bring him whatever material they had. His temper was flaring and both the captain and lieutenant were trying hardily to calm him down The gist of his message was that for weeks now the department had been telling him they were close to making arrests, but as of now he hadn't been made aware of any. The captain, cupping his hand over the phone, whispered to Lt. Meeker that before they go over there he wanted those two guys arrested that they had discussed before. Lt. Meeker nodded his head. The conversation lasted about fifteen minutes with the mayor doing all of the talking and ended with the captain just trying to survive with his job still intact.

Lt. Meeker went back to his office and got on the intercom to

Sergeant Calloway. "Ray, Meeker here."

"Yes lieutenant."

"Captain and I just got off the horn with the mayor and he's back on the rampage. We have to bring in those two guys the eyewitness ID'd; at least for questioning."

"What do you want to charge them with?"

"Oh I don't know, figure out something. We can get them in here on suspicion of illegal gun possession for starters. You can come up with anything else but get them in here. I need to be able to tell the mayor we got somebody."

"Okay lieutenant, I'm on it."

Lt. Meeker hung up and starting putting together all the material that he had that might loosen the collar of the mayor and give the public some confidence that the police department was making progress. He wasn't looking forward to appearing at the press conference because he knew that the reporters were hungry and anxious to lay blame on somebody. He grabbed his briefcase and his coat and headed down to the captain's office. Soon as he walked in the captain asked him if he was ready to go and did he have something to calm the mayor. He said he thought so, and the captain responded saying all right let's go.

On the way to the mayor's office, Captain Tillery kept asking about the missing half of that document with the drug details on it. Lt. Meeker responded saying that at the top of his list was getting into that warehouse to do a search, but right now he had nothing to get a search warrant on. The captain told him he'd better come up with something even if he had to do a midnight run himself. He then said quickly:

"You know I'm kidding, right?"

It was obvious to Meeker that even though the captain said he was kidding, deep down inside he knew that the message was clear – get in any way you can.

After a short ride the two officers got out of the car and hurried up to the mayor's office. The receptionist buzzed the mayor and informed him his appointments had arrived. She wasted no time in escorting them into the conference room where the meeting was to be held. The mayor was still in his office on the phone, but the receptionist told the officers to be seated and that he'd be in shortly. Minutes later he walked into the room with a scowl on his face and just looked at the duo several minutes before saying anything; not even hello. Finally, he opened up with: "You know who that was on the phone just now?" and before they could answer he said:

"That was the District Leader for the FBI wanting to have a meeting with me tomorrow. Gentlemen, it seems that we have a bigger problem here than I thought and you're going to tell me how to solve it, right? He wants to talk to me about some suspected heavy drug traffic that's been coming into our fair city and they've been tracking it. Okay guys, talk to me and make it good."

The captain looked at the lieutenant and his face showed his embarrassment at being caught totally off guard with this new wrinkle. Not knowing exactly how to respond, he was grateful when the lieutenant jumped in and said:

"Yes Mr. Mayor we are aware that there may be some new activity in that area and my men are on top of it."

"Oh yeah, lieutenant, tell me exactly what does that mean when you say you're on top of it."

"Well sir, even as we speak right now, an arrest warrant is being issued to pick up two men that we suspect may be instrumental and the keys to all that's been happening lately including the trafficking."

"Is that right, captain?"

"Yes sir, we're moving on it right now."

"Go ahead lieutenant tell me more about this bust. Is it something that I can tell the press this afternoon?"

"Yes sir. I even have something else here that I want to show you, that we are following up on."

After saying that, he could see that the mayor's countenance was a little more relaxed and the tension level in the room went down about 20 degrees. Lt. Meeker pulled out the half document with the shipment information on it and began to explain how they were going about securing the other half. He also told about the CONN's eyewitness being very helpful in identifying the guys they're picking up. The mayor grimaced at the mention of the CONN's and asked if Meeker had any sway with them to get them off his back. Lt. Meeker answered by saying that he was working closely with them and he would see what he could do. From that point on the meeting moved to producing a believable presentation that would give the press what they wanted and the public what they needed. Captain Tillery and Lieutenant Meeker breathed a sigh of relief as they broke the meeting and departed. They would be back that afternoon for the press conference.

Sergeant Calloway with the arrest warrant in hand for both Hakeem and Claudius (Hammer) gathered two patrolmen in a marked vehicle and headed over to the Minute Mart where they suspected the men would be. It was about 1:30 PM when they pulled up to the store and when the officers went inside there was no sign of them. The store manager was asked if he had seen either of them and the reply was no. Neither one of them had been in there that day. Calloway's next move was to go to the current addresses that they had on file and see if they could catch them there. They arrived at Hakeem's building and went inside to his apartment. After knocking on the door several times and getting no answer, they considered forcing their way in, but Sgt. Calloway hesitated. On their way in he saw that there was a super in the building so he went down to his apartment and asked if he had a key to Hakeem's place. After showing him the warrant, the super agreed to let them in.

Upon entering the apartment, there was no sign of Hakeem. Calloway began wondering whether he had been tipped that they were coming. He then reflected back on when the raid had been made on the store and they found nothing. Could that have been a tip off also? A scary thought crossed his mind. Was someone in the department leaking information? From Hakeem's place they proceeded to Hammer's and got the same results. There was no way other than being alerted in advance that they would have known we were coming, Calloway thought. After the second attempt, he called into headquarters to let the lieutenant know what was happening.

Lt. Meeker was at the conference busy fielding questions from the press and the public and also touting the fact that some arrests were being made. It was going to be extremely embarrassing when the news got out that the suspects they were trying to arrest couldn't be found. At this point neither the captain, the lieutenant or the mayor, knew this. Sgt.

Calloway was determined to bring these guys in before he let his lieutenant down so he gave up trying to call and went on a street search. Several times he rode by M&M's in his unmarked car hoping to spot any of the gang that he might be able to convince to give them up. The street search was not going well and after three hours, Sgt. Calloway was tired. He tried calling Lt. Meeker again but apparently after the press conference, the mayor was taking him and the captain to a late lunch.

At 5:00 O'clock Sgt. Calloway was frustrated at his exhaustive efforts and ready to call it a day. In a last attempt he decided that he would go by the store one more time. This time instead of driving by he parked on the far corner and waited. Fortune was with him because after about ten minutes he spotted both Hakeem and Hammer coming out of the store in a real hurry and jumping into a waiting car. Quickly he radioed for a patrol car to assist and he pulled up along side the suspect car. Before he could say anything, the duo must have recognized him so their car pulled off and the chase was on. Again on the radio, Sgt. Calloway gave the location and direction he was headed in.

The car sped down 7th avenue toward City Stadium weaving in and out of traffic reaching speeds of 60+ MPH. Sgt. Calloway alerted the desk that he needed more help and patrol cars were dispatched to join the pursuit. Hakeem's car turned left on 2nd street and appeared to be headed out of the city. However, when they reached the intersection of 2nd and 6th avenue, they were cut off by three patrol cars and hemmed in. The suspects stopped their vehicle jumped out and started running toward the old abandoned buildings near the corner. The footrace was on and it seemed that the two suspects were in better shape than the cops and could possibly get away. However, coming in from the other side were two more cops who had the angle and were able to catch and subdue the duo. Once on the ground and handcuffed, Sgt. Calloway caught up and took charge. After thanking the other officers, he looked at Hakeem and Hammer smiling and placed them under arrest. He read them the Miranda Rights and laughingly told them that he was only going to bring them in before for questioning, but now he was charging them with reckless driving, speeding, endangering lives, avoiding arrest and assaulting an officer in that little struggle. While the pair sat in the back of the patrol car, Sgt. Calloway just couldn't wait to contact Lt. Meeker.

Sarafina woke up early this morning and dragged herself out of bed. She walked over to her dresser mirror and looked at herself. The reflection that stared back at her wanted to erase last night and have a do over. The construction project inside her head was slowing down, but she was still feeling the taps of small hammers. She eased her way into the bathroom and downed a few more aspirins before heading to the kitchen for her morning cup of coffee. The boys had not awakened yet and she was glad for just a few minutes to herself. However, it wasn't long before she heard someone stirring and she called out.":

"Jameel is that you?"

"Yeah mom its me. You aw-ight?" "Yes 'J' I feel a little better."

Jameel walked into the kitchen and sat down. Then he said:

"You know when I came in you were already in bed so I looked in to see if you were okay. I saw that painting you got on the floor in there. There's something wrong with that picture 'cause when I looked at it real good you know the people in there started movin. They was doin all kinda stuff, havin sex and ereything. I almos fell on the floor. I started rubbin my eyes, but it was really there so I jus got outta there."

Sarafina sat up straight and her eyes widened and she looked hard at him. "Did you really see that?"

"Yeah mom, I think so."

"Did you do any thing last night? You weren't drinking were you?"

Jameel knew he was caught so he just confessed and said: "Yeah mom, I was at a friend's house and I had a little somethin."

"What kinda little somethin?"

"I had a little bit of that same stuff you was drinkin." Somewhat embarrassed Sarafina said:

"Well I guess that explains it for both of us. We are seeing things, `cause of that stuff. No more for me what about you?"

Jameel laughed and said: " After what I saw last night, definitely no more for me." They both laughed and she asked him to go wake his brother up so you guys can get ready for school.

In school Jameel was avoiding Dolitha as best he could because he didn't want to have to explain to her why he didn't meet her after school and why he didn't call. His best efforts however were unsuccessful because it seemed that whenever she wanted to find him she could. She came up behind him in the hallway when they were changing classes and tapped his shoulder.

"You tryin to duck me?" she said.

"Naw, you know betta."

"Why you ain call me last night?"

"I was out tryna fine a job an it got too late. I know yo moms don want me callin there all hours so I didn't."

"I tol you before, my mom is aw-ight wit me. She wouldn mine at all. Anyway did you find somethin?"

"No, I hafta keep lookin. I'll be out again tonite too." "You can call me when you come in even if it late, okay?" "Yeah aw-ight."

"You gonna meet me afta school today or you leavin early again?" "Yeah, I think I'm gonna leave early, I'll talk wit you later."

Dolitha was looking at him kind of funny and it made him feel uncomfortable. He knew she could tell when he was lying, but he had to go with it.

"Okay I'll wait for your call."

Jameel knew that tonight he had an appointment with the C's leaders and he was trying to keep his head on straight so that when he did meet with them he came across as really wanting to get in. He hadn't seen Sista so far today and he wondered whether she made it in after last night. She had as many drinks as he had and he thought to himself, if she felt like he did last night, maybe she took the day. It wasn't long though before he spotted her in the hallway during his next class change. She saw him also and smiled.

They were headed in opposite directions, but he managed to

communicate to her that he would see her at the deli during lunch. She nodded okay and they moved on.

When the lunch period came Jameel was actually sneaking out trying to avoid Dolitha and he had to laugh at himself for doing it. He walked in the deli and Sista was there with her usual crew, but when she saw him come in she made them get up. Jameel eased over and sat down beside her. She started to kiss him, but he drew back to let her know by his move that she shouldn't here. She got the message and backed off, but looked at him hard. He asked her how she was feeling and then she smiled again and said she had felt better. He got up to go get him a sandwich and asked if she wanted something. She said no, she couldn't eat anything solid yet and she already had some water. When he came back he asked her if everything was set for tonight. She said yes and that he should be at the store at 8. He agreed and gently rubbed her leg under the table where no one could see. She smiled and asked him when he was coming back over. He told her soon and then finished eating and left.

Jameel got home that afternoon and found the apartment empty. This wasn't one of the days that Sarafina usually went to the Unemployment Center for her counseling sessions so he wondered where she might be. Cinque came in a few minutes later and not seeing mom went straight to the kitchen to see if she had fixed anything for them to eat. When he saw that she had, he was satisfied and content thinking that she may have just stepped out. Jameel though was a little more concerned and went to their bedroom looking for a note or something that she may have left them. There was nothing there so he went into the living room. There was nothing there either. He became a little concerned, but not enough to cause worry so he went in the kitchen and fixed his plate.

Around 7:00 PM the phone rang and he went in to answer it thinking that it may be mom.

"Hello, Jameel here."

"Hi `J', this is Sista. Listen I got some bad news for ya. I jus got word that Hakeem and Hammer got picked up so they ain gonna be at the store tonight. I don know all the details but you shouldn even go near there for a while. I know you said you need some dough, but until I can see whas up I don even know what I'm gonna do for myself. Right now Buster is next up so I hafta get hold of him. I'll get backatcha soon as I know more."

"Wow thas cold. Why they get caught now?"

"I dono, cops musta been layin for `em. Look I gotta go, talk to you later." "Aw-ight see ya later, bye."

Down at police headquarters Hakeem and Hammer had been put through the booking process and were waiting to be questioned. Captain

Tillery had gone home from the lunch with the mayor, but Lt. Meeker had finally got the message that Sgt. Calloway left him and was back at the station. He came into the room with a wide grin and grabbed Calloway's hand and shook it hard.

"Way to go man, way to go, good job. I understand you got them on some multiple charges. That's good, real good, where are they now?"

"They're separated in the interrogation rooms, which one you want to take first?" "Think I'd like to talk with Mr. Hakeem first, I believe he's the main guy."

The lieutenant and Sgt.Calloway walked down to interrogation room #5 where Hakeem was being held and went in. Hakeem just sat and stared at them without saying a word. He looked very relaxed as if this was no big deal. Lt. Meeker spoke first.

"Well Mr. Brown seems like you got yourself a little bit of trouble here. What happened your car's gas pedal got stuck and you couldn't stop. Oh no wait a minute I know, you didn't realize you were being chased is that it?"

Hakeem just continued to stare at the lieutenant saying nothing.

"Okay I'm gonna ask you this just once. Now you know we got all your history here and you're looking at doing some serious time if this goes to court. But I'm willing to work with you if you want to cooperate because I know that you're not the brains behind the operation. I've got two questions for you. First, do you have weapons stashed in that Minute Mart and why didn't we find them? Second you've been bringing drugs into this city big time, how are you doing it?"

Hakeem just put his hand to his mouth, yawned then leaned back in his chair and looked at the lieutenant. Sgt. Calloway then chimed in.

"Listen Mr. Brown, don't be stupid. You want to go down by yourself for this whole thing. You can make it a little easy on yourself if you help us. If you don't cooperate, then we're going to make this same offer to your boy down the hall. You think he can hold out like you can. I don't think so. If he gives the main man up, then your deal is gone and so are you. What do you say?"

Hakeem rolled his head around and around in the chair and then stretched and yawned again. This action irritated the lieutenant and his temper started to show. He got right into Hakeem's face and said:

"You think this is a joke, Mr. Brown? You think I'm down here having fun? I've got a mind to just forget you and go lean on your buddy, he's not as hard as you is he?"

These words must have gotten to Hakeem's inner thoughts, because he was thinking to himself, no Hammer ain't strong like me, he jus might give up Mr. M and then I'm done too. He finally opened his mouth and started to talk.

"Look I know you guys ain really got nothin but that traffic mess an that ain gonna be e'nuf to do nothin wit me. But I'll tell you what, you lemme walk an I'll give you the stash."

"Just the stash Mr. Brown, what does that mean?"

"It mean I tell where the guns are an why ya'll couldn fine 'em; but thas it." Lt. Meeker backed off and sat down in his chair.

"Well that's a start Mr. Brown, but not good enough. Like I said, I don't really want you, I want your boss. Am I making myself clear? You understand where I'm going?"

"Yeah, I know you want me to give up the big man and get snuffed. You think I'm crazy right?"

"You give him to us and we'll keep you safe. You don't then we'll put the word out that you did and then where can you hide?"

Hakeem just laughed at that and went back to staring.

The lieutenant a little embarrassed at Hakeem calling his bluff, turned around looked at Sgt. Calloway and smiled.

"Okay Mr. Brown, here's what we're going to do. You're going to tell us where the weapons are how we can find them and when the next shipment is coming in then I'm going to recommend that you get some leniency at your trial. How's that?"

"What chu mean by leniency?"

"I mean I ask the judge not to throw away the key on you forever." "You gonna put somethin down in writin?"

"As soon as you write down where the weapons are, how we get to them and when the next shipment is coming, then we can exchange notes. Is that good enough for you?"

Hakeem sat back in his chair again and thought it over. "Aw-ight les go, where the paper?"

The lieutenant stepped out of the room leaving Sergeant Calloway alone with Hakeem and went and got a legal pad. He returned and Hakeem put down how to get into the secret room behind the main store and what weapons he thought were still there. He also told them that he really didn't know when the next shipment was coming in because he had not got the call yet telling him. He would not go into how that communication worked. Lt. Meeker satisfied that he had enough now to move ahead, put some concessions down that he knew wouldn't hold water and gave them to Hakeem. Little did Mr. Brown know, not being as legally savy as he thought, that what was there written on the paper was practically worthless in a courtroom. Hakeem was returned to his cell and both Meeker and Calloway moved on to interview Mr.Miller (Hammer).

"Well Mr. Miller seems like you got yourself some big trouble here."

They started in with the same routine that had been used on Hakeem. They embellished Hammer's interrogation a bit by telling him that they had already gotten the information they needed from Mr. Brown and they were just giving him a chance to come clean. Hammer initially took the same position as Hakeem and just stared at the legal duo. It wasn't until they told Mr. Miller about the hidden room and that they knew how to get into it, that Hammer was convinced Hakeem had said something. He started volunteering information trying to get his own deal, but the information was nothing new. Neither one of the suspects would roll over on the big man. From this both the lieutenant and the sergeant knew, that whatever hold this guy had on his underlings it was strong enough for them to go to jail rather than give him up. This was definitely not good for their investigation. Hammer was returned to his cell and Meeker and Calloway feeling that they had earned their pay for the day went home.

At 8:30 PM the Peterson phone rang again and it was Sista for Jameel.

"Jameel, Sista again can you come and meet me right now at the library? I talked to Buster and he wanna talk wit chu `bout gettin in. We also gonna talk `bout whas comin down soon. You comin?"

"Yeah I can be there in fifteen minutes."

"Aw-ight come to the science room in the back. Later." "Aw-ight, see ya."

Sarafina had not come back yet and Jameel wasn't sure what was going on, but he knew that he had to take advantage of this opportunity if he was going to start making some quick money. He told Cinque to stay in case mom called and if it started getting late he would call. Cinque agreed, but not before asking `J' what he thought was happening with their mother. Jameel said she was probably at one of the CONN's meetings, but he knew inside that this wasn't the case because she had not gone for several weeks.

At the library Jameel walked into the science room and spotted Sista sitting where she said she'd be, talking to a man who looked to be about the same age as him. He casually walked over to their table and stood. Sista, still talking to the guy, motioned for `J' to sit down. She finished what she had to say and started the introductions.

"Buster this is Jameel, Jameel Buster. Buster's takin ova for right now 'til we get word on whas gonna happen with Hakeem. I tol him you want in so ya'll needa talk. I'm gonna go upstairs for a half hour then I'll be back. That should give ya'll time to work it out. See ya."

She looked at both of them then got up and left. Buster looked Jameel up and down and then started the conversation:

"Man, you the one that got all shot up at Higyb's right?" "Yeah, whas that got to do wit this?"

"Nothin man, I jus wanna make sure who you is. You know Hakeem ain in fava of you comin in at all, but Sista's callin the shot. I dono if either Hakeem or Hammer comin out no time soon so I gotta test you an see if you qualify."

"What I gotta do?"

"First I'm gonna go wit you on a run an see how you handle that. Then you gonna make a pick up by yoself and introduce yoself to some people. I won be wit chu but I'll be watchin from the car. You got a piece?"

"No, I ain got nothin, what I need that for?"

"Thas aw-ight, I'll get you somethin from the store jus in case."

"I'm gonna set you up for Thursday night to do this thing. You gotta meet me at the store at 7:30. You in?"

"Yeah man, I'll be there."

Jameel inside was really having a problem with this guy who couldn't have been more than a year older than him being able to test him like a school child, but he reconciled himself by saying if this is how I have to start, so be it. Right on time Sista came down the stairs and rejoined them.

"Ya'll got things all worked out, I hope 'cause I don wanna know nothin 'bout that part of things. Buster you know that we due to get somethin comin in prably next week. Now Hakeem usually get the call, but since we don know if he gonna be out, I'm gonna get word to Mr. M, that you gonna handle it. Now I dono how he gonna act when he fine out about Hakeem an Hammer, but I know he won't like his stuff gettin hung up so we gotta pick it up and then move it. You down wit that?"

"Yeah, you know I'm down." "Jameel you good?"

"Yeah I'm wit it."

"Aw-ight Buster soon as I hear back from Mr. M I'll call you. Gimme yo cell number again so I can put it in here right now."

The group broke up and everybody left the library. Jameel before he went outside decided to call home and see about his mom. Cinque picked up and said that she was there, but she had been drinking again and she was sleeping. This upset Jameel more and it was hurting him, because she said just last night that she was through with that. He didn't know what he could say, because she was still his mother. It just made him want to get this C thing going so he could start getting some money. This he thought was the solution for him and her.

He got home about 10:00 O'clock and like he did before he peeked in on his mom. She was sleeping soundly. Out of curiosity he turned on the light and went over to the painting. It was still on the floor and he wondered why she hadn't hung it. He got real close to it this time to see if it was going to do what he saw last night. Nothing happened, the people, though in some real suggestive poses, didn't move or anything so he got up turned the lights off and left the room. He said to himself, that gin must have done a job on his head and he was seeing things because of it. He was still feeling though that there was something different about that painting.

Captain Tillery came into headquarters Wednesday morning feeling much better than he had for the last few days. The fact that the mayor had taken him and Lt. Meeker to lunch yesterday meant that he was pleased with how the press conference went. The local reporters ran a story in the first edition that for a change provided the public with a ray of hope and a view of the light at the end of the tunnel. They seized on the police report about the pending arrests and the possibility that this could lead to identifying the major players in the drug and violence game. The captain had a copy of the paper and walked into his office prepared to pat his lieutenant on the back. When he punched in his extension on the intercom and got no response he decided to take a walk down there.

When he got to the lieutenant's office it didn't appear that he had arrived yet so he inquired of some other staff whether anyone had seen him. No one had seen him, but one officer said that he knew he and Sgt. Calloway were here late last night because they were grilling some suspects they brought in. This made the captain feel good again knowing that he had in the house the confirmation of what had been given to the press at the conference. When he got back to his office he called Meeker on his cell.

"Hello, Lt. Meeker."

"Lieutenant, this is Captain Tillery how are you?" " I'm fine captain you been looking for me?"

"Well I just stopped by your office to show you the headlines. Did you see today's paper yet?"

"No sir not yet, good news?"

"Yeah good enough to give us some breathing room. I understand you have our guys here in house. Are we getting close to the top guy?"

"Well not really sir. Those guys we have will get us the weapons we're looking for, but they wouldn't give up the big guy. By the way, I was right about those weapons being in that store. Our guests told me about a hidden room in the back and how we can get in there."

"That sounds great. When are you going in?"

"Right now I'm over at the judge's office talking to her about getting another search warrant before I write up the papers. Captain I gotta tell you, she's not cooperating this time. She said she already gave us a shot at that store and we embarrassed her. She's not signing off on another warrant. I'm not sure how to handle this."

"All right don't worry about it come on back. I'm going to call the mayor and see if we can get him to persuade her."

"Okay cap, be there soon."

Captain Tillery didn't waste a minute before he had the mayor on the phone telling him about the hurdle he'd come up against with the judge. The mayor, still feeling good himself having seen the morning news, told the captain that he would talk to the judge. However, he also cautioned Tillery that this time they had better find those weapons or he would be in the doghouse again. The captain told him that he had the highest confidence in finding them this time and hung up.

Later that day, Lt. Meeker was on the phone with Reverend Joyner talking about how the CONN's had recently maligned the mayor with their verbal blasts regarding his ineffective administration. He continued that the mayor had asked him to try and get them to back off. He especially asked about Sarafina in that he hadn't seen nor heard from her lately. Reverend Joyner hesitated for a minute trying to collect his thoughts and consider what he wanted to let the lieutenant know about the status of the group. He then offered that the collective CONN's and New Life community action group had reached a very low membership level and he didn't think there would be any more attacks on the mayor. As far as Sarafina was concerned, again he hesitated, I believe that she's wrestling with some personal issues and she's no longer leading the way for the group.

Lt. Meeker replied that he was sorry to hear that because it seemed to him that she was very effective in getting that group involved in what he and his department needed help with. Reverend Joyner agreed and told him that he was actively trying to intervene with her plight and get her to come back, but right now it wasn't working. He concluded the conversation by saying:

" You can tell the mayor that you talked with me and I said that he need not worry about the CONN's ruining his re-election bid." Lt. Meeker heard all that the reverend was telling him, even that which he was not saying, so he was able to conclude that if his department was going to successfully end this city's nightmare, he was on his own.

That afternoon when Jameel and Cinque got home from school Sarafina was there.

Jameel was anxious to find out where she was last night and he went into the living room where she was watching television. He sat down next to her and respectfully asked:

"Mom you said you wasn't gonna drink that stuff no more didn't you?"

"You're right, but yesterday afternoon after I finished making your dinner, I went back into the bedroom to lie down and I looked at that picture again. I saw what you said you saw the other night, the people in there was havin a good time an it seem like they was invitin me in. Somethin kept tellin me to go to a place where they are havin that kinda fun. So I went over to the Big A an there they really was havin fun jus like the picture said, so I sat down. Somebody bought me a drink and then another before I knew I was back here and in bed."

"Mom, that picture ain no good. Where you get it?" "It was a gift from Asa."

"Somethin wrong wit it, we should throw it out." "I can't do that, it was a gift."

"But it makin you do bad things ain it?"

"Oh no baby I'll be all right, don you worry, now you go on and eat your dinner."

Jameel didn't want to argue with her, but he knew that something had to be done with the picture. He got up and went into the kitchen where Cinque had already started eating.

"Cinque, have you seen that picture in mom's room?" "What picture? What chu talkin 'bout?"

"There's a picture in her room on the floor. Guess you haven't looked at it." "No, I don go in there less she tell me to, so I ain seen no picture or nothin else." "Well neva mind, I jus aksed."

Jameel stopped talking and started eating.

Thursday came around and all that Jameel could think about was what he'd been assigned to do tonight. At school he was ducking both Sista and Dolitha and the rest of his crew, even Cinque because he didn't want to be questioned about what he might be doing the rest of the day. When school let out, instead of meeting the group to walk home together he went out the side doors and rushed away from the building. He crossed Avon Avenue and headed down to the deli where he had been eating the last few days.

There was hardly anyone there now so he got a soda sat in the back and waited until he thought all of his school friends had left the area. He then called home and told Sarafina that he was going to be home late tonight because he was going to see about a job. In a way he was right, but it wasn't the whole truth.

For the next few hours Jameel just walked around with a feeling of anxiety in the pit of his stomach. He was trying to picture in his mind what tonight might be all about, but the only thing he could imagine was what he had seen in the movies. Not knowing what to expect, he was hoping that this run that Buster was talking about meant only going somewhere and seeing the operation at work. Finally it was about 7:15 and he starting walking toward the store. The closer he got, the more the butterflies fluttered in his gut. From a short distance away he could see that some of the club members were in their usual positions outside the hang. Even though Hakeem and Hammer had been picked up, the soldiers were still loitering around there like nothing happened.

When Jameel approached, one of them stepped up to him and asked where he was going. Quickly, the butterflies left and Jameel was in his combat mode.

"I'm goin inside, Buster lookin for me" he said.

The soldier not knowing what arrangements had been made moved aside and Jameel went in the store. Buster was sitting in the corner where Razor used to call his office. He saw Jameel come in and motioned him over. He asked him was he ready to go and Jameel said yes. Buster got up and went in the back and disappeared out of sight. A few minutes later he came back with something in his hand. He handed it to Jameel.

"Here take this, you might need it. You know how to use it don you?" He handed Jameel a 38 Special revolver.

"Yeah man I know how, but what om gonna need this for?" Buster looked back at him smiled and said:

"You never know. Aw-ight les go."

They went outside and got into a waiting car driven by one of the soldiers that had been standing around inside the store.

Once in the car Jameel's butterflies came back and he was having a hard time trying to look cool like the others. A short while later the car pulled up into the back of the warehouse over on 5th Avenue near the outskirts of the city. Already in the back was a trailer with two cars surrounding it and several men alongside. As Buster's ride approached, all but two of the men moved toward the trailer and went inside. The other two men watched Buster park and escorted him into the trailer. It was obvious that the men had some serious hardware beneath their jackets and Jameel felt like this was a scene from one of the gangster movies he had seen.

Inside an older man was sitting at a table alongside one of his soldiers and the troops that were standing around outside just stood near him inside. Buster walked in boldly and pulled up a chair at the table. No names were exchanged, but Buster and the older man shook hands and started talking. It seems that this was the start of a new arrangement and negotiations were beginning right here. At times it got a little testy and everybody came to attention, but cooler heads prevailed and it passed. To Jameel, who had no idea how this stuff really worked, it was kind of exciting and he found himself enjoying it. The meeting ended with an agreement that when the next shipment came in it would be exchanged right here inside the warehouse. The details, time and date would be communicated through the usual channels that they both knew. Buster got up and nodded to his men and they walked out and left the area.

When they got back to the store, Jameel was wondering if this was all there was to this first test so he asked Buster.

"Yo man whas next?" Buster responded:

"I'm gonna show you to the rest of the crew and you may have to deal wit one of 'em."

Jameel had no idea what he was talking about, but he said okay. Buster then walked outside and called the guys together and said some kind of code word that Jameel didn't understand. The next thing he knew he was being escorted around the building into an alley alongside the store and one of the bigger soldiers cold cocked him in the back of his head. The rest of the members made a ring around the two of them and Jameel feeling like a brick had just hit him fell to the ground. He turned around and his vision was a little bleary, but he could see the soldier coming at him again so he instinctively put his hands up to cover his face. It wasn't his face that needed protection. He felt a hard kick to his abdomen and he was back down on the ground again. His mind was reeling and all he could think of was that this was it for him. Somehow he avoided the next blow and was able to roll over from the next poorly aimed kick. He struggled to his feet and managed to also avoid the next punch. Then his pugilistic skills that had been taught to him by his military veteran father kicked in and he gained mounting confidence as he avoided each of his opponent's subsequent blows. For the next several minutes the two went at it hot and heavy with Jameel finally gaining the upper hand and exhausting his opponent to the point where he was completely spent. At that point Jameel knocked him down and was on top pummeling him severly. Buster finally motioned to the ringside soldiers to grab Jameel and pull him off.

"Aw-ight man, you passed the first test. Go on inside to the bathroom and get cleaned up. Then come into my office."

Jameel still wobbly from his encounter stood up, brushed himself off, took a deep breath and walked with a rocking motion inside. When he finished cleaning himself off as best he could, being that there was a knot on his head that nothing in the bathroom could fix, he went over to the office. Buster smiled at him and told him he did okay for the first night, but tomorrow he'd be on his own when he would be making a pick up. He liked the way Jameel handled himself and told him that he'd be okay if he stayed cool.

Finished for the night, Jameel was told to go home and be back there at the same time tomorrow for his final test. Jameel, still a little edgy about the whole thing, started walking home in the cool night air taking deep breaths trying to slow down his heart rate.

When he got home both Cinque and Sarafina were there. Cinque was, as usual playing his NFL video game that he loved and Sarafina was on the phone. He was glad to see her there and also that he was able to get into the bathroom without being seen so he could attend to his head. He finished and poked his head into the living room to say hello. Sarafina nodded her acknowledgement without looking at him and kept on talking. From the gist of the conversation, Jameel could tell that she was talking to Asa. He wasn't happy about that, but what could he do he knew what was happening. He went into the kitchen and got himself something to eat that had been left for him. He thought to himself that even though mom wasn't acting like she used to, she sure could cook and the meals when they had them were delicious.

When Sarafina got off the phone she came in and asked Jameel how he made out. He tried not to look at her directly, but to no avail because she was able to notice his head and asked what happened. With some quick thinking he said that he was running from a dog around that big hardware chain and he fell and hit it on the sidewalk. Satisfied with the answer she went back to the first question. He told her that they were not hiring right now, but he had something else going that he could make some money. She didn't press him further and just said good.

Then she told him she was going to dinner again with Asa tomorrow and she might be coming in late. Jameel cringed when she said that, but he said okay. He asked though if she was going to be drinking. She didn't answer, but left the kitchen and went back into the living room. He sat there just thinking what it was besides getting some money to help pay the bills that he could do to get her away from this man who he perceived as nothing but trouble. He kept associating the man with the picture and coming up with evil.

Asa Leisar finished his conversation with Sarafina and called his brother in New York.

"If you're looking for Al you got him, if not you got the wrong number. At the sound of the tone leave your message."

Asa left a message to be called right away because it was important. Moments later his phone rang. It was Al who was screening his calls.

"Big brother what's up with you, where you been?' he said. I haven't seen you in a week."

"I've been working my show over here and now I need you to help me" Asa said. "That's good. I'm glad you called because I've been doing the same thing over here and the prospects are great. I have many who are ready to be claimed. Tell me about your prospects."

"I have one that I'm working on that is so good, I'm continually amused at how easy the total conquest is going to be. It is a previously God fearing woman who was His and now she's coming to me. Right now though she needs immediate employment so I'm making up a job in which I need you to set something up for me with your business dealings. She must be allowed to make some decent wages, but she must not be able to be free or independent. I want to claim her totally."

"I think I can do that. With my big prospect I have a greedy man who wants nothing more than to get rich no matter what the cost. He is a leader of many, and I'm hoping to get them all. Maybe we can do something that will accommodate both of us. Do you have something in mind?"

" I'm not sure, but let's put our heads together and see what we can come up with. I'm having dinner with her tomorrow night and I would like to be able to tell her that I have something she can start doing next week. What can that be?"

"Well I have my prospect putting together a plan in which he and his people will be coming over here to steal a large shipment of contraband coming into this country. The deal has been put off several times, as I am holding it up to get his excitement up to its maximum level and get the greed level up for his lackeys. Perhaps you can have your person be a liaison as a planning secretary working out of an office near you. You can set it up as an import/export business where she will be talking to people that I'll give you. In reality she'll be talking to my guy and getting his information to me. She need not know whom she's really dealing with and neither will he. What do you think, brother?"

"That sounds brilliant Al, when can we start?"

"You can tell her tomorrow that you will be sending her to an interview in the office that you're going to set up and then do whatever you need to make it happen. I will take care of my end and he will be on notice to start working with your person. We will collaborate on details once you are set up. Good?"

"Excellent! I'll call you again late Saturday afternoon and let you know where we stand. Goodnight!"

"Yes, have an excellent night."

The two brothers with a knack for plotting evil were well on their way to initiating a scheme in which they could claim the souls of those who they had set out to capture.

However, while they were moving ahead with their plans, there was one who was also watching; one who knew how to overcome evil plots and how to reclaim all who have been lost. Throughout the history of mankind, the deceiver and his deceptions have been loosed on this earth. Evil has been called good and good evil and the acceptance of the reversal has become a standard. Though the plots continue, the end is coming and neither the Leisars nor their followers will prevail.

Friday night came and both Sarafina and Jameel were preparing to go out. Neither one said much to the other because it was like a cat and mouse game where they were trying to avoid prying into each ones plans for the evening. Jameel was ready first and he started to head out around 7 PM. Before leaving though, he was trying to see what his mother would be wearing, but she was careful not to reveal anything while he was still there. He did ask her through the closed bedroom door what time she would be coming home, but the reply was that she wasn't sure yet, so he left it at that and walked out. A short time later she came out dressed to please as she had before and went downstairs to meet Asa who was picking her up. Cinque remained in his room oblivious to all that was going on.

The car was waiting right outside the building. Asa opened the door and helped her in.

On the way to the restaurant he told her how nice she looked and that he had been looking forward to tonight all day. The conversation was generally light covering everything from the weather to how her day went. That is until he asked about the painting he had given her. He asked if she had been looking at it and whether she was enjoying it. She thought this was a rather strange question because he knew she really wasn't into art and she just accepted it because he was giving it as a gift. Then she told him that she liked it and didn't let the question bother her anymore.

Before long they arrived at their favorite eatery and went inside. The waiter again showed them to the special corner in the rear of the house that they had come to call their hideaway. The wine, which Asa had pre-ordered was waiting for them on the table and the waiter after he had seated them, asked if he should pour. Asa said yes and the glasses were filled. Sarafina out of curiosity was looking to see what kind of wine they were drinking, but she did not recognize the name on the label. She knew she wasn't a wine expert, but it seemed to her that this was one that she had never even heard of, not even from TV. It went down smoothly and stimulated her appetite. The meal was ordered and it seemed that it came out more quickly than it had on previous occasions. They wined and dined and the hours passed by quickly. During the evening's conversation he had hinted that he had something special to tell her but he wanted to wait until they got to his place. She coyly said to him:

"I think I'm going straight home tonight." He picking up on the ruse countered by saying:

"Well I guess you don't want to hear the good surprise." "Well I guess it will have to wait." she said playfully.

"I guess so," he said looking away.

The playful banter went on for another few minutes until her curiosity got the best of her and she conceded agreeing to go home with him again.

As they rode to his place, the full moon cast a brilliant light on the city and the stars were out in full array. The wine was doing its job and she was feeling very relaxed in the comfort of his sedan. They reached the destination and she was escorted into what again seemed like the dreamscape of her early recollection. He took her coat motioned her to the couch and without asking went to prepare her a glass of his special wine. He returned and they both drank while he started to tell her about his special surprise. The explanation about the new job and her function sounded very exciting to her and she felt relaxed knowing she was going to be returning to work. She smiled and thanked him and that was his signal to begin the foreplay.

From that point on the scene was a repeat of earlier adventures culminating in almost the same dramatic ending. Even though she no longer saw the red dragon, she was still a little leery. By now she had totally abandoned her semi commitment to go home and was content to enjoy the evening to the fullest. The clock seemed to stop and all awareness of time passing became as if she was peering through a cloudy mist in a dense fog. During the act she was again peering at the ceiling to see whether the images that she had seen before would again be visiting them. Tonight they were absent and she drifted off into a deep sleep.

Jameel arrived at M&M's but this time he was greeted differently then he was yesterday. The soldiers standing around showed a new respect for him. How could he know that the challenge he had overcome yesterday was from one of their best men and he now enjoyed some rank he wasn't even aware of? Inside, though he was early, Buster was already waiting for him with the same piece that he had given him last night. He was asked if he was ready and he said he was. Buster explained to him what the whole plan was for tonight. He was told that he was going over to the back of Big Al's bar over on 6th avenue and 11th street and he was going to pick up a package of stuff that belonged to Mr. M. the big man. He was also cautioned when he told these new contacts who he was, not to ask too many questions, but be sure that the weight of the package felt like it could weigh five pounds. To be sure that Jameel knew what five pounds felt like, Buster gave him a package similar to what he would be getting so he could feel the weight. He finally told him not to worry that he and one of the other soldiers would be in the car close enough to see everything. Satisfied that Jameel knew his role, he motioned for him to follow him outside.

They got in the same car that they used last night and headed to Big Al's bar. It was getting kind of cold now, but it was a bright night and Jameel felt like with the brightness something warm like the sun was with him. When they got to Big Al's Jameel remembered that this was the place where his mom had said she was the other night so he instinctively looked around to see whether her car was in the area. Buster's car pulled around back and went to a far corner in the parking lot where another car was sitting. He pulled up to within fifteen yards of the car and flashed the headlights. The lights on the other car flashed back twice and Buster drove nearer, but not too close. Jameel was told to get out go over and meet his new contacts and be ready for anything.

The flutter in Jameel's stomach sent a nervous tingle down his spine and he almost stumbled as he got out of the car. The two men that got out of the other car came over to meet him at the halfway point. Standing about ten feet apart, Jameel told them who he was and they just looked at him hard not saying anything at first. Then one of the men asked him a question that he had no idea what he was talking about. Buster hadn't told him anything about what the man was asking.

"What chu think we fools or somthin'?" the man said when Jameel failed to answer correctly.

"You think we jus gonna give you this an you dono nothin."

He turned around to the other guy and said: "Smoke this m   " and Jameel fearing for his life started to reach for the piece that Buster gave him. In his excitement, his eyes were going bleary and a mist was forming, but he could see that the other guy was raising his hand and the next thing he knew shots were fired at him. He managed to get hands on his weapon and returned fire. He could hardly believe it, but the shooter went down and as he fired again so did the other man. He quickly composed himself just enough to run over and grab the package then turn around and head for his car. Buster had the door open and he scrambled inside. The engine roared and then all you could hear was the sound of tires screeching as the rear end shifted from side to side in making a hasty exit from the lot. Inside Jameel laid his head back on the headrest and heavily breathed a sigh of relief.

Chapter 12 - The Setup

At the Big A on Friday nights there was usually a big crowd shaking and writhing on the dance floor to loud music. Except for the people sitting or standing around near the back door, it was almost impossible to hear anything going on outside. However, this night those few people by the door heard the gunshots outside and one of them alerted Albert, the owner, to call police. Two men in that bar area courageously walked out the back door and looked in the direction of where they thought the shots came from. What they saw were taillights of a dark colored car racing out of the parking lot and two bodies lying on the ground beside a dark SUV in the far corner. Not wanting to get heavily involved, they went back inside told Albert what they saw then continued partying.

Within five minutes a patrol car responding to the call arrived and two officers went in the bar. They found Albert and questioned him briefly. He told them that he didn't hear anything himself, but he pointed out the two men who heard the shots and went outside. The officers asked the two men to come with them outside where they questioned them. After a few minutes of questioning, the officers let the men return to the bar and they went over to the corner and started searching. What they found was nothing; no car, no bodies and no shell casings. Thinking that this was some kind of a prank, they went back inside and found the two men again. After a more intense questioning this time, the men finally convinced them that they really did hear shots and saw bodies. The officers having no more to go on, decided there was nothing else they could do, called in their report and went back on patrol.

When Buster, Jameel and the other soldier arrived back at the hang, Jameel was still trying to maintain his cool front, but was shaking inside.

Buster told Jameel to give him back the piece. Jameel at this point couldn't handle it anymore and he went off on Buster.

"Man, why you set me up like that? I jus wasted two dudes `cause you didn tell me what I needa know."

"Ah chill out man, you ain done nothin." "What chu mean you saw it?"

Buster popped open the revolver dumped out the cartridges and showed them to Jameel. "Blanks man, blanks. Those guys you shot at shootin blanks too. They part of our crew. Ain nothin wrong wit `em an they be here soon. So chill man, you pass the test. I jus hadda be sure you could do it when the time came."

Jameel wasn't sure whether to be totally angry or relieved that he hadn't really shot anybody. He just looked at Buster and said:

"Aw-ight so now what?"

"Now you in an you just wait `till I get the call for the real deal an then I let you know."

"So when I start makin some money?"

"Soon man, soon. But since you jus passed yo test I'm gonna spot you a hunderd. You can get me back later."

Buster whipped out his bankroll peeled off a $100 dollar bill and gave it to Jameel. Jameel tried to hide his emotions, but his eyes gave him away as he accepted the money. Buster could see that he was impressed so he said to him:

"Don worry man, once you get rollin, yo bank account can git strong too. You jus be cool an do what I tell you."

Jameel still wasn't comfortable with this guy who was about his age, being able to control him like this, but with the feel of the large bill in his pocket and the promise of more, he made concessions.

When he got home it was about 11 PM, Cinque was in bed and Sarafina was not there.

He tried dialing her cell phone again hoping that it was back on, but the out of service message was still there. He then went to the kitchen to see if there was something to eat and made himself a plate out of some leftovers. He was really starting to worry about his mother now. She was staying out drinking a lot more and staying home less.

Reflecting on what he had done tonight, he was trying to reconcile himself to believe that what he was getting into would be for a short time and he would get enough money to stop soon. Before he left the kitchen, just out of curiosity he looked in the cabinet where he had put the gin bottle before and there it was; another bottle half full. He stared at the bottle for several minutes and then poured himself a glass and drank it.

Asa took Sarafina home the next morning then he went back home. She eased in the apartment door hoping that neither one of the boys was up yet, she was right. It was only about 9:00 O'clock and Jameel had taken a few drinks so he wasn't getting up anytime soon, while Cinque had gotten accustomed to sleeping even later on Saturday now since both mom and Jameel were staying out later on Friday nights. She went into the kitchen poured herself her morning coffee and sat down. She noticed that the cabinet door where she kept the gin was slightly ajar and she knew she closed it, so she looked inside and fell back in her chair. The level of the bottle was well below where she left it and she knew in a moment why this was. She said to herself, what can I say to him he sees me doing it and he's growing up. Sadly, she just closed the door tight and went and got in the bed.

Asa Leisar got back to his place and immediately began to hash out his plot. He looked in the newspapers and located several places that had office space available in the downtown area close to his office. Marking the ones he thought might work for him he made his calls. There was one that sounded ideal for what he had in mind, so he set an appointment for this afternoon and hung up. Then he started putting together a plan the way he thought an Import/Export business should operate. He named his project, Peerless Treasures, Inc., because he felt that what he was seeking was an unequalled treasure for him and his brother. Details were plotted, schemes were put in place and then he contemplated whom else he was going to need to get involved in his operation.

Around 2:00 PM he felt he had it all worked out so he called his brother. This time he got him on the first try and they discussed the plans that Asa had come up with. Al agreed it should work and said that he would get in touch with Ricoh, his prospect, and let him know. He told Asa that there should be no problem from his end, because Ricoh would be anxious to get his part going. Contented that they had an infallible plot working, both the brothers said goodbye and spent the rest of the day implementing the plot.

When Jameel finally got up it was almost 11:00 AM and he slowly worked his way into the bathroom. Feeling again like he had after leaving Sista's not too long ago, he said to himself:

"Why did I do that?"

Having no good answer, he got in the shower and tried to wash away the blahs. After coming out and getting dressed, he peeked in on Sarafina to see how she was. She was still sleeping. Cinque meanwhile was taking this all in and asked Jameel if he was having a problem too. Knowing what he was referring to, Jameel laughed and said no, not me. An hour or so later, Sarafina got up, showered, got dressed and went out again. Nothing was said to the boys and they were getting really worried about what was going on. She returned a short time later with a bag of groceries and another bag. Jameel wasn't sure, but he was guessing what was in the smaller bag so he followed her into the kitchen.

"What chu get mom?"

"Oh jus a couple of things I know we're out of. We ain got no more bread right?" "Yeah I think so."

Jameel saw her put away the bread, milk and juice, but by the time he came into the kitchen, the little bag had disappeared. He knew that she had disposed of it and didn't want him to see, so he said nothing and went back into his room.

He had had enough of this deception and being in the house was getting to him so he went out headed to Rajon's. This time, minutes later Cinque followed him out the door headed toward the recreation center to shoot some hoops with his friends. Neither boy said anything to their mother, they just walked out. Sarafina knew she was losing control of them, but didn't feel like this was a big thing anymore so she poured herself a drink and watched TV. An odd thing happened though while she was watching. A Noonday movie came on that was all about a woman who was married to a preacher and living the so-called good life. The TV family was just like hers with two boys, they were active in the community just like hers, and then he got killed in a car accident, almost like hers.

She then met a man who came along to help her, but in reality he was the devil leading her down an unrighteous path and out to claim her soul. In the end, after she had sunk to her lowest depth and ready to end her life, she had a direct encounter with God. After her epiphany she is restored and put back on the right track to salvation. She falls on her knees praising the One who saves her and it ends.

A shudder ran down Sarafina's spine and she had an eerie feeling that it wasn't just a coincidence that she was watching this movie at this time. However, when the movie ended she dismissed the feeling and got herself another drink. This time though after she consumed the drink she went into the bedroom and sat on her bed looking up at the picture she had mounted on the wall. The apartment door opened and Cinque was returning from his basketball outing. He walked in and went by his mother's room and saw her on her knees with her hands folded talking to the picture. It scared him at first and he didn't know what to do. But when she sensed he was watching, she got up and sat on the bed for a minute and then lay down.

"Mom, mom you aw-ight?" he said. Getting no answer he went in and shook her. "Tired, tired so-o tired" she mumbled.

Cinque could smell the alcohol on her so he just let her lie on the bed and he went out and closed the door.

When Jameel got back home, Cinque filled him in on all that he saw. Jameel then peeked in the room and she was still sleeping, but everything seemed to be okay. Cinque asked him what they were going to do and Jameel responded that he didn't know. He thought about trying to reach Reverend Joyner, but he didn't want to have to explain all that his mother had been doing. He then thought about calling Lydia and looked around for her telephone number. He remembered that the CONN's roster used to be on the living room coffee table, but when he looked there it was gone. He couldn't think of whom else to call so he gave up. The boys spent the rest of the night just watching television and playing video games while she slept through the night.

Sunday was rather quiet for the family. Jameel got up and fixed breakfast for him and Cinque while Sarafina continued to sleep. When she did get up, she apologized to the boys again for how she had been acting lately and told them everything was going to be all right soon because she was going back to work. Jameel felt good when he heard that and wondered whether this was the start of things returning to what they were. He asked her what she was going to be doing and she told him that she would know better on Wednesday after her interview. Still not feeling great she managed to pull herself together enough to go into the living room and watch the news.

Later that afternoon the phone rang and it was for Jameel. "Jameel here, whas up?"

"Jameel, its Buster can you come down to the store tonight `bout 8. Some of the guys gonna be there I want you to meet."

"Yeah, I can do that, see ya there."

Sarafina over hearing part of the conversation asked `J' who that was and he told her just a new friend he had met when he was looking for work. Satisfied with the answer she continued to watch TV and he went back to his room.

Eight O' clock came around and Jameel told Sarafina that he was going out for a little while. Still nursing a bit of a hangover, she didn't question where he was going, but did ask what time he'd be back. He just said not too long and left. He got down to the store and when he looked inside it seemed like no one was there, but when he got close to the door in the dim light he could see some of the guys sitting around on the floor. He couldn't tell what was going on, but one of them spotted him and opened the door. As soon as he walked in the smell of their favorite plant was in the air and he was greeted with a firm hug from Buster. Buster told him to sit down beside him and then introduced him to the troops sitting around the room. After the introductions, Buster passed the smoke to `J' and told him to join the party.

Jameel, not accustomed to the weed, hesitated at first, but not wanting to appear like he wasn't one of them took a deep drag. He coughed for about five minutes and the whole gang laughed, but after the second and third attempts he started feeling a new sensation that was making him feel pretty good. He continued with them in the party for an hour or so and then he was feeling mellow.

Buster told him that he heard something was going to be happening soon and it was going to be big. Jameel only half heard him, but nodded his head. The group then broke up and left the store.

Jameel riding on cloud 9 didn't feel like going home so he found a phone and called Sista. Slurring through his words at first, he was able to let her know he wanted to come over. She told him to come on, but wondered why he was talking like that. It didn't even occur to her what he had gotten into. When he arrived, she opened the door and it was obvious to her what he had been doing. She was no stranger to seeing her brother and the rest of the gang in this state, but she was a little surprised to see him this way. She really liked him and didn't want him to get like them. He stumbled into the apartment and over to the couch. She asked him if he wanted some coffee or some water, but he said no he just wanted her. Torn between wanting to respond and knowing his state of mind, she just sat down on the couch beside him and held him. Before long he was all over her and his kisses even in this condition were too much for her to resist.

When it was over and he had slept for a while, he woke up and she was standing over him just looking.

"You feel betta now?" she asked. "Yeah that was good, but I'm starvin."

"You got the munchies. Here eat this" and she gave him some chips with some dip. He gobbled them down and drank a half bottle of water. She then sat on the bed beside him and told him that she had heard from Mr. M and he wasn't happy about Hakeem and Hammer getting busted and he wanted them out. He told me to get Buster to bail them out tomorrow. Also he said that the next shipment would be coming in week after next and he wanted them back in charge. Now you know they don't know that you're in so it may be a little bit of a problem, but I'll handle it. You just keep cool."

Jameel agreed and said whatever she wanted him to do he would. After that he reached for her and love play act two started.

When Jameel got home it was after midnight and he opened the door very carefully. Nobody was up and he eased his way to his room. Not even going to the bathroom, he changed his clothes and got in the bed. Feeling very satisfied, he went into a deep sleep within minutes of laying his head on the pillow. This time, Sarafina who heard him come in but didn't say anything, poked her head into his room to see if he was okay. She was a little relieved to see that he was okay and sleeping soundly. Looking at him in the bed, she realized that she was no longer looking at a boy, but this was a man in her house.

At police headquarters on Monday, Lt. Meeker was all fired up about getting his search warrant to go back into the Minute Mart. It seems that the mayor was able to persuade the judge that it would be in her best interest to sign off on the warrant given the unstable climate of the city's citizens. While Meeker was setting the stage to take his men down there, he got word from Captain Tillery to hold off making the move until further notice. Wondering why he was being told to back off after he had painstakingly gone through all that he did to get here, he went down to the captain's office. Without knocking he barged in. The captain was on the phone and was surprised by Meeker's entry, but he motioned for him to sit down. He could tell from the lieutenant's facial expression that he was upset and he figured it was because of the hold. When he got off the phone he told Meeker to calm down before he got himself in trouble and he would explain what's happening. Lt. Meeker regained his composure and sat up straight in his chair eager to hear what the captain had to say.

Captain Tillery started telling him that over the weekend, the night crew had spotted that Bentley they had picked up on a few weeks back, not only at the store, but also at the warehouse over on 5th Avenue in the wee hours of the morning. We don't want to go crashing in there now because we suspect that something big is getting ready to come down and we don't want to spook them. I was just talking with the mayor, and he told me that the FBI has found out who the link at the airport is and they're waiting for the next arrival before they move in on him. The thing is they don't want to spook him either. They want the guy that he answers to and they think it's the same guy who owns the Bentley, the store, the plant and the warehouse. Relax lieutenant we're getting close, real close to solving this whole thing and I think it's going to happen soon.

Lt. Meeker satisfied with the explanation went back to his office and called off the dog team that he had assembled to make his bust. Sergeant Calloway was also disappointed about the stand down, but when he was told the reason why he also agreed there were bigger fish to be landed than the ones they had. Meeker then went down to the cells to talk to their guests again. Both Hakeem and Hammer were glad to see the lieutenant come because they thought he was going to tell them that the deal he had promised them was going through and they were going to be let out. Of course they didn't know that even while Meeker was talking with them, Buster was making arrangements per Mr. M's instructions, to get them bailed out.

Lieutenant Meeker asked them if there was anything they hadn't told him and that he was giving them one more chance to tell him everything. Suspicious that Meeker was pulling a fast one to get out of the deal he promised them, Hakeem asked him if was playing some kind of game and he wasn't stupid. Meeker calmed him down by telling him there was no game being played here, but he just wanted to know everything that they did. When Hakeem heard this and he didn't hear anything about getting out, he asked when that was going to happen. Lt. Meeker told him that he had to work through some things and it was going to take a day or so. Hakeem not happy with the answer, told the lieutenant he was tired of waiting and to hurry up with his deal or he would change his mind about letting him know about the next shipment. Lt. Meeker just smiled at him and said:

"What's the matter you don't like my hotel?" and turned around and walked out.

Later that afternoon, the papers came down and both Hakeem and Hammer were released. They were let out before either Captain Tillery or Lieutenant Meeker were told about it. When they found out, both were extremely irate demanding to know who got them out. They knew that once Hakeem got out, whatever weapons were in the store would be gone by the time they implemented another search and they would again wind up looking like fools; and so would the judge. The word that came back regarding the bail out was that it was through a bond posted by an anonymous benefactor. Lt. Meeker rushed out to find who the bail bondsman was and question him. He got to the bondsman, but was told that he couldn't release that information. Disappointed that he was right, Meeker returned to headquarters to try and figure what his next step should be to protect the department and the judge from the mayor.

Hakeem and Hammer upon their release went straight to the store. Buster wasn't there and the store manager didn't know where he was so they decided to go to their respective apartments and come back later. Hakeem before leaving looked around the store marveling that the veiled business was still doing well. He got to his apartment and noticed that it was not the way that he left it. He ran down to the super's apartment and questioned him about who had been in his place. The super with some fear in his voice told him that he had no choice because the cops showed him a warrant and forced him to open the door. Hakeem after hearing that backed off and went back to his place. Once inside, he dialed Buster's cell number and got him.

"Yo Buster, this Hakeem where you at? I'm in my own crib now, they finally released me"

"Hey man good to hear. Glad you out, whas up?"

"Look we gotta get the tools outta the store an move 'em to the warehouse right away."

"Why we doin that, they safe in there ain they?" "Naw man not no more, I hadda give it up?" "What chu mean?"

"Don be stupid man, I hadda tell them cops `bout the place to save my butt. I didn't think I was gettin out otherwise."

"Man you know big man ain gonna like that."

"How he gonna know, you gonna tell `em? All he ever worry `bout is we give `em his money when he come to git it. He don care what we got or ain got in there."

"Naw man, you know I ain tellin, but I jus think he gonna fine out."

"Man you don worry `bout that, jus meet me tonight wit some of the soldiers an some cars an we gonna move that stuff outta there before the cops raid the place."

"Yeah aw-ight what time you gonna be there?" "Meet there at 8."

"Yeah, cool. Jus one more thing though, you know we got a new guy." "Oh yeah who?"

"It's Jameel, you know the one that got all shot up at Higgyb's." "Jameel, how you let `em in, `cause of Sista?"

"Yeah she wanted it." "You test `em?"

"Yeah man, did it myself, he aw-ight."

"Well I can't deal wit that now, I'll talk wit Sista tomorrow. Aw-ight lemme go, I'll see ya later."

"Yeah man cool, later."

Not long after Buster hung up with Hakeem, he got a call from one of Mr. M's people. He wanted to know whether the business with Hakeem and Hammer had been taken care of. Buster assured them that it had and that both men were back on the streets. The word came back that Mr. M wanted to see both of them tonight at the store at 10:00 PM and don't be late. Buster immediately got back on the phone to Hakeem and told him what had just happened. Hakeem after several choice words said all right and his plan to move the stuff would have to wait until tomorrow. He told Buster to call Hammer and tell him to make sure he got to the store tonight too.

At 10, Hakeem, Hammer, Buster and a soldier were in the store waiting for Mr. M. Almost right on time, the Bentley parked around the corner and three men in suits got out and went in the store. They entered into the secret room and Mr. M. took the big chair. He lit right into Hakeem telling him that he wasn't happy about him screwing up and getting picked up for being stupid. He went on that this operation was too important to him to get messed up by a fool and there was no room in his business for fools. Hakeem totally submissive told the man that he was sorry and it wouldn't happen again. Mr. M. lowered his voice and settled back into his chair. Then he started telling about a very large deal that would be coming to the airport next week and he wanted no slip up's with the pick up and delivery. When he finished giving the details to Hakeem and feeling sure that he understood his role; Mr. M. and his soldiers got into the Bentley and left. It was now about Midnight and they were surprised by a patrol car coming in the opposite direction toward the store. Mr. M. cautioned his driver to maintain his composure and just keep driving. The patrol car passed them and kept going. However, the eyes of Mr. Malcolm Long were again watching the whole scene from his window across the street.

The next morning Captain Tillery came rushing into his office earlier than usual and hoping that the lieutenant would also be there. He was still peeved that the two men they had in custody yesterday had been released before they knew it. Knowing they would go straight to the store and remove the weapons they had confessed were there, he was scrambling trying to put together another dog team to carry out the warrant. After checking messages in his own office, he went to Lt. Meeker's to see if he had arrived.

Not seeing him, he started looking for the documentation on who was set up for the original team. Rifling through the papers on his desk, he came across the order authorizing the lieutenant, a SWAT team and two officers to initiate the search. He picked up the order and just as he was about to leave, the lieutenant came in. Without even saying hello the captain said:

"We've got to carry this out right now, before those guys get rid of the evidence." Lieutenant Meeker agreed wholeheartedly and got on the intercom paging the men involved in the action.

Fifteen minutes later the team was assembled and the police vehicles were rolling toward the Minute Mart. It was only 8:45 AM and the store was not officially open, but the store manager and his clerks were inside setting up for the day. Lt. Meeker rushed up to the door and banged on it. The store manager, tired of seeing this man again, came to the door with an angry look on his face. He opened the door and asked what the lieutenant wanted. Lt. Meeker presented him with the warrant, pushed him aside and motioned his men to enter. The team went straight to the rear room of the building and seeing nothing inside, stopped. Lt. Meeker then came in and said:

"Okay gents, watch the magic."

As he had been directed per Hakeem's instructions he went over to the picture on the wall and right in the center, well disguised from normal observation was a small flower. The center of the flower in what looked like the stigma was a button that controlled the sliding doors. Meeker pushed the button and slowly the doors slid open revealing a large room with a big conference table and plush chairs inside.

The men were surprised as they entered and even more surprised at what they saw. In front of them and all around them, neatly stacked like an armory, were weapons of all sorts. They found automatic rifles, handguns, shotguns and even some bulletproof vests. In addition, there was enough ammunition to fuel these weapons and equip a small army. Lt. Meeker sat down in one of the plush chairs and just laughed. Soon the men and even the captain joined him. It was if they had discovered a goldmine and they were all sharing in the loot. The captain instructed the team to put on their gloves and carefully carry the weapons out without smudging any possible fingerprints. This time the mission was successful and Lt. Meeker couldn't wait to get back to headquarters and file his official report.

Over in the Bricks complex Ricoh was on the phone with Big Al. It had been some time since he heard from Al and he was getting antsy about the big caper Al had originally told him about at the party he threw. Al, after doing his usual job in calming him down, told him that the plans that Ricoh had provided were good, but there were some things that had to be done before the execution of the actual job. Then he proceeded to tell him about the import/export business that was going to be put in the loop. He explained to Ricoh that there was going to be a woman contact that he would start interfacing with and she would be the key to the final details. He was to expect a call on Thursday afternoon and the woman would introduce herself and say a codeword so that he would know she is the right one. Ricoh anxiously agreed and told Al again that he was ready. Al told him soon amigo, soon and hung up.

Later that afternoon Sarafina received the call that she was expecting from Asa. He told her earlier that he would be calling today to give her the details on her interview tomorrow. He told her that the interview was really just a formality and she would be working for the Peerless Treasures, Inc. Import/Export Company based in New York but she would be working out of the satellite office right here. She was also told to be there promptly at 10:00 AM and make sure she had proper identification. Sarafina got real excited and started asking a lot of questions about what she was going to be doing. Asa sidestepped the barrage and just told her that everything would be explained to her at the session tomorrow. Feeling good about having a job, she said okay, I'll be there and hung up. Asa then got hold of his brother and confirmed that everything was in place and it was on. Al confirmed his role. He was going to conduct the interview and provide her with what she needed to know.

Not too long after the police had completed their raid and left, Hakeem, Hammer and a few of the soldiers pulled up to the store in several cars and an SUV. The store manager seeing them come up ran to the door and excitedly told them what had happened. Hakeem issued a string of expletives and motioned to Hammer to follow him. He told the rest of the crew to disappear and he would contact them later, but he wanted Hammer to go with him to his house. Once inside the apartment, Hakeem was beside himself with frustration and it was clear to Hammer that he was right on the edge.

Hammer tried to calm him down, but Hakeem explained to him that now that the police have the weapons they would be coming back for them. Hammer reminded him that he was the one who told the cops how to get in the secret room. Hakeem acknowledged that but said that was a ruse just to get out of the joint, because he was going to get the weapons out of there before they could pull off the raid and all they would find was an empty room. Mr. M messed up that plan good. Right now he was pacing the floor trying to figure what he could do. He couldn't decide whether he was more afraid of being picked up again by the police or Mr. M finding out that the room had been compromised.

It was almost as if he talked him up, because his cell phone rang and it was one of Mr. M's soldiers. He wanted to know if Hakeem was able to talk to him now. Hakeem stuttered at first trying to buy a minute to think of what to tell Mr. M. He finally said yes put him on. Mr. M came on and wanted to go over a couple of last minute changes in what he had told him last night. Hakeem said okay and he was listening. Mr. M. told him to write down what he was going to tell him so he doesn't forget. Hakeem told him to wait a minute while he got something to write with. Mr. M. gave him the changes and then, suspecting something was wrong from the shaky sound of Hakeem's voice, asked if everything was all right. Hakeem blurted out quickly yes everything's fine. Mr. M. still somewhat uneasy by his tone said okay and hung up, but off the phone he instructed his soldiers to go down to the store and check it out.

Mr. M.'s henchmen got to the store went inside and asked for Hakeem. The store manager, not knowing who these men were and still reeling from the raid this morning, wasn't sure what to tell them. They didn't look like cops, but in the suits they didn't look like Hakeem's people either, so he just said that Hakeem wasn't there and he didn't know where he was. The men not wanting to hear that asked if he knew where he might be.

The store manager said no, but getting the strong feeling that these men were not to be trifled with, volunteered that he had been here a while ago and may be at home now. Satisfied with this, the men looked around the store to see if everything was in place and then left. Because the store seemed in order, they didn't go to Hakeem's place but returned to the plant.

Hakeem sensing that things were starting to fall apart, told Hammer that he could feel that Mr. M. didn't believe him when he said everything was all right. He then said that the next shipment was due to come in on Wednesday of next week and they were supposed to be at the airport by 3:00 PM with the big van. Mr. M. had also said that he was aware someone had tipped the feds so there would be some changes in how he was to interact with the contact at the port. The contact would be calling the night before to let him know the change details. Hammer wasn't as shaken as Hakeem and asked why he was freaking out. Hakeem all pent up and annoyed at the question, verbally jumped on Hammer and told him that he should be worried too because he would go down if this thing blew up, just like he would. Hammer sensing Hakeem was really right on the edge, backed off and said nothing else.

Cinque and Jameel walked in the door about their usual time and were pleased to smell the aroma of barbecued chicken. They went into the kitchen and Sarafina was there cooking and singing. They hadn't seen her this happy for days and they wondered what the change was all about. Jameel asked her why she was so happy and she said she'd tell them at dinner. The boys thrilled at the possibility that their old mom was back, went into their room and started the usual evening routines. At dinner, Sarafina couldn't wait to tell the boys that she was going back to work tomorrow and she would be leaving around 9:30 to go on her interview. Jameel questioned if it was just an interview, why she said she had the job. She responded that Asa told her the interview was just formality and she already had the job. Jameel wasn't that familiar about how job interviews worked, but he was still suspicious just because it was coming from that Mr. Leisar.

Wednesday morning came and Sarafina got up early feeling excited, but confident. She woke the boys up and made sure that they were into their routines preparing to go to school. She saw them off and then went back in her room to lie down for just a short time. On the way she couldn't help but look at the picture. She didn't want to look, but somehow the picture had a way of enticing her whenever she passed by it. The scene once again of all the people just partying and having fun, was drawing her in, but this time she fought the feeling and instead of lying down, left the bedroom and went into the living room.

Before long it was 9:30 and she finished her final preparations for the interview. She left the apartment went down to her car and was on her way. She had a pretty good idea of where the place was so she wasn't worried about getting lost. Once in the block where the address she was given said the office was she was a little surprised that it was not in an office building, but was just a small storefront. There was no sign on the door or the windows or anything, but the address number was plainly visible so she parked the car and went in. The office was plainly furnished with a receptionist desk right at the door and then a partition closing the front area from the back. There was no one at the desk, so she waited a minute to see if someone would come out, but nothing happened. She started loudly clearing her throat to try and get some attention and soon a man came out who introduced himself as Alivedi Leisar. She was trying to subtlety make a connection, but she wasn't sure she should ask. He invited her into the back beyond the partition and there was a private office and several medium sized cubicles. She was directed into the office and invited to sit down. Mr. Leisar seemed very professional and began the interview by asking her to tell a little bit about herself. She was a little uncomfortable with this but managed to say what she thought he wanted to hear. It appeared that he was pleased with her response so he started to tell her about the operation that she was joining. He also explained that since this was a brand new office, the signs had not been put up yet, but they would be coming soon. When he finished telling her the duties, it seemed to her like this was going to be fun. When he told her what she would be earning, she had to struggle to maintain her composure because it was a lot more than what she was making before.

He finished talking and asked that she join him while he showed her cubicle and the rest of the office. They started in the very back with the rear exit which led out to a parking area. She was glad to see that because it would save her time looking for a space in the morning. Then he showed her the restrooms, both men and women. She was also pleased at this because the women's room was very clean. Finally they got to her cubicle that was right at the front just behind the entrance partition and near his office. She stepped into it and sat down in a nicely appointed executive type adjustable chair. In front of her were the usual things, a large spacious desk with plenty of drawers, a telephone, a computer with its own printer and a portable upright closet for her coat. She was extremely pleased at this arrangement and was ready to start. He told her that she could begin now if she wanted to or she could start tomorrow morning. She elected to start now.

He told her that they do have a receptionist who would be coming early tomorrow, but for now any calls that came in he would handle. The first thing he gave her was a list of names that she should become familiar with and to get used to saying the company name. She looked at the names and they all seemed strange sounding, but she didn't let that bother her. The next thing he gave her was a list of code words that were to be associated with each day of the week. In other words for Monday it was this, for Tuesday it was something else, etc. She thought this a little strange, but he explained to her that in the import/export business sometimes competitors would try to steal your product shipments if they could get your codes. This made some semblance of sense to her so she was fine with it. The type of phone she had was a call director model in which she could see all the calls that came in and switch them if she had to. She also thought this was strange, because if they had a receptionist why would they want her to have that control. Again, she was just happy to be here and nothing bothered her. The rest of the day was uneventful because there were only two calls that came in and he took them.

When she came in the next day at 9:00 AM, the receptionist was already there and she introduced herself. She was a fairly young woman maybe in her late twenty's and quite attractive. Right from the start they hit it off and by lunchtime they were both talking like old friends. Mr. Leisar had not come in that morning, but he called and issued instructions for Sarafina to call a Mr. Edwards, introduce herself, listen to and write down the details that he would give her and be sure to use the code word for today at the very beginning. Sarafina looked on the chart to see if his name was there and sure enough there was a Ricoh Edwards along with a telephone number. She called

Mr. Edwards, and as instructed gave the code word, and the conversation began. Mr. Edwards provided her with some information that seemed very strange. He was giving her dates that he could provide special large vehicles and descriptions of the vehicles. She acknowledged exactly what he said and wrote it down. Only one other call came in that morning, it was a wrong number.

As the day progressed, the number of calls started picking up. Mixed with the legitimate business calls were several wrong numbers. Sarafina figured that this must be due to the phone number being new and the callers were looking for the former holder of the number. The legitimate calls were seeking to get on Mr. Leisar's distribution list for those who would receive his special product when it became available. They referred to the import as Euphoria Dolls and to Sarafina it sounded like a toy. She diligently took the information and began to catalogue it to present to her boss when he came in. There were even some visitors that came in off the street looking for these dolls. The receptionist was also under the same impression that these were some imported dolls and she and Sarafina joked about being in the toy business.

It was very late in the afternoon when Al came in. He told his girls that he had been out drumming up new business and this would be happening from time to time. Sarafina gave him her list and he looked at it and was pleased. He asked her if she could work late on some evenings, perhaps starting tomorrow because he was preparing for a large shipment to come in. She said yes, it wouldn't be a problem and continued working. A little after 5 a call came in from Mr. Edwards who sounded frantic and wanted to speak directly to Mr. Leisar. The receptionist had already left for the day so she took the call. Mr. Edwards was insistent on speaking to Mr. Leisar immediately and said it was very important. Al was on another line, and Sarafina wasn't sure whether she should interrupt him or not, so she told Mr. Edwards what was happening and asked him if he could wait. He screamed back no and told her to get him right now. Sarafina responding to his attitutde walked into Mr. Leisars's office and told him the situation. He terminated his call and picked up Mr. Edwards.

Sarafina was still in the room when Mr. Leisar told Ricoh with a stern voice that he was never to talk to her like that again and that whatever he had to say could wait until he was ready to talk to him. She couldn't hear his response, but it seems that his attitude got better in a hurry and he calmed down. Mr. Leisar then dismissed Sarafina and she went back to her desk. Her curiosity was really tempting her to pick up on her extension and listen to what that was all about, but she resisted packed up and called it a day. For her first full day, she was happy and feeling like she was going to enjoy this new position and looked forward to getting her first pay check.

The days went by quickly and Sarafina was into her third week. From all that she could understand there was this big shipment coming in from South America and between Mr. Edwards and Mr. Leisar and a couple of other key people, all the arrangements were being funneled through her. She was excited about being an integral part of the operation and felt important. The only concern she had was that it was becoming more frequent that Al would ask her to work late. She was getting more tired with each extended day. Even though she was back working and seemingly getting her debts under control, she was still seeing Asa and drinking more. Al noticed that she was starting to appear tired one evening and offered her what he said was a picker upper. It was a pill that he said it would make her feel better. He had gained her trust by now so she took it.

Moments later she started feeling a new sense of energy. She was feeling a sense of being invincible and able to go another ten hours. Fortunately, he only needed her another hour and she went home. This new feeling she had was propelling her to new heights and she liked it. By the time she got home, it was if her whole body had been renewed and she could go on forever. When she walked in the door she was still in her happy mood and the boys could tell there was something different. They just assumed that she had a good day on the job. Since she had been working later she had made arrangements with the boys to get their own meals if she wasn't there and that seemed to be working okay. It wasn't very late but suddenly she started feeling tired again, almost drained. She went into her room to retire to bed, but the picture caught her attention. She stared at it and like before the party inside was in full swing and the naked bodies were engaged in their activities having a good time. By now she was accustomed to seeing this and she was so tired she just went to bed.

More and more each day she craved that feeling of energy and wellness and Mr. Al Leisar was there to accommodate her with the pills. Between ingesting the pills and drinking her gin late at night, her mornings were getting to be more challenging to get started. Both the brothers Leisar seemed to be helping her along this path, and she was hooked. As she got more into her addiction, family life was taking a back seat and the boys were totally frustrated not knowing what to do. It didn't really bother Jameel because he was busy into his own thing as he was getting more into smoking the plant and doing the soldier things with the C's. Cinque was at a loss to do anything so he just went along with whatever happened.

It was early afternoon Tuesday, the day before Mr. M's big shipment was due to come in at the airport. Hakeem for the past few days had been ducking the police, Mr. M's people even Hammer. He was feeling trapped by his own posse and the old feeling of top dog in control had eluded him. He was now anxiously waiting for the call from the airport contact and as the day progressed and he heard nothing, he was getting worried.

Mr. M. had thoroughly impressed upon him how important this

delivery was and he was still reeling from his recent mistakes. Finally the phone rang and he jumped on it.

"Hakeem here who dis?"

"Hakeem, port contact X, are you ready?" "Yeah man om ready whas the deal?"

"Have the big van at the usual area in P1 at exactly 3:00 PM tomorrow. You'll have about fifteen minutes to get in, get the stuff and get out of there. I know we're being watched so timing is critical. If you mess it up you're on your own, I don't know you. Bring only two others besides yourself, got it?"

"Yeah man I got it. See ya then."

Captain Tillery, Lt. Meeker and now the mayor were feeling a new sense of accomplishment after having captured the large cache of weapons and now getting close to tying it to somebody big. The FBI was even providing information directly to the police about what they had on the trafficking between continents and were certain that something was due to happen soon. Although they couldn't provide an exact date and time, they were sure that it would be this week. The mayor was encouraging his troops with all his ability to stay on top of anything that might give them an edge in making the bust and capturing the headlines. Inside he felt certain that if they could do this it would ensure his re-election when the time came.

Lt. Meeker had been lobbying to close the Minute Mart down after the raid, but Captain Tillery insisted that they leave it alone until they could nail the owner for his role. He knew that they were very close and closing the store would just serve to let the enemy know their plan. He reminded Meeker that they had received another report from the night shift that the Bentley had been seen in the late night hours around the store. In addition, the officers were able to get a good look at the occupants of the car and they would be able to identify them again.

"Let's just keep this under cover until we need it, but let us not spook the horse we're trying to catch." he said.

Being as close as they are he wanted to make sure that things were all in place so that when the final arrests were made, they would have a case that even the rookie prosecutor could prove.

Hakeem got on the phone and called Hammer. He wasn't sure he was going to get him, because since they had been in the joint he knew neither one of them had paid their bills. He felt though that since his service was still on, maybe his is too.

"Hammer that you?"

"Yeah `keem om here whas up?"

"I jus got the call from the port contact. Its on for tomorrow. We still got the big van right?"

"Yeah."

"Is it ready to roll?"

"Yeah I think so, but I betta check wit Buster to be sure."

"Aw-ight do that. When you git Buster, tell him he goin wit us an to meet in front of the school at 2:30 PM, don go to the store. You come there too."

"Aw-ight `keem I'll tell `em. Where you at now?"

"Om at my place now but goin out in a few. Gonna roll by the hang an see if it still bein watched. I ain goin in, but jus gonna drive by."

"Hey man can you swing by here an git me, I wanna check it out too?"

"Naw man no can do, I ain comin down there `cause they prably watchin you too. I know they be ridin through here almos ereyday, but I keep slippin out the back so they don see me."

"Yeah you right, I betta start doin that too. Aw-ight lemme go call Buster an let `em know whas goin on. Talk at chu later."

"Aw-ight, later."

Hammer tried calling Buster, but got no answer. He left a message and wondered where Buster could be that he wouldn't answer his cell. He then started thinking on something Hakeem said about things beginning to fall apart. Hammer wasn't one to panic easily, but when he saw the look in his leader's eyes, it made him wonder if he wasn't right. He didn't know Mr. M. as well as Hakeem or definitely Sista, but from all that he had heard about him he was high up on the big time operators list. The circulating word is that he is known not to take any prisoners when anything started to point to him. Keeping this in mind, Hammer was beginning to think that maybe he should start planning a way out for himself. If this deal tomorrow gets messed up in any way and whoever is watching can connect it with Mr. M., then both him and Hakeem would have a hard time getting away from the man. The thought put a new spin on how he needed to look at things when it came to the preservation of the C's and the protection of his own continuation.

At MHS Dolitha was noticing a big change in Jameel. Not only was he was avoiding her more, but his very persona was different. He was acting more sluggish and when he did see her he was not as responsive to her quips as he usually was. She tried to talk to him after school, but lately he always had to rush off somewhere saying he was going to work, but she never learned where he was working. It was making her very nervous to see what was happening to him, but there was nothing she could do. She also noticed that his relationship with the C members had changed and he was more into what they were doing than before. She suspected that he was in, but she didn't want to let herself believe it until one afternoon she came up on Jameel and Sista in a hallway and they were too close together for her not to know that a lot between them had changed. She didn't want to sneak up on them, so she just observed at a distance for a few minutes to be sure what she was seeing was really what she thought. There was no doubt. However, she was not ready to concede her interests and just go away so she started figuring out a way to get him back into her.

After school that day, Dolitha cornered him before he could escape and she asked him point blank what was going on between him and Sista. He tried to deny it at first, but when she told him she saw them together in the hallway he confessed that he had been seeing her, but it was nothing. Jameel knew that Dolitha could always tell when he was lying so he didn't. Trying to keep her from moving on, Jameel told her that she was still first and he would not see Sista anymore. This is exactly what she wanted to hear, but she knew there was more she had to do to make sure that he didn't go back. She made him promise that tonight he would come by her house to study with her. Jameel feeling like if he wanted to keep her he'd better skip the C's tonight and see her. So that's what he did.

Days were beginning to melt into other days and Sarafina was not sure even when she went to work what day it was. Al was giving her a lot of space and allowing her to come in late or not at all. He still provided her with the pills and knew that his brother was plying her with all the gin she wanted. Together they reveled in their vision that this soul was near total conquest and would soon relinquish the spirit. In addition, as a bonus she had made a major contribution for Mr. Al Leisar in setting up Ricoh and his followers to become a major conquest of souls for him. The time was quickly approaching when this whole deception would be ended, the conquered souls deposited in the reservoir and they could move on to their next prospects.

Today she sat staring at the picture, sharing the party spirit of the characters. She wasn't even making an attempt to go to work nor was she intending to call anybody. It was about 10:00 AM, Cinque had left for school and she wasn't sure whether Jameel even came home at all last night. Moved by the urging of the characters, she got up and poured herself a glass of gin and went back to the party. Her eyes were getting blurry and she knew that she had been losing weight, but when she stared in the dresser mirror the shock of what was reflected back to her scared her. At first she blamed her cloudy eyesight for not revealing a true image, but when she massaged her eyes several times and took another look she was sure that the image was real. She staggered back to the bed and fell on it. The thoughts flying around in her head were running to and fro trying to make sense of all that was happening to her. She was caught up in what seemed like an eternal nightmare having no end. The images that flashed before her weren't those of humans, but of something wicked and evil. When she saw the dragon on the ceiling that night at Asa's she knew now that was the beginning of something evil coming into her life, but she was helpless to do anything about it. Finally it occurred to her that the picture he gifted her with was a living evil spirit that had the power to induce images inside her head that made her want to do things contrary to her true self. She tried to get up, tried to move, but it felt like an extremely heavy weight was pressing down on her chest and she couldn't. With eyes wide open she stared at the ceiling while the room started to dance and whirl. The pills she had taken earlier and the gin that she just drank were mixing together in a concoction that was playing havoc with her body. Suddenly her breathing slowed, her heart was slowing and she seemed to be drifting in space into a twilight zone.

Chapter 13 - The Return

For weeks now the city had been undergoing a transition from what used to be a progressing metropolis to an urban settlement existing under a dark cloud hanging over the entire geographic area. The rising crime rate is attributed to the gangs gaining new resurgence after a brief respite and the reluctance of the citizens to confront them.

Groups like the CONN's combined with the New Life Temple of God community activist committee have stepped back due to the lack of effective leadership. Fear of coming out of their houses after hours has risen to new heights and the people hiss at the ineffective role of the police department.

Recently the newspapers and radio reporters had given the people a new sense of hope when they reported that certain arrests were made. The light at the end of the crime tunnel seemed to be burning brighter and brighter and they felt that they were moving closer to coming out, but when these same reporters had to announce that the arrested suspects were set free and to date no further action taken, the darkness of the clouds descended lower. Only those who were courageous enough to venture out at night because of their mutual protection were happy at what was happening in the city. The mayor, the city council, and the police were feeling extreme pressure at having to solve a problem that seemed to have sprung up overnight.

It had gotten to the point that the city's industry was being affected. Large businesses were beginning to relocate and the smaller ones were closing because of lack of support. Train ridership wase down, busses were underutilized and even at the airport, which was an anchor for the metropolis, passengers have elected to come and go via other options. Airport operations had drawn particular scrutiny because the FBI had become aware of high-level international drug trafficking.

Today was a very special day at the airport for Hakeem and Hammer. The time had come when Mr. M's special package was due to arrive and the challenge was on to retrieve it. Since early this morning, Hakeem was up going over the plan and making sure that his posse understood it. Together with Hammer he checked the van, the counterfeit ID credentials, should they be needed, and even the escape route to be sure that all was in order. By one o'clock his nervous energy had reached a point that he had to light up his favorite smoke to calm him down. Hammer noticing his anxiety and his method of relieving it, spoke reminding him about needing to be clear when they went to the airport. Hakeem took exception to Hammer's observation and told him to back off he'd be fine.

2:30 came and the group mounted the van and headed out. During the ride to the airport Hakeem seemed to regain his composure, but Hammer was still watching him wondering if he was okay. Hakeem started to nod a few times and Hammer cautioned him about Mr. M's mention of no slip up's. The mere mention of Mr. M. straightened him up and his eyes refocused. At 2:55, they reached the P1 area where they were supposed to meet contact X and be passed by the first line of security. 3:00 O'clock came and went, no X. Hakeem's calm disappeared and panic set in. Here they were sitting at a checkpoint in broad daylight and knowing that the feds were all around, he was about to turn around and speed out of there. Hammer grabbed the wheel and hollered at him: "Wait man, look here he comes." Contact X was walking at a fast pace moving toward the van.

"All right you guys the timing schedule is off so you got only ten minutes. I've already cleared it with the next point so just go straight to the bin and pick it up. Don't stop for nothing. Get it and get out of here quickly."

Hakeem gunned the vehicle to the area where the storage bin was and pulled along side. The four occupants jumped out and entered the bin. There were several stacks of boxes marked with coffee signs. Hammer ran back to the van threw open the doors and the transfer was on. They quickly formed an assembly line and started moving the boxes out. In just a little over the ten-minute mark all of the boxes were loaded and the men jumped back in the van. Hakeem sat in the front passenger seat as Hammer took the wheel. He raced through the gate and they were out of the airport exit in five minutes.

Hakeem sat back in his seat and breathed a sigh of relief, but inside he had the feeling that this was too easy. He kept looking behind to see if they were being followed. He did notice one or two cars that to him looked like unmarked police vehicles, but when they turned off he charged the suspicion to his imagination. Then he said:

"Hammer, somethin ain right here."

"What chu talkin `bout man. We got the stuff don we."

"Yeah we got it, but it was too easy. You know we was bein watched, why nothing happen."

"Ah man you trippin. Jus chill, we'll be at the warehouse soon."

Hakeem took Hammer's advice and laid his head back, but deep down inside something was telling him all was not what it should be. They arrived at the warehouse and started taking the boxes in when Hakeem still feeling uneasy about the whole thing, noticed there were some cars across the street that were not usually there. He told one of the soldiers to go over and check it out and see what's up. The soldier carried out the order and reported back that they were empty. Hammer was still checking Hakeem out and getting more suspicious about him. He was wondering whether he was about to crack. In an attempt to cool the situation, Hammer told him he needed to go home and stay until he got it together; he would finish up here. Hakeem responded saying he was fine and he would stay until the job was done. After that, Hammer was done with this conversation and left it alone.

Cinque came home that day feeling pretty good. He had a good day in school for himself and the basketball team, that he had qualified for, was off to a good start. He entered the apartment and as usual went straight to the kitchen to see what goodies were available. Seeing none he started for his room when he saw that his mom's door was open. Thinking she was home and if she were in there sleeping the door would be closed, so he went over. She was there in the bed, but something didn't look right. She was leaning half out of it with her arms draped on the side. He went over to her and as he got closer he could see that there was some distress. Her breathing was extremely shallow almost not at all and when he shook her she hardly responded. He opened her eyes and a blank stare came back at him so he knew this wasn't right. He tried shaking her again several times and got the same response. In a state of panic he called 911 and barely got the information out that they needed. His stuttering made it difficult for the dispatcher to understand what he was trying to say which just delayed the EMTs in responding to the call. Finally the address was established and confirmed and the ambulance was on its way. Minutes later the medical team was rushing up the stairs and banging on the apartment door. Cinque quickly opened it and directed them to the room. Once inside the team made a quick examination and determined that medical help beyond their capability was needed so she was bundled up and carried out. Cinque locked the door ran down the stairs and jumped in the ambulance alongside his mom. Seeing her with the oxygen mask on and hardly breathing reminded him of the night that Jameel got shot and he was reliving the event all over again.

With sirens blaring and emergency lights flashing the ambulance sped away headed toward Mercy General. As the paramedics continued to administer medical treatment to Sarafina one of them kept asking Cinque what happened. He told them that he didn't know because when he got in from school this is how she was. They had basically already assessed that this was a drug overdose case and were treating accordingly. It was now a matter of determining what had been ingested so they could make the proper report. Inside the emergency entrance the receiving medical team rushed into action and carted her to a private room where the doctor determined that she should be admitted.

Cinque was called to the desk and asked about all the pertinent information, insurance coverage and the other usual questions. The receptionist at first tried to be patient, but was getting a little angry at his lack of knowledge about her insurance coverage or any other related facts. She logged in the data that she could ascertain and told him to take a seat in the waiting area.

Cinque was very upset and wondering how to get word to Jameel without leaving the hospital. It finally occurred to him that his brother might be at Dolitha's house where he had been going after school lately. He had no idea what her telephone number was so he located a public telephone and hoped that a directory was there. He found one and tore open the book rifling through the pages scanning for her address. He knew the street but wasn't sure of the house number or her mother's whole name. When he got to the section with the Davenports listed, there were several on her street and his frustration level grew. He only had enough change to make two calls so it was going to be a real gamble on hitting the right one in that number of tries.

While he was contemplating which of the numbers he would call, the hospital emergency team was rolling Sarafina into the operating room for an immediate procedure. She was clinging to life and it wasn't clear even to the doctors just how much she had ingested of the pills or the alcohol or how long ago she did it. Mercy General was known for being a good facility and even in her delirium she must have felt she was in good hands, because they could tell she was fighting to survive.

Ever since the day Dolitha had confronted him with the question about his relationship with Sista, Jameel had been more attentive to her. He was not only walking her home almost daily, but now he was often going upstairs to sit for a while. Her mother was usually there sitting on the couch in the living room watching TV, but when the duo came in she would greet them and say a few words to Jameel and then disappear into her room. Jameel could see that she had some kind of impairment, but it wasn't clear what it was and he never asked Dolitha to explain. He knew it was Dolitha who ran the house and took care of the business, but until the first time they got together in her room, he didn't realize how much her mother didn't bother her.

Today was one of those days when Jameel was feeling especially loving and when they got to Dolitha's house and went upstairs he was curious about her mother not being in her usual spot to greet them. He asked where she was and Dolitha told him that her mother's sister came to get her last night to take her home with her to visit for a few days. Upon hearing this Jameel's eyes lit up and he could hardly wait to get her into the bedroom. He had never felt comfortable before knowing that her mother was just a couple of rooms away, but now having the apartment to themselves his inhibitions were no more. He quickly steered her to the room and began kissing her passionately and undressing her. She knew he was ready just by the hints he kept making on the walk home, but she didn't realize that his extra passion was due to the unconstrained feelings caused by the freedom of being completely alone with her.

It didn't take long for her to respond before the two of them were locked in the deepest throes of any passionate encounter they ever had. Though it was not their first time together, this time it seemed like all the others were lifeless compared to the height of emotions streaming from both of them now. The conclusion this time allowed them to mutually melt into a blissful state of satisfaction and they both drifted off to sleep. She heard the phone ringing, but had no desire to get up and answer it. He was no more inclined to get up then she was so they both lay there for a long time. After another half hour, he looked at the clock and realized he had been told to meet his crew at the hang fifteen minutes ago. He had also been told that there was something big coming down and if he wanted to get in on it to be there. He jumped up threw on his clothes and almost ran out the door providing only a short quick explanation to her.

He got to the store just in time to catch Buster getting ready to pull off. Buster told him angrily that he was about to get cut out of his first deal and that the next time he would get left. Jameel apologized and said it was unavoidable. Buster not wanting to hear that told him how it was about the business and nobody was exempt, reluctantly accepted the apology and they moved on. There were only three of them in the car, but Buster told him that they were meeting Hakeem and Hammer at the warehouse. It was now close to 7:30 and darkness was setting in. As they got close to the warehouse, the soldier who was driving slowed down and surveyed the area. This was the same soldier that was in on bringing the shipment there so when he saw the same cars that were there before he became suspicious and told Buster.

Buster took in what he was saying and immediately called Hakeem. Hakeem answered and said he and Hammer were already inside and acknowledged they saw the cars too and had already checked them out, so come on in. Buster told the driver it was okay and to pull in around the back. The car went into the back and the crew got out and went inside. Just like before they allowed only the minimum lighting and stacked the boxes in a corner with each of them taking a stand in the four corners. Jameel was told as the new guy that his role was to watch out for the client's car coming and alert them when they arrived. Jameel felt a kind of excitement inside knowing that this was his first real day on the job and could lead to a very large paycheck.

It was not more than ten minutes later before a large black extended van pulled into the back of the warehouse followed by a regular size car. They pulled into the same spot that was used when Jameel was first brought to the deal. Three men got out of the car and then the driver of the van joined them. Jameel who was standing outside alerted Buster who told the rest of the crew to get ready. A thought flashed across Jameel's mind, he started to think about the prank that Buster had pulled on him when he was being tested. He thought to himself, this won't be a test and supposed the real thing goes down that happened that night. Buster didn't give him any tool tonight so he felt naked and unprepared. The men were quickly approaching so he put the thought out of his mind and tried to put on his most fierce face to greet them.

As they got up to him, he checked them out to make sure they were carrying the briefcase they were supposed to have and then gave the special knock on the door. Buster opened it and they all went inside. The lights were kept low with only a main light illuminating the desk and chairs. Hakeem and Hammer were seated on one side and the older guy from the visiting team with one of his soldiers sat opposite them. The two other soldiers just stood by the door. Jameel stood next to them knowing he had help in each corner should he need it. The older guy opened the dialogue and said:

"Okay lesee it." Hakeem returned with:

"Show me the money."

Jameel almost blew it by starting to laugh because the talk sounded so corny like the lines from an old movie. However, he quickly muffled the laugh and turned it into a short cough so as not to draw too much attention to him.

The visiting soldier with the briefcase placed it on the desk and opened it. Hakeem turned it around and picked up several stacks and fanned them. Convinced it was all there he motioned to the soldier in the far corner to bring over a box. The older guy opened the box and picked up a bag at random and pierced a small hole in it. He tasted the product and invited one of the others to do likewise. The soldier beside him also tasted and they both agreed that it was top notch quality. The money was handed over and the van driver said he was going out to bring the van up to the door. Hakeem motioned to Jameel that he should go with him. So he did. Jameel walked right with him to the van to make sure he wasn't going to do anything unexpected. Jameel got in the van with him and they backed right up to the warehouse freight delivery dock. Jameel and the driver got out and went back inside to let the transfer begin.

When the door was opened the next time, so many lights came on from outside it was like the sun had suddenly come out and it was daytime. Red lights were flashing and there were so many cars and police vans there it seemed like the whole force was in on this bust. Cops dressed in riot gear rushed the entrance and with weapons pointed commanded that all inside get down on the floor. It happened so fast, that none of the occupants inside had a chance to react and scramble out the office back door to the inside of the warehouse where if they could have gotten to, they could have easily disappeared in to one of many hiding places. Hakeem and the rest of his posse, now including Jameel, just sat stunned in disbelief wondering how this could be happening.

The arresting officer seeing the look of astonishment on Hakeem's face decided to tell him about the hidden cameras built into the cars across the street. He told him that they had been on candid camera ever since they brought the stuff into the warehouse and indeed had been followed from the airport by several FBI cars taking turns in the chase. Hakeem just looked at him with a blank stare and thought to himself, his gut feeling had been right all along. Both the C's and their guests were loaded into the police vans and transported to headquarters. Jameel with his head hung low and his face in his hands could hardly keep himself from breaking down and crying, but his pride prevented it.

The phone rang again several times and finally Dolitha answered it. "Hello this is Dolitha."

Barely able to get the words out Cinque said: "Dolitha this is Cinque my brother there?"

Hearing the anxiety in his voice she said quickly: "No he lef a while ago, somethin the matta?"

"Yeah, my mom in the hospital doin real bad. Where he go?"

"I'm not sure, but prably went to M&Ms where he usually go. You want me to fine him?"

"Yeah 'cause I gotta stay here. Fine him an tell 'em to get here now."

She said okay and starting getting dressed. Not knowing whether he really went to the hang or not she thought she should get Rajon before going down there by herself. She made her way over to his place and knocked on the door.

"Who dere?"

"Rajon, its Dolitha open the door."

Rajon really surprised to see her at his place opened the door and said: "Hey girl whas up?"

"Jameel's mom in the hospital and we needa fine him. He lef me a while ago but he mus notta gone home. I think he might a gone to M&M's but I don wanna go there by myself. Can you go wit me?"

"I dono girl, you know I don go down there 'cause they been tryna get me in wit them for a long time."

"Rajon, you his best friend you gotta help him. His mom's in the hospital. What kinda frined you be?"

"Ah aw-ight, aw-ight lemme get my coat."

Dolitha and Rajon quickly scampered down the stairs and onto the street. From his place M&M's was a bit of a walk, but they almost ran there so it didn't take long. When they got there two of the C's were standing around outside even though it was a bit chilly. Seeing Rajon one of the soldiers laughingly said: "You finally comin to join up?"

"Naw man, lookin for Jameel. He here?"

"He was here but he went somewhere wit Buster. Dono know if he comin back." "This important man, you know where he went?"

"Man you know I can't tell you even if I knew. What chu lookin for him for?" "His mom's went to the hospital an he don know it. I gotta fine him."

Dolitha then stepped up and said: "If you know how to reach Buster please call 'em and aks him to tell Jameel so he can git to the hospital."

"Yeah aw-ight I can do that."

Rajon and Dolitha then turned around and headed back to her house. On the way she was trying to think where else he might have gone. It crossed her mind that he might have gone to Sista's, but she didn't want to let herself believe that because he had just been with her. She swallowed her pride though and when they got to her house she found Sista's phone num-ber and called her. Sista answered and after getting over the initial shock of hearing Dolitha who never called her, asked what she wanted. When Dolitha told her what was happening, Sista said she would join the search and get the message to him. Dolitha thanked her tongue-in-cheek and hung up. Rajon sitting with her suggested that she try to reach that preacher that runs the church she goes to. Dolitha agreed and looked up the number for the church. She wasn't quite sure what the name of it was but she knew about where it was located.

Scanning through the churches in the city, she found one that she thought could be the right one since it was listed in the right area. Fortunately, she hit it on the first try and got Reverend Joyner.

"Hello, Reverend Joyner."

"Reverend Joyner this is Dolitha Davenport. You don know me, but om a friend of Jameel. You know, Miss Petterson's son."

"Yes okay is he all right?"

"Yeah he's aw-ight, but Miss Petterson's in the hospital an I can't fine him now." "When did she go to the hospital?"

"Sometime today, I think. I jus found out." "She's at Mercy General, right?"

"Yeah, I think so, you goin there?" "Yes, what did you say your name was?" "I'm Dolitha, Jameel's girl."

"Okay Dolitha thank you for calling me. Would you give me your telephone number? If I find Jameel before you do I'll ask him to call you."

Dolitha gave him the number and hung up. She and Rajon just sat there trying to figure where else Jameel might be. Nothing came to mind.

At the hospital the surgical team was just coming out of the operating room when Rev. Joyner arrived. After checking in at the desk, he was told to go to the waiting area and someone would let him know her status soon. In the waiting room he saw Cinque pacing around nervously. Cinque saw him come in and ran to him putting his arms around him and holding on. Reverend Joyner held him and tried to comfort his spirit. They both sat down and Rev. Joyner asked him what happened. Cinque, not knowing all the details told him that all he knew was that when he came home she was in the bed hardly breathing. Reverend Joyner thought that she may have had a heart attack not wanting to even entertain any other cause.

After a short time a doctor came in the room and asked for Cinque first, but when he saw how young he was, he turned to the reverend and asked if he was related to her.

Reverend Joyner identified himself as her pastor and the doctor started talking to him instead of Cinque. The doctor told him that she had ingested a large volume of alcohol along with some pills that they believed to possibly be methamphetamines. The combination had seriously impaired her liver and kidneys and they weren't sure how she would respond to how they were treating her. They had drained her of as much as they could, but now it was a wait and see situation. Rev. Joyner thanked the doctor and then reflected on how not too long ago he had been here for her son. The doctor told them they could continue to wait here if they wanted to, but there was nothing else could be done until tomorrow. Reverend Joyner gave the receptionist his telephone number and asked to be called if there was any change in her condition. He then turned to Cinque and asked him where his brother was. Cinque told him that he was trying hard to find him, but couldn't. Reverend Joyner offered to drive him home thinking maybe his brother was there.

They got to the Peterson house and Cinque let the Reverend in. Upon opening the door, Cinque called out for Jameel, but received no response. The Reverend walked around the apartment with Cinque and looked in every room. No Jameel. While he was still there the phone rang. Cinque thinking it might be Jameel ran to the phone and picked it up.

"Hello Cinque here this Jameel?"

"Hello this is Asatani Leisar from the employment center, is Sarafina there?" Reverend Joyner heard Cinque repeat Asa's name and wondered whether he should talk to him. He waited to see how the conversation would go before deciding.

"No. She ain here, she in the hospital" Cinque told him.

Upon hearing this he got real excited and said: "Is she at Mercy General?" "Yeah."

"What happened to her?"

"I dono when I came home from school she was sick so I called 911 and they took her."

Asa smiling and thinking that the time had come when he would step in to make his final claim, pressed Cinque to tell him more about what he saw, but Cinque just repeated what he had just told him. Asa finished the call by telling Cinque he was going over to the hospital to see her. Before Reverend Joyner could ask Cinque to let him speak to the man, he hung up. The Reverend then asked him who that man was and Cinque told him he was the man his mom had been going out with. Rev. Joyner suspected that this was the same man he saw the night he came by to minister to her. He didn't get a good look at him then, but from the way that Sarafina was dressed, he suspected that he couldn't be a good influence on her. He asked Cinque if he was going to be all right and when the response was yes, he started out the door.

Just as he was leaving, the phone rang again and this time it was Jameel. He was making his allotted phone call after he had been processed at headquarters. Jameel was surprised that Cinque answered the phone because he did so very rarely and immediately asked where mom was. Cinque told him and Jameel, who was standing up, fell back in his chair. He pressed Cinque for details, but Cinque could only tell him what he had told everybody. Cinque then asked him where he was and Jameel was ashamed to tell him, but he had to. The reverend had stopped at the door and turned around when the phone rang. Upon hearing Cinque's conversation, he came back in the room. Cinque told Jameel that he was there and asked him if he wanted to speak to the reverend. Jameel was embarrassed, but he said yes because there was no one else who could do anything for him right now.

Once on the phone Jameel nervously told what happened and said that he had to stay there overnight until he could be arraigned in the morning. He said also that he didn't know what happens after that, but he didn't think he would be getting out soon.

Reverend Joyner explained to him what the process was and told him that if a bail would be set, he would come and get him. From what Jameel had told him he wasn't sure whether there would be bail, but he would call his friend the mayor and try to get him out. Especially since his mother was in the hospital and he hadn't seen her yet. Jameel thanked him and was told his time was up so he had to hang up. Reverend Joyner could hardly believe all that was happening to this family at the same time, but he felt strongly that there were some other than natural forces at work. Again he asked if Cinque was all right and then he left.

It only took a few minutes after he hung up with Cinque before Mr. Asatani Leisar was on the phone with Mr. Alivedi Leisar, his brother, jubilantly telling him the details of the latest event. Together they celebrated in anticipation of the final stages of their mutual conquest of this soul. Big Al then told Asa how close he was also to capturing Ricoh and his people thanks to all the help that he had gotten from Sarafina. They agreed that tomorrow night they would go up to the hospital and perform the ritual that would allow them to make the offer to her. Asa reminded Al that if he got to the hospital before him, not to go up to see her alone. Al questioned why he had to wait, but Asa just said: "Trust me, I know" and hung up.

Cinque was really having a hard time digesting all that was happening in his family. He went into the kitchen to get something to eat, but found he was not really that hungry so he made a P&J sandwich and poured a glass of milk. Things had seemed to be getting better when Sarafina went back to work, but then quickly everything got worse and she was drinking more and staying home less. He didn't know about the pills, but he knew that alcohol alone didn't make people act like she was. When he left the kitchen before getting ready for bed he went into her room and looked at the picture. To him even though the scene was lewd picturing some raunchy activities, he couldn't see anything wrong with it like Jameel was telling him. He stared at it for several minutes until he finally determined that it was just a nasty picture, left the room and went to bed.

The morning came and Cinque felt as if he hadn't slept at all. He struggled out of bed and was deciding whether to go to school or not, but because he knew that this is what his mother would have wanted, he did. When he got outside he met up with both Dolitha and Rajon who were just passing by his building. They joined forces and of course the topic of the day today was Jameel. Dolitha asked if he had heard anymore about Jameel and Cinque hesitated to tell her the truth. He chose rather to talk about his mother saying that she was still in bad shape. Dolitha immediately picked up on his avoidance of her question and pressed him for an answer. When he told her where he was, she stopped walking immediately and hollered:

"What?"

Cinque had to calm her down before they could proceed. He told her he didn't know all the details and wouldn't until later on today when he would be talking to their preacher at the church. Dolitha made it very clear to Cinque that when that happened she waned to be there and he was to let her know so she could come over. Cinque told her that he didn't know what time he was going to call, but if she wanted to she could come home with him and wait. He told her he was going to try and get a ride to the hospital right after school and she could come too if she wanted. She said yes she did and she would also try to get a ride.

All day at school none of the trio seemed like they wanted to be there worried about Jameel. Time seemed to stand still and the clock wouldn't move. Dolitha at one point of the day passed Sista in the hallway and even though they were cordial to each other when Sista asked about Jameel, Dolitha had a hard time keeping herself from telling her where he was. There was no way for her to know that in a short time she wouldn't have to tell her anything, the C club members in the school would have gotten the word and advised her about what happened last night. Until then though, Sista suspected that something had gone wrong and she was feeling the anxiety of not knowing. She kept herself composed and went on about her routine until the guys came up to her.

When the final bell for the day rang, both Cinque and Dolitha hurried out the door to the waiting car outside. One of Dolitha's girlfriend's mother who came to pick her up from school, when she heard about Jameel's mother being in the hospital volunteered to give them a ride. From the school the hospital was just a short ride and within fifteen minutes they were there. Dolitha thanked her girlfriend and her mother and she and Cinque got out and went inside. At the receptionist desk they inquired about Mrs. Peterson and were told that she had slipped into a coma and was not allowed any visitors. Cinque couldn't handle it anymore and he broke down crying. Dolitha walked him over to the waiting room and tried to console him. They sat down and in a few minutes he got himself together. They weren't sure what to do next because they didn't have a ride home and to walk was a little too far. While they were sitting there Reverend Joyner came in and went up to the desk. He was told the same thing initially, but when he said that he was her pastor, the receptionist agreed to let him go up. As he started toward the elevators, Cinque saw him and ran over.

"Reverend Joyner, Reverend Joyner they lettin you go up?" Reverend Joyner turned to Cinque and said: "Yes, won't they let you?"

"No, they tol me she in a coma an I can't see her."

Reverend Joyner then turned around and went back to the receptionist and asked her to let the kids go up with him; he would be responsible. She reluctantly agreed and told them not to stay too long or she'd get in trouble. The reverend agreed and they got in the elevator.

On the ICU floor they were again confronted, this time by the head nurse on the floor. When he explained who he was, she assumed that he had come to pray for her and so she let them go in. They got to her room and stopped when they saw her hooked up to a monitor and other tubes inserted in her veins. The sight was hard to accept even for the reverend. Again Cinque had difficulty dealing with the situation and he almost lost it.

Dolitha put her arms around his shoulders and held him tightly. He held up. Reverend Joyner then kneeled beside the bed and put one hand on her arm while he held his Bible in the other and began to pray.

"Father God, in the name of Jesus I come to you on behalf of the soul that lies here before me. You Lord who brought her into this world and who has the power over life and death hear my cry. I thank you for being the God that is full of mercy and grace, the One who gave us His only begotten Son so that we might be redeemed of our sins. Lord please hear me and grant my petition that this woman whom you have already blessed in a mighty way, one whom you have attended to in times past bring her back so that she may continue to serve you. Bring her back from whatever may have drawn her down the road to iniquity, and wrap your loving arms around her so that she may be protected from the evil one. Lord I pray fervently and with all my might and from the depths of my heart that you would be responsive to this prayer. I ask this blessing in the mighty and matchless name of Jesus the Christ. Amen.

Reverend Joyner concluded his prayer and got up off his knees. He turned to the kids and said: "That's all we can do here. Now it's up to Him what the fate of your mother shall be." Cinque and Dolitha joined him as they walked out of the room. They had already left the room so they didn't see when a warm glow came over Sarafina and her eyes blinked three times and opened briefly before closing again. The trio went down in the elevator to the desk and signed out. Somehow, although he couldn't explain why, Cinque felt a lot better. The reverend asked how they were getting home and when they told him they didn't know he promised to take them. During the ride he told Cinque that he had been in touch with the mayor and with Lt. Meeker and that a bail setting for Jameel's case would be determined tomorrow. He also told him he thought because it was his first time in trouble he would probably get off lightly and that he would pay his bail if that were the case. Anyway, Jameel could be home tomorrow.

Dolitha and Cinque were happy to hear that and got home feeling pretty good.

Later that night, at the hospital, close to eight o'clock in walked the Leisar brothers. Unbelievably there was no one at the desk and no security anywhere around. They moved behind the desk went through some files and located Sarafina's room. Mercy General was a reputable hospital, but if there was any downside, hospital security was it. The brothers moving with alacrity as if on a special mission didn't use the elevator, but negotiated the stairs two at a time up to the third floor. They quickly moved down the hall with no challenges and made their way to her room. When they walked in she was no longer comatose, but in a state of semi consciousness and moved her head when she spotted them. Asa wasn't sure whether this was a good sign or not, but he approached closer to the bed and took her hand. Through glazed eyes she seemed to recognize him, but couldn't talk. He greeted her and told her that he was there to save her.

Big Al came alongside of him and pulled out from the case he had with him some sort of talisman that he placed on her body. He took his brother's hand with one of his and with his other held hers and they started to chant some kind of incantation. Sarafina could hear them, but she couldn't speak or move. Asa kept telling her that she was his and to get well all she had to do was to agree with him and say the words:

"I belong to you."

Her eyes were glazed and vision was dim, but she could hear him clearly chanting and encouraging her to say the words.

He squeezed her hand several times and kept insisting that she say the words. She was looking at both men directly, but somehow they no longer seemed like men but something inhuman. The images reminded her of what she had seen in her apartment that she thought was a dream, now she couldn't be sure if it was real or not. The more he insisted, the more she was trying to speak. He promised her riches and power and told her that she would never have to work again, just say the words. In her compromised state and through his power of persuasion her mind was telling her that she just wanted to get this over with and be well again. She was struggling to speak, but the incoherence was more babble then anything. He kept prompting her and saying the words before her, but she just couldn't form them on her own. After several attempts and with great effort she was close to achieving the goal and the words were starting to come together.

Her mouth was open as her head swirled around and she was starting to speak when suddenly the room lit up with an indescribable brilliance. The brightness was so intense it was as if a thousand high wattage halogen lamps had been turned on. She closed her eyes tight and tried to put her hand over them to cover, but without success. She felt the room growing warm and her mind took her back to the time when she was in the hospital chapel praying for her son. She opened her eyes slowly and the brightness no longer affected them for she could see the image of a man suspended in mid air right in the center of the room. He had the appearance of an angel, but his eyes were glowing with the intensity of a burning fire. He lifted up his hand pointed to the brothers and they immediately froze in place. The talisman that had been placed on her chest fell on the floor and melted.

Even though her vision was still dim she could see that in their frozen state the Leisar brothers with mouths and eyes wide open were in fear. The angel moved closer to them and standing directly in front of them said:

"I am Michael angel of the Lord God Almighty who has been sent here to intercede for this His servant. How is it that you are not afraid to put forth your hand to destroy the Lord's anointed? Hear the words that I speak to you, be banished from this place and approach this woman no more."

Again with a wave of his hand the two men disappeared, the light went out Sarafina's head rolled back onto the pillow and she went into a deep sleep.

In her sleep state she wasn't sure what was happening to her, but the angel that she saw in the room with her was now speaking in a dream.

"Fear not my child for the Lord is with you even until the end of days.

For the Lord has called you like a woman forsaken and grieved in spirit. Like a youthful wife when you were refused.

for a mere moment I have forsaken you, But with great mercies I will gather you. With a little wrath I hid My face from you for a moment; But with everlasting kindness I will have mercy on you. Says the Lord, your Redeemer." (Isa.54:6-8)

Upon hearing these words, she became aware that something in her body was changing. She felt a cleansing taking place and a renewal of spirit that she hadn't felt since the days before she met Asa. With the feeling of rejuvenation came a sound uninterrupted sleep not as one who is comatose, but one who slumbers in the Joy of the Lord.

The next morning came and Sarafina woke up early, even before the nurses came in to check on her. Although she now had full control of her limbs and was able to move, she just lay there staring up at the ceiling wondering about all that seemingly happened last night. Not sure whether it was real or all a dream, she looked on the floor where the talisman had melted and sure enough there was a spot in the shape of the trinket. Marveling in the appearance of the angel that spoke to her she felt compelled to get up and go to the chapel to give thanks for her recovery.

When the nurses came in they were surprised to find her not only awake and very talkative, but full of energy. She started to tell them about her revelation last night, but hesitated because she thought they might think that she had been hallucinating. They removed the monitor connection and all tubing then took her vital signs. One of them remarked that she was in great shape and she couldn't see any reason why the attending physician shouldn't let her go home. Sarafina was extremely happy to hear that because she was anxious to go home and see about her boys. While they were all standing around and the nurses were talking about her miraculous recovery, the doctor came in and was also surprised to see her awake and sitting up. He took the nurses report and examined her declaring that she was ready to go home. Before he released her though he asked that she just lay down for another half hour because he wanted to do a final check to be sure, given her condition last night.

It was now around 10:30 and while she was waiting for the doctor to come back and give her a final release in walked Lydia. She was so surprised to see her, words escaped. Lydia with a big grin walked over to her hugged her and told her that she had been thinking about her for a long time, but last night she had a dream that told her she must come here today. She couldn't explain the dream, but it was so compelling that she took off from work to come. She also said she wasn't even sure that Sarafina was still here, but a voice inside her head told her to go. Sarafina related to her about her dream and they both laughed. The doctor then came back and asked Lydia if she could wait outside for a few minutes while he made his final examination. Upon completion of this exam, he marveled also at the recovery and signed off on her release.

As she packed her things, Sarafina asked Lydia if she wanted to join her in the chapel. Lydia admitted that she was not big on that kind of thing, but after last night and having been at Reverend Joyner's services lately she said she thought she'd better go. They went down to the chapel and it was just as Sarafina remembered it. The blank cross was still there hanging high in the rear of the room. She took Lydia by the hand and led her up to the cross and knelt down and prayed like she hadn't done in some time. Lydia was stunned to hear her because she had never heard this from her before.

"Heavenly Father, My Lord and My God once again I come into your

presence and before your throne of grace to say thank you. With a bowed head and a humbled heart I thank you for sparing me from the depths of despair and restraining me from continuing down the path of destruction. You Lord God who are mighty to save and gracious to restore have determined my fate. You who have all power in Your hands have seen fit to redeem me from the evil one who would have destroyed me had it not been for you.

Father I just thank you for all that you have done for me and continue to do in my life. Lord thank you for seeing me through this trial and travail in which I have failed You. I know that it was only You who could prevent the fate that was assigned to me by those who would do me harm, You came when I needed you most. I will trust in you with all my heart and seek to do your will in all that I do from here to the end of my days. Lord grant unto me the wisdom that I will need to carry out your mission as it has been given to me and I will perform to the best of my abilities that You have given. I ask that you receive my request and answer my prayer that I may serve you all the days of my life. I pray this prayer in the precious name of Jesus. Amen!

When Sarafina finished praying she was about to get up from her knees when she turned to Lydia to see the tears streaming down her face. Lydia had never heard her pray, but the words that she spoke even though they were coming from her lips seemed to have come from somewhere else. She told Sarafina that she felt something inside of her moving like an inner sense of peace that she had never felt before. Sarafina hugged her and told her that the Holy Spirit had reached her and she needed to go to church with her on Sunday and get ready to be baptized. They got up together walked out and Lydia drove her home.

Sarafina walked into her apartment not knowing what to expect since she had been away. She walked into the boy's room and though messy it was not any more than it would be had she been there. She then went into the kitchen to see what was left of the food. The refrigerator was practically empty and she wondered what the guys had been eating, until she looked in the trashcan. Pizza boxes and fast food wrappers filled it. She then looked in the cabinet where she had kept the liquor bottle before. There was a bottle there, but it was practically empty. She couldn't remember how she left it, but thinking back on how Jameel had started drinking, she wondered if he hadn't brought it to that level. She took it out and poured the remainder into the sink and flushed it. Her next step was into the bedroom.

Boldly she stepped up to the picture that had been mounted on the wall, and again started feeling a strange sensation, but this time she felt the strength to remove it from the hooks and set it outside the apartment. She sat down on the bed and reflected on all that had happened to her while that picture was in the room. The thoughts that came into her mind were chilling and she tried to dismiss them. Then she thought again about the appearance of the angel in the hospital room and what he did to Asa and his brother. She wondered what happened to them, which prompted her to call her office and see. She dialed the number and the receptionist answered:

"Good morning Peerless Treasures how can I help you" she said. "Hi this is Sarafina how you doin?"

"Sarafina is that you? Where are you I've been wondering about you and whether you were even coming back here."

"I've been in the hospital but I'm okay now. Is Mr. Leisar there?"

"No I haven't seen or heard from him for the last two days. I don't even know if he's coming back. The phones haven't been ringing and I just sit here passing the time away doing crossword puzzles. Do you know what's going on?"

"No. What about that big shipment that we been workin so hard on, did it come in?" "As much as I know it's supposed to happen this week on Friday. I know you made all the arrangements except the date, but that's what it looks like."

"Okay, don tell him I called I wanna surprise him when I come there, right?" "Yeah okay I won't. When you coming in?"

"I'm not sure yet, but soon. See ya then." "Okay bye."

Sarafina didin't know from that conversation whether the man had been really banished to somewhere or he was back home. She then tried calling Asa in his office and got the same message from one of his assistants. This made her wonder even more whether they had really disappeared so this time she left a message for him to call her. She knew that if he was still around she would have to confront him at some point, so why not now. Feeling a new sense of confidence and a renewed spirit she felt capable of handling anything. In her spirit she knew that this man was evil and somehow she had to deal with it. While she was reflecting on how to handle that situation, the door opened and in walked Cinque holding the picture.

He was so happy to see her that he hugged her too tightly and she had to gasp for air. "Wow, now thas a welcome home. How are you baby?"

"I'm fine mom when you git here?"

"This mornin an I'm fine too. I'm throwin that picture out so you can just take it down to the garbage bin and dump it later. Where's Jameel?

"Mom you betta sit down for this." "Whas wrong?"

"Well Jameel's in jail, but he should be comin home sometime tomorrow Reverend Joyner said."

"Oh my God! In jail for what?"

"He got caught wit some of them C boys an they had some drugs. But Reverend Joyner said since it his first time, he should get off."

"Well I guess I better call Reverend Joyner and get the story." "Do he know you home?"

"No not yet, but I'm goin to call him right now."

Sarafina hurried to the living room and dialed his number. He was not at the church office and she didn't have his cell number handy so she left a message asking him to call her after he checked his messages. She was tempted to call Lt. Meeker, but she didn't want to do that until after she talked with her pastor. She got up and asked Cinque if he was hungry. He said yes and she told him that she had to go to the store to get some groceries and she would fix him a good meal. Again he asked her if she was all right, wondering inside if she really had been cured from the alcohol thing. She said yes and she would be right back.

She got outside in the parking lot and her car seemed to be in good order, but she wondered whether it was going to start since it had been sitting for a while. When she got in and turned the key she was thankful that it turned over on the second try. As she headed to the supermarket, she looked around the neighborhood to see what changes had taken place. She laughed to herself when she thought that she was looking at it again almost as if she had been away on a long vacation. She had only been in the hospital a few days, but her recollection of the hood had gone cold long before she went there. After picking up the groceries she returned home and prepared a good home cooked meal for Cinque.

After dinner she went back in the living room to watch TV. It wasn't long before the phone rang and it was Reverend Joyner. She could hardly let him get his hello out before she was asking him about Jameel. He told her the whole story as far as he knew it and that Jameel had gotten caught up in something that he shouldn't have and was arrested. He went on to explain how he had talked to the mayor and the police lieutenant to try and get them to be lenient on him. It had worked and tomorrow they could go down in the morning and bail him out. The reverend said further that the boy should be okay, but he was now concerned about her. She started in telling him about her encounter last night with the men and with the angel and now she's fine. He praised and thanked God and told her that he had been there earlier and prayed for her. She told him she was grateful and that she was ready to come back to the church and rejoin the CONN's. He was delighted to hear that and told her what state the CONN's and his group had fallen into. She confirmed her commitment to restart the group and promised to do it soon.

At police headquarters the next day both Reverend Joyner and

Sarafina went down early looking to get Jameel out of the lock up. They met Lt. Meeker on the way in and he was glad to see her, but felt sorry about her son. He asked her how it was that he could have gotten mixed up with the same people that she was fighting against. She told him that it was partly her fault because she herself had gotten mixed up in something that she shouldn't have and stopped being his mother. Lt. Meeker wasn't quite sure what she was saying, but he didn't pursue it. Rather he told one of his men to go down and get Jameel and bring him up. All of the paper work had been completed and when Jameel was brought up to his office, he was so embarrassed and ashamed to see his mother and the reverend that he just hung his head and walked in. Sarafina went to him and hugged him while Reverend Joyner placed his arm around his shoulder and told him that everyone makes mistakes, but he must learn from this one. They left the building and Reverend Joyner went his way while the Peterson's went theirs.

On the way home Sarafina asked her son how he got mixed up with the gang when he knew that she was trying to stop them. He could hardly speak when he told her about his desire to make some money to help her out of their financial situation and that was the only way he could make enough. She told him she understood his wanting to help, but she hoped that he learned that was not the way to do it. She then told him too about her encounter and that she had learned something also. Their talk seemed to ease the tension for both of them and she wanted to know if he was going to go to church with her on Sunday. He was thrilled to hear that she was going back and said he would be glad to go with her. In the back of his mind however, he knew there were some things that he had to do with the C's. He was still mindful of something Sista told him about once you're in, you can't get out and right now he didn't know how he was going to do it.

Asa and Alivedi were in Asa's house still reeling from the violent dispatch that had been given to them by the angel. They were huddled together trying to figure out how in the confrontation they lost. After offering up a solicitation to their god they determined that they may have lost one, but the other sheep were still ready for the sacrifice and they would double the effort to claim them. Asa checked his telephone messages at his office and was surprised to hear that Sarafina had left him one. He looked at his brother and said:

"Could it be that all is not lost with her?"

Big Al reminded him of the words that were told to them at the hospital and said that they should let that one go and concentrate on the others. Asa reluctantly agreed not wanting to admit defeat nor concede anything to the higher authority. He sat down with his brother and the plot to make the big shipment pick up was finalized. Friday would be the big day. Big Al got on the phone to Ricoh and fired him up one more time by telling him the time was now and Friday was the day.

Inside the Peterson apartment Sarafina was going through all of her papers trying to find the CONN's roster and meeting notes. It seems that during the time she was under the influence of the picture things were misplaced and in disarray. She searched through the drawers in her dresser, through the shelves in her closet and even under her mattress without success. With one last ditch effort she seemed to recall that in one of her stupors she had fallen on the floor by the couch with the papers in her hand, so she looked under it. There, pushed back from the edge were a bunch of documents bundled together with a clip. She reached under and pulled them to her. There was all the information that she was looking for.

Finding the roster she scanned down to find all the key people as she remembered their dedication and started calling. Many were surprised to hear her voice and thought that she had given up out of frustration. Others had heard that she was sick and couldn't attend any more. For whatever reason they thought she abandoned them, they were all glad that she called and were ready to let her lead them again. She asked if they could come to an emergency meeting Thursday night. Without any hesitation all of them said yes and they volunteered to spread the word to get others to come out.

She then called Reverend Joyner and told him about her calls and when she spoke to him he was excited about the results and said that he would have all of his people that he could get in touch with also come out.

When she walked into the recreation center on Thursday night, she wasn't sure what to expect. The number of people that were already there, waiting for her and Lydia to come in was overwhelming. Her heart jumped at seeing the numbers and she knew that it was more than just her that was making this happen. She looked around the room and was thrilled to see not only her old favorites like Malcolm Long and Janet Johnson, but Reverend Joyner and Lieutenant Meeker were seated in the back row. She moved to the front of the room stood behind the podium and delivered such an emotional welcome back opening that it bordered on it being a sermon. She told them about what she had gone through and what it meant to her that they still believed in her and she was ready to finish what they had started out to do. The crowd applauded and many said Amen. The rest of the evening was spent revamping old plans and getting the patrols back on track.

After the formal meeting, Lt. Meeker and the reverend came over and congratulated her on her ability to re-galvanize the group so quickly. Lt. Meeker told her that he was happy to have been able to get Jameel home and that he would certainly put in a good word for him when the matter came before the judge. He also told her that he could still use her help in getting the final pieces put together in his construction plan to nail the mastermind behind the whole operation. He went on to tell her that even though he had evidence enough to bring a good case against the soldiers, it was not enough to get the big man. She replied that she was excited to get back on the right track and would do whatever she and the group could do to help the police.

Hakeem, Hammer and a few of the soldiers who were arrested that night at the warehouse were denied bail because of their prior records and remained in the lockup. When the word got back to Mr. M. he was so angry that not only did his people get snatched, but the major shipment that he had worked so hard to coordinate the movement of was now sitting in the police storeroom, he sent his henchmen down to the store to bring him somebody, anybody that he could come down on. The street network had already picked up on this vibe so none of the gang was anywhere near the store for days after the arrests. The gang without a functional leader was turning to Sista for directions, but she told them that that was not part of what she did. Now they were leaderless and running scared from the big man, so they were virtually impotent and at the mercy of the rival B's. If they only knew that the B's were being set up by another source even more deadly than Mr. M, then fear of their rivals would cease to be a problem.

At headquarters Friday morning Lt. Meeker and Captain Tillery were going over all the pieces that they had to the puzzle and coming up with the same scenario. It was clearly apparent that the main pieces were still missing and in order to get them they needed more help. They rehashed over and over what they had and who else they could go after to find what they needed. It wasn't until early that afternoon, when the phone rang and it was Sarafina for the lieutenant that a new direction for finding their missing pieces came in.

"Hello, Lt. Meeker."

"Lt. Meeker this is Mrs. Peterson how are you?"

"I'm fine Mrs. Peterson good to hear from you how are you?

"I'm doin fine now an I got some news that may be good for you." "Sounds great, I could use some good news about now. What you got?"

"You remember the man named Malcolm Long who lives across from the Minute Mart and ID'd those men for you?"

"Yeah, I remember what about him?"

"Well he called me this mornin an said he heard some men at the plant talkin 'bout some piece of paper thas in that warehouse that they gotta get out right away 'cause it got a lotta information on it 'bout the whole operation. He didn know what they was talkin 'bout but it sound real important."

"Thank you Mrs. Peterson, this could be what we're looking for. Thank you so much and tell Mr. Long thank you for us."

"Okay good. Bye."

The lieutenant got off the phone and turned to the captain saying:

"I think this may be it. You know that document that we found in the store raid that was torn in half?"

"Yeah, what about it?"

"Well this tip may lead us to the other half." "Okay I'll bite where are we going?"

"According to what I was just told, back to the warehouse and search that office in the daylight. Maybe even look for some hidden rooms there too."

The captain looked at him and they both laughed. A short time later with warrants in hand they were putting together another team to enter the warehouse. There was absolutely no problem in getting the judges' signature this time because the results of the last bust had brought some real positive acclaims for both her and the mayor.

By 3:00 PM the team was assembled and ready to roll. Since the warehouse was vacant they didn't anticipate there should be any problem with the raid. When they got there they saw a tractor trailer parked in the rear and this drew some suspicion about another shipment that may have come in that they and the feds missed. Cautiously they sent one of their cars up to the big rig while the other blocked off the exit. With guns drawn they approached the vehicle and found a sleeping driver inside. An officer banged on the window and the startled driver almost jumped through it. After regaining his wits, he rolled down the window. Some routine questioning took place and it was determined that the man had just pulled in off the highway after a long drive from out of state and he saw the vacant building with an easy access yard so he pulled over to sleep for a while before proceeding to his delivery in the city. All of his credentials checked out so they allowed him to go back to sleep while they conducted their search.

The team then went back to the shipping dock and entered the building through the same doors they had entered in the other night. This time once inside, having the broad daylight brighten up the room they could easily see that except for the desk and few chairs, there was nothing else there. Lt. Meeker jokingly told the crew that it was impossible for any kind of hidden room to be in this place. They searched the desk thoroughly even turned over the chairs and found nothing. Then they turned their attention to the walls and the ceiling with no luck. He was not be deterred and his instincts were kicking in again so he started banging on the walls in several places.

Finally he came to a spot where the sound wasn't like the rest of the room so he instructed his men to go out to the car and get something to punch a hole here. Sure enough it was hollow and behind it was a shelf with an old safe just like the one he found in the store. Quickly he pulled it out and broke it open. He was so excited that his hands were shaking when he tried to force it open. After many tries the lock gave way and he looked inside. He couldn't believe what he was seeing and his heart started racing. He called the captain over and they both looked at it for several minutes. There in front of them along with several other vital pieces of evidence, was the thing.

Chapter 14 - The Judgement

All the indicators were pointing to it being a gorgeous Saturday morning and it was forecast to be a beautiful day. As the sun was making its ascent over the eastern horizon the pilot of the tugboat was steering the big freighter into a berth at the dock. Compared to the weather that the ship's captain had encountered late yesterday while navigating through the infamous Bermuda Triangle, the calming relief he felt in reaching his final destination was welcomed. Because of the triangle's tropical storm conditions, the ship arrived well behind schedule arriving on the day after its due date.

To Ricoh, upon hearing about another delay from Big Al, last night, his anxiety was about to soar out of control. In the middle of his excitement and having to retell his posse about another delay in the shipment, he was having a hard time keeping them in line.

Except for the high expectation of what the final yield financially was going to be, he would have abandoned this effort after the first few times that Al put it off. To him each time the reason given had been somewhat suspect, but because of his relationship with his new contact named Ms. Peterson, he hung in. Now that he was told that the ship was nearing entry and just a few miles from port, he was busy firing up his soldiers one more time.

He was up early this morning checking out the van, the credentials, in fact going over the whole routine as it had been explained to him on how the deal should go down. The soldiers who would be involved in the run were coming into his apartment one by one until they were all accounted for. Even though he had rehearsed with them many times since they were first told about the venture, he wanted to go over it one more time and he did. Feeling comfortable that everyone knew his role, he told them to sit back and relax while they waited for that go phone call from Al. PK, his lieutenant, sensed his excitement and tried to calm him down by offering him a smoke. Ricoh refused saying that he was ready to go and didn't need a boost.

At exactly 10:00 AM the phone rang and it was Al. His instructions were that the crew was to meet him and his brother at Pier 5 at precisely 1:00 PM come right up to the gate and look for him. Further he was to make sure he had the right credentials ready as he had been instructed, and to look the role that they had planned. Ricoh confirmed all the instructions and told Al that he had everything ready. He hung up and asked his crew if anybody needed a booster or a drink or something before they left, because he wanted everybody to be calm when they hit the docks. There was no response so he assumed that all was in order.

Around 11:00 the group was in the van and they were rolling toward the bridge to take them into the big city. PK was driving while Ricoh rode shotgun. They were appropriately dressed and had been practicing using correct language in order to convince the guards at the gate that they were who they were pretending to be. This was difficult at first, because they were so accustomed to speaking in the jargon of the street, but after a while they could turn it on and off as needed. As they were riding, it occurred to Ricoh that the one thing he had forgotten to do was double check with Slick Willie that the storage bin for the product was ready. He pulled out his cell and dialed the number.

"Yeah, this Willie."

"Willie, Ricoh how ya doin?"

"I'm good man whas up?"

"Jus wanna make sure you ready to take delivery later today." "Yeah, I'm ready. What time you gittin here?"

"If ereything go right, should be 'bout 3:00 O'clock. We gonna pull right up to the doors, right?"

"Yeah thas cool, I'll be ready." "Aw-ight see ya then."

"Aw-ight, later."

Having taken care of that detail, Ricoh put his head back and enjoyed the ride. A short time later they were rolling over the bridge and entering the big city. They headed toward the docks and were running just about right on schedule. When they reached Pier 5 they pulled up to the gate and spotted Al talking to a uniformed guard. Ricoh said to PK:

"All right here we go, get it together."

The guys in the back hid under the tarps and became motionless. There was hardly any activity going on at the docks today because it was Saturday and the ship that came in was supposed to have arrived yesterday. The offload for this late arrival had been done early in the morning by a hastily assembled longshoreman gang Special clearance had to be made in order to authorize the pick-up, but with Al's connections that wasn't a problem. The merchandise had been moved to the area in the yard where they were to pick it up. The only problem Al foresaw was what could come up now, because he didn't know anything about this new guard or how dedicated he was to his work.

PK pulled the van right up to the gate and the guard came over.

"May I see your work order please?" he said while looking in the vehicle.

"Here it is sir" Ricoh said and handed him the documents that Al had given him. "Okay may I see your identification please?"

PK pulled out his and handed it to him, Ricoh did the same.

The guard looked them over for a few minutes then handed them back and said: "Will you be needing assistance sir, we're kind of shorthanded today?"

"No thankyou we can manage. We'll be fine." Ricoh said.

"Okay go through the gate turn left and follow the arrows to area 10, there you'll find your bin.

On your way out you don't have to stop here, just blow the horn and I'll open the gate." "Thank you sir." PK said.

The guard went back inside the gatehouse and opened the gate. PK eased the van forward and followed the arrows. Ricoh started laughing saying:

"You don look like no fed to me, is he stupid or what?"

PK had to laugh too as they got up to the target area. When they got there, Ricoh jumped out and applied the combination to the locks that he was given and opened up the bin. There inside were at least 30 boxes of what was marked as supermarket supplies for a major chain. After looking through the rear windows to make sure there was no one around, the crew hopped out the back doors and the transfer began. Less than twenty minutes later the transfer was complete and the van was rolling back toward the gate. Al was now sitting in his car with his brother just a short distance away from the gate waiting for them to come out. They approached the gate blew the horn and the gate opened. Once outside, Al spotted them and pulled in behind them and they all headed back toward the bridge.

Once they got near the Bricks Complex, Ricoh called Slick Willie again to let him know they were close. Willie told them to just come down the ramp to the door and he would see them when they got there. Ten minutes later they were pulling up to the doors and Willie opened them. Ricoh directed Al where to park and the Leisar brothers moved in that direction. The crew started offloading the cargo and placing the boxes on the hand trucks Willie provided. Al motioned to Ricoh that he wanted to talk to him. Ricoh told him to follow him and they headed to Willie's apartment. Inside Asa did the talking and started to tell Ricoh about a commitment that he needed from him before the final sale could be made and the buyer for the goods sent to him. Ricoh looked at Al, because he hadn't heard anything about this part of the deal, but when Al just nodded his head he figured it was all right. Asa pulled out a contract and handed it to Ricoh.

Ricoh started reading the document as best he could because there were some clauses in there that he didn't understand. As he read it the references to souls being given up in exchange for wealth and privileges while on this earth made no sense to him. He looked at the last page and there were lines for six signatures including his, PK's, Willie's and the three soldiers. When he got to that part he stopped and asked Al what it was all about. Al took on a new strange look that caused a shudder to run down Ricoh's spine. He turned to look at his brother and his form was the same. Willie was in the room and he couldn't believe what he was seeing, there was something scary about both men, but he wasn't sure what to do. Asa started talking again, but this time his voice was raspy as he told Ricoh that the riches that he was about to get came with a price, but it would be worth it once he and the others signed the papers.

Ricoh felt like he had been placed in some kind of trance when he agreed to sign. His mind wasn't clear and he was having trouble believing what his eyes were recording. He told Willie to go out and bring the other guys in so they could sign too. Willie left the room as instructed and brought the other three in. Once all of the signatures were in place, there was one more act that Asa told them he needed from them and that was a drop of each man's blood. Still acting under the spell that had been cast over him, Ricoh commanded his troops to comply and it was done. When all was completed, Asa pocketed the contract and he and his brother went back to looking normal again. The spell was lifted and Ricoh feeling like he just woke up from a dream, asked what happened. Asa, with a very calming voice, explained that the men were finished storing the goods and he was now ready for the next step. A buyer would be coming by on Monday to get the product and deliver him the money. When Asa told him the payoff figure, Ricoh tried as hard as he could not to be overwhelmed, but his eyes betrayed him. Al told him that this was just the beginning and if he continued to serve them he would do well. Ricoh went and sat on the couch just smiling and looking at Willie who was in a state of shock along with the others. Asa and Al having accomplished their mission said goodbye and left.

Jameel and Cinque, smelling the aroma of bacon, eggs and pancakes coming from the kitchen again, couldn't wait to get out of bed and get in the kitchen. It had been some time since they had a big breakfast and they stumbled over each other trying to get to the bathroom first. Sarafina had a new resurgence of energy and was not only cooking again on a regular basis, but was feeling good about it. That is until she received the mail and saw the bills. She realized quickly that she would probably be out of work again after the bout with Asa and his brother and the little money she had saved was awfully low.

She pondered in her mind just what she could do now as far as getting more unemployment checks since Asa was almost the headman at that office and he would surely deny her claim. Today was a nice day though and she wasn't going to let that bother her now, so she went to the living room and turned on the TV.

Jameel after breakfast played video games with his brother until around noon when he decided he was going to Dolitha's. He asked his mother if there was anything she wanted him to do before he left and when that was cleared he walked out the door. There was hardly anybody out on this beautiful day and as he walked he couldn't help but feel like everything was going his way. He hadn't given any more thought to the C's and how he was going to make his exit, but with the main guys behind bars for now, and the rest of the group laying low from Mr. M, he felt all right. The biggest thing for him was that he was glad to see his mom back to her old self and even though he knew the money situation was still the same, somehow things looked different.

At Dolitha's he bounded up the stairs and knocked on the door. Thinking he should have called first, he wasn't sure she was even there when nobody answered right away. He knocked again and finally she came to the door looking a little tired and worn out. Right away he asked her what was wrong and she told him that she hadn't been feeling well and that she had been throwing up. It never occurred to him that this meant anything so he asked her what she had been eating. When she told him it wasn't the food she was eating, but something else. This got his attention. Her mother was back and greeted Jameel in her usual manor before leaving them alone. He then pressed Dolitha to explain what she was talking about and the next thing he knew that good, good feeling that he came in with was gone. She told him she thought she was pregnant and Monday she would know for sure when she went to the clinic. He just looked at her for several minutes not knowing what to say and she looked back at him wondering how he felt about it. The minutes passed and nothing was said, but finally he broke the ice and asked her what they would do if she were? She looked at him and smiled and asked him what he wanted her to do? Then he asked her if her mother knew and she said she wouldn't tell her until she was sure. For the first time since they had been together he didn't know what to say.

Back at the Peterson house Sarafina spent the rest of the day going through some of her old notes from CONN meetings and some that she took from her new job. Although she couldn't clearly make the connection between her function at Peerless Treasures and anything illegal, she was getting more suspicious when she recalled the telephone conversations between that Mr. Edwards and herself. The fact that he kept giving her new vehicle and personnel data and she would respond with new pick up dates for the same shipment bothered her. Also when he talked about the dolls it wasn't like he was referring to any toys. The more she contemplated the transactions, the more it seemed like there was a dark side to these imports. She made up her mind to let Lt. Meeker know on Monday who she was dealing with and what she thought.

Saturday night in the Bricks Complex, Ricoh and his boys were feeling so good about their stash that they threw another of his wild parties. As much as he wanted to let them, he had to restrain his attendees from getting into the product that he had secured. Even though it was supposed to be a secret, as his posse got higher into their cloud 9 atmosphere, the more the word spread about what he had. When one of the ladies of the night came to him to tempt him to open up the stash, Ricoh was hard pressed not to comply, but when he thought about the consequences, he sobered up. The party ran through most of the night into the early morning hours and everybody was feeling good when suddenly an apparition of Big Al appeared out of nowhere. He stood before Ricoh in a mist like form reminded him of his contract and how he had been sworn to secrecy with a severe penalty for any violations. Ricoh abruptly ended the party.

On Sunday just like in days past, Sarafina was going to church and pushing the boys to come with her. However, she no longer demanded that they go, but was more cajoling. She noticed that Jameel seemed to be in the doldrums and she asked what the matter was. Not wanting to reveal the reason for his despondency, he told her that he was probably just catching a cold or something and he'd be fine. She asked if he was still going and he said yes. An hour later they were all headed out the door going to New Life.

Reverend Joyner had prepared a sermon for today that reviewed his earlier message on community responsibility and Nehemiah and how it related to the congregation even now. He was extending that theme even further when he delved into the life of Jesus as a community activist and organizer. As per normal, his invigorating rhythm and powerful delivery instilled new spirit in the people and they were excited to get back on the right track. Just prior to closing the service, he formally recognized before the whole congregation, Sarafina and her family and welcomed them back. Amen's and hallelujahs erupted from the sanctuary and the people were glad to see her in the usual seat again.

When Monday came around, all of headquarters was buzzing about the most recent raid and what it turned up. Lt. Meeker and Captain Tillery had brought the safe into his office and were now putting the pieces together. The contents of the latest find contained a .38 caliber handgun, a very old package of the product and the missing half of the document they sought. When they placed the two halves along side each other and aligned them, it revealed the plans for several shipments from the past, for then and sometime in the future. It named names, telephone numbers, storage places and specific instructions on how the deals were struck. Both the captain and lieutenant were laughing with so much joy at having found the final pieces to the puzzle they could hardly contain themselves. With high excitement they called other staff into the office and exclaimed how they had solved the riddle. Patting each on the back and congratulating everybody on a job well done, the captain dialed the mayor to give him the good news. Before he could complete the call however, Lt. Meeker cautioned to wait until they had a chance to get the big man and bring him in. The captain immediately agreed and thought that having a whole case prepared, would be significantly better than half of one. Then he instructed the lieutenant to get started on making the bust.

While they were all still celebrating, the phone rang. It was Sarafina for Meeker. She started telling him all about what had been going on with the Peerless Treasures business. Very interested in what she was saying, he revealed to her that he thought the federal boys would be interested in checking this one out. Then he asked if she could come down there today when he called his contact with them. It would be extremely helpful. She agreed and they set a time for her to come in. The lieutenant told Captain Tillery about the phone call and they were having difficulty believing the run of success that they were having. If they could be credited for another drug bust as a result of her information, especially with the FBI, then they could both be looking for increases if not promotions. The celebration continued.

At 11:00 AM, as agreed, Sarafina came into headquarters and sat with Lt. Meeker.

After greeting her he wasted no time in calling his contact and informing him about what he had. The contact told him that they knew about the shipment that had come in over the weekend and were tracking the movement. What they didn't have though was what he was giving them now. That was the link that they needed between the shipper and the coordinating agency in this country. Sarafina supplied the company name, the person she worked for and all the information about what she knew. The FBI contact took the information and said he would call them back later after running this by his team. After the lieutenant hung up, Sarafina asked him whether she would be arrested because of what she did, he assured her that after all she did to help him, there was no way he was going to let that happen.

Sarafina left headquarters and went home. Lt. Meeker assembled his team and they were headed to the Gateway Safe and Lock plant with an arrest warrant for Mr. Antonio Mizzetti in hand. They entered the plant and again were confronted by Mr. Lukinbill the plant manager. When he was told why they were there, he started stuttering and making excuses about knowing nothing about the boss other then this plant's business. As they were talking to Lukinbill, the officers stationed outside saw some men running out the back door and getting into a Bentley. They alerted Meeker and he responded telling them to stop the men. It was too late as the Bentley tore out of the parking area and onto the streets. Meeker ran out of the office jumped into his car and the chase was on.

The Bentley roared out of the lot and turned onto 6th Avenue headed toward the highway. Lt. Meeker radioed for help and within a few blocks of the plant the big luxury vehicle was hemmed in and forced to pull over. The occupants included Mr. Mizzetti and three of his henchmen who were immediately arrested. There was no resistance, but when searched the soldiers gave up several handguns and two switch blade knives.

While being informed of his rights, Mr. M. told the police officer that he could skip all that because they had nothing to hold him on.

Lt. Meeker could hardly wait to bring this group in. He called ahead to the captain and informed him of what they had and the captain responded with his own delight. Overall so far it was a good day at the station. When the team arrived the men were processed and placed in the appropriate holding areas. It happened the mayor was on the phone with Tillery when the men were brought in and the captain couldn't resist telling him what was happening. The mayor got excited too just thinking about the positive news headlines he would be getting from all of this recent positive police action.

However, he was not told exactly who the police were going after next.

When Lt. Meeker returned to his office he had a message from his contact at the bureau. The message said that they had tracked the movement of the shipment out of New York and into your city. He was instructed to call back as soon as he got the message. Meeker responded and connected with his contact. The FBI investigation had traced the shipments' movement to the Bricks Complex and had identified the owners of the Peerless Treasures business. They were sending a team to the Bricks right now and if he wanted to be in on it, to meet him there in twenty-minutes. Meeker was again having trouble taking this all in. This was too much good fortune for him to process all at once.

He told the agent that he and his men would meet him there in an unmarked car on his schedule.

The three officers jumped into Meeker's car and rushed to the Bricks. They weren't sure what the feds would be driving, but they knew it couldn't be hard to identify. Surely it wasn't and right in front of building #1 they saw two vehicles with government plates parked with the men still in them. Meeker pulled along side the first one and rolled down his window. He asked for his contact and hit it right on the first try. They introduced themselves and shared the action plan. The feds were going in as the buyer that they had learned was supposed to show up today. The men inside wouldn't know what the buyer looks like so it should be easy. Once they were in and have tested and secured the product, arrests would be made. The feds claimed the collar, but told Meeker he could share in the glory since it was in his jurisdiction. Meeker told the feds that he had absolutely no problem with that and they set the plan in motion.

Not having the details about exactly where the shipment was being stored, the fed team on a whim guessed that it would be in the basement delivery area. They went around back and down the ramp to the delivery doors. The lead man rang the entry bell and told Willie, who answered the door, who he was. Willie had no reason to suspect anything, invited him in and took him to his apartment where Ricoh, PK and the other soldiers who were in on the deal were waiting. The agent signaled to part of his team to follow him and they all went in. Inside Willie's place the meeting began. The agent wanted to see the product right away, but Ricoh wanted to play a little game feeling the power that he thought he had by having the goods, took him through some changes. He asked the agent where he was from and some other silly and unrelated deal questions.

The agent, tiring of this obvious charade, told Ricoh that he didn't have time for this and got up starting to leave. Ricoh immediately got down from his high horse and escorted the feds to the storage bin.

Once inside the bin and the product tested and secured, the fed team leader pressed the button on his lapel transmitter and the rest of his team and Meeker's boys moved in. It happened so fast that not Ricoh or his cronies could believe what was going on. They were all arrested and taken in.

At police headquarters Mr. Mizzetti was ranting and raving about his treatment and threatening to sue the whole city and each officer individually. He wanted to speak to the mayor right away and demanded that he have his lawyer come right now. When Captain Tillery was reminded who had been brought in he came down to processing pronto.

When Mr. M. saw him he demanded to know what was going on and why he was there. Captain Tillery pulled Lieutenant Meeker aside and pretended to question him about having a solid reason to hold this man. The lieutenant acknowledged the sham and assured him that they were on firm footing and this man was behind all their troubles. Captain Tillery then turned to Mizzetti and told him to relax that his council was on the way.

Meanwhile, word had gotten to the mayor about who had been arrested and brought in. He was now on the phone with the captain.

"Tillery, are you crazy?" the mayor screamed. Do you know who that man you're holding is?

"Yes and no Mr. Mayor."

"Now what the Hell does that mean?"

" You see all the roads led to his house and we just followed one and found the prize." "Well you better be right because if this thing blows up we're all going to pay for it. I trust you have all the evidence you need to nail him?"

"Yes sir, I'm sure we got enough.." "Okay, just keep me informed. Goodbye." "Will do. Bye."

The real buyer showed up at the Bricks later that day and followed his instructions to go to the delivery entrance. After knocking on the doors many times and getting no response, he left and called Al. Al, who was furious at hearing his report, tried calling Ricoh. No answer. Since he was at the Peerless office already, he decided to physically go down to the Bricks and pay a visit. Arriving there he looked around to see if all was clear and went to the back. He got the same result as the buyer and this sent him into a quandary because even though he and his brother had gotten what they sought initially, the buyer was next on their target list and now he was spooked.

Back at police headquarters, a well-dressed man stormed in demanding to see his client immediately. The sergeant was having difficulty calming or restraining the man and the commotion was heard right down to the captain's office. Almost at the same time, Captain Tillery and Lieutenant Meeker came forward and inquired about the man's business. This was Mr. Mizzetti's attorney with papers in hand demanding his release. It seems that a preliminary hearing had already been conducted and the judge had set bail that had been paid. After perusing the papers, the captain turned to the man and ensured him his client would be released, but not before his final processing. Still somewhat irate, he calmed down, but told the officers that he was not leaving without him.

Several minutes later, Mr. M. was brought up before the group. He also was still ranting about the indignities he suffered and threatening to sue the whole department and the city. His attorney pulled him into a corner and tried to convince him to limit his threats with some success. The pair then walked out the door and disappeared.

Lieutenant Meeker and the captain turned to each other and laughed knowing that they had lit a fire under the most important man in town; the kingpin of a major operation in their city.

The case they had built and were now ready to take before the courts was almost infallible with the documents they possessed.

At school, although Jameel's body was present his mind was clearly focused on something else. Dolitha didn't show up today and he knew where she was. He tried to act like everything was okay, but anyone who knew him well could tell that something was bothering him. Cinque had even asked him this morning before leaving the house what was wrong. He shrugged it off and just said he had a cold. When he ran into Sista, she was pressing him to tell her whether it was his situation after the arrest that was bothering him or was it something else. He had not been seeing her lately and she was getting a little suspicious about what was happening. She told him that as far as the arrest thing was concerned, everything would be all right because the big man would fix it. She didn't know then, that the big man's situation was also in need of some fixing.

At the Peerless Treasures office Big Al was on the phone with his brother talking about how things seem to be getting interrupted. The contract that they had on the B's was not sufficient to satisfy their appetite and they were busy scheming on how to recover the buyer and his crew. Asa said to Al that the fact the police and the FBI were now involved presented some new challenges, but nothing they couldn't overcome with some more precise plans. While they discussed some new possible strategies, Asa still would not concede he was giving up on Sarafina and was intent on pursuing the issue. Try as he might, Al could not convince him to drop it.

The opportunity he was seeking for a new confrontation was not delayed because he saw through his office window Sarafina walking in. She had decided she was not waiting to be fired by Al, but would go down to the unemployment center and talk to Asa first because he got her the job. She recalled the scene at the hospital, but not clearly. It was not clear in her mind about the relationship between the two men that had visited her. To her, even though she knew there was some inherent evil about this man, she wanted to test the waters and see if he would help her get her checks restarted. He called her over and told her to be seated. She went in and looked at him hard to see if there was something that would give her a clear indicator on what really happened at the hospital. He started asking her about where she'd been as if nothing had happened.

When she started telling him about all that she had been through and especially about the job he had gotten her, she looked at him very intently trying to determine if he was covering up anything. Being the master of disguise as he was, he divulged nothing, either in speech or actions. By the time she finished telling him that she wasn't going back to the job anymore and that she had even alerted the police about the operation, his demeanor slipped slightly and she saw a small dent in his armor. To Asa he was thinking to himself, now he knew what went wrong with their original plans. He was more intent now than ever to claim her.

It was obvious to him that she had no recollection of what really happened at the hospital, so he continued in his disguise and pretending to be her ally. He told her that he would draw up the papers she would need to make some legal claim about the illegality of the job and then he could reinstate her claims. Once that was done she could continue to draw her checks. While he was telling her this, he was really developing a plan in his mind about how he was going to entrap her as he and his brother did with the B's. He concluded her visit by saying she would have to come back tomorrow and he would have the appropriate documents ready for her signature. He asked her if she could come back at 2:00 PM. She agreed and left the office.

Right after she left, he called his brother at Peerless and told him the whole story. Al responded that he suspected she may have been the link to the police, but he wasn't sure. Asa then told him about his new plan. Al wasn't in total agreement with any action against her and he reminded Asa again about the encounter at the hospital with the angel. Asa was not relenting or willing to compromise and said that he was not afraid of that spirit. Asa continued describing what would be in the new contract document and that he would need him here in his office tomorrow so that they both could complete the deal.

Al reluctantly agreed and the plan was set in motion.

Sarafina left the office not knowing how to feel. The attraction that she had felt before was no longer there, but there was still something about this man that she could not get over. Outwardly she wanted to believe that he was really going to help her, but inside her spirit was telling her to be aware of the power that he once held over her. She still wanted to test her theory about the relationship between the two men, so instead of going directly home, she decided to swing by the Peerless office and see what was happening. When she neared the office she could see that some business signs had been put up but they didn't look like any type of sign that was intended to have permanency. In fact, as she got closer they appeared to be just tacked on and could be removed on a moment's notice.

Originally, her thought was to just drive by, but when she saw the flimsy signage, her curiosity got the better of her about what was going on inside. She turned and pulled into the parking lot and went up to the rear entrance. She tried the door handle but found the door locked. Slowly she went around to the front looking in the side window for any activity. The window blinds were closed tight so only the slightest glimmer of light could have gotten through. When she got to the front door she found that locked too, but saw through partially closed blinds that her old co-worker the receptionist was seated at the desk. Sarafina rang the entrance intercom bell and the speaker came on.

"Hello this is Peerless may I help you?"

Sarafina identified herself and the receptionist glad to hear her voice pressed the buzzer and the door opened. Once inside they hugged each other and both started to talk at once. The mutual admiration exchange lasted several minutes, as both were glad to see the other. Finally, Sarafina asked if the boss was there. The receptionist told her he had been there earlier today, but left just a little while ago in kind of a hurry. She then went on to tell Sarafina all about the strange things that had been going on in the office. Sarafina asked what kind of strange things.

The receptionist told her that she came in early one morning and when she opened the door and was headed back to the ladies room to freshen up, when she passed by his office the door was partially open and there was an odd light emanating from it. Not knowing whether he was in there, she moved closer to see what was causing it and she saw a form in there that didn't look like him. In fact it didn't even look human, but it was kneeling and chanting to something in the wall. When it saw her the door closed by itself and she ran to the back. She finished in the lavatory and when she came back to the front he came out of the office and everything was normal. He just said good morning like nothing happened and the rest of the day was fine.

This was all Sarafina needed to hear to confirm in her mind that everything she thought she saw at the hospital was real and the two men who came to her there were these Leisar brothers. She went home feeling more assured about the angel's intervention on her behalf and now more aware that whatever was in store for her tomorrow she knew she had a real ally. As she entered the building, she stopped by the mailbox and picked up her mail. The bills were still coming, but now she didn't feel as threatened as she once did and she just lumped together and took them upstairs. Somehow the feeling of hope was rising in her and the belief that everything was going to be all right was growing stronger each time she reflected back on what the angel said to her in the hospital.

Inside the apartment she busied herself while she waited for the boys to come in by preparing dinner and listening to the radio. The news coming on was a mixture of good news about how the police department was regaining the confidence of the people because of the recent arrests that had been made and the bad news about one of their leading citizens being accused of being a bad guy. She knew that the information she provided to Lt. Meeker was solid so she was surprised at the media's reluctance to condemn the man. Not until the final court trial and conviction would they believe that he was the instrument being used by another power to cause the problems in the city.

Jameel and Cinque came in together at their usual time. On Jameel's face she could still see the despondency that he had in the morning. She asked again what was wrong and the reply again was:

"I must be catching a cold."

Being his mother and knowing her son, she knew it was much more than that, but she didn't pry, thinking that when he was ready he would tell her. They finished dinner and Cinque went to his room to do his homework, but Jameel said he was going out for a while. When he said this, she wanted to ask where he was going, but seeing the look on his face, she had a strong sense of where he was headed followed by her intuitive sense of what was wrong.

He arrived at Dolitha's place and hurried up the stairs. When she opened the door, she looked radiant and faced him with a broad smile. He walked inside not knowing whether to breath a sigh of relief or prepare for the worst. She grabbed him and kissed him deeply then led him to the couch. Looking at him without saying a word she was waiting for him to ask. When he didn't take the bait, she blurted out, yes I am and you are the one. Upon hearing this, his heart skipped a beat and his breathing was uneven. He turned from her leaned his head back on the edge then asked when. She responded telling him that the projected date was some time in mid July. She then took his hand looked straight at him and asked:

"You want me to get rid of it?"

He sat up and looked back at her and said: "I dono, I jus can't believe it right now."

He stayed for a little while longer and they just sat on the couch listening to music not saying anything or going near her room. The mood they shared was different from anything they had felt before. The realization that they were no longer kids, but adults and about to become parents, was setting in and how to handle it was not clear. When he left he told her not to worry and he would see her tomorrow. They kissed and he left headed home.

At home he walked in the door and Sarafina looked at him knowing already what was happening. She felt what he was going through, but just allowed him to come to her when he was ready. He went in the kitchen got a glass of water and sat at the table. She came in shortly after under the guise of getting some water too and she sat down looking at him. He looked back at her and through teary eyes said:

" I really messed up now. I got in trouble, did ereything you said not to with the gangs and now I jus found out Dolitha's gonna have a baby. I dono what to do."

Sarafina got up, walked around the table, stood behind and put her arms around him. She gave him a big hug then said:

"Son, things are never as bad as they seem at first. I'm going to call Reverend Joyner right now and ask him if we can see him tomorrow. Don you worry, we can work things out somehow."

Jameel wrapped his arms around his mother's and just moaned. For a few minutes they shared the empathy and then Sarafina went into the living room and dialed.

"Hello, Reverend Joyner."

"Hi Rev. Joyner this is Sister Peterson how are you?" "I'm truly blessed sister how are you doing?"

"Well I'm getting back to normal, but I need to talk 'bout somethin for my son."

"Okay which one?"

"The older boy, Jameel. You already know about the gang trouble, but now his girlfriend is pregnant and he need yo help. Can we see you tomorrow?"

"Of course sister I can see you at 7:00 tomorrow night here in my study. Until then though please remember that God does not abandon His children and there is nothing too hard for Him to take care of."

"Oh thank you Rev. we'll see you then, goodnight. "Sure thing Sister Peterson, goodnight."

She hung up the phone and told Jameel what was going to happen and he agreed to go. After that they both retired to their rooms.

Jameel told Cinque what was happening and all he could respond with was: "Wow man, she really knocked up? What chu gonna do?"

Jameel told him about the meeting with the preacher tomorrow and after that he would know better what to do. Cinque just said wow again and went to bed. Jameel retired too.

Sarafina lay in bed for a long time just staring at the ceiling not able to go to sleep.

She was going over in her mind all the things that had taken place over the last few months and wondering why it was happening to her family. She remembered the first incident with Cinque being taken away because somebody lied about him. Then she reflected on Jameel getting shot because somebody mistook him for someone else. Then she thought about the picture, the gift she received and how it had impacted her. Finally she admitted that because of that gift she had succumbed to the lust of her body for someone she thought was her helper. Turning these things over and over in her mind, she finally drifted off into a deep sleep.

At the height of her REM state while she was in the throes of dealing with her transgressions an angel appeared before her and began to speak. He told her that because she was getting so close to doing a big task for the Lord by inspiring the people of her community to confront evil, Satan stepped in to test her strength. All that was happening to her and her family was to see just how strong her faith was and to determine where she would break. The Lord allowed this, just as He did with Job, because he knew that with her He had a diamond in the rough and the sparkle that was within would not fade. The dream ended with a final advisory from the angel about tomorrow's final encounter with evil.

She was told that when she went into the employment center, the document that Asa would present to her was really a contract for her soul that would be couched in legal jargon meant to disguise its real intent. The angel instructed her to read carefully the whole document and when she came to the end, look carefully at the signature line for both her and him. Notice carefully the name where he should sign. It will say Asatani Leisar on one line and Alivedi Leisar his brother on the other. These are the agents of the evil one and here is what the names really mean. Asatani Leisar is a cryptogram meaning - Satan Is A Evil Liar and Alivedi Leisar means - the Devil Is A Liar. When she heard these words she felt a deep sense of revelation and discovery and her troubled sleep became peaceful until morning.

At the Gateway Safe And Lock plant on Wednesday morning Mr. Mizzetti was having a meeting with his henchmen and Mr. Lukinbill inside his private office. He was desperately trying to erase all ties to him with the gangs and the drug action and he was grilling his people about who in the plant besides that Peterson woman could have known anything about his business. His angry tone in talking with them had them all afraid to say the wrong thing and so it became a futile effort. Mr. Lukinbill was groveling and saying that he didn't even know about his outside connections and he certainly wasn't aware that his reports knew anything. Mr. M. got overly excited with his response and told him to get out of his office, he was useless. Mr. Lukinbill made a hasty exit, not knowing whether he still had a job. The three remaining soldiers were straining to come up with anybody they could think of inside the plant that may have had a clue about what was going on, but they drew blanks.

Mr. M. not satisfied with getting no answers told his soldiers to go down to the store again tonight and go through the meeting room with a fine tooth comb and make sure nothing is there to connect him to anything. After another minute, it occurred to him that there was something at the warehouse, so he told them when they finished at the store to go to the warehouse and get it. He was not aware that the police had already been there. Having received their orders, the men returned to their work in the plant. As one of them walked by Malcolm Long's machine he stared at him hard as if trying to recall whether he could possibly be the informant. He couldn't remember any point where Mr. Long could have heard anything to know about the outside operation, so he dismissed the thought and went back to his area.

Mr. M. meanwhile was on the phone trying to explain to his organization heads just what happened to the shipment they had negotiated with their international connections. Although the thermostat in the room indicated a comfortable temperature, the sweat rolling down Mr. M's forehead said the climate was extremely hot. Even in his position near the top, his superiors were not accepting that their goods were now in the hands of the police. The instructions to him were to get back the product or come up with the equivalent street value, which was about 2.5 million dollars. The time given to make restitution was one week from today's call and he was to deliver the goods personally. After hearing this, his mind went into overdrive trying to come up with just how he could pull it off. Getting the goods from the police was practically impossible and producing that kind of money right away was too. Then he looked in his desk drawer to see if his passport was still there.

When Sarafina woke up this morning she felt refreshed at having been given the warning about what was destined to happen this afternoon. After feeding them and giving encouragement to Jameel telling him again that everything was going to be all right, she got the boys off to school. It was still early, but she was anxious to call Lt. Meeker and let him know that she was going to be meeting with the brother of the man who ran the Peerless Treasures business. She wanted to tell him also, that she suspected that there was a connection between them and all that was going on just like with Mr. M. She waited another hour and then made her call. Lt. Meeker had just come in, but he was glad to hear from her as usual and appreciative to get her latest tip. He asked her what time her meeting was and told her that he would be there.

Sarafina arrived at the center right on schedule, but this time her luck with finding a parking space was not holding. She wondered whether this was a bad sign or an omen as she continued to circle the lot. After circling a few times, finally someone was coming out when she was near enough to pull in.

It was a little after 2:00 when she got in the elevator, feeling a sense of trepidation and anxiety not knowing exactly what to expect, but having foreknowledge of an evil plot. When she walked into the commons area and explained to the receptionist that she had an appointment with Mr. Leisar, she was told to have a seat and he would be right with her. She looked over to where his office was, but couldn't see him. The butterflies in her stomach were having a ball and she was contemplating going to the ladies room before the meeting to take an aspirin for her nerves. Before the decision was made, the receptionist called her back to the desk and told her that Mr. Leisar would meet with her in the small conference room down the hall. She had never been in that room before and it made her even more suspicious about what was going to happen. Cautiously, she walked down the corridor until she reached the room that was at the end of the hall in a very private area.

The door was closed so she knocked. A voice quickly responded telling her to come in, which she did. There seated on one side of the conference table was Asa Leisar and across from him was the other Leisar. She had to steady herself to keep from stumbling because the shock of seeing both of them together again threw her off. All that the angel in the dream had foretold was coming to be. She grabbed the closest chair in front of her and started to sit down before she fell, but Asa asked her if she would come a little closer. Slowly she got up again and moved a few chairs over. Al greeted her and asked her how she was doing and started to explain to her why he was there. She wasn't really paying much attention to what he was saying, but the gist of what she could make out was that he was not angry at her for filing her complaint and he was going to help her restart her benefits.

Asa went on to explain to her the document in his hand and that she might find it a little confusing, but it was a special arrangement. She said it would be okay, but just wanted to read through it. As he handed it to her he looked at her very hard and she was getting woozy. Her eyes were becoming bleary and she thought she was seeing him change right before her eyes. She tried to read the paper in front of her, but each sentence seemed to be moving. Rubbing her eyes, she placed the document on the table to steady it, but there was no difference in what the print looked like. In her mind she was remembering what the angel said in her dream and she was looking especially for words that related to soul. It was becoming more difficult as each minute went by and she convinced herself to just go to the last page and look for the names that the angel warned her about. When she got there, she focused as well as she could and sure enough there were three signature lines. There was one for her and one for each brother.

She knew right away that this was the trap that had been set for her, but somehow she felt unable to resist and was about to sign when Asa snatched the pen from her hand causing a prick to her finger and a drop of blood fell on the page. He apologized profusely saying he was so sorry because he thought she was about to sign on the wrong line, but he quickly handed the pen back to her so she could complete the task. She mumbled okay and was about to sign when this time her hand opened involuntarily and the pen fell to the floor. Then even through the glaze in her eyes she could see a figure hovering near the ceiling in the corner of the room. Right away she felt her strength returning and her eyesight clearing as she focused on the corner figure. With a wave of his hand the angel blew the papers off the table onto the floor and the brothers got up scrambling to retrieve them. As soon as they put the document back on the table in front of her, the door opened and in walked Lt. Meeker with Sgt. Calloway and one of his officers. Asa was startled, but recovered quickly and demanded to know why the cops had barged into his office. Lt. Meeker pulled out his document and explained to the brothers that this was a warrant for the arrest of both of them for complicity in drug trafficking. The brothers looked at each other in amazement, but said nothing.

Sarafina feeling much better now, looked over to the corner of the room where the figure was, but it was gone. She turned and thanked the lieutenant for believing her and showing up when he did. As the officers escorted the brothers out, he turned back to her and thanked her for all her help. She got up and followed them out, but as she walked the thought occurred to her that she had not gotten what she came there for so she went to the desk and asked who could help her reinstate her benefits. The receptionist made another appointment for her to come back tomorrow and see another counselor. Sarafina accepted the time, but then she explained what her situation was and what she needed and asked if the person she would be seeing could take care of it. Assured that they could, she left the center headed home.

At school, Dolitha was back in class and she and Jameel had a long talk at lunch about their futures. He told her he was going to meet with his pastor tonight and asked her if she wanted to come. She immediately asked him if he wanted her to and he said yes. When he got home he was still feeling the pressure of knowing what he was facing and it must have shown on his face. Sarafina greeted him at the door and told him to cheer up and then she told him about her day hoping that her encounter with the angel would give him some encouragement. He kind of smiled and thanked her for telling him that, but he wasn't so sure that it would happen for him. Then he told her he had invited Dolitha to come and mom thought that was a great idea. Cinque came in a few minutes later and they all sat down to dinner before going back out to see the preacher.

Before going to the church it was agreed that Sarafina would swing by Dolitha's house and pick her up. Once there, Jameel went upstairs to get her and a short time later down they both came. Sarafina hadn't seen her for some time and when she took a good look at her now she was impressed at how beautiful she is and nicely dressed. The couple got in the car and started for the church. During the ride, in the beginning there was silence. Dolitha wasn't sure how Sarafina felt about the situation. Did she blame her for what happened; did she want her to abort, these were things going through her mind. Sarafina sensing the tension spoke first saying that she remembers how it was to be young and in love and that she understood what the kids were going through now.

Dolitha hearing these words breathed a sigh of relief and felt more relaxed. The rest of the ride took on a different atmosphere and the conversation was light as they talked about everything, but the baby.

At the church Reverend Joyner welcomed them into his study with open arms saying he was so glad to see all. Jameel started to introduce Dolitha, but the reverend told him that they had already met at the hospital when his mother was there. He then invited them all to sit down on the couch and lounge chairs that had been arranged in a semi- circle. He asked them if they wanted anything to drink or snack on and told them what he had. As an icebreaker he started talking about the wonderful work that Sarafina was doing in the community and that anybody associated with her must be all right. Dolitha smiled and this put her somewhat at ease. He then asked Jameel how he felt about her and what was happening. The question caught him off guard and he wasn't sure how to respond. He couldn't say that he loved her because he honestly didn't know. As far as the coming event he wasn't sure how he felt about that either. He hesitated for minutes and when he finally spoke his voice was shaky and unsure. What he said was that he thought he was too young to be anybody's father and how he felt about her was still growing. Dolitha lowered her head when he said that and was about to cry.

Reverend Joyner thanked him for his honesty and said that it was a good start for them. He then got up and placed his arms around Dolitha's shoulders and asked her how she felt about him and the baby. Without hesitation, she said she loved him with all her heart and would like to have the baby. Next he turned to Sarafina and asked her the same thing. She said she would be supportive of whatever the kids wanted to do. The reverend quickly corrected her by saying that they were no longer kids and this was a very adult situation. He then started to counsel all of them about the gift of God through this child. The fact that he or she was now a reality and being formed in the womb was not by accident. For it has been determined that what will be has already begun. He went on to say that the responsibility for the care and nurturing of this gift was to be shared by all of them.

The session lasted about two hours during which he advised the young couple to cling to each other through this period and learn to appreciate the wonderful gift that they have been given. He didn't advise them to get married right away and looked straight at Jameel when he said not to marry for the wrong reason. But he cautioned them about the needs of the child to have both parents as he grew up and if that were not available then the child would be destined for a void in his life. At the end he asked them to join hands with him as he entered into prayer for the welfare of the baby and for divine guidance on how to deal with the upcoming trials they would all face. He prayed also that they would one day come together as a family and love one another. The couple and Sarafina left that night feeling more confident about what may lie ahead and ready to face tomorrow.

On the way back to Dolitha's house Sarafina asked her had she decided what she was going to do. Before answering Sarafina she turned to Jameel and said she was going to have the baby. He looked back at her grinned and said:

"Fine thas what we gonna do."

When he said that she squeezed his hand and then looked at Sarafina who was also smiling. They dropped her off and it was now just mom and her son. Sarafina told him that she would do all she could to see that everything would be done right and if he wanted to marry her she would help him with that too. He said he wasn't ready to get married yet, but he would do right for his baby. Sarafina was glad to hear him say that and said no more about it that night.

Things were really starting to come together for the city's police department and their beleaguered status. The evidence from the warehouse and the store and now eyewitnesses were coming forward eagerly, even the one from the Bricks who felt comfortable enough now to speak, to lend their voices to the matter. The prosecutor was putting together a solid case and the news media was supportive by running positive journal accounts on all phases. Even the crime rate was down. With the leaders from both gangs put away without bail and the ranking leader now cowering not from the police, but from his own, things were seemingly returning to normal. The joint community group was having their bi-weekly meeting tonight and the mood was expected to be upbeat.

Sarafina along with Lydia was busy preparing for the meeting and excited about all that the group had achieved in the last few weeks since her return to the front. They were going over the reports that the patrols prepared and it became obvious that they were being very effective. Though no one could really say that it was because of the patrols that the streets were safe to walk again at night or whether it was due to the arrests of the leaders, what could be said is that the citizens who volunteered were having fun doing it. The mood in the community was more open and more of the neighbors were signing up to contribute their time to the cause. The duo could hardly wait to get to the meeting tonight to share the patrol reports and thank the people for what they had accomplished so far, but to also remind them that this effort was not an event, but should be an ongoing vigilance for the sake of all.

Seven O'clock came and the meeting room in the recreation center was once again filled to capacity. This time not only were Lieutenant Meeker and Reverend Joyner there; but were joined by Captain Tillery and Sergeant Calloway. Sarafina and Lydia went up to the podium and opened the meeting. This time she invited Reverend Joyner to come up and start it out with a prayer of thanksgiving. He almost ran to the front happy to perform this task and welcomed the opportunity. Sarafina launched her reading of the patrol reports from the last cycle and commended all who were involved. She was so excited at the level of achievements and the progress from what started out as just a few women sitting around a table talking about we got to do something, to this room filled with willing workers ready to serve.

As she reflected on her own challenges a change came over her and a glow emanated from her body as the words coming from her mouth seemed not to be her own.

"My friends and my extended family, as I stand here before you humble as I know how to be, a message has been given to me to stand in the gap for you. At the beginning of this work, even as at the beginning of the world when man was placed here to be fruitful and multiply and subdue the earth, man was instructed to follow God's rules. Down through the annals of time, man has not only turned away from heeding His statutes and commandments but has redefined the Word according to his whims. Now he calls good evil and evil good and runs after the dictates of his own imagination. He lusts after the pleasures of the flesh and markets his vanity to the young and defenseless. In seeking after his own rise to power, he has abandoned caring for the indigent and needy. I am a living witness to how easy it is to be persuaded by the wiles of the evil one and to be led down a path of destruction. Even all of you are witnesses to the devastation and destruction caused by the assent to power of those who are inwardly guided by the adversary. It is not because we are weak physically, but because we are destitute spiritually lacking the desire to study His word so that we show ourselves approved. We continue to accept that which we know is wrong and condemn that which we know is right. The time is fast approaching when even in His infinite patience we will have exhausted the grace which He has afforded man for generations. We cannot continue to run away from the cry of the helpless and to elect as leaders those who would hasten our destruction. I, even I have known the depths of despair and have been given over to the desires of the flesh and seeing not what is real, but what the adversary wanted me to see. In the gleam of my longing eyes I have seen only that which would condemn the flesh and burn up the true passion for the one who saves and restores. But in His wisdom I was only lent for a short time to that period in which I was able to see how far man has fallen. When I was awakened and the veil was lifted from my clouded eyes I was able to see clearly the true light and separate it from the darkness that had befallen me. Now that I am awake I challenge all of you to learn to see clearly and separate the darkness from the light so that you too will be able to stand in the gap for someone else. We have come together for a cause and it has worked so far, but if we want to make the improvements permanent then I encourage all of you to study God's word. In this book of guidance and solutions you will see that if we don't change our ways now, then our time left here on this earth will not be long."

She ended her address and the glow dissipated. All eyes in the room were fixated on her and the silence was so loud it was deafening. As they stared at her she realized she had been talking, but couldn't remember starting or stopping, so she turned to Lydia who was standing behind her and asked her to take over because she felt feint. Lydia stepped in and asked Reverend Joyner if he would close the meeting as he began it. Before he closed, he encouraged the crowd to take up the mantle and continue the good work that has begun in each one of them. He went on to say to them not to become weary in well doing for in due time they shall reap the benefits, if they don't feint. After that Rev. Joyner gave the benediction and a powerful spirit came over the room as all of the people departed.

The ensuing months after that night saw dramatic changes in the community. The gang activity was now almost non-existent, the arrested gang members had been brought to trial and convicted, the big man, Mr. Mizzetti, was also convicted, but there was some concern about the inappropriate sentencing. Many of the citizens believed it was too lenient, but how could they know that Mr. M.'s bosses were anxiously waiting for his release so that they could administer their own form of justice. Jameel was given probation for two years and obligated to do community service for 1 year which he gladly accepted to join the CONN's and work with them. Dolitha and Jameel were going to become parents in about a month and they both accepted Christ as their Savior and were baptized at New Life Temple of God. The properties of Mr. Mizzetti were confiscated under the drug laws and the Gateway Plant was sold. Under the new ownership Janet Johnson was promoted to the General Manager position. She then rehired Sarafina as the new Office Manager at twice the salary she had at Peerless. The Leisar brothers never got to trial because as they were being held in custody, one night they simply disappeared from the cells. However, according to Lt. Meeker, a rumor has it that in a city just outside of Las Vegas, a new import/export company had just emerged called Leisar Trading Unlimited and the owners were reported to look just like the brothers. As for Lt. Meeker and Sergeant Calloway they both received promotions. The mayor ascended high on the polls for re-election and the fact that he gave a political celebration party in appreciation for the services of the CONN's and New Life community group, didn't hurt. Sista, who was somehow not indicted, after the trials left the city and was last heard of doing quite well using her assets in New York with the top man in business operations. Cinque and Jameel finished out the school year successfully with Jameel looking forward to graduating next year. Cinque was now planning to try out for the football team at the end the summer. Rajon, who had considered dropping out decided to remain in school with his friend, was just happy that he had the C's off his back trying to recruit him.

Life in the city has returned to what it used to be when Sarafina first moved there.

During the period of surging violence and other crimes against the people, the dark cloud that hovered over the metropolis seemed to absorb all of the good and spit back all of the evil. Not only was Sarafina and her family victims of the evil influence of Satan's soldiers, but all who came in contact with them were subjected to the one thing that he is best known for. The one evil thing that from the beginning of time, when life on this planet was introduced in the form of man, to the current age where man's technological achievements have elevated him to magnificent heights; is still here. Exposure to that one thing is sure and unavoidable as man continues to live out his life in this age.

Discerning when one has been exposed is not always as easy a task as one might hope. As the Peterson family came to understand, after experiencing many trials and tribulations as foretold in the Great Book, and having been able to finally stand and thwart the fiery darts of the evil one, the race is not given to the mighty nor to the swift, but to he who endures to the end. Right from the beginning, all the evil that has ensued thereafter can be attributed to the plans of the master of deception the one who can convince us all to believe, trust and accept **"The Liar's Gift."**

The End